THE GATES OF TIME

THE STARSEA CYCLE BOOK NINE

KYLE WEST

Copyright © 2023 by Kyle West

All rights reserved.

No part of this book may be reproduced in any form or by any electronic or mechanical means, including information storage and retrieval systems, without written permission from the author, except for the use of brief quotations in a book review.

Cover Art by Deranged Doctor Design.

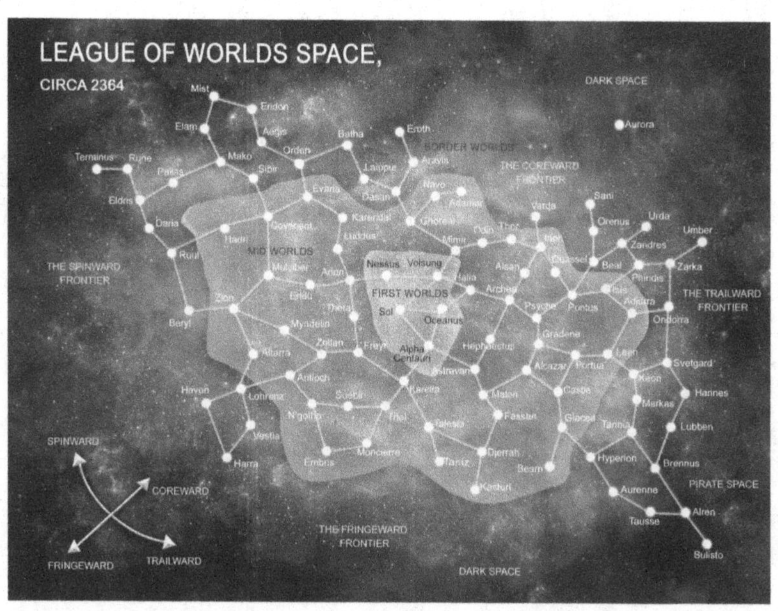

LEAGUE OF WORLDS SPACE,
CIRCA 2364
DARK SPACE
Mist
Eridon
Elam
Aegis
Batha
Eroth
Aurora
Orden
BORDER WORLDS
Terminus
Rune
Mako
Laupur
Arayla
THE COREWARD
FRONTIER
Sibir
Pallas
Navo
Sani
Eldris
Evaria
Dasin
Adama
Varda
Orenus
Urda
Daria
Covenant
Karendal
Ghoreal
Umber
Hadir
Luddus
Mimir
Odin
Thor
Trier
Zandres
Beal
Zarka
MID WORLDS
Ruul
Mulciber
Nessus Volsung
Alsan
Quassel
Phindis
THE TRAILWARD
FRONTIER
THE SPINWARD
FRONTIER
Zion
Eridu
Ardan
FIRST WORLDS
Italia
Archea
Isis
Adastra
Thera
Sol
Psyche
Pontus
Ondorra
Beryl
Myndelin
Oceanus
Gradena
Zoltan
Freya
Hephaestus
Laen
Altarra
Alpha
Centaun
Svelgard
Havon
Antioch
Ilaretta
Astravan
Alcazar
Portua
Xeon
Hannes
Lohrena
Susiia
Maton
Casbe
Markas
N'golfa
Ihel
Fasstin
Glaces
Tanna
Lubben
Vestia
Moncierre
Talesia
Djerrah
Hyperion
Brennus
SPINWARD
Harra
Embris
Taniz
Kashuri
Beam
Aurenne
PIRATE SPACE
COREWARD
Alren
Tausse
FRINGEWARD
TRAILWARD
THE FRINGEWARD
FRONTIER
DARK SPACE
Bulisto

1

"THERE IT IS," Lucian announced, gazing out of the main viewscreen. "The Grand Dome of Nessus."

Blood Wyvern descended toward the immense, translucent dome, beneath which sprawled a vast city filled with innumerable towering skyscrapers, most of them radiating with vibrant, multicolored neon lights. The Grand Dome was not the only one on the surface; hundreds were scattered across Nessus's barren landscape, all interconnected and harboring bustling cities. Although the planet lacked an atmosphere, it had become home to hundreds of millions.

"Beautiful," Serah said. She glanced at Lucian thoughtfully. "You know . . . they're hosting a *massive* tournament here for MFS. All the top players will be there."

"MFS? What are you—?" Lucian paused for a moment in realization. "Oh." He gaped at her in disbelief. "They have *tournaments* for Medieval Farming Simulator? You can't be serious."

"MFS is more than just a game; it's a way of life. *Harvest the past. Cultivate your legacy.*"

"That's catchy."

"I'd be in the tournament myself, but I haven't had enough time to invest in my farm. All my favorite players will be there: Sower of Seeds, Crop Whisperer, Barnyard Baller. Even Plowmaster69."

Lucian couldn't suppress a snicker. "Wow, the Plowmaster himself will be there?"

"Yes, *she* will be there. And *she* arguably has the most impressive farming empire on all Aranis. She commands over ten thousand serfs! Ten thousand, Lucian. Not NPCs, but actual players her knights have captured!"

"She sounds delightful."

"And it's set to start tonight! Can we go? Please, please, *please*?"

"We don't have time. We have to concentrate on the mission, remember? Our vacation's over. Billions of lives are in the balance."

"Well, even *we* need some R&R. I know we've had a few weeks to ourselves, but what's one more day?"

Before Lucian could reply, she turned back to the viewscreen, where her blue eyes mirrored the glow of the approaching skyscrapers. "This is going to be fun!"

The ship nestled into the spaceport hangar. Lucian consulted his slate for directions to the hotel Fergus had reserved for them.

"The Galactic Grand," Lucian said. "Fancy."

"I've already done my research," Serah chimed in. "Our suite is five hundred credits a night! We have our own concierge, the entire top floor, even a pool bar!"

"How could we survive without a pool bar? Anyway, it's just a ten-minute walk from here."

Lucian ensured the ship was secured before they exited the hangar and stepped onto the main promenade of the spaceport.

———

UPON REACHING the penthouse of the Galactic Grand, the door slid open automatically. They were welcomed by a vast open area filled with columns, gauzy red carpet, white marble floors, and a breathtaking view of a sea of lights at the forefront of the Glitz Strip. For five hundred credits a night, Lucian had to admit the view *was* stunning.

Everyone was already there, gathered by the windows, drinking cocktails and eating finger foods spread out on the dining room table.

His mother was the first to turn, beaming him a smile. "Lucian!"

He was suddenly surrounded. It had only been a few weeks since they parted, but they were acting like it had been months.

"Miss me that much, eh?"

"Oh, I won't even try to hide it!" Linus gushed. "Life is just so boring without you, my boy."

"It's good to see you," Emma said, giving both him and Serah a hug. "How was your vacation?"

"Wonderful," Lucian replied. "We saw a lot of stuff."

"*Did* a lot of stuff, too," Serah added.

"TMI," Fergus said. "Either way, I'm glad you're rested. Hungry? Thirsty? We have our own bar and drink mixer. Can make practically anything you want."

"I'll have an old-fashioned," Lucian said.

"Frozen strawberry margarita for me," Serah said. "No! Harvey Wallbanger!"

"Done and done," Fergus said easily. "Welcome to Galactic Grand, the finest hotel in all the Worlds. I've always wanted to stay here in the penthouse. Bucket list item. They say the staff will lick your boots if you ask them."

"They will," Linus confirmed. "Mine are positively sparkling!"

"Now *that's* TMI," Serah said.

"Lucian," Plato said, sidling up and giving him a hug, "good to see you."

Lucian smiled. "Yeah, you too. All rested up?"

"Rested *and* fed," Plato said, patting his belly. "I feel like I could take on the Worlds!"

"That's what we're here to do. But maybe we can relax first. Catch up."

"Speaking of catching up," Plato said, nodding toward the window, "talk to him."

Lucian looked up to see the only person who had yet to greet him. Jagar stood facing out the window. He stood regally, and Lucian could've sworn he hadn't seemed so tall before. Jagar had always had a slight stoop to his back, but that seemed to be gone now.

And when Jagar turned, Lucian's breath was taken from him. His face was *completely* different. Well, it was the same face, but old wrinkles had vanished while his form seemed stronger than ever before. He was a good twenty or thirty years younger. He cracked a knowing grin.

Before Lucian could even react, Serah gasped. "Holy rotting crap balls, Jagar!"

At this exclamation, Jagar merely lifted a single brow, with just as much sandy brown as gray in it. "I bought myself a few years, let's just say."

"No kidding!" Lucian said. "That must've cost you a fortune."

"Well, I was lucky enough to come into one. I won't go into the details, but I followed someone's advice and erased about thirty years off my life."

Lucian had to admit, even in his fifties, Jagar was a handsome devil. He looked like a movie star, and the silver at his temples only lent him an extra layer of dignity. He could see why Ansaldra had gone for him.

"Drained about half my stash," Jagar went on, "but I'd say it was worth it. Especially if I'm to keep up with you young bucks."

Lucian laughed. "You were doing a pretty good job of it already, but I see your point."

Lucian noted Khairu's absence, but from what he had gathered, she was at the Volsung Academy, helping to stabilize things there.

They spent the next few hours catching up, and Lucian had fun enjoying their company. He'd missed this, and it wasn't often they had the chance to talk about something other than saving the universe.

But, as always, things went back in that direction. As everyone grew quiet, it was time to talk business. They all looked at him to lead. He was no longer uncomfortable with that role. He had grown into it.

"I'll get right to it," he said. "We have a decision to make. An important one. We know Sharo—AKA the Ancient One—went to Mako. That's where his fleet is. As long as he exists, he'll be a threat."

"Let's take him out," Fergus said. "You have all Eight Orbs and Lightspear. You should make quick work of it, right?" He chuckled. "Might even make it home in time for dinner."

A few people snickered at his joke, though it was half-hearted.

"I wish it were that easy."

"Why *wouldn't* it be?" Linus asked. "You wiped the floor with him above Earth! I couldn't believe my eyes when the entire *Alkasen* fleet just vanished. Just do even a *fraction* of that, and he's done for!"

"That took time to set up. I don't think the Ancient One will just sit back and let me build my ether reserves until I can pull off something like that, especially without the distraction of the entire *Alkasen* fleet. However, I have another idea."

Everyone waited for him to gather his thoughts.

"Every minute we wait allows the *Alkasen* to regroup. We assume it'll be quick and easy to go after the Ancient One. But he has access to Space-Time Magic, just like me. And more than that, he has his own tricks up his sleeve. The Ancient One is the source of the same Shadow Magic that Xara Mallis had. We saw Sharo use it on *Holy Fire*. We shouldn't underestimate him. Worse, he knows we're coming. Taking the Ancient One down might be harder than we expected."

"But you have to face him at *some* point," Fergus said. "Right?"

Lucian steeled himself a bit. He wasn't sure how they would react to his idea. It sounded crazy even to him.

"Hear me out. I don't *have* to face him."

"What are you suggesting, lad?" Jagar asked.

"I have all Eight Orbs. Maybe it's time for me to return them to the Heart of Creation sooner rather than later. Skip the whole fighting bit entirely."

2

LUCIAN WATCHED as they processed this news. From their widened eyes and surprised expressions, this was clearly not what they had expected.

"It's . . . an idea," Emma said, breaking the silence, her voice uncertain. "I just don't know if it's a *good* idea. Wouldn't that just leave the Worlds open to the Ancient One? Sounds risky."

Lucian realized he'd have to do more convincing. "I *can* find the First Gate. All we have to do is follow the Seven-Fold Path. And with Space-Time and Dynamism, I can move us even faster with a warping bubble. It won't take years to find the First Gate. Potentially, we could be there in just a few months. Maybe even less. I mean, you guys saw how fast I got the ship moving when we went to shut down all the Border Gates."

"We know that," Mira said, "but do you *really* think it'll only take a few months? The First Gate is quite far. You said that yourself. We don't know how many star systems the original Starsea Empire had. We might have to travel clear across the galaxy, and even with magic, that's a long way."

"It's far, yes. But not as far as that. When I searched for the

First Gate all those months ago, it felt as if it was in reach. If I had to guess, about a hundred Gates. I know, it seems like a lot. It would take months. But with this new warping bubble I've discovered, it won't take years. A long way, sure, but definitely not across the entire galaxy. Keep in mind I'm not saying we *should* do this. I'm saying if we returned the Orbs now, it would force the Ancient One to react to us rather than the other way around."

"I'm with Emma," Fergus said. "He can do a lot of damage to the League if we leave. It's hard to say just how *much* damage. Would a few months be enough time for him to kill millions of people? Or would it be even worse than that? You mentioned Shadow Magic, Lucian. To me, that's the gravest threat. We don't know what it's capable of. If we take too long to get to the First Gate, there might not be a League worth saving by the time we're through."

It was an excellent point, and one Lucian didn't have an answer to, at least not in this moment.

"Now, I'm going to side with Lucian a bit," Serah said. "If we wait and the Ancient One proves harder to take down than we thought, we could waste a lot of time while the *Alkasen* regroup for another attack. By then, it'll be too late." She turned to Lucian. "Maybe you can do that future-delving thing to figure things out."

"It wouldn't be so simple. Anything involving the Ancient One directly will be hard to predict. He has Space-Time Magic, so he can block me from seeing any futures that have to do with him. The point is, no matter *what* we decide, there will be conflict with the Ancient One."

"I guess," Serah conceded.

"So, where will this Seven-Fold Path take us, roughly speaking?" Emma asked. "You felt that out already, so do you know anything specific?"

"I know we can start around Nai Shairen. I can portal us there easily. From there, though, it's uncharted territory."

"About a hundred Gates, you said," Fergus said. "All in Dark Space, too. And with you holding all Eight Orbs, they're going to close in on us like a noose. They can detect them, after all."

"Not us!" Serah said. "We'll go really fast, right?"

"Not fast enough to elude detection," Fergus warned. "They'll probably have weapons or even magic that can slow us down. As fast as Lucian can move the ship, can we really outrun torpedoes? Enough of those, and even *Blood Wyvern's* cloaking won't save the day. This is all a gamble, and a big one."

Serah looked at Lucian worriedly. "Of course, there's nowhere to refuel on the way, so Lucian will have to Atomicize new fuel units. In theory, though, we could keep picking up speed as fast as he can make the fuel, right?"

"That depends," Emma said. As soon as she whipped out her slate, Lucian knew she was about to hit them with some advanced calculations. "*Blood Wyvern's* max speed is about ten percent of the speed of light; it can get there on half a tank of fuel. Theoretically, it *can* go faster, but the ship simply won't speed up when it doesn't have the fuel to slow down. It's a security measure."

"We're mages, though," Serah said. "We can just *create* fuel. Or at least, Lucian can."

"I can easily override the programming," Emma agreed. "But you get diminishing returns the faster you speed up. It just takes more and more energy to keep accelerating."

"Say what now?" Serah asked.

"I don't have the exact calculations, but *Blood Wyvern's* navicomputer will tell us. The faster we go, the more mass *Blood Wyvern* takes on. Therefore, the energy required to get the ship from ten percent light—its top theoretical speed—to fifteen percent, for example, is significantly greater than getting it from zero to five percent. And that already takes a mind-bending amount of energy and some funky quantum stuff."

"And speed might not matter much, anyway," Fergus added.

"After all, the warping bubble circumvents the need for speed. Speed is still valuable to have, but most of the legwork is done by the bubble."

"That's right," Lucian said. "With the warp bubble, it'll only take a few days to pass through each star system, regardless of our speed. However, there *is* a downside. It takes a lot of ether, and that will make us easy to spot by any mage powerful enough to detect it. We need to balance speed and warping."

"So, the primary danger is being detected," Mira said. "I doubt the Swarmers have anything fast enough to catch us, but if they figure out what we're doing, they can easily shoot us down."

"Why wouldn't they just let us go?" Emma asked. "If we're going to the First Gate, we're doing exactly what they want. Destroying us risks losing the Orbs in outer space."

Lucian knew that was a good point, but also remembered Silumko telling him they would try to get the Orbs back themselves, if only to have insurance in the case Lucian went his own way. From their perspective, it was safest for them to retrieve the Orbs from Lucian in the safest manner possible.

What that might look like, Lucian couldn't say. The *Alkasen* would likely try to use magic to disable the ship.

"One more thing," Mira said. "What happens when we return the Orbs? How can we prepare the League for a future without the Gates?"

Lucian knew she had asked an impossible question, the one he didn't really want to deal with. No matter what they did, millions, if not billions, of people would die. Most of the League simply could not survive for long without Earth and the Solar System. And, of course, Earth itself would struggle without the raw materials and food provided by the League planets. The League of Worlds was a trade network of dizzying complexity, and if he returned the Orbs, magic would be gone for good.

And yet, *not* returning the Orbs guaranteed that reality itself, one day, would cease to exist. It was impossible to say when the lights would go out, but Lucian had no reason to doubt Silumko's words.

"I don't know," Lucian said.

"Should we speak to the Hegemon about this?" Emma asked. "Maybe give her some time to make sure each world is self-sufficient?"

"She would *never* go for that," Fergus said. "What person wants to go backward in progress? To be the Hegemon responsible for the deaths of billions? Hundreds of worlds, forever separated, with no way to bridge the gap. After the initial chaos, Earth would probably be okay, along with anything in the Solar System. But the worlds outside of Earth would regress. Things would work for a few centuries, but inevitably, without the population, knowledge, and resources of the home world, they would have to start from scratch. Worlds like Volsung or Chiron would probably keep a lot of their technology. The people on completely hostile worlds, like Oceanus or Nessus, would likely be doomed. It's a horrible problem, one with no simple answer."

Everyone looked at Lucian. He hated how this decision was up to him. He was the one with the Orbs, the Chosen of the Manifold, who was supposed to return them to the Heart of Creation. For as long as he could remember, that was his path.

And if he followed that path, it would change history forever. There was no way he could have it all. If he kept the Orbs, it meant eternal war with the Ascendant Beings and the *Alkasen*.

"Let's set this discussion aside for now," he finally said. "I don't know what's right. There are no good choices, as far as I can tell. I'm holding out for a third option. I don't know if it exists, but it's easy to get stuck on dichotomies. Maybe if we can imagine the solution, we can achieve it."

"It's impossible to say," Fergus said. "But we'll keep our ear to the ground and see if we can find anything."

"So, what's the consensus?" Mira asked. "Go after the Ancient One? Or leave the League behind and hunt for the First Gate?"

"Let's decide tomorrow morning," Lucian said. "After all, we're on Nessus, and it would be a shame not to explore while we're here. So go out, have some fun, and we can decide tomorrow morning."

"That's the best idea I've heard yet," Serah said. "If we hurry, we can still make the tournament!"

"What tournament?" Emma asked.

"MFS! You should join us."

She held up a hand. "Oh, no. I have a very strict no third-wheeling policy."

"Very sensible," Linus said.

"Come on!" Serah said. "You won't be the third wheel, I promise!"

"You're speaking as if I haven't already planned out my entire night. I'm going to eat dinner, then see a show that looks interesting. Then it's lights out."

"Boo!" Serah said. "Well, when Lucian and I are done, we're coming to get you. I mean, if we're *really* going into Dark Space like we talked about, then we need this to be the most epic night of our lives!"

"I think I'm going to try my hand at gambling," Linus said. "Only, I'm a little low on creds. Could you spot me a few, Lucian? I'll pay you back with interest when I win big."

"I'll transfer you a hundred," Lucian said. Thanks to the League's stipend, he had more than enough to spare. "Go nuts."

"Thank you, kind sir!"

"If you like gambling, I know a good place," Jagar said. "It's been a while, but if it's still there, the liquor flows and the women are beautiful."

Linus laughed and gave an exaggerated bow. "Point the way, my good man! I am, as ever, your humblest servant."

"I hear Nessus is a foodie's paradise," Plato said. "They have a Night Market here that is said to be second to none. Over ten thousand food stalls with every cuisine you can imagine!"

"Count me and Mira in," Fergus said. He glanced at her. "I mean, if that's all right with you?"

"Actually," Mira said, "I have my own ideas for what we might do."

"Oh?" Fergus asked, raising an eyebrow.

Lucian clapped his hands. "All right, I think I'm ready. Serah?"

Serah was practically yanking on Lucian's hand. "Come on, come on, come on!"

All Lucian could do was shrug his shoulders and follow.

3

THEY ENTERED the neon-lit street below, and it was all Lucian could do to keep up with Serah in the thick crowds.

"Wait up!" he said.

Serah seemed oblivious, eager to get to the venue as quickly as possible. "Come on! We're going to miss the bus!"

"We don't have to take the bus! I've got the creds for a taxi."

"The bus is *here*, though," Serah said. "Let's go! We're going to miss it."

Serah was already climbing inside. Lucian followed.

It was only once they were sitting down, and the bus hovering down the street, that Serah noticed the sour expression on his face. "Aw, come on! Don't tell me you're in a mood at a time like this."

"Of course not. Why would I be?"

She squeezed his leg playfully. "You getting sick of me already? We've only spent every waking moment with each other for the past few weeks."

"No, I'm not sick of you."

"Is it because you don't want to see the tournament?"

Lucian realized that was exactly the reason. Seeing a bunch of cyber medieval farmer nerds fighting it out over the fate of a fictional virtual world was not his idea of a good time. But he couldn't say so out loud because this was important to her.

"I'm also just worried about everything we talked about. It's hard to snap out of all that."

"Yeah, makes sense. Do you want to talk about it?"

"I just need a distraction. Maybe after the tournament, we could go get drinks or something."

"Yeah, I'd be down for that!"

Serah looked out the window, her face reflecting the neon lights of the massive skyscrapers. Even now that she had escaped Psyche and had seen a few things, she still had a wide-eyed sense of wonder.

She turned back to him. "I'm sorry. It's probably selfish of me wanting to do this, when we have so much else going on . . ."

"It's not that. I'm just . . . complicated, I guess."

"Oh, so complicated. You are positively broody. We'll do something you like after. The night is still young, after all."

The bus pulled to a stop in front of a massive skyscraper, glittering brightly under Nessus's eternal night sky. The distant dome above them was so clear that it looked as if nothing separated them from the vacuum of space. The street was strangely empty, considering the general busyness of the Glitz Strip.

"Are you *sure* this is the right place?"

"Positive!" Serah piped. "Let's go in!"

But when they reached the front doors, the interior was empty, though well-lit.

"What's going on?" Serah asked. She started beating on the doors. "Hey! Open up!"

"They're going to think you're trying to break in," Lucian said. He peered into the empty lobby. "This can't be it."

Serah held up her slate. "Hey, where's the MFS tournament?"

The slate's automated female voice responded. "I'm sorry. It seems the Medieval Farming Simulator Tournament was held yesterday at this venue. Is there anything else I can help you with?"

"No!" Serah wailed. "How could I have gotten the date wrong?" She looked as if she wanted to throw her slate. "This useless hunk of junk! You gave me bad info! This is horrible. *Truly* horrible."

"What do we do now, then?"

But Serah was already looking into the distance, above some buildings across the street. Her blue eyes went wide as the sounds of screams echoed from the distance.

"Awesome!"

She headed in that direction, and Lucian knew there would be no stopping her from going on the roller coaster.

———

Within the hour, they were at the very top of that ride, a coaster that seemed to go up and up, only to go straight down at unreal speed, flying above the busy streets. In fact, the amusement park appeared to blend with the city.

Serah was screaming her head off, her eyes a mix of exhilaration and fear. Even Lucian had to admit that they didn't make coasters this fast back on Earth.

They stayed there until way past midnight, Lucian never remembering when he'd had so much fun. Things got better when the rest of the group joined them, except for his mother and Fergus. Lucian didn't even want to think about what those two were up to.

Lucian even got recognized a few times, and eventually, it got to be too much. Reporters were already there, wanting to get his opinion on every event going on in the League.

"That's enough," Linus said. "Make way for the Chosen One!"

Lucian wanted to tell him to cut it out, but people actually listened to him, much to Lucian's surprise.

"It's time to head back," Lucian said. "It must be two in the morning."

Emma stifled a yawn. "I don't think this place *ever* sleeps."

"That's Nessus for you," Jagar said.

"Did you win big?" Lucian asked.

Jagar chuckled. "Oh, I certainly did."

"You should've seen him!" Linus said. "I never knew Jagar was such a lady's man."

"Oh?" Serah asked. "Do tell!"

Jagar was looking around, seeking any potential threats. Whatever recreation he had been up to earlier, he was all business now.

"Relax, Jagar," Lucian said.

Once again, the crowd was gathering around them. Lucian wondered if he could ever go anywhere by himself again.

"All right, we *really* need to go," Lucian said. "Where's Plato?"

"Getting a funnel cake," Serah said.

Lucian suppressed his annoyance. "I thought he already got one."

"He did, but they messed up his order. He wanted one with chocolate and cherries, but they gave him powdered sugar and hazelnut."

Lucian couldn't care less. "Linus, can you find him?"

"Already on it."

Linus weaved through the throng. Lucian tried to back away from the mass of people, all of them pointing their slates toward him. He felt uneasy being surrounded by so many people. It brought to mind the fight on board the *Alkasen* cruiser, where he had killed well over a hundred of his human brethren. He felt his skin break out in a cold sweat.

Serah put a hand on his arm, seeming to sense his tension.

That was when, out of the corner of his eye, Lucian sensed a shifting shadow.

He turned his head, scanning the crowd for any sign of danger. But there was nothing but the usual hustle and bustle of the amusement park.

But Lucian's instincts told him that something was off. It reminded him of when the Ancient One's shadow had been following him.

Maybe it was nothing, but maybe it wasn't.

"Jagar, keep an eye out," Lucian said, his voice low and urgent.

Jagar nodded, his hand instinctively moving toward his shockspear.

Emma looked at them both. "What's going on?"

"I'm not sure," Lucian admitted. "But something feels off."

Plato returned, a half-eaten funnel cake in his hand. "What's the hold-up, guys?"

"*You* are," Linus scolded. He saw Lucian's face. "Eh? Did something happen?"

"Lucian feels like something's up," Jagar said, his eyes scanning the crowd. "We should head back to the hotel."

Plato raised an eyebrow. "What *kind* of something?"

"I don't know," Lucian said. "But Jagar has the right idea."

That was when he saw it—a glint of metal in the hand of a man pushing toward them.

4

INSTANTLY, Lucian raised a dual Binding and Psionic shield just in time to absorb the impact of a metal slug. The attacker's handgun whirred as multiple shots were fired, even as more assailants revealed themselves, also opening fire.

Screams emanated from the crowd, people panicking and fleeing from the attack. After a few seconds, Lucian identified at least a dozen men who remained, each dressed in muted colors. Their violet-glowing eyes showed Psionic possession. But who was controlling them?

By now, the crowd had all but dispersed, leaving Lucian and his friends to face the assassins.

Lucian enhanced the strength of his magical shield, launching himself forward while summoning Lightspear in his hand. The ethereal weapon manifested, a streak of white-hot magical energy.

He drove the deadly weapon directly into the nearest assassin's chest, the attacker letting out an almost inhuman shriek before his body disintegrated into ash.

The other attackers were dispatched in quick succession by

the others. However, even *more* assassins emerged from nearby storefronts, alleyways, and even ride entrances. It seemed as if a small army of Bonded Preserved had infiltrated the Grand Dome, all set on taking out Lucian.

As Lucian and the others continued to fight, he noticed something odd. Every time an assassin died, a strange shadow escaped its body, seeking a new person to occupy. These shadows seemed either unable or unwilling to enter Lucian's friends, but there were still plenty of bystanders who hadn't escaped. As soon as these shadows entered them, they immediately turned against Lucian. More shadows still roved the amusement park, seeking their next victims.

"Stop killing them!" Lucian said. "This isn't the *Alkasen*. It's the Ancient One."

The others halted immediately. A shadow went directly toward Lucian, which he impaled with Lightspear. The shadow shriveled and died in less than a second.

It was as he had feared. Lightspear was the only thing that could stop them, but by now, hundreds of these shadows were loose, spreading like a virus. It seemed for every person the shadows killed, three or even four would be set loose, causing the attack to spiral out of control.

It was easy to see what would happen unless Lucian could somehow stop it.

"I have to hunt down every one of these shadows," he said. "Lightspear's the only thing that can kill them."

"You can't kill them faster than they can spread," Jagar said. "That's just math."

Lucian recognized Jagar was right. "Then we have to find the Ancient One. He's the source."

"Shadow Magic," Serah said. "It has to be, right?"

Right now, it was too dangerous for Lucian's friends exposed to this battlefield. Eventually, the shadows would regroup and attack in even greater numbers. The only option was to get them to safety and figure out the next steps.

While maintaining his shield, Lucian redirected his ether to create a portal back to the spaceship. Within a moment, an ovoid portal appeared before them, revealing the central hub of *Blood Wyvern* on the other side.

"Come on, get in!" Lucian said. "I have to find my mom and Fergus. You guys get the ship into orbit. Use the autopilot."

There was no argument. Everyone sprinted through the portal and into *Blood Wyvern's* wardroom beyond, leaving Lucian behind.

Once alone, Lucian fought with a fervor such as he had never known. He entered the Ether, becoming one with Lightspear and attacking every shadow in sight. Using Binding and Gravitonic Magic, he made his way back to the hotel over the city's towers.

Hey! Serah said, reaching him by Psionic link. *Your mom and Fergus are already on board.*

They are?

Yeah. You should come here, Lucian. These shadows are everywhere! There's no way you can get them all with just Lightspear.

Lucian fought on, trying to see if he could push the shadows back. He reached for the Orb of Radiance, gathering as much ether as he could manage and then letting loose a nova of intense light. It scattered the shadows, but only for a moment. They regrouped, the air above turning dark with their influence.

Lucian cursed. Even he had to admit that it was a losing battle. Given time, even he would be completely overwhelmed.

He warped himself aboard *Blood Wyvern*, which, to his relief, was well on its way off-world.

He ran to the bridge, where everyone had gathered. "Is everyone okay?"

Serah nodded, her eyes wide with fear. Emma and the others looked shaken, but unharmed.

Plato was the first to speak. "What in the Worlds *was* that? Where did those shadows come from?"

Lucian's mind was spinning. "It has to be the Ancient One. Only he can use magic like that. Lightspear is the only thing that can counter it."

"Do you think the Ancient One is on Nessus?" Fergus asked.

Lucian didn't think that was the case. He would have sensed such a powerful presence. And yet, he didn't see how it was possible. Maybe he had sent a few of his Prophets to infiltrate the Grand Dome, perhaps using a portal.

By now, they had entered Nessus's orbit, and already, dozens of messages and hails were lighting their dashboard, which Lucian muted. There were even a few explosions visible on the surface below.

Emma shook her head at the carnage. "If we let this go unchecked, the entire Grand Dome could be turned into his personal army. That's thousands of people. Potentially millions." Her face blanched. "And worse, it can spread off-world, too."

"So, what do we do?" Jagar asked. "If the League acts fast, maybe Nessus can be quarantined. We can stop the spread and allow it to burn itself out."

"Burn itself out?" Serah asked. "It's probably already too late!"

"We must contact Hegemon Madi and explain the situation," Jagar said grimly. "There are no easy answers here . . . I do not envy the hard choice she will be forced to make."

"Hard choice?" Emma asked. "And what do you think that will be? Bombard the entire planet until nothing's left?"

"I won't hear of it," Fergus said with conviction. "You think she'd bomb Nessus off the galactic map? That's millions of people. There has to be another way!"

"Every minute that passes, more are turning," Jagar said. "Like Lucian said, this isn't the *Alkasen*. If their Bond of Creation could spread like this, they would have used it long ago. This is the

Ancient One's doing. A Shadow Bond, if you will. We have to deal with *him* to put a stop to it."

"If the Ancient One was capable of this all along, why start now?" Serah asked.

It was a good question, but one Lucian didn't have the answer to. "That's hard to say. What I know is that Jagar is right. We need to find the Hegemon. She's still in the Solar System, and it will take hours for the news to reach her. We can get to her even faster. One thing I can say for sure is that the Ancient One isn't on this world. Jagar's also right that the Ancient One is the source of this *Shadow Bond*."

Emma frowned in thought. "If the Ancient One isn't here, then where is he?"

"It's possible he's still on Mako since that's where the remnants of his fleet were found. He might be using the planet as a base."

"Let's go there," Serah said.

Lucian thought it over. "Here's the plan. I propose splitting up our team. One team will go directly to the Hegemon and explain the situation. The other will go after the Ancient One."

"I agree," Mira said. "Who will go?"

Lucian looked around at the others. He knew he would have to choose carefully. His mother would go to the Hegemon. As the Grand Admiral of the Starsea Fleet, she was the right person to lead this team. And for obvious reasons, she couldn't directly go after the Ancient One as a non-mage. It would simply be too dangerous.

Fergus would also go with his mother. The mages would look to him for guidance in the dark days ahead.

Then there were Linus and Plato. Both were strong mages in their own right, but they hadn't been fighting with Lucian as long as the others. Fergus might need some additional support in managing the Mage Division or the Irion Mages, and Linus and Plato would both be there to offer it.

Lucian wanted Emma with him. She was arguably the most powerful mage he had access to. And Serah would stay with him as well, for obvious reasons.

That left Jagar. His brown eyes were fierce, and his younger body would make him that much stronger of a physical fighter. He had already been formidable north of eighty years old. Lucian couldn't pass up the opportunity to fight beside him again.

As for a pilot, he'd have to get Khairu and hope she would help. Not only would she be a pilot, but she'd round off his team's weaknesses as a Dynamist. While Lucian was extremely powerful in all the Aspects, it would be nice to have someone to shield Dynamism while he focused on other things.

Lucian considered Selene for a moment, but they had little enough time as it was. Every hour counted, and going after Khairu would take some time already. Selene would remain on Psyche.

"Here's the plan," Lucian said. "I want no arguments. My mom, Fergus, Plato, and Linus will be part of the Hegemon team. You guys will tell her exactly what's going on with this attack by the Ancient One."

"But we *don't* know exactly what is going on," Linus protested.

"I understand. Think about this, though. I'm sure there are already witnesses and broadcasts that caught our fight, and to the untrained eye, it will look a lot like we caused it. We need to get to Madi before that news does. Serah, Emma, Jagar, and I will go after the Ancient One in the Mako System. We'll also pick up Khairu from Volsung as quickly as possible. We'll need a pilot."

"Just the five of us," Serah said. "Wow, all this is moving fast. Are we *sure* he's on Mako?"

"Trust me, I'd know if he was here," Lucian said. "He wouldn't risk fighting me directly, but he'd have no problem sending his minions to do his dirty work. Whatever this magic is, it's highly dangerous. I guess he could be somewhere besides Mako by now, but that's the first place we should look."

"Okay. So, what now?" Serah asked.

"We head back to Earth and the fleet and touch base with Madi. The Sentinels and Mwangi should be strong enough to create a portal to Nessus. I'll have to let all of you work out the details because we're going to have to leave pretty quickly once we drop you off."

"I suppose you'll be taking *Blood Wyvern*, then?" Mira asked.

Lucian nodded. "Yes. Serah, Emma, Jagar, and I will take *Blood Wyvern* to the Volsung Academy and pick up Khairu. The autopilot can handle that much. Once we get her, we'll head to Mako and take out the Ancient One." He looked around at everyone. "Questions?"

There were none. All were ready to follow him and carry out his orders.

"Let's go."

5

THEY EMERGED from the portal a few thousand kilometers away from the Starsea Fleet, which was still in orbit above Earth. Within moments, they approached the flagship, *Mekong*. The dashboard of *Blood Wyvern* lit with a hail request, which Mira answered.

Admiral Thorin's deep voice resonated from the other end. "Admiral Abrantes. This is a surprise."

"Admiral Thorin. We're back with unfortunate news. We need to call the Hegemon, the Cabinet, and all the admirals for an emergency meeting. Arrange it. I'll be on the *Mekong's* bridge in half an hour."

"I'm sure it can be arranged, but I doubt the Hegemon can be summoned so quickly. She is in her palace in Geneva, after all."

"Get her here as quickly as possible. It's time-sensitive and billions of lives could be at stake."

There was a moment's pause, but Thorin recovered quickly. "I will relay your message."

"For security reasons, keep this between us for now."

"Of course, Grand Admiral."

Mira closed the line.

Within fifteen minutes, *Blood Wyvern* docked in its usual hangar. Mira, Fergus, Linus, and Plato stood in the ship's wardroom.

"I suppose this is goodbye," Mira said. She seemed to put on a brave face, but Lucian could tell she was worried.

He didn't blame her. "We'll have this sorted out soon. You'll see."

She offered a wan smile, as if knowing that wasn't true, but she didn't challenge it. "We'll hold down the fort here. You'd better get moving, son. I love you."

After everyone said their goodbyes, there was no time to waste. Lucian and the others returned to the bridge and instructed the autopilot to head out into space.

Within a minute, he created the portal to Volsung, instructing the ship to land on the island of Transcend Mount.

Less than fifteen minutes later, they were touching down among deep snowdrifts, with the icy ocean extending in all directions. It was the depths of a northern Volsung winter, with temperatures well below zero. They suited up and headed out, battling the north wind as they pushed toward the Academy entrance.

Just being here again filled Lucian with melancholy. The northern latitudes of Volsung were truly a dreary place, but there was also a strange sense of heaviness that he couldn't place. Something that went beyond the climate.

The Transcends were waiting for him near the central brazier that provided ample warmth, apparently sensing his arrival. Every Transcend, save for one.

"Sorcerer-Ascendant," Transcend Red began. "This is a surprise."

From their somber expressions, Lucian could immediately tell something was wrong.

He looked up and down the line. "Where is Transcend White?"

The silence that followed was telling.

"She isn't well, Sorcerer-Ascendant," Transcend Red said. "She hasn't been for the past week."

"How bad is it?"

Transcend Red's face was pale. "We fear she may not be long for the Worlds, Sorcerer-Ascendant. She has deteriorated quickly and refuses all longevity treatments."

Lucian's heart skipped a beat at the news, a chill settling over him that had nothing to do with Volsung's winter cold.

"Let's not delay then," he said, struggling to keep his voice steady. "I need to see her."

"She instructed no one was to disturb her, but I think in your case, we can make an exception." She turned to Transcend Violet. "Would you take him there and make sure she's ready to see him?"

Transcend Violet didn't object. The others seemed to look to Transcend Red to take the lead. "Of course."

Lucian nodded, turning to the others. "Catch them up on what's happening. I'll meet up with you later."

The others nodded as Lucian headed for Transcend White's tower with Transcend Violet.

"Is she okay?"

Transcend Violet shook her head regretfully. "She's dying, Lucian. All this stress over the last few months has been too much for her."

"How did it happen so fast? It's only been a few weeks since the Siege of Earth."

"At her age, a shift in the wind is all it takes. She projects strength, and no one can match her will or her intellect. But her body has not kept pace."

Lucian couldn't help but feel somewhat responsible for that.

It wasn't long before they reached her door. Transcend Violet entered directly. Two male Talents stood there, their eyes widening before registering recognition.

"Sorcerer-Ascendant," one of them said. "She's upstairs resting."

"I can let her know you're here," Transcend Violet offered.

She ascended the circular staircase, and Lucian waited a couple of minutes in her office. He'd been here twice, so long ago that it almost felt like another life. The scene was much the same as he remembered; the fireplace was blazing hot and casting the walls and various knickknacks in a warm glow. It seemed impossible that Transcend White wouldn't occupy that chair behind that stately desk. She was a force that had shaped the history of humanity and magekind for decades.

If she was dying, Lucian didn't know what the mages would do without her.

Transcend Violet returned and nodded for him to go up. He climbed the stairs to a bedroom with high ceilings and tall windows that offered breathtaking views of the surrounding iced-over ocean. The walls were adorned with framed, digital artwork depicting scenes of what appeared to be humanity's history. A four-poster bed, draped in rich velvet, sat in the center of the room.

And in that bed was Transcend White herself, propped up by pillows. Her wrinkled face was serene, but her dark eyes still held all their fire. But she seemed thinner than ever before, and for the first time, he saw her in humble pajamas rather than the radiant vestments of her office. In such a light, he realized just how frail she was.

"Lucian," she said, her voice somewhat raspy but still strong. "Come closer."

He did so, unsure where to begin. "I'm sorry for disturbing you like this, Transcend White. And I hate to hear such terrible news about your health."

"Bah. It's long overdue, if you ask me. The most pertinent

question of my life has been answered; without that question hounding me, it's as if my spirit is ready to rest, so to speak."

"You mean Vera?"

Transcend White nodded. "Yes. Sad and terrible business. But what can one do? She made her choice, and I made mine. Not the ending I was hoping for, but it's the ending I must go to the grave knowing." She looked at him closely. "But you didn't come to hear about an old woman's troubles."

"I need Khairu to help pilot our ship. Things have gone from bad to worse."

"Indeed?"

Lucian gave her a quick update, and her face darkened at the news.

"The fight is far from over, it seems. You'll have to learn to continue it without me. You've been doing that, anyway. If I could help, I would, though you know you don't need to ask me for permission. You're the Sorcerer-Ascendant, after all."

He understood her point. He outranked her now, which was still a strange thought. "It was more of a courtesy. And of course, after speaking to the Transcends, I wanted to see you, too. And maybe to get some advice while I'm here."

She gave a slight chuckle. "The older I get, the more I realize the vanity of it all. I've accumulated knowledge, yes, and I understand how people work. But I don't think my experience will be helpful to you in defeating the Ancient One." Her eyes became misty, apparently with remembrance. "Believe it or not, I was once your age. In fact, the first time I came into this tower, it was to meet Arian himself, who was then the Sorcerer-Ascendant of Magekind. He was a mentor to me, albeit for a short time."

Such a thing was hard for Lucian to imagine, but he supposed it must have been so. She was old enough to attend the Volsung Academy while Arian was the Sorcerer-Ascendant. Her sister, of course, had attended with her. He wondered how that dynamic had played out.

"A lot of things have happened since then," she said. "At the end of my life, despite how high I have risen, I've played things too safely."

He supposed everyone had regrets in life. He wasn't sure of Transcend White's regrets, but it wasn't his place to poke and prod. It seemed she wanted someone to listen to her.

She gave a small smile. "Vera, of course, was the opposite. Brave, not afraid to take a risk. At some point, our paths diverged, and she dedicated her life to something she truly believed in. What I considered a fable. She was so sure the fraying could be solved that she went to dark places she should never have gone. Perhaps she needed me there to temper her worst proclivities. Who can say? I had the chance to go with her, and I turned her down. There's an alternate life, eh? What we could have been had we met each other in the middle."

"You couldn't have known what would happen. And maybe it needed to happen that way."

"Perhaps. Yes, it's easy to blame oneself using hindsight. What's hard though? Forgiveness. Forgiveness is difficult, but it's the most important thing. Life is too short for anything else. It's a lesson even I must remember."

"What do you think?" Lucian asked. "Is it a good plan to go after the Ancient One like this? Would it be better just to abandon everything, try to bring the Orbs back?"

"I can't answer that for you, Lucian. You'll have to trust your instincts. If you don't have that, what *do* you have? Questions can only lead you so far. At some point, you must be your own answer. Something tells me, though, that you don't have much time to decide. Whether or not you want to, you must face him. It won't be easy. It won't be fair. As powerful as you have become, he has something you don't in this strange Shadow Magic, if it can even be called such."

"Do you think it's a new Aspect?"

"Who knows? It's like nothing I've ever heard of. After everything that's happened, would it be so impossible?"

He realized it wouldn't be. "Will you be all right, Transcend White?"

"Vivienne," she insisted. "Stars above, it's been so long since anyone's called me that. Don't worry about me, Lucian. I'm just an old woman, frail, weak, and ineffectual. I will go where everyone goes when they die. And my Focus will go to the Manifold."

"Vivienne," he said, surprised at how natural it felt to call her that. It made her just a person, not the distant and powerful master of the Volsung Academy.

She smiled in memory. "Oh, how I was so excited to be a mage. I can still feel the cool wind from the prow of the ship. I can hear the excited buzz of conversation from all the others, just hoping they would be selected to train here. The Volsung Academy, the greatest mage school in all the Worlds. Not even Vera could have spoiled my mood that beautiful day. We got into a bit of a tiff. Landed us bathroom duty on day one." She attempted to laugh, but only ended up coughing. Lucian offered her water from the nearby nightstand, which she drank gratefully. "It was a long time back, but if I close my eyes, it's almost as if I'm there. Reliving everything. It's all gone in a blink. That day, those years, that were all so real, as real as this. No one remembers anymore. No one but me. It's . . . the cruelest thing. For all of my sister's faults, we at least shared that."

She was silent for a time. He felt a tear come to his eye as he realized how this strong and proud woman had finally been humbled by age and time.

"You want my advice? I can tell you this much. Hold Serah close. Hold whatever matters close. The universe is a dark place, so we must be stars for each other."

At that moment, she settled into silence, seeming to lose her energy to talk.

"Don't waste any more time on me, Lucian. I suspect by the time you return it will all be over for me. Go now. Believe in yourself. Embrace who you are. Live your truth."

He felt lump, realizing he was saying goodbye. "I will, Vivienne. Thank you. For everything."

"Go, Lucian. Be the hope we need."

He reached for her hand, held it for a moment, before letting go and leaving the room. He felt a profound sadness, but also a sense of determination. Transcend White's words were a potent reminder of the gravity of his task and the fleeting nature of life.

Lucian rejoined the others. He couldn't articulate his feelings, at least at that moment. Khairu was already waiting. Just from his gaze, it seemed they picked up on his mood. That they needed to act, and they needed to act now.

"Take care of her," Lucian said to the gathering of Transcends. "And . . . as the senior Transcend, Transcend Green is in charge until we can hold a proper election. That's how it's written in the Volsung Academy Charter, right?"

Transcend Red blinked at that. Clearly, she had assumed control, bullying her way to the top. But from her face, it seemed she would respect Lucian's wishes. She couldn't go against the Academy's own bylaws.

"The Academy will be in good hands," Transcend Green assured Lucian.

"Whatever plans Transcend White had for the new Tower on Psyche, please set them aside for now. Be on the lookout for a message from Grand Admiral Abrantes, or maybe even the Hegemon."

"We will do so," Transcend Green said.

Lucian looked at his companions. "Let's not waste any more time."

Once on the ship, he explained things more fully. As they left the island behind, he couldn't help but glance back at the

Academy below, particularly at the tower on the northeastern side.

While she wasn't long for the Worlds, her words would stay with him, providing guidance and strength in the dark days ahead.

6

ONCE THEY ARRIVED in the Mako System, it didn't take long to find the remnants of the former Believer Fleet. Most of the debris had scattered in various directions in space, but the broken hulls of the larger vessels remained relatively intact.

They approached the vicinity of the *Holy Fire*, which was so battered and destroyed that it was beyond repair. Already, some automated League salvage crews were on site, assessing what could be recovered from the wreckage.

"We won't find anything here," Jagar said.

He gazed toward Mako itself, the place where he had trained long ago under Lakhmu's guidance. A place where he had trained with the likes of Ansaldra, Xara, Vera, and Sharo.

"To think that it would all come back here," Jagar mused.

Lucian looked toward the planet. Even from this distance, he could feel the powerful pull of the ether emanating from the Source of Power.

But there was something else, too. A dark presence that reminded Lucian of his battle with the Ancient One.

"That's where he is," Lucian said. "And somehow, he's using the Source of Power to attack us. Controlling his shadows from afar."

"Is that even possible?" Serah asked. "That's scary."

"It's the only thing that makes sense. It also explains why he can make these Shadow Bonds now, but not before. He needs the power of the Source to pull it off. He's channeling it somehow."

Emma frowned as she considered the problem. "If he has access to so much ether, he'll be hard to stop."

"All five of us against him, the Source of Power, and all the Focuses he's absorbed along the way," Serah said. "Do we have a plan, or are we just going in guns blazing?"

"Well," Jagar said, "it's hardly something we can plan for. I say we just go duke it out. Lucian has to drive that spear of his right into him. That's the long and short of it. We do that, then we can focus on returning those Orbs to the Heart of Creation."

It sounded like a plan to Lucian. "All right. There's a spot I remember by the lake with the cave. The ship should fit there. After we land, we can go inside and check things out."

"Ready when you are," Emma said.

"Me, too," Serah said. "Let's go kick some Shadow Man ass."

Khairu piloted the ship toward the planet. It wasn't long before *Blood Wyvern* was cutting through the thick atmosphere. Within minutes, they were hovering above the ruined complex of the Mako Academy. The sight of ash and charred timbers reminded Lucian of the tragedy that had occurred here, with Lakhmu sacrificing his life to remove Vera's brand.

He didn't want to linger too long. "See that valley over there? Fly that way and slow down when you see a lake. There are a lot of trees, but there should be a clearing not too far from the cave entrance."

Khairu followed his directions, and within half an hour, they landed. They exited the ship and headed for the water's edge.

The heat was intense, so Lucian raised a reverse Thermal shield to protect them from the harsh sun and oppressive humidity.

Lucian guided them across the lake, creating a pathway perfectly counterbalanced against the pull of Mako's gravity, allowing them to walk across. All too soon, they reached the dark, foreboding entrance of the cave.

While Lucian was streaming Radiance to mask their presence, he knew it was still likely a being as powerful as the Ancient One could sense the Orbs.

"Be ready for anything," he said.

He carefully led them across the water inside the cave, only letting go of Gravitonics when they had reached the interior shoreline.

Lucian created a bright sphere of light to ward off any unwelcome wildlife that might be lurking. To his relief, the cave was empty.

He gestured toward the tunnel ahead, and as they moved forward, he couldn't help but feel that something was different this time.

He didn't want to take any risks, so he took a couple of minutes to forge a powerful seven-sealed shield, while Emma created a shield of her own blocking Space-Time, covering every base they could. Lucian summoned Lightspear while the others readied their own shockspears. They approached the cliff at the end of the tunnel, where the Source's light shone with an unreal, blinding radiance. Lucian warded the light to see more easily, but there was no sign of the Ancient One.

At last, they reached the cliff that led down to the Source. As they peered downward, something else caught Lucian's attention: something unexpected yet unmistakable. The portal hung in the air, perpendicular to the floor, with a dark sinuous line connecting it to the Source of Power. It was ringed with darkness, while its interior thrummed with deep violet energy.

"A portal," Emma said.

"Let's check it out," Jagar suggested.

"Don't mind if I do," Serah said.

She generated an anti-gravity aura large enough to cover them all. Instantly, Lucian felt lighter on his feet.

They stepped off the cliff and descended slowly toward the chamber floor, landing lightly about ten paces from the ovoid portal. While its border was white, on the other side lay pure darkness, with no clue where it might lead. There was no sign of the Ancient One, either in this chamber or beyond, though they couldn't be sure without stepping through.

"Of all the things in the Worlds, this was probably the last thing I expected to see," Khairu said.

Lucian was already heading toward it.

"Lucian!" Serah called. "It could be a trap. What if it's Shadow Magic?"

He paused, thinking for a moment. "There is some magic here I don't recognize, but it's forming the shell of the brand. That means it will not affect the stream's function."

"Even so," Emma said. "It's a risk to go in there."

"What *is* the function of the stream?" Jagar asked.

"I'm sensing every Aspect, but Space-Time is the strongest component."

"That makes sense," Emma said. "It's a portal."

"Except the stream is *reversed* in this portal," Lucian said. "I've never seen one quite like it. But I'm pretty sure the Ancient One himself drove Sharo to step through it. If we want to find him, then we need to go inside."

They were all silent for a long moment, considering. There was just no telling what would be on the other side. It was obvious the portal could only exist by continually siphoning ether from the Source of Power. That was precisely why the Ancient One had created it here.

"If we're going to do this, let's go," Jagar said. "But we should all try to enter at the same time, and make sure we're creating a powerful shield and come out guns blazing."

It was a wise suggestion.

"Line up," Lucian said. "Fall into step with me."

He waited a moment to ensure everyone was ready. Once they were all lined up, they began walking forward in sync.

As they approached, Lucian felt a strange distortion emanating from the portal. It was unlike any typical portal, but he remained determined to go through all the same.

When they entered, Lucian felt himself stretched. He opened his mouth to scream, but no sound came out. Everything was dark, yet paradoxically, blindingly bright. He couldn't make sense of where he was or where he was going.

The sensation lasted anywhere from a few seconds to several hours. It was impossible to say. When Lucian and the others snapped back to reality, they found the portal behind them, along with a sense of vertigo and dizziness, as if he'd just stepped off a carousel.

Once his double vision corrected, he could tell it was the same chamber, but there were subtle differences that were difficult to quantify. The air seemed cooler, with less moisture. The rock formations had changed in ways he couldn't quite pinpoint. The sound of water dripping echoed from somewhere above them.

He looked around, relieved to see that everyone had made it. "Everyone all right?"

"*That* was a trip," Serah said. She sniffed the air tentatively. "Smells drier than before, if that even makes sense."

"Feels weird," Emma said. "It's the same but . . . *different*. Why would it spit us out in the same place?"

Jagar surveyed the area, appearing not to trust his surroundings.

"Let's head for the cave entrance," Lucian suggested. "He isn't here."

Lucian sensed something else too, something different not just in the environment, but within himself. But he couldn't focus on that for now. They needed to find the Ancient One. No one else could have created that bizarre portal.

To his surprise, there was a crude staircase carved into the cliff, so obvious that he wasn't sure how they had missed it before. The others eyed it warily, but they had no choice but to ascend.

The tunnel, too, had changed. The walls were smooth, and stranger still, ancient runes covered the surface—writings that hadn't been there before.

"This is getting weird," Jagar said.

Lucian had an idea, but it was still too early to say.

They exited the tunnel and found the lake completely absent, replaced instead by an empty cavern. There was little other adornment. In the distance, Lucian could see the cave mouth's dim light. He guessed it was nighttime.

He released his Thermal shield, realizing it was no longer necessary. The air blowing from the entrance was mild, quite different from the sultry air he had been expecting.

As they reached the cave entrance, Lucian's suspicions were confirmed. Instead of the familiar landscape, the outside world was completely transformed. The once-vibrant lake had vanished, replaced by a valley filled with deciduous trees. The stars were many and bright, casting ample light on the scene. The air was cool and pleasant, holding a sweet fragrance, a far cry from Mako's sweltering heat.

Yet, the overall shape of the land remained similar, with subtle differences that were hard to identify. Most astonishing of all, the distant mountain peaks, near where the Mako Academy would be, were capped with snow.

It was Mako all right, but a different version. Lucian wasn't sure exactly what was happening, but the distorting effect of the portal was making sense, along with the reversed Space-Time stream.

Lucian felt a sinking realization that this mission would prove more complex than he had initially expected. The Ancient One was out there somewhere. But where *was* this place? Or perhaps the more pertinent question was, *when* was this place?

Emma seemed to echo his thoughts. "This is going to sound crazy, but I'm thinking we might have traveled in time."

"Yeah," Lucian said. "I was thinking the same thing."

Again, the altered landscape stared back at them, defying them to think of another explanation. But no alternative explanation seemed plausible.

"Okay," Jagar said. "If we've traveled in time, can we figure out what year it is?"

"This must be far removed from our own time," Emma explained. "The climate is very different, considerably cooler. Earth-like worlds often have warmer and cooler periods, cycles that can last tens of thousands of years or longer. I don't know Mako's specific situation, but for such a drastic difference, we must be in one of the cooler periods. The trees are also an entirely different species compared to when we entered. I'd guess we've moved millions of years into either the past or the future."

"Okay," Khairu said. "Is there a way to confirm it?"

"There's no GalNet to look up the information," Lucian said, checking his slate just to be sure. "I don't know if that would help in this situation, anyway."

"We already have a clue," Emma pointed out. "Those runes appear well-maintained, and there are stairs. Clearly, some civilization exists. What civilization might have been on this world in the past?"

"Starsea?" Serah guessed.

Emma nodded. "Yes, it's either them or an even more distant past. Ten million years ago, during the Builders' time when the

Gates were first created by the Ancient One. That would be the First Starsea Empire, not the Second One."

"That's wild if true," Lucian said.

"Maybe so, but it makes sense," Emma said. "The Ancient One first came into our reality ten million years ago. He was also present during the time of the Second Starsea Empire, one million years ago. Maybe he created this time gate so that he could lead us to a place where he had an advantage over us."

"So, just to clarify, the Ancients from a million years ago and the Builders from ten million years ago are two separate species, right?" Serah asked.

Emma nodded. "That's my assumption. To put things in perspective, human civilization is closer in time to the Ancients, the Second Starsea, than the Ancients are to the Builders, the First Starsea. One million years separate us from the Ancients, while nine million years separate them from the Builders. There was no overlap between the two, as far as we know. We already know what the Ancients look like because we've seen them before. They're reptilian, tall, long-limbed, with gray or blue skin, red eyes . . . as for the Builders, who can say what *they* were like? Given the significant difference in plant life here, my guess is we're ten million years in the past. It's hard to imagine even a million years causing this much change, but I leave room for the possibility."

"Okay, why could we not be in the future?" Lucian asked.

"Well, it's possible. But those runes would have to correspond to a future and distant civilization that is most likely not humanity. It would either be an entirely different species, or a species into which humans have evolved."

"Not impossible," Khairu said. "But speculation is fruitless. How can we actually verify the time? Knowing that will help us understand what we're dealing with."

"I already have an idea," Emma said, glancing up at the night sky. "I have the star positions from our own time saved on my slate. All we'd have to do is to compare them to *this* night sky, and that should give us a year, within a certain margin of error."

"You have star positions saved on your slate?" Serah asked.

"I'm an astronomy nerd," Emma said. "Always have been. We can compare the positions of the stars in the sky here to my data and run a simulation to determine which time period it best corresponds to."

"That would require a significant amount of processing power," Khairu said. "That power relies on GalNet servers, and there's no GalNet here."

"I have a high-quality slate," Emma said. "The best money can buy. It will take some time, but I'm confident it can run the simulation."

"It's like you were prepared," Lucian said.

"Never underestimate the power of a good slate," Emma said.

She was already aiming her slate at the sky to take a reading. After completing the task and spending a couple of minutes working with the slate, she lowered the device. "All right. It's estimating two hours."

"That's quite a wait," Khairu said.

"Maybe it's for the best," Lucian said. "It's nighttime here, so we might as well take advantage of it. Knowing Mako, we don't have much time before daybreak. Let's get a few hours of sleep inside the cave, then we can review the results in the morning."

"Sounds like a plan," Jagar said.

They retreated into the cave. Lucian was eager to explore this new reality, but while things were still unfamiliar, he didn't want to stray too far from the gate. They hadn't gotten any rest since the Ancient One's attack on Nessus, and he knew his team would be better for it.

They didn't have much outside basic gear in their packs because they hadn't expected this bizarre turn of events. But they had enough to make a stew over a makeshift fire. He didn't sense the Ancient One at all, meaning he was far away from this location. He knew the cave was likely being monitored, so he set a powerful Radiant ward to mask their Focuses from detection.

If they were discovered, the time gate was right behind them. Escaping back to their own time and trying again would be easy.

"I'll keep watch," Jagar said. "All of you get some rest."

Lucian nodded gratefully and closed his eyes.

7

LUCIAN SLEPT for an indeterminate amount of time before something caused his eyes to snap open, his heart pounding in his chest.

He rose, but the cave was dark and silent. He conjured a basic Radiant stream, finding the action surprisingly difficult, and spotted Jagar sitting on a rock, looking toward the mouth of the cave. It was still night outside. Only a few hours could have elapsed.

But despite the silence, Lucian sensed a distinct danger permeating the air. If magic was this hard to stream, it could only be for one reason.

Someone, or perhaps a group of *someones*, was warding them.

He approached Jagar as silently as he could. The older man noticed his movement and reached out Psionically.

Everything all right?

We're being warded. Can't you sense it?

Jagar frowned in obvious confusion. *No, I don't. What makes you so sure?*

I feel . . . weaker. There can be no other explanation.

At that very moment, a guttural war cry pierced the air from the direction of the cave mouth.

Everyone was up in an instant, shockspears out. Lucian watched as over a dozen Ancient warriors entered the cave, flowing white robes, gray reptilian skin, and shockspears alight with magic. Their red eyes glowed menacingly in the darkness as their discordant and harsh language filled the air.

More were entering from behind them, until about two dozen warriors faced them down, forming a semicircle that forced them deeper back into the cave. The longer they waited, the worse this would get.

Lucian instinctively summoned Lightspear, while reaching for his Orbs to draw as much ether as possible. The Orbs would get them out of this situation, just as they had so many times in the past.

But to his dismay, he only felt a gaping void in his Focus where his Orbs *should* have been.

Panic set in immediately. He kept reaching in vain, but after a few seconds, it became obvious.

He didn't *have* the Orbs.

He still held Lightspear in his hand, apparently not having lost that. But without the Orbs, he didn't know how they could stand against so many of these warrior mages.

There was only one thing they could do, especially as more of the warriors piled in from the cave entrance.

"Retreat!" Lucian commanded. "Head back to the gate now!"

They cast him quick glances, but as soon as the order registered, they sprang into action, backing away toward the tunnel.

But the Ancients wouldn't let them escape so easily. Their shockspears crackled with electricity, while magical blasts of fire scorched the ground before them, creating a wall of flames that blocked access to the tunnel. Lucian extinguished them by Atomically creating some water while cooling the area with reverse

Thermalism. This action, which would have been so simple before, took far more effort than it should have.

Without his Orbs, he simply couldn't draw ether quickly enough.

As they leaped across the remains of the fires, Serah stumbled. Lucian streamed a quick tether to give her a boost, and she landed safely on the other side. He could see the fear in her blue eyes, and that fear only fueled his determination to get them out of this ambush.

Serah wasn't the only one with a close call. Jagar narrowly dodged a shockspear that whizzed past his head, its electricity humming. Emma unleashed a powerful kinetic blast, knocking several mages off their feet, buying them precious seconds.

But the Ancient warriors would not be so easily resisted. Khairu attempted to absorb a lightning bolt aimed at Serah with a magnetic shield, but the impact knocked them both to the ground, leaving them vulnerable. Serah rolled away just as another mage lunged at her with a shockspear.

Lucian's heart clenched with fear; the thought of losing her was unbearable. Gritting his teeth, he launched Lightspear at the Ancient, scoring a direct hit. The warrior instantly disintegrated into a pile of ash, and Serah rolled safely away to rejoin the others.

The mages were gathering for another attack. Lucian knew they needed more space to retreat, but he couldn't beat them back with simple streams. What he needed was sorcery.

The Shadow Realm faded, replaced by the Ether. Perhaps he didn't have his Orbs, but he still had Lakhmu's lessons. Combining Radiance, Binding, and Psionics, he streamed a shattering laser, sweeping it toward the mouth of the cave. Dozens of mages fell to the attack, instantly disintegrating as soon as the pulsating beam of light made contact. The laser only lasted a few seconds before Lucian's ether was extinguished.

It gave enough of a reprieve to retreat into the tunnel leading to the gate.

Lucian drew more ether from the Manifold itself, gaining just enough to create a Binding barrier over the tunnel entrance. Already, he felt the shield being battered by the Ancients' magic. Under that assault, it would only give them a few extra seconds.

They fled down the tunnel, down the stairs, and back to the time gate. Without a moment's hesitation, they plunged through, leaving the mages and this perilous reality behind.

Lucian again felt himself being stretched as time itself slipped away. After what seemed hours, the group found themselves back in familiar territory, the cave of the modern day they were accustomed to.

"Everyone all right?" Emma asked.

Lucian's emotions were a whirlwind, and losing his Orbs was more of a blow than the sudden ambush. Clearly, the time travel had caused them to disappear somehow.

Back in his own time, however, the Orbs should be back in his possession.

Just to be sure, he reached for them.

He found only a gaping emptiness.

Lucian felt an icy dread as the others struggled to catch their breath. Their faces were a mix of relief and lingering fear.

Serah, her eyes still wide, noticed Lucian's state. "Hey, you all right? What's wrong?"

Lucian sank to the ground, unable to believe what had happened. Everything they had done over the past two years had been completely erased by a single poor decision.

Of course, that had been the purpose of the time gate. The Ancient One had somehow known it would strip him of his Orbs, and worse, Lucian couldn't understand *why* it had happened.

But he didn't know what could have been done to prevent it. They had to go after the Ancient One or risk the Shadow Bond spreading to even more people.

He wasn't sure what he could have done differently.

"Lucian?" Emma asked. "It's all right. We're alive. Clearly, we can't do anything against the Ancient One like this, so we just need to focus on returning the Orbs now. Right? Lucian?"

Lucian's heart raced as he turned to face his friends. He'd never seen them look so concerned.

He must have been quite the sight. At last, he forced himself to say it.

"They're gone."

"What do you mean, *gone*?" Khairu asked. "Of course, the Ancients are gone. They haven't followed us here. Maybe they're not capable of doing so."

"No," he said. "*The Orbs* are gone. I don't have them anymore."

Jagar shook his head. "What are you talking about? That can't be right . . ."

"Seriously?" Serah asked, fear returning to her eyes. "How is that possible?"

"I don't know. It just is."

He walked toward the side of the chamber, where the stairs would have been in the other time period, what Lucian now knew to be the past. The stairs were gone here, completely erased.

They were back in the present all right.

"Maybe we can head back," Emma said, doubtfully. "When did you notice they were gone?"

"Right before the attack, I noticed something was off. I thought we were being warded, but Jagar confirmed we weren't. I . . . was just sensing my own natural power. A power that's much weaker without the Orbs." He shook his head. "I suppose I lost them as soon as we passed through that thing."

"But . . . why?" Serah asked. "And how?"

Lucian remained silent. He didn't have the answers, and truth be told, it was all too much to consider. He was still in a state of disbelief. After getting so many things right, he'd truly and royally messed up humanity's one chance of survival.

"Maybe they're in the portal itself," Khairu said. "It's confusing in there. Probably some weird quantum stuff going on. Perhaps in that state, the Orbs sort of come loose from a mage's Focus." She shrugged. "I've got nothing else."

"Well, the last thing I want to do is go back there," Emma said, "but if we need to for the sake of finding the Orbs, then we shouldn't hesitate."

Lucian saw her point. He didn't relish the idea, either, but he saw no other choice.

"Everyone, stay here," he said. "It was my mistake, so I'll just risk myself."

Before they could counter him, he strode toward the portal.

But when he was just a few steps away, it suddenly contracted and winked out of existence.

8

ALL OF THEM stared at where the gate had been for a long moment in shock. Only the Source of Power remained behind it, thrumming with potential.

"Hey!" Serah shouted. "What happened?"

Lucian stared in shock. Now that he had lost his Orbs, the Ancient One's plan was complete. He'd kept the gate open long enough for them to enter it, and then to return empty-handed. The Ancient mages may have been planted there specifically to drive Lucian and the others back into the gate, effectively cutting them off from the Orbs.

Lucian gazed at the Source of Power, the massive energy rift that still pulsed with potential. The Ancient One had used it to create a time gate without the aid of the Orbs.

Perhaps Lucian could attempt the same thing.

Before he could think further about how to go about it, Jagar created a flame in his hands. The warrior nodded, as if confirming a fact.

"I felt no poison from streaming that," Jagar said. "That means the Orbs are active here. Someone possesses all Seven."

"What?" Khairu asked. "How can that be?"

Lucian reached for his Focus again to be certain. But that was when he realized something.

He had only tried to detect the seven *original* Orbs. He hadn't tried to reach out for Space-Time, which occupied another part of his Focus.

He reached for it, and with a start, he understood that perhaps not all was lost.

He couldn't help but smile. True, the Orb would be useless without the others to empower it. But it was something.

"I have the Orb of Space-Time," he said. "I just assumed it was gone with the rest."

Emma closed her eyes in relief. "It's something, right? Ether isn't toxic. Magic is functioning properly."

Jagar nodded. "Aye, that's right. I felt the same thing in that cave during the fight. Magic was working as it should have. Meaning someone there had all Seven Orbs, too."

"The Ancient One?" Serah wondered.

Jagar nodded. "It could be no one else."

"You have a theory?" Emma inquired.

Jagar hesitated as he considered. "The Orbs are unique objects, right? There can only be one of them. Can you imagine having two Orbs of Binding, for example?"

Lucian saw his point. The very thought of it seemed contradictory.

"That's logical," Emma agreed.

"Assuming that's true," Jagar continued, "when we went to the past—a past where the Ancient One exists—he already held all Seven Orbs. As such, Lucian wouldn't have been able to keep *his* Orbs if we arrived a time after the Ancient One had gathered all seven."

"If that's true," Serah said, "then Lucian would have his Orbs again once he came back to this time. Correct?"

"And why would Lucian have been the one to lose his Orbs in the first place?" Khairu asked. "Why not the Ancient One?"

Jagar looked at them both. "My guess it, it's because the Ancient One already *had* them. So when someone else comes along who has them too, reality may default to the one who already holds them previously in the timeline, so to speak. At least, that's my theory. As for Serah's question, that's the trickier one. If we are indeed in the present, then maybe something about the past has changed. My idea is that we've created a whole new timeline. A timeline where the Ancient One has kept the Orbs this entire time."

"What are you talking about?" Serah asked. "That's crazy."

"There's merit to the idea," Emma said. She was examining her slate. "It's as I suspected."

"What?" Lucian asked, hungry for any piece of information that might give them answers.

"My slate is done processing the stars from the time we just came from. At first, I thought we were ten million years in the past, but it turns out I was wrong. It was actually one million years ago."

"Meaning?" Serah asked.

"The Ancient One, using the Second Immortal as an avatar—that avatar might even be Sharo Khalin—had the Orbs in the past, right? But when we escaped back to our own time, we might have created an alternate timeline, as Jagar said."

"Are we sure it's the Ancient One who has the Orbs?"

Emma continued her line of thought. "That's the most likely answer. My theory is that Sharo Khalin, directed by the Ancient One, created the time gate we went through, intending it as a trap that would strip Lucian of the Orbs. When we returned to *this* reality, we did so without stopping the Ancient One a million years ago. This led to an alternate timeline where Starsea never fell and could repel the *Alkasen*."

"That would mean he's still alive," Jagar said.

"Yes, that's likely," Emma answered. "However, there are other possibilities, too. For instance, Starsea could have fallen, but another human in this timeline might have gathered the Orbs, becoming the Third Immortal."

"Xara Mallis?" Khairu asked in disbelief.

"It's possible. We won't know until we go out there. We traveled to the past and failed to stop the Ancient One. Therefore, he survived all this time with no one challenging him, right up to the present day."

"We're not even certain we're back in modern times yet," Serah said. "Maybe the gate transported us to an entirely different era, or maybe the gate can access *any* point in time."

"Well, if that's the case, it's too late to test the theory," Emma said. "The gate is gone. The Ancient One likely caused that to keep us from going back once we realized our mistake."

"So, if the Ancient One still has the Orbs," Serah said, "why does Lucian still have the Orb of Space-Time?"

Lucian knew the answer to that one. "The Second Immortal never got the Orb of Space-Time. The First Immortal did. During his war with the *Alkasen* ten million years ago, he sent the Orbs forward in time. That's what Silumko told me on Nai Elyn. The only exception was the Orb of Space-Time. That one didn't move forward with the others, and presumably, the *Alkasen* got their hands on it. A series of events happened between then and when Arian discovered it—events we can't be certain about. But that's not the point. The point is that the Ancient One didn't have the Orb of Space-Time one million years ago, and no other being did, either. That's why I still have it."

"My head hurts," Serah said.

"It makes sense, though it is mind-bending," Emma said. "It's further evidence that we visited the time of the Second Starsea, around a million years ago."

"Okay, let's assume all this is true," Khairu said. "That would mean that the Ancient One and the Second Immortal are still alive. Or perhaps we're in an alternate version of our world where Xara Mallis is in control. All of human history could be entirely different!"

"We won't know what we're dealing with until we leave this cave," Emma said. "But no matter *who* has the Orbs, one thing is certain." She looked at Lucian. "They'll want to find you and get the Orb of Space-Time. And if the Ancient One is in control, he'll know to look for you here. After all, he's the one who created the gate, and it was probably designed to collapse as soon as someone went back through it. He might know how to detect that."

"That's not guaranteed," Jagar said.

"No, it's not. But we should behave as if he *can*, if only because it's safer."

"That would mean he's been waiting for a million years for this very moment," Serah said. "There's no way he can know the exact date we were going to appear!"

"Maybe, maybe not," Emma said. "He could know we're here. So, we should get our bearings and figure things out."

"One thing's clear," Lucian said.

"What?" Serah asked.

"For *our* version of reality to exist, we were supposed to deal with the Ancient One in the past we just came from. That's what led to this new timeline where I no longer have the Orbs."

"Yeah, maybe," Khairu said. "But without the Orbs, it wasn't a battle we could win."

Lucian nodded. "Either way, if we want to return to our own timeline, we have to complete the loop, so to speak."

"Complete the loop?" Serah asked. "What does that mean?"

"It means I have to gain control of the Orbs in *this* timeline and use them to create our own time gate. Then, we use that gate to go back to the past and deal with the Ancient One there."

"But you'd still lack the Orbs," Emma said. "As soon as you gather the Orbs here and go to the past, you'd just lose them again. That means defeating him not just once, in this alternate reality, but twice. You'd also have to beat him again in the past as well, and both times without the benefit of the Orbs."

"Rotting hell, this is so messed up," Serah said. "Okay, so why can't Lucian just create his own time gate? The Ancient One did it without the Orbs, so maybe Lucian can, too."

"I need the Source of Power to do it," Lucian said. "And the only moment in time I have a memory of is the one where we're being attacked. That's not going to go well."

From everyone's silence, it seemed they got his point.

But it was similarly impossible in this time period since someone, most likely the Ancient One, controlled all the Orbs. Lucian had nothing more than Lightspear and the practically useless Orb of Space-Time, which would only allow him to stream indefinitely without fraying.

"I know this seems insane," Lucian said, "but maybe this is how things are supposed to happen. The Ancient One believes he's rewriting history to his benefit, but what if he's wrong? What if there's still a way to stop him, against all odds? If all of this was *supposed* to happen, that means all the tools to defeat him exist in *this* time period. We just have to find them."

"That's supposing all of this has happened before," Khairu said. "In a manner of speaking. That would mean in *our* timeline, we succeeded in this alternate timeline, defeated the Ancient One, and then traveled to the past to defeat him again. It stretches credulity a bit."

"But it's all we have. So, we have no choice but to believe it's possible. What's the other option? Giving up? We've come too far to do that."

"That's a good point," Emma said. "It's a reason to go on, at least."

The others nodded in agreement. This was far beyond Lucian's comprehension, and he was certain there were many other complications he simply hadn't considered yet.

However, there was no other path forward. They would have to figure this out one step at a time. He couldn't dwell on it too much, or he would be overwhelmed with doubts.

"We'll start by getting out of this cave. We'll find a safe place to stay. Then, Emma can use her slate to get a star reading to confirm the time. Assuming the stars correspond to modern times, that would be further evidence of everything we've just talked about."

"And after that?" Khairu asked.

"We'll find the Ancient One. He's somewhere in this reality. I still have Lightspear, and that might be all I really need to kill him."

Lucian knew it wasn't that simple, but maybe it *was*. There *had* to be a way out of this.

At least, he had to convince himself of that, or he would lose all hope.

"We should move out," he said.

He led the way to the cliff and climbed. He had no choice but to face this uncertain reality. The others were depending on him.

But inside, he was reeling from everything that had happened. He wasn't sure what the future held, but they had to go out and face it all the same.

9

WHEN THEY REACHED the cavern lake, the temperature was cooler than in the present they knew, but substantially warmer than the past they had just visited. Lucian wasn't sure what to make of that yet.

Without the Orbs, Lucian realized he was no longer the strongest in every individual Aspect. He would have to rely on his friends to cover his weaknesses.

It was Serah who created a pathway of anti-grav discs to cross the lake toward the entrance, outside of which was a small island absent in their own time period.

Serah took a break, and Lucian took over by tethering everyone toward the central island one by one. His manipulation of ether seemed to go in slow motion. It took him far longer to gather the required amount of ether. Although the Orb of Space-Time enabled him to gather ether faster than if he didn't have any Orbs at all, it was still substantially less than what he was used to.

They took a brief break on the island, and Serah frowned in thought.

"Don't get me wrong, it's rotting hot here, but it's not as bad as our own time. I wonder why."

"It might be winter," Emma said. "We'll have to wait until nighttime for me to check the sky and confirm we are actually in the present."

Once they were settled onto the far shoreline, Lucian was drenched with sweat. The spot where they had parked the spaceship was completely vacant. Its absence was further evidence that this reality was entirely separate from the one they had left behind.

"Okay," Serah said. "Now what? I'm hot, tired, and hungry." She looked at the lake. "Say, Khairu. Can you fry that water with electricity? I could go for some fish."

"How do you know there's fish in there?"

"It's water. *Of course* there are fish."

"Not necessarily. This isn't Earth, Volsung, or even Psyche. This world has a completely different biome."

"Well, *critters*, then. I'm not above a nice snake. I'm not picky."

No one else seemed to have the heart to talk, including Lucian. It was easy to see why. There was no telling what awaited them here. For all they knew, this planet was completely uninhabited, and there was no way off.

But the Ancient One—or at least, the person holding all the Orbs—was here.

Lucian just had to find the next right thing to do. It was too much to think in grand terms.

"Yes, food would be a start," he said. "We don't have anything to lose by trying."

He reached for Dynamism and Radiance, creating an aura that allowed him to detect electrical impulses in the surrounding environment, no matter how minor. Within the lake, he saw several creatures that could be described as fish, though, being on an alien planet, they had likely taken a different evolutionary path, as Khairu had pointed out.

Whatever they were, they were dinner.

Lucian found a likely spot, pointed his spear, and shot a lightning bolt at the water's surface.

Not a moment later, they had a dozen creatures to choose from, all of them eel-like in composition, while a couple had entirely too many legs.

"On second thought," Serah said, "I'm not so hungry anymore."

"Those things look poisonous," Emma said, her nose wrinkling. "And they *stink*."

Lucian had to agree. "Well, if there's nothing we can eat here, we're screwed. Lakhmu survived on this planet, and he had to have eaten the local wildlife and plants."

Jagar gave a noncommittal grunt. "Well, I lived a few years on Mako when I was a lad, and I don't recall ever eating anything from the lowlands. This area is avoided."

"So, all the good eating's up in those mountains, huh?" Serah asked.

"You might say that."

"That's what we'll do," Lucian said. "Head uphill. Maybe head for the Mako Academy. Best-case scenario, it's there. Worst-case, we'll get a good view to scope out the terrain."

"Where is it?" Serah asked.

Lucian nodded toward the slope rising before them. "If we follow that up, it'll get us close. It would be a good idea to get a bit of altitude before nightfall. It'll be cooler, for one. As for food, the human body can survive a month without it."

"A *month*?" Serah asked. "You're crazy. I don't think I could survive a day without eating."

"I'm sure we'll figure out the food situation. The Academy site isn't too far from here. Maybe a couple of days away at most, and we can get there faster using magic. Unless anyone has a better idea, let's plan on that."

"What do we do if the Academy isn't there?" Serah asked.

"I don't know. Explore the planet, see if we can find anything."

"Lovely."

"I know it's not ideal, but we'll learn more as time goes on. Let's try not to get overwhelmed in the meantime. Find the next thing to do. Easy enough, right? And right now, the next thing is heading toward the mountain and maybe finding something better to eat."

From the others' silence, it didn't seem as if they bought that. Lucian wasn't sure he did, either, but as the leader, he had to say something encouraging. The minute they saw him give up hope, they would, too.

He started his way up the slope, and the others followed.

Night fell a few hours later, and after they found a somewhat sheltered spot on a cliff, Jagar built up a fire while Emma got out her slate and scanned the clear night sky.

An hour later, she had a match.

"Modern day," she said. "Just like we thought. We can be anywhere five hundred years forward or backward in time, or as little as a few months, or even within a few hours of when we left."

"But why is it so different?" Khairu asked.

"Well, the stars have shifted enough to place us in Mako's cool season," Emma said. "We are obviously in some alternate version of the planet. There are no GalNet signals, though my slate is picking up lots of radio chatter above. Most of the signals are encrypted, so I can't get a lock."

At that moment, their conversation was silenced by the unmistakable sound of a spaceship passing overhead.

Lucian quickly doused the fire with magically created water, motioning for the others to back up against the cliff face. He also streamed a reverse Thermal aura to hide their heat signatures.

But as the heavy transport or freighter passed overhead, it was clear it wasn't looking for them. It didn't slow, its engines making a deep and resonant rumble like the growl of a hungry beast. Lucian felt the vibration in his bones.

It was several minutes before the echoes died on the surrounding mountain slopes, and night creatures resumed their former chorus. The ship was heading in the general direction of the Academy.

Lucian smiled. "So, there *are* people after all."

"A good sign," Khairu conceded, "but what would a heavy ship like that be doing on a world as isolated as Mako?"

"Maybe it's not as isolated in this timeline," Emma said.

"Either way," Lucian said, "we have a lead. That ship was heading toward the Academy. And we should definitely follow it and get some more intel."

They settled down to sleep, Lucian creating a defensive ward just in case.

They were still strangers here, and it made sense to be careful.

———

LUCIAN AWOKE the next morning with an unwelcome pang of hunger. However, he wasn't worried about eating. He reasoned that any place with people advanced enough to use spaceships must have food.

Within minutes, they resumed their hike up the mountain. The going was tougher, but with Lucian's Binding Magic and Serah's Gravitonics, they made quick progress.

Lucian couldn't help but notice how much more difficult it was to stream Binding. His primary was Psionics, and without the Orbs, he was reduced to the same limitations as every other mage, unless he entered the Ether and used sorcery. Sorcery was risky, as it used so much ether that it was easily detectable by other mages.

The upper slopes of the mountains were cooler. Eventually,

they came across a trail heading up the mountain. The trail widened into a proper road, though it remained unpaved.

Finally, the trees thinned as they reached the mountain ridge. On the other side would be the site of the Mako Academy, and hopefully, the ship they'd seen last night.

But as they crested the ridge, Lucian and his companions were stunned by the sight before them.

Spread out before them was a sprawling city, a strange contrast of primitive architecture and technological sophistication. Behind a circular stone wall, buildings primarily made of wood and stone rose. Yet interspersed among these rustic dwellings were gleaming metal towers that rose at least forty or fifty stories. In the distance, Lucian spied contrails of ascending spacecrafts, showing that this city was a hub not only for the surrounding area but worlds outside this one.

Lucian quickly ducked behind the ridge, and the others followed suit.

"What *is* this place?" Serah asked. "That's where the Academy is supposed to be!"

Lucian shook his head. "Who knows? I didn't see anyone down there. Did you?"

Everyone shook their heads.

"Seems a strange spot for a city," Khairu said.

"Well, it seems like our only option to learn more," Lucian said.

"What if we can't understand them?" Serah asked. "They have to be speaking different language, right?"

It was a real consideration. After all, a timeline this diverged from theirs would not speak Standard English.

"Psionic Magic can translate easily enough," Lucian said. "That's how I spoke to Silumko. Just let me do the talking."

"What about us, though?" Emma asked. "We need to understand what is said, too."

Lucian saw that this could be an issue. "It'll take a lot of ether, but I can create a Psionic ward that affects all of us. I'd have to brand each of you, and then your brand will understand everything I can. More than that, if you *speak* through the brand, you'll be able to speak back in the person's language I'm Psionically connected to."

"That's possible?" Serah asked.

"It is," Jagar said. "I did something similar to speak to the wyverns, however, I never took it as far as what Lucian's saying."

"To keep the ward and brands active, though, I'll have to use sorcery. And I'll need someone to shield us with Radiance, because it'll take a lot of magic to make it happen."

"I can shield," Emma said. "So, we'll really be able to understand everything?"

Lucian nodded. "Yes, it should work, as long as I'm Psionically connected with whoever you're talking to. You'll simply just be reading my mind through your own brand, so to speak."

"How long will it take to set up?" Khairu asked.

"A few minutes, probably. Emma, you ready?"

She nodded, and Lucian felt her Radiant ward go up, hopefully powerful enough to cover his magic.

He reached directly into the Manifold, allowing his intuition to guide him. He created each brand in succession, each designed to be a conduit of a primary brand, the one Lucian streamed on himself. All that was required was to connect the primary brand to his target, and the rest would synchronize.

A few minutes later, he let go of the stream, taking a moment to regather his strength.

"Our brands should work now," Lucian said.

"I have a strong Radiant ward up," Emma said.

"If we get into trouble, the rest of you need to pick up the slack," Lucian said. "I only have enough ether left for basic streams. But hopefully, it doesn't come to that. Our goal is to learn more about this world."

"What if something goes wrong?" Jagar asked.

"Do what we always do."

"Kick ass and chew bubble gum, and we're all out of gum?" Serah asked.

Lucian nodded. "Something like that. Wait for my signal before getting violent."

"Sounds reasonable," Serah said. "Ready when you are, Lucian."

The group descended cautiously toward the city.

10

AS THEY APPROACHED THE CITY, Lucian's curiosity was piqued by the fusion of ancient and modern. What was the purpose of the wall? Why were there buildings that looked so primitive along with the futuristic towers advanced enough to be from his own time? What people lived here? And *were* they even human?

One of those questions was answered as they approached what appeared to be the city's main gate, where two Ancient guards stood watch. Lucian felt his stomach drop at the sight. Maybe there were no humans in this reality at all.

The guards' uniforms were made of a lightweight, flexible material that covered their bodies from neck to toe. The fabric had an iridescent sheen, shimmering with shades of silver. They also wore chest plates made of a sleek, metallic alloy, which seamlessly blended with the fabric. In short, the armor was definitely futuristic, a strange contrast to the stone wall behind them. On their hips were holstered shockspears. Mages, then.

The guards eyed the approaching group warily but made no

move to attack or apprehend them. Humans weren't a surprise or unwelcome. Perhaps this was a society where Ancients and humans coexisted. The thought was a strange one, but Lucian supposed anything could be possible.

Lucian took a deep breath and stepped forward, ready to communicate using his Psionic Magic.

When the nearer guard spoke in a harsh, garbled tongue, not too different from the Ancient language he'd learned by speaking with Silumko, Lucian connected to the Ancient's mind to understand the message.

"Where is your master, human?"

Lucian quickly parsed the guard's thoughts. He quickly discovered that in this society, almost all humans were enslaved, the property of an Ancient master. That they were alone, without an Ancient escort, immediately made them suspicious. It would make it almost impossible to navigate not just this city, but all Ancient society.

Lucian would have to play along, at least for now.

"Our master sent us outside the gate," Lucian quickly explained, his words and voice automatically forming the harsh Ancient dialect.

The second guard chortled. "And who is your master, short-lifer?"

"Short-lifer?"

"And half-brain," the other added.

Again, Lucian parsed their thoughts for information, and quickly learned that the Ancients had a naturally longer lifespan and saw themselves as superior to humans because of that. That explained the pejorative of "short-lifer." As for half-brain, they probably saw Lucian as stupid for not understanding something as simple as the first insult.

"Who is your master, short-lifer, or do you have half a tongue, too?"

Lucian quickly sifted through the Ancient's thoughts and pulled the name of an important Ancient who lived in the city. "The Grand Benefactor Sipho. Ever heard of him?"

Now, both guards definitely seemed more suspicious, almost reaching for their shockspears. It was clear the name meant something to them. Lucian gave them a small mental push, increasing their fear of crossing paths with the Ancient noble and his supposed slaves.

"The Grand Benefactor," the first guard said. "I've never heard of him having slaves like you. Ones with weapons and no escorts. One is rare enough. But five?"

"And I've seen none of you before," the second guard added. "It is difficult to tell your kind apart, but I think we would have noticed five humans leaving our walls without an escort."

Lucian's mind quickly formed an answer, using knowledge of Ancient society gathered from the guards' memories. "The Grand Benefactor recalled us from Nai Shairen, where we completed our studies at the Xolani Celestial Academy. As for why you didn't see us leave the walls, we were dropped off to conduct business for our master."

"What kind of business?" the first guard asked.

"None of yours. Take it up with the Grand Benefactor."

The two guards seemed shocked by this response, but Lucian knew the guards could react in one of two ways. Either they would punish him harshly, or they would see them as particularly high-ranking humans who were confident enough in their position as favored servants to not care either way.

From the guards' hesitation, it seemed as if they were going with the second option.

Lucian continued. "We are loyal servants of the Grand Benefactor. We will fight to the death in his honor." Lucian's eyes narrowed. "Or anyone who questions his methods."

"All right, all right," the second guard said. "You can go in. But you short-lifers better be careful. You might not be so lucky next time."

The first guard gave a withering glare with his baleful red eyes, but finally, he nodded toward the gate, which rolled back.

They strode past the gate and into the town.

"Nice work," Emma said.

"Obstacle one cleared," Serah said. She smiled. "The Ancient language sounds so awesome! All that growling and clicking, it's impossible to say anything without sounding angry!"

"You're strangely happy about that," Khairu observed.

"I can switch languages if that bothers you."

"Pipe down," Jagar said. "We're trying to blend in, remember?"

Upon entering the city, Lucian immediately saw that most of the inhabitants were Ancients, dressed in loose-fitting robes of varying quality. The street ahead circled up the rounded peak of the mountain, while on both sides rose buildings of stone and wood, interspersed with more advanced buildings of metal. Quite a few Ancients cast glances their way, and many held advanced devices similar to the slates Lucian knew from his own time.

"Try to look natural," Lucian said. "Like you've been here a thousand times before."

"Sure thing," Serah said. "Strolling through an alternate time-line filled with Ancients with human slaves is just another Tuesday for us."

Several Ancients watched as they passed, seeming to marvel at their strange speech.

"What now?" Khairu asked. "Eventually, someone's going to apprehend us."

"Look," Emma said, pointing. "There are some people over there!"

Indeed, toward their right in a narrow alley were two humans, both men, wearing humble clothing and haggling with a merchant, also human. All three had brown skin, black hair, and thick beards, while wearing roughly woven clothing.

Lucian approached, readying himself to use Psionics to speak to them. He reached out to the nearer of the two humans' minds, parsing his thoughts and quickly discovering they spoke the same language as the Ancients, though they also had their own tongue that was nowhere even close to Ancient.

Lucian spoke to them in their local dialect, knowing it might win their trust.

Once the connection was firm, Lucian called out. "Hello there, friends!"

The two men turned, shocked, each of them offering a hasty bow. Lucian realized that compared to them, their clothing looked quite rich and futuristic, something a wealthy Ancient might wear.

"Rise," Lucian said, deciding it was best to play the part. "I'm looking for information."

"What kind of information, Highborn?"

Neither man would look Lucian directly in the eye. He wanted to tell them there was no need to scrape and bow, but he realized that might look suspicious to others around them.

"We are new here, on an errand from our master," Lucian said. "We want to learn the history of this world and the local customs. That sort of thing."

The men exchanged a nervous glance, but neither dared question him. "The Royal Library is where you should look, Highborn. All knowledge is kept there."

"And where is the Royal Library?"

The man pointed. "Top of the mountain, in the palace." The bearded man looked at him curiously, apparently over some of his earlier trepidation. "You speak our language well, Highborn. Though your accent is strange to me."

"We come from Nai Shairen, the Crown of the Starsea Empire

itself," Lucian said easily. "We learned many things at the Xolani Celestial Academy."

"Ah, yes. I see the tales of that wondrous place have not been exaggerated." The man bowed again. "It was this one's pleasure to serve you, Highborn."

The men scurried away down a nearby alley and around a corner, seeming to want to put as much distance as possible between themselves and Lucian. The merchant, too, was gone, apparently having slipped off during the interaction.

"Strange," Serah said. "If it's this hard to talk to the townsfolk, then who *can* we talk to?"

"Maybe we should change clothing to blend in with the human locals," Khairu said.

It was a good idea. Lucian couldn't help but notice that the merchant who had abandoned his wares sold clothing, the same kind as these two men wore.

"Let's grab some of these," he said.

"It looks scratchy," Serah said, running her hands over the roughly woven fabric. "But if it'll save the galaxy, well, I guess I can deal with it."

They pilfered the goods quickly, no one being any the wiser, before heading a couple of streets over, where they found even more humans, apparently having entered their side of the city. They found an isolated alley where they quickly changed. Jagar had also procured a pack; into this, they placed their old clothing in case they needed it later.

"What now?" Serah asked, once all of them were changed. "It looks like I'm wearing a sack. A potato sack."

"Yeah, I'm with you," Emma said, somewhat prissily. "I wouldn't be caught dead wearing this."

"Let's keep exploring," Lucian said. "Try to keep a low profile, all right? We blend in, and that's what matters."

"Do we want to check out this Royal Library?" Khairu asked. "Could be a good way to pick up some information."

"Maybe later," Lucian said. "I think we need to learn more about where we are first. Find other humans and learn about this world. I'm curious about how things got to be this way."

"All right," Khairu said. "After you."

Lucian led them out of the alleyway and back into the streets of the Ancient city.

11

LUCIAN GUIDED the group through the city's labyrinthine streets, observing throngs of people going about their business. As they blended in with the crowd, no one cast Lucian or his companions a second glance. There were few Ancients here, and in this part of town, it seemed humans were left to their own devices, although Lucian had no doubts the Ancients had ways of keeping tabs on their subjects.

Here, the buildings were mostly modest, constructed of wood and stone, with none of the gleaming towers of the main square. The air was perfumed with the aroma of sizzling street food, and the dirt roads buzzed with the murmur of strange languages.

"Any ideas on where to collect information?" Jagar asked.

Serah pointed to a wooden sign hanging above a nearby establishment. "In Medieval Farming Simulator, taverns and inns are the best places to learn new things. That looks like a tavern if I ever saw one."

Lucian examined the wooden placard creaking in the wind. Though the runes were indecipherable, the image of a full tankard spoke volumes. Some things were universal across time, cultures, and even realities. It was undoubtedly a bar or tavern.

Lucian couldn't help but chuckle. "Here I was, thinking video games would never be useful."

"I'm not a noob."

Lucian turned to the others. "Remember, keep your spears hidden. And if you want to talk, just trust the brand. Talk *through* it, if that makes sense. Try not to overthink it, or you might mess up."

"I'm a textbook overthinker," Emma said. "I'll probably just stay quiet."

"Are you sure this will work?" Serah asked.

"Of course," Lucian said, though he wasn't entirely confident. "My point being, as long as I can switch my Focus to the right person, we should be able to communicate pretty seamlessly. Until we learn the language, this is the only way to do it."

"Learn the language?" Emma asked. "That seems a tall order."

Lucian was already getting the feeling they might be in this reality a long time, but with sorcery and Psionics, there might be ways to speed the process along.

"Roger roger," Serah said. "After you, fearless leader."

With that, they entered the dimly lit tavern, where laughter and chatter filled the air, accompanied by the spicy, pungent scent of smoke. The disheveled patrons, with their worn, soiled clothing, betrayed their lower social standing compared to the Ancients. Despite this, the atmosphere was warm and welcoming. There seemed to be some sort of solidarity among the humans, a camaraderie that was lacking among strangers in their own reality. Lucian supposed systemic oppression by the Ancients was responsible for that.

As they settled at an empty table near the back, Lucian suddenly felt nervous. What if he bungled the ward and all his words came out as gibberish?

Soon, a tired-looking serving girl approached them, her garments frayed, and her forehead marked with a distinctive scar.

"What can I get you?" she asked wearily in the local human dialect.

The group's eyes widened in surprise, comprehending her words despite the unfamiliar language. The ward was working exactly as Lucian had expected.

Realizing they would need to pay for their order, Lucian distracted her with a question. "What's good here, anyway?"

"If you're in the mood for a drink, our ale is quite popular. Some say it's reminiscent of the venom of the Zarthaxian viper. Personally, I think the viper's venom might be a *touch* more palatable."

"That bad, huh?" Serah asked.

To Lucian's amazement, her words also came out in the local human dialect, and yet he understood her perfectly.

"What about food?" Jagar asked, also in the same language. This was working far better than Lucian had expected.

She gave a wry chuckle. "Well, our fare is a hit-or-miss affair. You could try the Grastian Stew. It's a local favorite, though the consistency often makes it more of a sludge. If you're lucky, it might remind you of something your mother tried to make while she was experimenting in the kitchen. Otherwise, you might be chewing on something that tastes like the aftermath of the viper's dinner."

"You're doing a good job of selling this place," Emma observed.

Before the server could respond, Serah butted in. "We'll have one of the Grastian Stews, please." As everyone gave her a strange look, she shrugged. "I could eat *anything* at this point."

"Your funeral," the server said. "So, that's five ales and a pot of stew for the table?"

"This won't kill us, will it?" Lucian asked, half-jokingly.

"Well, truth be told, not much on Grastia agrees with offworlders, or so I've been told. But no, it won't kill you. I eat it almost every day, and I'm still here." She flashed a smile, revealing several missing teeth.

Grastia. Lucian realized Mako must have a different name in this reality.

"I don't recognize your faces," the server continued amiably. "You must've just got here. Unlucky you. Where are you in from?"

"Nai Shairen," Lucian replied. "On an errand."

The girl's eyes widened, momentarily filled with fear, before she quickly recovered. "That's a long haul from the capital."

"We were hoping for a bit of information," Lucian said. "We'll pay well."

Reaching out with Psionic Magic, Lucian stoked her emotions, hoping the effect would incite her greed. He felt a pang of guilt for manipulating her in such an unseemly way, but they had few other options.

Whatever the case, the ploy seemed to work. "What kind of information? I have other tables, so make it quick."

"What's the best way to get off-world?" Lucian asked. "Our ship broke down and I don't know a good local place to get parts."

She frowned, looking skeptical. Something Lucian had said was off, though it wasn't immediately obvious what that was. "Well, you'll find plenty of junk shops on the east side, where the masters live. Of course, you'll need money and a Writ of Transit, signed and sealed. But since you're already here, I'm sure you've got that. Right?"

"Of course," Lucian said easily. "I was just wondering if it was standard across all worlds."

"This place might be a backwater dump, but we're still under the rule of Starsea. I wouldn't know what it's like out there. I've never been off this rock."

"Syrana!" a male voice barked from behind the bar.

She stiffened at the reprimand, giving a quick curtsy. "I'll be back with those drinks and stew."

Syrana hurried away as the gruff barkeep shook his head and went back to wiping his mugs.

"Money and a Writ of Transit," Serah mused, rubbing her hands in anticipation. "Looks like we'll be doing some thieving."

Khairu's forehead scrunched in thought. "I wonder how money works here. Is it something tangible, like gold? Or digital, like credits in our own reality?"

Emma observed the patrons in the tavern. "I've been watching a few of the tables, and it seems they're paying with some sort of data stick."

"So, it's digital," Lucian concluded.

Emma nodded. "I can't help but notice how backward everything is. There are spaceships and advanced buildings, but not on this side of town. Maybe in this reality, technology is heavily regulated. Some can use it, some can't. Humans seem to fall into the *can't* category."

Serah furrowed her brow. "How does *that* make sense?"

Jagar leaned in. "Control. The Ancient One might only allow technology to be used by certain people—either Ancients or those most loyal to him. Humans seem to be slaves here, or at the very least, comprising a lower caste. Outside of a few key pieces of tech, like these data sticks, they seem to be mostly barred from using advanced technology."

Emma tilted her head. "I wonder how humans are even here at all. It would mean Starsea never really expanded to Earth until recently."

Lucian nodded. "They've never found Ancient ruins on Earth, so that would make sense. The Ancients weren't there a million years ago, so maybe they never discovered the Gates leading to Earth until humans came about. That could be anywhere from modern times to even a hundred thousand years ago."

"I noticed different ethnicities of humans, too," Emma added. "That pushes the timeline up a bit. Humans have had time to evolve different skin colors and phenotypes. Our server has blue eyes, for example, which would have only evolved in the last ten thousand years. The discovery of Earth must be quite recent—at least relatively speaking. Either that, or they knew about Earth and just ignored it until humans had achieved a sufficient level of intelligence."

"Interesting idea," Serah agreed. "One thing's for sure. This timeline sure is weird."

At that moment, Syrana returned with several tankards of ale, expertly balanced, along with a big pot of stew. The smell was unusual, but Lucian's stomach rumbled, anyway. She placed the concoction on the table.

"Dinner is served," she said. "Anything else?"

"That's all for now," Lucian said. "Thank you."

Thankfully, she went off, apparently not expecting payment yet, a fact for which Lucian was grateful.

As Lucian and the group ate the thick, green stew and drank the weak ale, he didn't find the taste disagreeable. It definitely had an earthy taste, and bits of tough meat that had a gamey quality. Perhaps it was hunger, but he finished one bowl and ladled himself another.

As they continued eating, Lucian couldn't help but notice the lingering stares from a rough-looking group of men nearby. Although the din of the tavern muffled the men's words, it was clear Lucian's group was the butt of their jokes. They laughed raucously, and one of them even splashed a bit of his drink on Jagar, though he played it off as an accident. Jagar gave a harsh look of warning, but this only made the men laugh even harder.

The men only grew bolder. Reaching out with his Psionic Magic, Lucian even caught some lewd comments about the women. For the first time, he realized they were the only women among the patrons, and their presence seemed to defy some sort of social norm. The culture here seemed to be far more patriarchal than Lucian's own.

"We should leave," Lucian said.

"What about paying?" Emma asked.

"Well, we don't have any money. I'll wait until the server comes back, then make her think we paid."

"That's so evil!" Emma said.

"I've got a better idea," Serah said. "Why don't we convince those chuckleheads to pay for us?"

She nodded toward the other table, and unfortunately, the gesture wasn't missed. Almost immediately, they stood and approached their table.

Lucian held back his sigh as he, Khairu, and Jagar rose to meet them.

12

BEFORE ANY OF those rowdy drunks could get a word out, Lucian spoke first. "Is there a problem?"

The lead man, who was burly and beady-eyed, sneered. "What's it to you, outsider? If you have something to say about us, say it to my face and see how it fares."

Lucian had a few choice words for him, but he had to make himself hold them back. "I have nothing to say at all. We were just about to leave."

"Not until I've had my say, outsider."

Lucian was fast losing patience, but Khairu stepped in, her response more measured. "I suggest you return to your table and leave us be. Your next round's on us."

The men looked at each other and laughed. The surrounding crowd parted, anticipating a fight.

The man shook his head vehemently, pointing at Khairu. "That won't be good enough, love. If I let a girl like you buy a drink for me, what's that say about me, eh? So that puts us back at square one. I'll speak plainly. I don't like your faces, so what are you going to do about it?"

"Nothing," Lucian said. He turned to the others. "We're leaving."

The server, Syrana, just came back. "Not without paying!"

Lucian quickly established a Psionic link with the lead bully. *Tell her you'll settle our tab.*

The man's eyes instantly went glassy with a slight violet sheen. Lucian streamed a bit of Radiant Magic to hide the effect.

"I'm sorry. Look, let me square things with you. Your table's on me, yeah?"

"Oi!" one of his chums shouted. "You've gone soft in the head, Varn?"

The man reached into his pocket to pay, but this was too much for the others. The man who had spoken up stepped forward.

"You asked for this."

Before Lucian could defuse the situation, the drunken man lunged at Khairu. She easily sidestepped him as the rest of his group joined the fray.

Lucian sprang into action, tethering the feet of two men lunging at Jagar together, causing them to collapse in a tangled heap. One drunk went for Serah, but she knocked him clear across a neighboring table with a punch amplified by Gravitonic Magic. Jagar didn't use magic at all, simply throwing punches so hard and fast that the other two attackers couldn't even react.

It was over in a flash. The men beat a hasty retreat, and the tavern fell silent. The remaining patrons stared at Lucian's group in shock and fear.

"Magic," someone said.

The word was unmistakable in the silent room. Perhaps they had not been as subtle as Lucian had thought.

Those who hadn't left during the fight beat a hasty retreat. Only a few bystanders remained, along with the bartender who had scolded Syrana, who gazed at them wide-eyed.

"That was magic," he said. "I know it when I see it!"

"You saw nothing," Lucian said. He turned to the others. "Come on."

The barkeep held up a hand. "No, stay! This is important. Trust me." The bartender licked his lips, having difficulty recovering from what he'd just seen. "I never would have guessed I'd live to see this day."

"What are you talking about?" Lucian asked, glancing at the door to check for the authorities.

The barkeep hesitated, then beckoned them closer. Lucian remained where he was.

"You really don't know?" the barkeep asked.

"Just get to the point!" Khairu said.

"The Prophecy of the Time Weaver," the barkeep whispered, his voice barely audible. "Don't ever tell anyone I told you about it. That old Ancient, Themba, sometimes comes in here. He told me all about it. He told me to be on the lookout for folks like you."

"Themba?" Lucian asked. "Who's that? And what's this about a prophecy?"

"Don't say the name. Anyway, the Prophecy speaks of a great hero, one of our kind, who comes from another world and saves humans from slavery. The Chosen, he's supposed to be called. Themba says we will know him because he can wield magic like the Ancients."

Lucian exchanged glances with his companions. "Chosen" was the first thing that seemed similar between their two timelines, even if the details were different. But that humans couldn't use magic at all was surprising. After considering this for a moment, Lucian supposed it made sense. Magic was supposed to only be useable to a species when the Orbs were held by a member of that species.

In this timeline, the Ancient One must have been possessing someone of the Ancient species. So, it made sense only Ancients could use magic. As for why Lucian and the others still could, he couldn't explain. Ultimately, the Manifold was the one that decided who was, and wasn't, a mage, and perhaps exceptions could be made.

"What is this Prophecy?" Lucian asked. "Who is this Time Weaver? And who is Themba? Where can we find him?"

He felt like he was shotgunning the guy with questions, but he had to learn as much as possible.

"The Time Weaver is an ancient and powerful being. A god, I guess you could say. As for Themba, he's an Ancient, but he's all right by us. He drinks here sometimes, though I haven't seen him in a few weeks. I remember what he said, though. I'll always remember that, because he has some strange ideas, even for an Ancient. He told me to keep an eye out for the Chosen. That he'd be a human that used magic. Not that I ever believed him. A human, using magic?" He gave a short, nervous laugh. "He proved me wrong."

"Tell me more about this Prophecy," Lucian said. "Where can we find Themba?"

"The Prophecy says the Chosen would have a shockspear, too, but not the kind like the Masters. It would be a crystal spear of pure magic, a spear he'll use to drive into the Heart of Shadow . . ."

Before Lucian could ask anything more, the tavern doors burst open. A group of Ancients stormed inside, wearing the same armor as the guards at the gates. Their red eyes locked on Lucian and his team. They wielded shockspears, and from their aggressive postures, they looked ready to fight.

The bartender fell to his knees. "Mercy, great one! I beg your favor."

"What's going on here?" the Ancient demanded. "Answer truly, and you may live. But be warned! One lie and I'll smite you where you kneel."

"Leave him alone," Lucian said.

The leader's gaze snapped toward him. "You dare interrupt

me, slave?"

"Leave," Lucian said. "Now."

The Ancient leered down at him, his red eyes murderous. He said nothing more, simply raising his hand, where a ball of electricity gathered and crackled within his grasp.

Lucian, without hesitation, summoned Lightspear and thrust it forward, reducing the Ancient to a heap of ash.

The barkeep gasped at this display as the remaining Ancients cried out in alarm. There was a moment's pause, of shock, as they lunged forward to avenge their fallen leader.

There was no more keeping a low profile. Khairu unleashed a fork of lightning at the first wave of attackers, with Serah, Khairu, and Jagar joining the fray, using both their spears and magic to fight back.

The skirmish was intense, but Lucian and his team were well-honed from their many fights together. It only took half a minute for the once-humble tavern to lie in ruins and all their enemies to be dead or fleeing. But it was only a matter of time before they regrouped and brought reinforcements.

"We need to get out of here," Lucian said.

Retreating behind the bar, they discovered the cowering barkeep.

"Find someplace safe," Lucian said.

It was all he could say before they dashed through the kitchen and emerged into a deserted alley. The cool, fresh air contrasted with the stifling atmosphere they had left behind.

They raced through the streets. Terrified humans scrambled out of their way as the garbled cries of Ancients echoed from behind. Ice spears whistled past. Serah raised a hasty Thermal shield, blocking any from stabbing them from behind.

Lucian headed for the city's edge, noting their proximity to the wall. As they reached the main street, the gates were just a quick sprint away.

Only to find that the gates were closed.

Gathering ether into his Focus, Lucian prepared a powerful reverse tether. As they neared the gatehouse, he released the energy, blowing the doors off their hinges with a thunderous boom. Beyond them lay a dense forest.

"Come on!" Lucian shouted.

Magical attacks glanced off their shields as they made for the trees. Within a few minutes, they were running deep into the thick foliage.

But Lucian knew they were hardly safe here. Lightspear did well enough in clearing a path, but their progress was terribly slow. They pushed on for half an hour, always keeping ahead of their pursuers by using their magic to knock down every tree and obstacle they could to cover their makeshift trail.

When they came to a deep ravine, Lucian let out a sigh of relief. If he could tether everyone across, it would seriously hamper the Ancients from coming after them.

He began doing so immediately. Just a few minutes later, everyone was safe on the other side with no signs of pursuit. They pressed on, distancing themselves from the city. They ran for hours, and soon, it was just the sounds of the nighttime forest and their labored breaths.

"Let's take a breather," Lucian said as soon as they had entered a clearing.

They collapsed where they stood, unable to think or do anything else.

Lucian almost wanted to call the expedition a failure, except for the information they'd learned about the Time Weaver's prophecy, and the person who had shared it with the bartender, a certain Ancient named Themba. What was their role in all this? Unfortunately, they had been ambushed before the bartender could give them more information.

Lucian eventually stood up, along with everyone else. With the Ancient city behind them, it felt as if they were back to square one: surviving in the wilds of an unfamiliar planet.

13

DEEP WITHIN THE FOREST, far from the city they had narrowly escaped, the group found themselves surrounded by lush foliage and towering trees that seemed alien in their grandeur. These trees possessed a cold, ethereal beauty, not unlike evergreens on Earth.

As the sun set, it cast an eerie, otherworldly glow through the leafy canopy, bathing their surroundings in autumnal beauty. Despite the enchanting atmosphere, a palpable sense of urgency weighed heavily on Lucian. It was hard not to feel as if he'd led the group to failure. Without the Orbs, his capabilities were limited, and having to rely on his own strength was quite the change.

But he couldn't let himself become discouraged. It was still on him to be the leader in this dark situation.

The others were silent, without direction. Lucian needed to give them something to do, a way out.

"We need to find this Themba guy," he said. "From what the bartender was saying, it seems like he's somewhere in that city."

"But how do we find him?" Emma asked. "We barely know

anything about this world and our cover is blown. As soon as we step back in, we'll get attacked."

The group fell silent, lost in thought. The rustling of leaves and distant calls of alien creatures heightened Lucian's sense of unease.

Lucian listened, hoping someone would suggest a better idea than the one already forming in his mind. But when no one said anything, he figured he'd have to share it.

"The idea I have is risky," he said.

"What?" Serah asked.

"Well, it's nothing fancy. Jagar and I will sneak in. As Psionics, we'll be able to manipulate people's minds, if needed. And since it's just the two of us, we won't stick out. Once we're inside, we'll hit up every bar and see if we can find out anything about Themba. The bartender mentioned Themba shared that info with him. Maybe he makes the rounds and does the same thing in other places."

"What makes you think anyone other than that bartender knows about him?" Emma asked.

"Because it seems like he's looking for me," he said. "That bartender is probably not the only one he's spoken to. If this Prophecy of the Time Weaver is real, then I'm sure word has already spread throughout the city. That will draw Themba out if he's anywhere nearby. He'll be looking for us, and if we're looking for him, it'll go faster."

"That's risky," Emma said. "If all that is true, then maybe he knows we came out this way. He can pick up our trail."

"That's not guaranteed," Serah said. "I'm with Lucian on this one. This is a lead we need to pursue."

"Maybe we should sleep on it," Khairu suggested. "It's late, and we shouldn't rush into this."

"A wise suggestion," Jagar agreed. "I think we'll be safe to sleep in this meadow tonight. Regardless, I can take first watch, while Emma can maintain her Radiant ward to conceal our presence."

"So, we have to sleep on the ground?" Serah asked.

"We can use magic to create a basic shelter," Emma replied. "It won't be pretty, but we just need protection from the elements and prying eyes. The Ancients are probably looking for us, but thankfully, this planet is covered with forests, valleys, and mountains. And there's a fog settling in. That should do a lot to hide our position."

As night gathered, they risked a small, smokeless fire. They found a small cleft at the edge of the clearing that would do a decent job of hiding the light. No one would know it was there unless they came within five meters of it.

Lucian slept uneasily, the intermittent nighttime sounds waking him up at various points. When morning came, Lucian awoke to see Jagar returning to the camp carrying a odd-looking creature with black, slimy skin that looked like a strange cross between a giant salamander and a fish. Lucian had to admit, it didn't look appetizing in the least.

"This one's safe to eat," Jagar said as he set to work skinning the creature and stripping off the meat. "Tastes better than it looks. We'd trap them sometimes in my Mako Academy days."

"I'll have to take your word for it."

The meat cooked quickly, and Lucian was surprised at the appetizing smell. He tried not to think about what it looked like as they sat down to eat. He had to admit, the taste and texture were reminiscent of fish, if chewier.

As they ate, the group discussed the plan from the previous evening.

"I don't have any better ideas on what to do," Khairu said. "So, if we go with Lucian's plan, how do we implement it?"

"We should wait until nightfall," Jagar said. "It will be easier to go unseen."

"Are you sure the two of you will be enough?" Emma asked.

"It'll be easier to go unnoticed," Lucian said. "They are looking for five of us, remember? With just two, we won't stick out as much."

"All right," she said. "We'll stay here in the forest, then."

"All of us can head over there together. We can set up on the edge of the forest, and then Jagar and I will come back when we've learned more."

"So, what's our job?" Serah asked. "Stay out of trouble?"

"Mainly, yeah. We'll communicate with you Psionically if we need backup, or if anything changes."

"So, we'll leave tonight, then?" Jagar asked.

"Sometime this afternoon, we'll head back to the city. Then we'll wait for full darkness to make our move."

"Which raises the question," Khairu said. "Just *how* will you get inside if the gates are closed?"

"Hopefully they won't be. But if they are, we'll have to improvise. Maybe a tether as a last resort."

"That can easily be seen," Khairu said.

"Sometimes, the walls of old cities will have posterns," Jagar said. "Secret doors the defense could use if they needed to go out during a siege. Perhaps they'll have the same thing here."

"That's a great idea," Lucian said. "We'll be on the lookout for that."

"I don't like it," Emma said, "but I also don't see any other choice."

"We'll just throw on our hoods if we have to go in," Jagar said. "There seem to be thousands of humans in that city. They won't be looking for us on the streets if they saw us in the forest."

"We'll need to play it safe for sure," Lucian said. "Security will probably be tighter. Thankfully, our clothing doesn't look out of place."

"Are you sure you're up for this?" Khairu asked.

Lucian understood the unvoiced part of her question: Are you strong enough to do this without the Orbs?

"I'm weaker without the Orbs, no question about that. But I haven't lost any knowledge of how to use my magic. It's just going to take a bit more time and thought. Let's try to stay positive, all right? I know this might be the hardest spot we've been in so far, and that's saying something. But finding Themba could be the key to getting back to our own time. We have to go for it."

From their silence, it didn't seem as if they were convinced. To be honest, Lucian wasn't sure he was, either.

"In the meantime," Jagar said, "we should rest and try to prepare ourselves as best we can. We can head back to the city in the afternoon. It'll take several hours to get back through the forest."

"Good idea," Lucian said. "Let's rest up and kill some time for now."

14

WITH THEIR COURSE of action decided, they began making their way back through the forest as the afternoon shadows lengthened. It wasn't difficult to retrace their path, but Lucian still had to hack their way through the obstacles they'd felled during their flight.

All too soon, they had reached the edge of the forest. All was quiet as they saw the city rising through the undergrowth.

"We'll keep watch here," Khairu said. "If anything happens, Serah will reach out."

"Be careful," Serah said, her expression worried. "Don't push yourself too hard."

He gave her a hug. "Don't worry. We'll be back before you know it."

Before Lucian could doubt himself, he and Jagar slipped into the night, up the slope toward the city.

The first thing Lucian did was create a reverse Radiant aura, darkening the immediate area around them. The stream also worked to mask their use of magic. To hide their heat signatures in the dark, Jagar created a reverse Thermal ward. Lucian was confident that neither of them would be seen.

Within a few minutes, they were close to the gates, only to find the doors firmly shut. It didn't surprise him, but it would make the job of getting in much more difficult.

What now? Jagar asked. *A tether would be too obvious.*

Let's explore along the wall. See if we can find another way in.

They went off to the right, walking along the wall as Lucian expanded the Radiant stream to look for any obvious points of weakness. With his vision sharpened, it wasn't long before he saw an unmistakable shape through the underbrush growing under the shadow of a tower.

It was a small, hidden door. A postern that Jagar had mentioned last night.

There's a door past that brush.

That growth is pretty thick, so they were probably trying to hide it. Any ideas on how to get past it?

I think we can work our way through. On the other side, getting inside should be simple enough. We just need to blast the door open.

Sounds good to me.

Keeping his hold on Radiance, Lucian approached the undergrowth, finding it difficult to gain entry since it was so thick. Cutting it with Lightspear would be too obvious. If he still had access to Space-Time Magic, he could easily phase through the wall, but as it stood, he had to get creative.

Ideas? Lucian asked.

Jagar considered for a moment. *Sometimes, a good kinetic push is all you need. It shouldn't make too much noise.*

Before Lucian could respond, Jagar threw out his hand, uprooting two of the small, spiny trees that barred their progress.

But much to Lucian's surprise, several other trees whipped toward them, apparently not liking Jagar's way of dealing with things.

Lucian threw up a hasty Binding shield, and the tree limbs

pounded against the blue barrier with ferocity, but they might as well have tried to break through a diamond wall. Jagar stood beside him, trying to make sense of the strange obstacle before them. The racket the trees were making was infernal, and if it went on much longer, would become impossible for the guards to miss.

They had to defeat the trees quickly and quietly.

Lucian reached for Psionics and Thermalism, a dualstream that he had used in the past to calm emotions. He wasn't sure if it would also work on plant life, but he supposed it was worth a shot.

Almost immediately, the aura took effect. The trees' frenzied attacks slowed until it sounded like nothing more than the breeze through the leaves. After another few seconds, the trees were completely still.

Breathless and sweating, Lucian let go of the Binding shield while keeping the emotional dampening aura active. He set it in a brand, so that he wouldn't have to continually stream. Even this action, something small with the Orbs, was very draining for him.

He checked the wall above; it didn't seem as if anything had alerted the guards. A stroke of luck.

Let's move, Lucian said.

How did you get them to stop?

Reverse Psionics and Thermalism.

Jagar nodded. *Good work. Let's get inside.*

The two of them pushed their way through the spiky vegetation, what had obviously been planted by the Ancients as a defense measure. Within a couple of minutes, they were standing before the metallic postern door, painted the same color and pattern as the stone blocks of the wall.

Lucian reached out for the metal, streaming Thermal Magic directly onto the hinges. After a couple of minutes, the heavy door fell clean off.

They ducked inside, finding themselves in a dimly lit corridor. Now out of range of the trees, Lucian let go of his calming aura to conserve his ether.

The corridor within was silent and completely dark. Lucian used Radiance to sharpen his vision.

Stay close behind me, he said.

Eventually, they reached a set of stairs, with no sign of another being, Ancient or human. Once at the top, they found a heavy wooden door. Lucian pressed his ear to the surface, but heard nothing on the other side.

"Here goes nothing," he said in a low voice.

Once again, he reached for Thermalism to melt the hinges. These didn't take much to fall off, being less durable than the ones on the outer wall. The door toppled toward them, but before it could clamor on the floor, he and Jagar caught it, leaning it against the wall.

Emerging from the top of the tower, they found themselves at the top of the wall. Lucian scanned the area and found there were no patrols. He then recreated his Radiant ward, and darkness gathered around them. They edged forward and peered over a crenellation and down into the city below.

Lucian glanced over at Jagar. *On the count of three, jump.*

There was no question on Jagar's face; he trusted Lucian to break his fall without asking for further details.

On three, they leaped over the side. The city sprawled out before them, presenting a stark contrast: the human side showcased yellow-tinted windows set within modest wooden structures, while gleaming towers dominated the opposite end. At the city's heart stood a fortress atop a high plateau. What might once have been a medieval stronghold was now infused with modern technology.

Lucian used Gravitonics to slow their fall before hitting the cobblestones beneath. They landed lightly on their feet and advanced into a dark alley across the street. They waited a moment to see if they were in the clear. When all was silent, Lucian let out a breath.

"Went smoother than expected," he said. "We're lucky the streets are so empty."

Jagar nodded toward a building across the street, from which the sound of conversation and music emanated. "Maybe because everyone's in there."

"A tavern."

"Just what we're looking for."

Lucian drew up his hood, and Jagar did likewise. The two men headed across the street at a natural gait, heading down some steps and into the loud establishment. Lucian dropped the Radiant ward, replacing it with a Psionic one that would allow him and Jagar to speak and understand the local language.

Inside, they found themselves in a lively tavern, bustling with patrons. The dimly lit room was filled with laughter, music, and the aroma of food, heady smoke, and ale. Lucian could hardly believe that they had just been on an almost-deserted street just moments ago.

Lucian and Jagar exchanged glances before sitting at a small table at the far end of the tavern, the only two that were open. As they sat down, a pretty barmaid with plump cheeks approached them and radiated a warm smile. "Evening, gentlemen. What can I get you?"

"Two ales, please," Lucian said.

He nodded his thanks as she smiled and hurried away to fetch their drinks.

As they waited, Lucian observed the crowd. Much to his surprise, it wasn't just human. There were Ancients as well, and if he didn't know better, all of them were enjoying the night together. Perhaps Themba was even among them.

"You seeing what I'm seeing?" Lucian asked.

"Aye, that I am. Strange. Clearly, things are a bit more complicated than we first thought."

The barmaid returned with their ales. "Here you are, gents," she said brightly.

"Thank you," Lucian said. "We'll keep our tab open." Before she could counter him, or demand proof that he was good for it, he flashed a winning smile while giving her a mental push. Her cheeks flushed as she batted her eyes.

"Of course, handsome," she managed. "For you, I can make an exception. Can I get you anything else? Anything at all?"

"Yes, actually. I have a question. Is there a curfew in effect for humans in this part of the city? The streets were so empty."

She laughed. "Not at all, doll face. You new in town?"

Lucian smiled, not at the blatant flirtation, but to get more information out of her. "I'm just curious why there are so many humans and Ancients hanging out together. I've never seen that in all my travels."

"Well, this here is an Abolitionist bar. Not all the Masters hate our guts, believe it or not. And many of them even want to see us win our freedom. They are a minority, but they are welcome in places like this."

"It's not illegal?" Jagar asked.

"For them, no. I don't know how else it is in the Starsea Empire, but here on Grastia, the Ancients have some measure of free speech, however little."

Lucian looked at a nearby table that had a mix of humans and Ancients. Two red-eyed Ancients were looking in their direction, one with blue skin and the other with gray.

"Anything else?" the barmaid pressed.

"Yes, one last thing. I'm looking for an old friend, an Ancient by the name of Themba. Have you heard of him?"

She frowned. "Hmm. Can't say that I have. Although Themba is a rather common name, as far as Ancients go."

"That's all. Thank you."

She smiled graciously and went to tend to her other tables.

Lucian glanced toward the door. "Let's get out of here. I think we're catching some attention from the locals."

Jagar gave a nondescript nod. The two men waited a few more seconds and headed for the door. Thankfully, neither was stopped as they stepped out into the street.

Lucian headed a few doors down, ducking into another establishment, this one far less busy and shabbier in appearance. It wasn't the place he'd willingly step into, though it would be useful to lie low for a bit. A few older men sat at the bar, but the tables were all but empty, aside from one man who sat in the far corner, whose tall form was obscured by shadow.

Lucian and Jagar exchanged a glance and sat at the center of the bar, where they could monitor the door.

As they settled down, a grizzled bartender approached them, his expression disinterested. "What'll it be, chaps?"

"Two ales," Jagar replied, keeping his voice low.

The bartender grunted and left to fetch their drinks.

"See that guy in the corner?" Lucian asked quietly.

Jagar nodded without even needing to look.

The bartender returned with their ales and set them on the table with a thud.

"That'll be twenty aurics."

Lucian smirked. "This can't be worth more than five."

The bartender chuckled. "Well, sometimes outsiders bite on the first offer. It'll be ten."

Lucian decided not to toy with the man any longer. "I'll pay as soon as you tell me who that man in the corner is."

The bartender's eyes flicked up, then back to Lucian. "Don't know his name. Keeps to himself, mostly, and he pays. I don't concern myself too much with Ancients."

Lucian had to restrain himself from looking again. Apparently, whom he had believed to be a human was actually an Ancient.

"That'll be ten," the bartender repeated, more firmly this time.

"Put it on my tab."

"I don't do tabs for first timers. Cough up the aurics, or there'll be trouble."

While Lucian fought for what to say, a shadow fell over him.

"I'll take care of these two," a deeply resonant voice said in the local human dialect.

Lucian turned to see the wiry old Ancient offer a data stick, which the bartender scanned. The bartender glanced at Lucian and Jagar, seeming curious.

"You two are lucky. Let me know if you want anything else."

Without waiting for an invitation, the old Ancient took a seat at the bar next to them. His wrinkled skin was pale, his eyes red, while his heavy brow ridge sported two small horns above each eye. Those red eyes bored into Lucian's without expression. He wore humble brown robes, well-made, but not attracting attention.

"You two shouldn't be in here. Not everyone in this city is as welcoming as they seem."

"Does that include you?" Jagar asked.

"Perhaps. Perhaps not. But I know why you're here, and I know *how* you're here."

Lucian was already suspecting they'd found who they were looking for.

"You two stick out like sore thumbs," the Ancient went on. "Fortunately, you have me to protect you."

Lucian hesitated for a moment. "And who are you?"

"Themba," the man replied simply.

"That's what I thought. We've been looking for you."

"Oh? And I've been looking for you as well. Longer than you know."

Themba showed no facial expressions other than a slight furrowing of his brow. This made it impossible to read his emotions. Lucian had noted the same thing when speaking to Silumko. It seemed to be what speaking to an Ancient was like.

"Listen," Themba said. "I think we have much to discuss, but we can't do it here. I have a house. It's not far. We'll be much safer speaking there."

"Why should we trust you?" Lucian asked.

"I'm a friend," the Ancient said without hesitation. "If the rumors from yesterday are true, then you are the one I'm looking for."

Lucian glanced at the bartender, but he was at the other end of the establishment, and no one was close enough to overhear.

Themba continued. "I'm much too old to beat around the bush. You need a guide in this strange world you find yourself in. Allow me to aid you. At any moment—"

That was when a mix of humans and Ancients, including the blue and gray-skinned ones from the previous tavern, crowded the doorway. The one with blue skin pointed a long, accusing finger directly at Lucian.

"There! That's them!"

15

JAGAR AND LUCIAN were already on their feet, ready to fight. Themba stood with them, and from his calm demeanor, he didn't seem concerned in the slightest. He merely folded his hands before his flowing brown robes. His red eyes stared hauntingly at the challengers in the doorway.

"Surrender yourselves!" the blue-skinned Ancient said. "Surrender or perish!"

"There is no need for violence," Themba said. "They are with me."

"And who are you, to consort with short-lifer scum?" the blue Ancient asked. "Leave now, old one, or you'll face the same fate."

"A pity."

Themba threw out his hand, streaming a raw burst of Psionic Magic that pushed all the attackers out of the doorway. He then created a Binding shield over the entrance. The bartender and the establishment's few patrons cowered in fear as Themba turned calmly toward Lucian and Jagar.

Lucian allowed Lightspear to appear in his hand, and Themba regarded the weapon coolly.

"You are the one I seek. Follow me and do everything I say."

Lucian nodded. "Right behind you."

Themba led them out a back door behind the bar. They fled into the alleyway behind the establishment, and Jagar slammed the door behind them. Lucian used his Binding Magic to reinforce the exit. It might buy them a few seconds.

The three sprinted down the alley, Themba quite swift on his long legs. Ahead, Lucian got a sense of just how tall he was—at least two meters. Lucian and Jagar were hard-pressed to keep up.

After several twists and turns through the empty cobblestoned streets, they found themselves in a small, hidden courtyard. They paused for a moment to catch their breath, scanning their surroundings for any signs of pursuit. Strangely, Themba didn't seem winded in the slightest.

Lucian looked at their mysterious new ally, wondering how far they could trust him. "Where are you taking us, Themba?"

"You'll see soon enough. That spear of yours . . . it can be none other than the Crystal Spear, mentioned in the Prophecy of the Time Weaver. You must be the Chosen, sent here from another world to destroy the Shadow Emperor. It's my sacred charge to aid you."

"Yesterday, the bartender mentioned you," Lucian said. "I wanted to be sure you were the right person."

"I am the one you seek. For many years, I've waited for your arrival and had almost given up hope. The Shadow Emperor will soon learn of you if he hasn't already."

The Shadow Emperor had to be the Ancient One, but Lucian didn't bring up the thought at the moment.

"You can't stay here on Grastia," Themba continued. "I have many questions, as I'm sure you do for me. But for now, we must focus on survival."

"How did you know where to find us?"

"I am well-versed in the Prophecy of the Time Weaver. It led me to this world, though we don't have to discuss it now.

We'll have plenty of time to speak when we're safely off this planet."

"You have a ship?"

"Yes. The wall is near."

Themba bounded off again, leading Lucian and Jagar through a maze of alleys, their footsteps echoing off the walls. Shabby tenements leaned over them, inducing a sense of claustrophobia.

At last, they stepped into the open air before the towering city wall, their last obstacle before the forest and safety.

The coast was clear, at least for now, so Lucian prepared to tether everyone to the top of the wall one by one. But this notion was quickly dashed as footsteps emanated from behind them.

Lucian would have to stream everyone across at the same time and do it without the aid of the Orb of Binding.

"Quickly!" Themba said.

Lucian entered the Ether and willed three Binding tethers into existence, immediately yanking them off the ground and toward the parapet of the wall. Once on top, they dashed to the other side.

"Jump!" Lucian said.

All three leaped, the ground rushing up to meet them. Just before making impact, Lucian streamed an anti-gravity aura. They landed, Themba touching down with a grace that belied his age. Clearly, this wasn't his first time in a situation like this.

As they ran toward the trees, several fireballs streaked through the night toward their position, but Jagar shielded them just in time.

It wasn't long before they entered the thick forest.

Lucian reached out for Serah. *We're back, though in a different spot.*

We're headed your way; we can see all the commotion. Just keep this connection open and we'll meet up soon.

Let's just meet by the ravine. It'll save time. Any trouble?

Other than this snake-like thing with feathers that almost swallowed Emma whole, no, we're perfectly peachy.

That . . . sounds terrifying. We found Themba. He says he has a ship ready.

A ship? Interesting. Well, we'll figure it all out in a minute.

It took about half an hour of cutting through the trees with Lightspear before they met up on the edge of the ravine. Lucian expanded his Psionic ward to encompass his friends so they could communicate with Themba.

Emma's eyes widened in relief and concern, her hair in disarray. "What happened? We saw some lights flashing from the city."

She, Serah, and Khairu looked at Themba curiously, but also with a bit of misgiving. Lucian didn't blame them. He was an Ancient, and they had yet to meet one who was an ally. His ghostly white skin, height, and hauntingly red eyes only lent to his somewhat menacing air.

"This is Themba," Lucian said. "He helped us escape, and he has information about the Time Weaver."

They made quick introductions before Themba spoke again, all business.

"We must get off world as quickly as possible."

"Lucian said you have a ship," Khairu said. "And yet, we're in the middle of the forest."

"Oh-ho," Themba said. "That we are."

Without waiting for a response, Themba walked to the very edge of the ravine itself, nodding toward it.

"It's down there. Fortuitous that we fled in this direction."

"Were you expecting us?" Khairu asked.

"Many questions. Just as many answers. Follow, and you will learn!"

Themba seemed to step over the edge, except instead of falling, there appeared to be a narrow path, well-hidden in the darkness.

"They won't find us down here," he said. "Be careful; the path is narrow."

Lucian created a light sphere bright enough to illuminate the way ahead. The depth of the ravine reminded him very much of Psyche.

They marched in silence for the better part of the night. Themba set a fast pace. Lucian and the others were hard-pressed to keep up. It went on like this for hours as they headed deeper into the ravine.

Just when Lucian was about to call for a halt, the path evened out, placing them before a stand of dense foliage. Themba parted the leaves, revealing a hidden cave entwined with vines and over-growth. Inside, the faint outline of a sleek, advanced-looking ship lay shrouded in darkness. It reminded Lucian very much of *Ethereal*, the first starship that had been requisitioned for their use.

"Rotting hell," Serah said. "Now *that's* a ship!"

"Our escape lies within," Themba said, gesturing toward the cave. "All questions will be answered on board."

"And where are we going, exactly?" Jagar asked. "And how do we know we can trust you?"

"You will have to decide that for yourself. Unless you have another way of procuring a ship, or another guide in this dark and dangerous universe, I'm your only chance."

From Jagar's silence, it seemed he couldn't disagree with that.

"The Shadow Emperor's agents are sure to be scouring this ravine within hours," Themba continued. "I doubt we can even escape the atmosphere unnoticed."

"My magic can help there," Lucian said.

"That's what I was hoping," Themba said. "*Tempus* has never failed me in all my years, and there have been many of those. Either way, this ship is our way off this planet."

"What's after that?" Lucian asked.

"Finding the Time Weaver, of course. According to his

Prophecy, which led me to you, he is the key to defeating the Shadow Emperor."

Lucian saw that there was no going back now. "Lead on, then."

The group readied themselves to board the strange ship and venture into the next stage of their journey.

16

AS LUCIAN STEPPED ABOARD *TEMPUS*, he instantly noticed it had been designed with Ancient proportions in mind. The control panels, buttons, and switches were positioned higher than he was used to, and all appeared well-maintained and carefully polished. Despite the overgrown nature of the cave, everything inside the ship seemed immaculate.

Lucian got the impression that Themba still lived and operated out of the ship. A well-worn and frequently used tool kit was stowed under a desk, while an odd assortment of relics was displayed on its surface. It bespoke a space that was constantly occupied, despite its orderly appearance.

Everyone fanned out around Lucian, taking in the main entry —a circular area with several branching corridors leading deeper into the ship.

"Have a look around," Themba said. "I'll be on the bridge getting things ready."

Lucian moved deeper into the ship, toward what appeared to be the crew quarters. It seemed there were eight individual pods, not unlike the ones he was accustomed to aboard interstellar liners. Each pod was at least ten feet long.

The wardroom, if it could be so called, was complete with an elongated table and oversized chairs bolted to the deck. The recreation area had long, comfortable sofas, but no other ornamentation. Lucian wondered how Ancients kept themselves entertained on long voyages, or even if they had the need for entertainment. Did they have movies, games, or even novels? It was a strange thought, but he looked forward to learning more.

The spaceship was a blend of efficiency, advanced technology, and comfort. Lucian couldn't help but be intrigued by its unique design and scale, something both recognizable and foreign.

Once finished with the tour, the five humans gathered on the bridge, where Themba was already at the helm, apparently quite comfortable piloting.

"Just in time," he said. "I was just about to take off."

"Wait a second," Lucian said. "I feel like we need to talk first before making any rash moves."

"I would recommend we leave immediately, but if answering questions will put you at ease, then we can spare some time."

"I think we should. You want to be our guide, and we just got here and have no idea what's going on."

"That's a fair point. What would you like to know?"

"Okay, first, do we have any leads to find this Time Weaver guy?"

Themba shook his head in a surprisingly human gesture. "Not a one. But I have some ideas about where we might start. I have a friend in a neighboring system. She's very knowledgeable about the history of the Starsea Empire, even where it concerns the Time Weaver."

"What can you tell us about the Time Weaver?" Lucian asked.

Themba was silent, seeming to gather his thoughts as he watched the strange runes of the Ancient language flicker across the screen.

"I can speak of that, in time. Right now, I'm more worried about surviving the Planet Guardians above. With everything that's happened on Grastia, any ship leaving this vicinity will be suspect." He looked at Lucian. "I trust you can shield this ship from detection?"

"I can," Lucian said.

"I can help, too," Emma said. "Radiance is my primary."

Themba nodded, his red eyes observing the group. "Strange, to think of humans using magic." His brow furrowed. "You must never use it where you'll be seen. If you haven't figured it out already, only the Ancients can use magic. If they were to discover five *humans* can use it, well, it could be disastrous. Already, word is probably spreading from Grastia, and eventually, it will reach the Shadow Emperor's ears."

"How soon?" Khairu asked.

"Well, Nai Shairen is twelve Gates from here. Typically, it takes a light-message about two weeks to travel that distance, though that depends on Gate distribution. And of course, two weeks for any orders to travel back to this sector of space. It is . . . difficult to predict what he might do with this news. He might write it off as a rumor. Or he might dedicate all his resources to investigating it. We should prepare for the possibility of him rallying the Seraphim to begin his hunt for the Chosen. That could happen in as soon as four weeks. Perhaps even less, if we are unlucky."

"The Seraphim?" Lucian asked.

"His personal guards, the most elite sorcerers in the galaxy, trained in the spear and deadly magic. If they find out about you, they will hunt for you without mercy."

"Would they know what we look like?" Serah asked. "We tried to be careful."

"Well, if my observations are any sign, you did a good job of hiding your appearance. And fortunately, on a world as remote and primitive as Grastia, you were likely not logged by any security cameras, especially in the parts of town you frequented. But if we visit more advanced worlds, you will not have that luxury."

"So, keep a low profile," Lucian said.

"Yes," Themba said. "No magic, under any circumstances. Assuming they didn't note your appearance, we should make it the entire way to Regalia safely, where my contact is. I will do whatever I can to aid you in your quest to find the Time Weaver. The Time Weaver is the key to defeating the Shadow Emperor. His prophecy says only he has a weapon that can destroy the Shadow Emperor. And the Chosen is the only one who can access this weapon. We will have to discover the rest on our own." Themba turned his red eyes on Lucian. "I know it can't be easy to follow a strange old Ancient like me. From what I've gathered, it seems Ancients are few where you come from."

"You might say that. I don't even know how to describe where we've come from."

"Well, we can get to that in time."

"So, to recap," Khairu said. "We need to locate the Time Weaver to get the weapon necessary to kill the Shadow Emperor. I'm confused, though. Doesn't Lucian *already* possess that weapon? As far as we know, Lightspear is the only weapon that can destroy him."

Themba's brow furrowed. "Yes, it's quite perplexing. The Crystal Spear—or Lightspear, as you call it—is the only weapon capable of destroying the Shadow Emperor according to the Time Weaver's own prophecy. I'm uncertain which weapon or power the prophecy is referring to. The weapon might signify knowledge exclusive to the Time Weaver, which the Chosen must possess to fulfill his destiny. Whatever the case, our priority is to find the Time Weaver. The prophecy is clear the Chosen cannot win against the Shadow Emperor without his aid."

Serah's brow creased. "Tell us more about this prophecy."

Themba leaned against a nearby console, his gaze far away. "The Prophecy not only alludes to the Chosen and his destiny to vanquish the Shadow Emperor, but also says that he's destined to save *all* realities, not only this one, but everything originating from the Light Realm."

"How do you know so much about this?" Khairu asked.

"The Prophecy of the Time Weaver is ancient indeed. It exists in a single copy, safeguarded in the Moon Tower of Nai Elyn."

"Nai Elyn," Khairu echoed. "Isn't that the Shadow Emperor's home?"

"How did you access it?" Emma asked. "I'd assume not just anyone would have that privilege."

"You're correct," Themba said. "The Shadow Emperor himself granted me access to study the Prophecy, a privilege reserved for the most potent and loyal Seraphim."

"You're a Seraphim?" Lucian asked. "I thought you just said they were the enemy."

Themba fell silent for a moment. "Yes, I was a Seraph. Once. My history is . . . complex. And yes, perhaps at odds with my current intentions. I will do my best to explain myself. What I saw in the prophecy forever changed me. I had a vision of a champion with a spear of light challenging the Shadow Emperor. They clashed on the surface of Nai Elyn itself, contesting for mastery of the Orbs. I knew the Chosen would overthrow the Shadow Emperor himself—something I'd previously considered impossible, given the length of the Shadow Emperor's reign spans beyond all reckoning."

"Approximately a million years," Emma said.

Emma's use of the term "years" translated automatically to the Ancient language equivalent, thus effectively conveying her point.

"That long?" Themba asked. "Well, I'm not surprised. The Starsea Empire experiences cycles of darkness and light, and who can determine how many of these have transpired? But that's a discussion for another time. Either way, my vision convinced me of the Ancient One's impending fall. Once I became convinced, I realized that my allegiance to him stemmed more from fear and compulsion than any other motivator. This realization inspired me to escape —no easy endeavor. Even now, my former Seraphim brethren are hunting me, and I owe my survival to my cautious disposition."

"How did you know where to find us?" Lucian asked.

"Again, it was the Prophecy of the Time Weaver. I had another vision, the emergence of the Chosen from a very particular place; a cave hidden behind a lake under starlight. And much to my surprise, I perceived the Chosen would be a human, the lowliest of all the Ancients' servants."

"Gee, thanks," Serah said.

"That's not my belief, of course, but the prevailing attitude of my species. It's unjust, and I do what I can to promote equality, despite my limited resources. Upon this revelation, I was overwhelmed with fear. I fled the Moon Tower, knowing that this knowledge would lead to my demise. For no one can deceive the Shadow Emperor and live to share the tale."

"How did you escape?" Lucian asked.

"That's a long story, and it bears little relevance to our current conversation. I sacrificed everything for my beliefs. My journey began with fleeing to the Empire's farthest reaches. Despite these measures, there have been a few near misses over the years. All my efforts were aimed at seeing the Time Weaver's prophecy come to fruition."

"But you told that bartender on Grastia," Emma said. "And then he told *us* about it."

"That happened much later. I planted seeds. I spoke with those I deemed trustworthy and asked them to keep an eye out for one like you. But before even that, I grappled with the truth of my visions. Initially, I was hesitant to accept them, but going against what I knew to be true would have driven me to madness and despair. So, for all these years, I've been working covertly, and now that I've met you, Lucian, I know my efforts weren't in vain."

"So, how did you determine where I would appear?" Lucian asked. "Throughout the Empire, there must be hundreds, if not thousands, of lakes and caves that match the Prophecy's description."

"That initially puzzled me. The image was etched into my memory, and I felt an urgent need to find this location before it was too late. As you pointed out, countless lakes in the Starsea Empire resemble the one on Grastia. I roamed aimlessly for years, frequently battling for my life to stay ahead of the Seraphim."

"How did you find the lake, then?" Emma asked.

Themba's brow furrowed. "I stopped looking at the lake and the cave from my vision and started paying attention to the stars."

"Of course," Emma said. "That's the same thing I did to figure out where and when we were."

"Well, I could have used your expertise. It took me ten years to reach the same conclusion. Once I studied the star positions, there it was—Grastia. That narrowed my search to a single planet. Even then, it took many years for me to find the right location. But with grit and determination, I discovered it."

"So, you've been waiting ever since?" Lucian asked.

"For over one hundred revolutions of this planet around its sun. I grew from a young Ancient into the elder you see now. We Ancients are aptly named, for our life span is uncommonly long for most sentient species, more than twice that of a human. But never did my faith waver. I set up residence in the nearest city and awaited any rumor. There were many false leads, of course. Just yesterday, I thought it was another false lead. But I investigated all the same. I questioned carefully and found out that there had been at least one human here using magic who had fled into the forest. I was preparing to follow you there until you returned, and I confirmed the rumors myself."

"And that's that," Serah said.

"In a manner of speaking. And now, we must continue with our journey. As outsiders, you will know practically nothing of the Starsea Empire. That's what I'm here for. Right now, I detect the use of an advanced Psionic ward that allows us to communicate. In time, you will learn our languages and customs enough to get around without raising suspicion. Our priority is to find the Time Weaver wherever he is in the Worlds. Already, we have lingered here for too long."

"Wait a minute," Khairu said. "You still haven't fully explained yourself. What if you're still working for the Shadow Emperor and he placed you here to intercept us?"

"I'm no loyalist," Themba said. "If ever we run across his agents, you will realize that. I was once a Seraph in the Shadow Emperor's employ. I was not highly placed enough to be in his Council, but I was high-ranking enough to have access to the Time Weaver's Prophecy. As unsatisfactory as this answer is, I'm afraid you have no choice but to trust me."

"I'm not sure we *can* trust you, given the circumstances," Khairu said. "All this about the Time Weaver sounds far-fetched. Just who is he? What is his role in all this?"

"There will be time to speak about this more at length. I have been as accommodating as possible, but now I must insist we begin our journey."

Khairu watched Lucian almost incredulously. "Lucian, are you sure about this?"

"We're going with him," Lucian said. "This is our best shot of recovering the Orbs and stopping the Ancient One. I have a lot of questions for Themba, too, but right now the priority is getting off this rock. And yes, finding the Time Weaver."

Khairu sighed, clearly not liking this one bit. "All right. But I've got my eye on you, Themba. You have a lot to answer for."

"Indeed. For now, take a seat and relax. As best as you can."

Themba looked at Lucian for a moment curiously but said

nothing. Lucian had the feeling it had something to do with calling the Shadow Emperor the Ancient One.

The ship hummed to life, the vibrations coursing through the deck. They took their seats, and as soon as they did so, the ship smoothly lifted off the floor of the hidden cave, rising above the ravine and the thick forest below.

Lucian nodded at Emma as he reached for the Radiant Aspect. "Streaming the shield now."

Emma joined with him, a powerful Radiant shield enveloping the vessel. Such was its strength that Lucian was confident it would make them invisible to all forms of detection unless a ship was within a few kilometers of them—an event none too likely given the vastness of space.

Within minutes, the star-filled night sky was quickly replaced by outer space. As Lucian gazed down on the forested world below, he couldn't believe he was still in an alternate reality, but one look at Themba's pale, alien face was enough to dash that notion.

"Adjusting course," Themba said.

"How long will it take to get to this Regalia?" Serah asked.

"This ship can reach ten percent of light speed, the fastest allowed by law. It has powerful Atomic and Gravitonic brands."

"What is the purpose of the Atomic brand?" Khairu asked.

"It replicates fuel."

Her eyes widened at this. "We don't have anyone who can make a brand like that."

"It has its uses, but also its limits."

"And the Gravitonic brand allows you to accelerate far beyond your inertial dampener's capacity," Lucian said.

Themba looked at him curiously. "Inertial dampener? What is that, exactly?"

"It's standard with any starfaring ship," Lucian said. "I'm not exactly sure how it works. It's a machine that counteracts the acceleration of any ship."

"An inertial dampening machine? I've never heard of such a thing. How does it function?"

"It has this thing called a graviton plenum," Emma explained. "It creates a bubble powerful enough to encompass the entire ship. So, when the ship moves, the bubble moves with it. The faster the ship goes, the more gravitons the plenum produces to keep up—to a point, of course. You can't accelerate past the dampener's capacity without becoming pancakes on the back wall."

"I see," Themba said. "So, it counters the force of inertia. And it operates without magic?"

Emma nodded. "Yes. The first ones were invented about two hundred years ago in our reality. Obviously, the technology has advanced remarkably since then."

"You keep mentioning your reality, as if you come from an entirely different existence. The Prophecy of the Time Weaver mentioned you come from another world, but nothing as different as another reality."

"In a way, it *is* another world," Emma said. "We're from an alternate reality. Your timeline and ours split about a million years ago."

"An alternate reality?"

"We'll explain later," Lucian said. "It's surprising that a civilization as advanced as this doesn't have inertial dampeners."

"Well, some forms of technology are forbidden by the Shadow Emperor. This *inertial dampener,* as you call it, could be one of them. If it were widely available, it would make travel between worlds far too easy."

"So, does any spaceship in this reality have to use Gravitonic Magic to slow down?" Serah asked.

"Yes. Either by employing a Gravitist mage or purchasing an incredibly expensive brand from a sorcerer powerful enough to create one. The second option is far costlier. There's no other way to travel between the stars. More than that, every sorcerer answers to the Shadow Emperor."

Jagar grunted. "There's no better way to control your subjects than to make them need you. If the Shadow Emperor controls the sorcerers, then he gets to dictate who can travel through space and who cannot."

Serah's brow furrowed. "Then how do *you* have access to a spaceship, Themba?"

"I'm a sorcerer. I'm powerful enough to create my own brands. I was a Seraph, remember?"

"Interesting," Serah said. "Magic in this reality seems far more advanced than back home. Most mages could never make brands like this. It's too dangerous."

"Yes," Themba agreed. "But you must remember, in this reality, the practice of magic is hundreds of thousands of years old. Sorcery is still dangerous, and it will always be to the uninitiated."

"Are there any other brands on this ship?" Lucian asked.

"Yes. Quite a few. All created with sorcery. However, like all brands, they need to be refreshed every few years. Don't worry; all my brands are in excellent condition. As for the first leg of our journey, we'll take about two weeks to reach Regalia. Unfortunately, our Gate is at the opposite end of this system, and it will take some time to reach it."

"What can you tell us about Regalia?" Khairu asked.

"Regalia is a moon—a city-world and a major trading crossroads. If anyone knows anything about the Time Weaver, it would be Zikhali."

"That's the name of your contact?" Lucian asked.

"Yes. We can trust her. For good measure, we might also trade ships with her, just to be on the safe side."

"Is the identity of this ship compromised?" Khairu asked.

"I have no reason to believe that," Themba said. "Still, we cannot be too careful."

In that moment, Lucian realized just how much they were at the mercy of this strange, old Ancient and the unknown reality in which they found themselves. What secrets did he hold? What twists and turns lay ahead?

Lucian couldn't say. They had just had to deal with that when the time came.

17

TEMPUS HUMMED with quiet activity as it traced a starlit path toward their next destination: the moon-city of Regalia. The two-week journey would provide a brief respite from the action on Mako—or Grastia, as it was called in this timeline.

The entire crew met in the central hub of the ship. Themba had called this meeting, and Lucian assumed the Ancient was going to teach them a bit more about what to expect in this reality. They had also taken the intervening time to catch him up on all the important details. He knew a few things about the reality they had come from, that Lucian was the Chosen there as well, and that he had possessed all Eight Orbs. Themba also knew about the Ancient One and his escape into the time gate, which resulted in the reality they all found themselves in.

It was hard for the Ancient to accept at first, but with a few follow-up questions, he acknowledged the reality of the situation.

Everyone waited as Themba watched them. Lucian still held his Psionic ward to ensure seamless communication. He was hoping they could find another solution because maintaining the ward significantly weakened his active streams. For now, though, this was all they had.

"It is time for you to learn more," Themba said. "But before we do that, there is something important we must take care of." He turned to Lucian. "Until now, you have been maintaining a complicated Psionic ward to allow communication. It's important that you not only learn the Ancient language but also some of our basic customs that will allow you to blend into Regalia. Doing so is the key to avoiding detection."

"How are we supposed to learn an entire language and culture in two weeks?" Serah asked. "That's impossible!"

"You won't learn it in the conventional way. I know magic that will allow you to absorb the proper information in far less time. You are likely already familiar with Psionic links. But what I have in mind is a bit more complicated: a Psionic mind-stream. A mind-stream doesn't pass along just words. It also passes along knowledge, memories, and information the sorcerer wants the subject to know. Very few are capable of such advanced magic. Thankfully, I am."

"I've never heard of such a thing," Khairu said with suspicion. "Will it allow you to read our minds?"

"Only if you allow it," Themba said. "But you don't need to worry about that. I will simply transfer some knowledge of our language and customs; basic information that will allow you to navigate Starsea society. It is an extremely intensive process, and honestly, it doesn't always work perfectly. It's far better to learn a language in the field. However, with time so limited, this is the only option we have."

"Let's go for it," Lucian said.

"After we're done with the Psionic impartation, we will only communicate in the High Ancient language aboard this ship. There are no guarantees that you will be fluent in the Ancient tongue by the end of this journey. The Ancient tongue is hard for the human palate, to where most humans cannot speak High

Ancient and must defer to the Low Tongue. Understanding, however, is quite easy. By the end of this Psionic impartation, I have full confidence you'll be able to understand most of what's being said without needing Lucian's ward. However, speaking may be another matter entirely. Some of you will, and others not. This remains to be seen. If we are lucky, all will understand and speak."

"Let's do this," Serah said.

Jagar grunted. "More like, let's get this over with."

"It's . . . unconventional," Emma said. "But I see no other way."

Themba's red eyes settled on Lucian, as if seeking permission to continue.

Lucian nodded. "We're ready when you are, Themba."

Themba nodded, his brow furrowing—an expression Lucian interpreted as contemplation, or perhaps even solemnity.

Themba's long, pale hands rose slowly, fingers splayed as he gestured toward the center of the room. Wisps of ethereal violet light swirled around his fingertips, coalescing into radiant, other-worldly streams of Psionic Magic.

Everyone remained breathless as those streams of light eddied and formed a purple aura encapsulating them all.

"This might feel a bit . . . *strange*," Themba said, his voice soft yet resonant in the hushed central compartment. His red eyes burned with a fierce, focused light, contrasting against the violet tendrils that continued to spiral outward from him.

The streams weaved through the air like threads forming a tapestry—a tapestry of sorcery. This many streams should have been impossible for any mage to control, but Themba was clearly not speaking idly about his former status as a Seraph in the halls of the Moon Tower of Nai Elyn.

The steady hum of *Tempus* seemed to lower, as if in reverence to the unfolding spectacle. The violet tendrils unfurled toward each crew member, gentle as whispers yet laced with potent magic. As they contacted Lucian's mind, a tingling sensation spread from the touchpoint—a ripple of paradoxical cold warmth that was as baffling as it was fascinating.

Lucian closed his eyes, accepting the link willingly. The magic cocooned his mind, the sensation both foreign and oddly comforting. His thoughts felt clouded at first, a heavy fog settling over his consciousness, as if he were in a trance. Then, a dam burst, and information poured into his brain. New concepts, strange words, and grammar flooded his senses, each piece of knowledge slotting into place as if it had always belonged.

A quick glance around him revealed his companions were experiencing something similar. Emma gasped in surprise. Khairu clenched her fists, while Serah's eyes were wide and amazed. Even Jagar's expression was one of shock.

And yet, no one recoiled at the barrage of knowledge. They all remained still, engulfed in the violet magic, surrendering to Themba's mind-stream. Lucian realized that Themba, at any point, could utterly destroy their minds with this power, and that he chose not to only proved he was an ally they could trust.

Themba was the eye of the Psionic storm, his concentration unwavering. He held the links steady, his gaze flitting between the humans as he monitored their absorption.

The session lasted for what seemed like an eternity. All of them stood, eyes glazed, unable to move or do anything else but comprehend the new language. Lucian understood that language was so much more than words; it held entire worlds and belief systems and was the soul of an entire race of sentient beings. It was no surprise to Lucian that the language was harsh, direct, and aggressive, yet not lacking in beauty, much like the Ancient people.

When Themba finally released the links, allowing the violet tendrils to dissolve back into ethereal wisps, the room shuddered back into reality, with time resuming its usual pace. The hum of *Tempus* rose back to its usual rhythm.

Everyone was blinking, completely silent. There was a sense

of calmness and surety from the new knowledge imparted. Lucian could only describe it as a mutual understanding, a unique bond forged through a shared experience. Through Themba's mind-stream, they had all taken their first step in integrating into this alien society.

Lucian broke from his reverie and looked at Themba, who stood on unsteady legs, a testament to the energy he'd spent. Despite his outward exhaustion, his red eyes were bright with satisfaction.

"I didn't expect humans to have such magical strength," he said, speaking the Ancient language, with Lucian understanding every word without even holding the ward. "You know enough to mix in with Ancient society, though of course, there will be gaps in your knowledge. It's my hope all of you will speak fluently by the time we arrive."

From the others' astounded reactions, it seemed as if they could all understand perfectly.

"Now comes the actual work," Themba continued. "To truly engage in the Ancient language, you will need to practice. This will require speaking to each other only in High Ancient from now on, even if it feels unnatural at first. The language is complex, with unique phonetics that are difficult for humans to speak. It's not just about memorizing words, but mastering the rhythm, the tone, and the click consonants that are integral to the language." He paused, meeting each of their gazes. "Practice, as they say, makes perfect. Speaking in Ancient will help your brains adapt faster, making the knowledge I've imparted more instinctive."

Lucian was the first to break the silence, his voice sounding alien to his own ears as he answered. "*Ngemfundo vukulu.*" He blinked in surprise at how easy it had been to make the strange sounds.

"It is indeed a great task," Themba translated, his head

nodding approvingly. "But I have faith in you. I have faith in *all* of you."

"What's crazy is that I understood exactly what you said," Serah said, her face pale. "*Dak'so ngoz!*"

"Now, *that's* an unusual phrase," Themba remarked. "It echoes our ancient lore of the underworld, but the idea of it rotting is intriguing."

"Rotting hell," Jagar said, in Standard English. "Doesn't exactly translate, nor roll off the tongue in Ancient."

"I beg to differ," Serah said. "*Dak'so ngoz! Dak'so ngoz! Dak'so ngoz!*"

Lucian couldn't help but snicker. "Hey, you sound like a goblin in that video game you play."

She put her hands on her hips. "I do *not!*"

"You kind of do," Emma said, stifling laughter.

"Stop making fun of me! I'm just leaning into the language, which is what all of *you* should be doing, too."

"This language has a certain . . . *harshness* to it," Khairu said, in Ancient, her eyes going wide at her ease of using the tongue. "However, Serah is correct. We need to practice and not only get used to the language, but all the idioms it has."

"*And* the idiom I just made up," Serah said.

With that, the room erupted in a cacophony of voices as the crewmates practiced, Themba presiding over them like an old master watching his pupils.

By the time they arrived, Lucian hoped they would have the language fully mastered.

18

LUCIAN and his companions fell into a familiar routine. Staying busy was the secret to staving off madness in space, and Themba always gave them things to do, whether it involved maintaining cleanliness and order, learning about the ship's operation, or studying Ancient history as the ship carved its path through the cosmic void.

Interestingly, Lucian discovered Ancient records dated back only about thirty thousand years. In this reality, a year based on one revolution of the Ancients' home world, Nai Shairen, which took slightly longer than Earth's: three hundred and eighty days.

While thirty thousand years was undoubtedly a long span of time, Lucian knew that a million standard years had passed since they'd traversed the time gate on Mako. Thirty thousand years was only three percent of the total timeline of Starsea. It was clear from the records that Starsea's history didn't extend farther back than that.

To Lucian, this paradox was deeply unsettling and demanded an explanation. That was nine hundred and seventy thousand years of history that had to be accounted for. What was the Ancient One doing that entire time?

One day, while they were eating in the galley, Lucian raised this question with Themba.

"The Starsea Empire has existed for over a million years," Lucian said. "Yet, I can't find any records older than thirty thousand years. Why is that?"

"Ah," Themba said. "This is an important subject. There is an answer to this riddle. That answer is that this isn't the first iteration of the Starsea Empire."

"What do you mean by that?" Emma asked.

"The Starsea Empire goes through cycles of creation and destruction. Cycles that are at the whim of the Shadow Emperor himself. We refer to these as the Void Cycles, periods of darkness and periods of thriving civilization. The periods of civilization can last as long as the current one, about thirty thousand years, while others are over within a few thousand years. Very little is known about the topic, but Seraphim scholars have pieced together a picture using limited evidence. Outside the Seraphim Sorcerers, this knowledge is practically unheard of."

"But . . . *why*?" Lucian asked. "What does he have to gain from destroying his empire?"

"It's more about what he stands to *lose*," Themba said solemnly. "Rather than lose control, he will annihilate his empire and start afresh. He is immortal. As long as he holds the Orbs, he will never die. Even if everything around him perishes, he will continue on. There are several theories why he does this, but the main one suggests that if anything threatens his rule, he simply erases everything to begin anew. The threat could come as a rebellion, or the reasons may be even more arbitrary. It is truly impossible to guess his motivations."

"How can he obliterate an entire *empire*?" Emma asked. "All by himself?"

"The Shadow Emperor's might is incomprehensible. He

reigns over all known sentient life and commands over a thousand suns. I'm afraid all of you have arrived at the peak of the Starsea Empire; it's my suspicion that when technology becomes this advanced, we are closer to another cataclysm than not."

"My guess is he sees technology as a threat," Khairu said. "No matter how hard he tries to suppress it, new tools and ideas find a way of spreading."

"Well said," Themba said. "The Shadow Emperor is not only the architect of calamity. He is also the source of rebirth. For after every cycle ends, he builds anew, after all the memory of the past has been extinguished, except perhaps in the oldest legends. And then, after thousands of years of darkness, even those legends transform until all original meaning is lost. Only then does he permit his subjects to rebuild."

"And you learned about this from your time as a Seraph?" Khairu asked.

Themba nodded. "Yes. The Shadow Emperor possesses a unique form of magic. A magic that manifests as a shadow, spreading from person to person, taking absolute control."

Lucian felt a chill as he realized this magic was like what he had observed in his own reality in the Grand Dome of Nessus. From the glances he shared with the others, it seemed they were thinking the same thing.

Themba continued. "All said, this has likely been the longest cycle by a wide margin. That's why I fear that if news of the Chosen reaches the Emperor's ears, even as a rumor, he may start a new Void Cycle, dooming everyone in the Starsea Empire to certain death."

"Billions would die," Lucian said.

"Indeed, that is so. Hundreds of billions. The Void Cycles serve as the Emperor's desperate fail-safe. Once his Shadow Magic has purged everything, he creates anew, spawning another empire from the ashes of the last. Perhaps he is seeking the perfect society with each iteration, one that will never rebel. But even if a million years have passed, he always falls short of his goal."

"What can you tell us about the Ancient One's magic?" Khairu asked. "Is it a new Aspect that no one else can use?"

"That is difficult to say. What I can tell you is that only the Emperor seems capable of it. It is from this he derives his name, the Shadow Emperor. In this way, he embodies the same essence as your Ancient One."

Lucian pondered everything Themba had said. He couldn't help but think that the attack of Nessus might have been the Ancient One's attempt to do something similar in their own reality.

At last, Lucian spoke. "I'm almost one hundred percent sure the Ancient One is the source of the Shadow Emperor in this reality. I followed him through a time gate a million years in the past. That's a past *both* of our realities share. But because I failed to defeat him in that past, I suspect it created an alternate reality when I went back through the gate. That's what created your reality, Themba. And the Ancient One has been here ever since, using his Shadow Magic to control things with these Void Cycles, as you described. And now with the Time Weaver in the mix, I'm at a loss for how to make sense of things . . ."

From Themba's silence, it seemed he was having difficulty comprehending things, too. Lucian didn't blame him.

"How does the Time Weaver fit into all of this?" Khairu asked.

"Ah," Themba said. "He is said to be an immortal time traveler, and unlike most other sentient beings, the Time Weaver can survive the devastation of a Void Cycle. Ever since these cycles began, the Time Weaver has evaded the Shadow Emperor's grasp and has propagated his prophecy of hope. He is an enigmatic figure, with his own lore and legends about him. He appears often in old stories, and these stories often have a hint of truth. But of course, he is most well-known for his prophecy, about a champion who would come armed with a spear of light to destroy the Shadow Emperor. Of course, the Emperor is aware of the prophecy, and ever vigilant. He would sooner usher in a new Void Cycle than risk the prophecy's fulfillment."

"So, let me get this straight," Serah said. "We've arrived at the tail-end of a cycle. And Lucian, the Chosen of the Manifold, is here, and if the Shadow Emperor ever learns about him, he'll just use his Shadow Magic to destroy everything?"

"It is a perilous situation, to be sure. With Lucian's arrival, we stand on the cusp of a new Void Cycle. The empire teeters on the brink of annihilation. One false move, and reality itself will unravel as the Shadow consumes us all. That magic, once unleashed, will only grow in power until none are left to withstand it."

"It seems . . . overwhelming," Lucian said. "From what you've said, it's almost as if the Time Weaver isn't real. Just a myth."

"Most think that," Themba said. "However, his prophecy led me to you, did it not? In my mind, that proves he is real. That it's led us this far means there is always hope. The Time Weaver prophesied that one day, the Shadow Emperor would fall. It is our task not merely to survive, but to fulfill that prophecy and change the course of the Empire's destiny."

All went silent for a moment as Themba's eyes looked at them one-by-one, finally settling on Lucian.

"Perhaps you came here by mistake, Lucian, but I don't think so. Your reality, and mine, are linked in ways that are not obvious at first glance. You are here for a reason. You are here to defeat the Shadow Emperor, and this Ancient One who controls him. And in that way, perhaps, you are also fated to save your own reality."

Themba's words hung heavy in the silence that followed. Lucian studied the faces of the others, each wearing expressions of shock, confusion, or grim determination. Jagar, in particular, looked shell-shocked, having remained silent throughout the entire conversation.

The immense weight of the Time Weaver's prophecy bore down on Lucian's shoulders. He knew they had to find him somewhere. Without the weapon Themba had talked about, they stood no chance against the Shadow Emperor. And they couldn't simply ignore the prophecy; after all, it had led Themba directly to Lucian. If it had been right in that case, then it was also probably right about the weapon Lucian needed.

Lucian looked at Themba. "In situations like this, when everything is so overwhelming, it helps to focus on the next small thing to do. Right now, that's figuring out what to do when we get to Regalia. I don't know how I can stop the Shadow Emperor without the Orbs. Now, I only have one, and it doesn't even work without the others."

He couldn't help but laugh at the situation. This was why he had vowed never to mess with time travel. His actions had influenced billions of beings across a million years of history, leading to the rise and fall of empires, all from his journey through the time gate on Mako. That it had only occurred a few days ago in his own time made it even more surreal.

He snapped back to reality and looked at the others.

"Themba's right. Maybe we're here to change the course of history, not only for this reality, but for our own. In a strange way, we are responsible for both. Our actions created them, after all. And from everything I've seen, this timeline is no less significant than ours."

Around the table, heads nodded, faces reflecting a mixture of determination, uncertainty, and hope. It was a lot to take in, but they still had time before they reached Regalia.

Maybe by then, things would make more sense.

19

THEY PASSED through their first Gate in this alternate timeline. The experience was much the same as in their own, although there was no real reason it *wouldn't* be. Unlike everything else, the Gates were an unchangeable constant, even by the Shadow Emperor.

The day before their arrival, Themba called everyone to the bridge of *Tempus*. Through the viewscreen, the swirling cosmos of deep space provided a resplendent backdrop to their meeting. Tomorrow, they would land on the grand metropolis of Regalia. Until now, Themba had been mostly quiet about his plans.

Now, that was about to change.

"Regalia is a massive trade port and crossroads for the Outer Empire, but being so far from the core of Starsea, it has a reputation. This can work to our advantage and detriment. Fifty billion sentients call Regalia home, and not just Ancients and humans. The Starsea Empire recognizes twelve different species as sentient within its territories, and all of them will be represented on Regalia in some capacity. I only say this to prepare you. If you've been studying, you should know the names of these species by now, along with their basic attributes. Mostly each species keeps to themselves, outside of reasons of trade. But without exception, Ancients are at the top of the hierarchy, with other races subservient to them to various degrees. Humans, unfortunately, are among the lowest. Of course, as we've already discussed, we must maintain the distasteful ruse of me being your master. This will give us the most freedom to act on our own. In public, I'm afraid a certain decorum must be followed. This is especially true when you are interacting with an Ancient. You are to keep your eyes lowered and only speak when spoken to."

"That's going to be a tough one," Serah said.

"Tell us more about this Zikhali," Khairu said, steering the conversation back to its original purpose. "You've mentioned she's an old friend, but you've told us nothing beyond that."

"Yes, an old friend," he said, his voice curiously soft.

"What's the story there?" Serah asked.

"She's capable and trustworthy. In the Regalia Deeps, she's known as the Shadowglide."

"What does that mean?" Lucian asked

"It's a creature that moves in the depths of the ocean part of Regalia. It blends with the shadows of the sea floor until it strikes with lightning speed."

"That sounds . . . terrifying," Serah said.

"Indeed," Themba agreed. "Zikhali is someone you want to have on your side."

"*Is* she on our side?" Emma asked.

"Yes."

"You seem confident of that," Khairu said, not hiding the skepticism in her voice.

"She helped me greatly during my exile. Kept me safe when no one else would, and she did so without the promise of a reward." He paused for a moment, reflective. "She has her fingers in many pies—smuggling, piracy, racketeering—but she has a moral compass, at least for the people and causes she cares about. I trust her, and you should, too."

Lucian had to wonder why someone of her nature would want to help Themba without a promise of reward. Nothing was ever truly free, and he had to wonder whether this Zikhali could be a blind spot for him.

"So, how is this supposed to go down?" Lucian asked.

"The first step is docking *Tempus* at a hangar the locals call the Harbinger's Nest. It's off the grid, so our entry will not be reported to the authorities."

"What if a government satellite logs our passing?" Khairu asked. "I've read the Empire keeps track of all ships entering and leaving a planet's atmosphere."

"We have a dummy transponder, so those satellites will log nothing more than that. They won't run anything as advanced as a full hull scan. A standard spaceport would do that, but at the Nest, that won't be an issue. The Nest is in the Deeps, where the presence of the Imperial Police is almost nonexistent."

"Okay, what happens after we've docked?" Emma asked.

"We meet Zikhali at the Shard, a dance club known only to those with certain . . . proclivities. It's been around since before Regalia was even called that."

"The fact that we're meeting her at all means she still needs convincing," Khairu observed.

"Yes, that's true. But I'm confident we can come to an agreement. She has already relayed she has information that might be of use to us. Something she doesn't want to risk being intercepted. Otherwise, there is no point to this. That she's meeting us speaks to her sincerity. It's true that we might have to give up *Tempus* in exchange and take a less capable vessel; that will be hard to stomach, because *Tempus* is a powerful ship, and the brands I placed on it are quite valuable and unique. It's quite possible Zikhali might even want it for herself. If not, she will find us a buyer who will give us a fair price. Her connections can rebuild the ship into something unrecognizable by the Empire, all while preserving its brands."

"Why can't we do the same thing with whatever ship we gain?" Jagar asked.

"Time. That process will take months, and months we do not have. Not when, at any moment, the Shadow Emperor could catch wind of us."

"So, assuming she's able to, what happens after Zikhali fences our ship?" Serah asked.

"I know she can find a buyer. We won't stick around long. Zikhali will arrange a clean, fully stocked ship for us. Once the transaction is complete, we leave Regalia with whatever information she has. The less time we spend there, the better."

The plan seemed good. As good as Lucian could hope, anyway. There were many moving pieces, and things could go wrong at any point. But their lives were in Themba's hands, and of course, Zikhali's.

With Regalia looming on the horizon, all Lucian could do was prepare himself as best he could.

———

IN THE QUIET of the night hours, Lucian's sleeping pod provided a much-needed refuge. He was grateful for the larger size because it meant Serah could fit in with him with some room to spare.

He stirred awake when Serah slipped in, her slender figure easily navigating the confines. She nestled in front of him, and Lucian wrapped his arms around her, the silence broken only by their shared breathing.

Normally, he wasn't one to fall asleep in this position. Serah's body was a literal furnace, but in the cold, dry air of space, the warmth was welcome. The Ancients, apparently, didn't believe in blankets—at least, not on spaceships, and he hadn't figured out how to work the controls for temperature.

He was about to fall asleep when she twisted to look at him. Her blue eyes appeared uncertain.

"What's wrong?" he asked, moving a strand of hair from her face. "Worried about tomorrow?"

She was quiet for a long time. Usually, she was quick to say what was bothering her. That she wasn't made Lucian realize something major was weighing her down.

"Something has really been eating at me. I'm not sure how to broach the subject . . ."

"You can tell me anything. I'm here and I'm listening."

Her eyes looked into his, still unsure. "I haven't said anything yet because things have been so stressful. And during our vacation, I didn't really want to bring you down. We'd just saved Earth. It seemed wrong to talk to you about something coming from my own insecurities."

"What do you mean?"

She sighed, as if steeling herself. "To be completely honest, I'm struggling with . . . jealousy, I guess you could say."

That was the last thing Lucian expected to hear. "Jealousy? About what?"

"I've tried not to think about it, but I can't stop. The only reason any of us are here now . . . the only reason this reality even *exists* . . . is because the Ancient One is still alive. And from what Emma said, you had the chance to end everything once and for all."

Lucian was confused for a moment. "Is this about me saving Emma?"

"I know it's not fair. And yet it's hard to get over the fact that you saved her instead of the entire universe."

"You think I should've let her die?"

"No, definitely not. It's just that she got something that I didn't. I tried to keep this to myself, but it's just been bothering me, even though I know it shouldn't. I guess in the back of my mind, there are worse doubts, too."

"Like what?"

She was quiet for a moment. "Like if you really love me over her."

Lucian saw her point. "Serah, she's just a friend. Nothing more. I love you, not her."

"I'm sorry to bring this up. I also know you've distanced yourself from her for my sake. But . . . the fact remains. You and she share a bond. Maybe it's just friendship. Maybe it's more."

"It's *not* more. I don't know what I can do to convince you."

"Would you have done it if it were Fergus, for example? Or Jagar, even?"

Lucian thought about it for a moment. "I don't know about that. It's true that Emma and I have something of a history. In the end, though, you were the one I wanted. The one that was right for me. That's why I'm with you, right?"

"Maybe you just felt bad about pushing me aside."

"No, that's not it. It's because I love you."

"More than her?"

"Yes! It's not even a question for me." Lucian hugged her close and buried her head beneath his chin. "This feels right to me. I can't imagine it any other way, nor do I want to."

"I'm sorry," Serah said. "I'm just sharing my feelings. That's what we're supposed to do, right?"

"Of course. I'm glad you shared, because you've given me the opportunity to remind you just how much you mean to me. And . . . maybe I haven't shown that to you enough."

"No, you have. There's so much on your mind. How can I even compare to that?"

"You're everything, Serah. You're the whole reason I'm doing this. I just want all this to be over so we can have a normal life together. If that's possible, then it's what I want."

"I want that too. To be honest, my insecurities probably won't vanish overnight. The fact remains: She got something that I never did—a grand gesture. Maybe you would do the same thing for me, but the situation has just never come up. But I'm in love with you, Lucian. That's what makes me act crazy sometimes."

"Your feelings are valid. I'm in love with you too. If I wasn't, I wouldn't have been strong enough to heal you or to face down Xara Mallis. I keep going because of that. Power, the Orbs, none of it matters to me. I just want a life with you. That's my true fight."

"I . . . want to believe that. But when I think about how we got our start, we never expected this. We were just trying to survive together on Psyche. At first, I thought we were just distracting each other from a foolish mission we were both caught up in. I expected us to die. Better to die with someone by your side, right? I mean, did you think of us as anything more than that?"

"It grew. Like you said, we were trying to survive. But after finding the Orb of Psionics, it felt more serious. Like it could actually be something, even if neither of us were looking for it."

"You never expected to leave Psyche or see Emma again. If you'd known, would you have gotten involved with me?"

"That's not true. I don't know how, but I knew from the moment I landed I was getting off Psyche. There was no doubt in my mind. If I was waiting for her, I wouldn't have pursued anything with you. But you won me over."

"How?"

"Because you make me laugh and smile. You help me get through the day. You always help me keep perspective. You're funny as hell, and I like that you don't take things too seriously. You . . . balance me like no one else ever could. And physically . . . well . . ."

". . .Yes?"

"Let's just say you're my type."

She laughed. "Well, I'll take it."

"So, have I convinced you?"

"And what about her? How do I compare? Physically, I mean."

"That's not even a question."

"Seriously, though. How do I stack up?"

"Well, you both are stunning. If I said she wasn't, well, I'd be lying, and you'd know that."

"Yes."

"But to me, it's no contest. It's not just physical, but every trial we've faced together, every moment we've shared, every inside joke."

She sighed. "I just need to cut it out, don't I?"

"Yeah. Maybe."

"Yeah," she said with a sigh. "Maybe."

Lucian held her close, yet he could still feel a barrier between them. As he held her, a nagging worry formed in the depths of his mind. Could Serah be right? Had he been so blind, unable to see what was glaringly apparent? Was he still nurturing a love for Emma, trying to suppress it out of respect for Serah?

He knew he loved Serah. Powerfully. But he'd saved Emma, where maybe, logically speaking, he *shouldn't* have. Emma herself had admitted that much.

But holding Serah close, he knew that wasn't the case. Serah was his person. She completed him in a way no one else in the universe ever could.

The only thing that hurt was the fact that she couldn't see it.

Eventually, she closed her eyes. He watched her for a while, her chest rising and falling rhythmically.

At last, he too closed his eyes and fell into a restless sleep.

———

THE NEXT MORNING, the crew gathered in the wardroom, with still a full day left to reach Regalia. Themba was on the bridge, minding the console, while the others were eating some meal packs. Ancient cuisine was markedly different from human food, incredibly bland to Lucian's taste. But the nutritional requirements of both species were similar, meaning everyone could practically eat the same thing.

"You really think we can trust this Themba?" Khairu asked. "He obviously has feelings for this Zikhali, and it seems to be clouding his judgment."

"Yeah. I noticed that, too," Jagar said.

"She's literally called the *Shadowglide*," Khairu went on. "It's a creature that hunts from the shadows and impales unsuspecting prey with a sword-like nose."

"I looked it up, too," Emma said. "Not a good way to go."

"What if *we're* the ones who are impaled?" Khairu went on. "I doubt we would be the first. Or what if Themba is the one turning us in for his own reasons?"

Lucian didn't have an answer for that. All he felt was a lack of control. Just days ago, he had been the one calling the shots. Entire fleets had followed him.

Now, in this reality, he was a slave and just had to hope for the best. And his conversation with Serah had unbalanced him.

"Are you okay?" Emma asked. "Both you and Serah are very quiet."

"That's . . . unusual," Khairu said, looking at Serah. "Are you feeling sick?"

"Not sick," Serah said quietly. "Far from it."

"We just didn't get much sleep last night," Lucian said. As soon as he finished speaking, he realized that had a certain implication.

"Well, can't fault you for that," Jagar said.

The others chuckled, but Lucian wasn't in the mood. "Let's focus here. Does anyone have any ideas? I trust him as far as I can throw him, for the record, but what other options do we have?"

"None to speak of," Khairu said.

"Maybe we don't trust him completely," Lucian said. "That's fair. But think about this. Every single one of us gave him access to our minds, and he did exactly what he said. I think he's proven himself enough for us to follow him onto Regalia."

"You said it yourself," Khairu said. "We don't have any other choice."

"It's not ideal," Lucian said. "The only thing going for him is that he hasn't led us astray yet. If this is all an act, it's a very elaborate one."

"I definitely think he's on the run from the Shadow Emperor," Emma said. "That part of his story seems to check out. I'm just not sure about this Zikhali business."

"Maybe he's hoping for a payout from her," Khairu said. "They might be working together."

"I don't know," Lucian said. "Seems unlikely."

"He could be listening to us now," Serah said. "Should we *really* be discussing this so openly?"

It was a good point, but they were speaking in Standard English. Unless Themba used Psionic Magic, it was not likely he would understand.

"Until he proves otherwise," Lucian said, "I'm going to assume he's being honest. Like I said, all of this is too crazy to be a lie. I could be wrong, but I don't think so."

"Maybe you can read his mind or something," Emma said.

"Without the Orb of Psionics, my powers are limited, especially against Themba. You saw how advanced his magic was."

"So what?" Khairu asked. "We just trust him?"

"Until he gives us reason otherwise, then yes. But that doesn't mean we lower our guard. We've been betrayed too many times for that."

"So, what's our Plan B?" Jagar asked.

"Themba said it himself. Regalia is a big world with fifty billion souls. It would be easy to get lost there and figure things out later."

"Yeah, maybe," Khairu said, doubtfully. "Trust is difficult for me. But like you said, we may have no choice."

"We'll figure this out. I promise you that."

"I just have a strange feeling about this Regalia stuff," Khairu said. "I can't put my finger on it."

"You have good instincts," Lucian said. "We'll just have to navigate it, like we always do."

"We have been through a lot so far," Emma said. "I've done some research on Regalia. The Deeps seem like a dangerous place. It's said that it's a place not even sunlight reaches. It's a haven for criminals and unsavory types. I'd recommend looking over the notes Themba sent us to get acquainted with the different species we'll encounter. From what I've seen so far, we're in for some strange sights."

"True enough," Lucian said. "We don't know what we're walking into, but we've walked into the unknown before and come out the other side."

Khairu crossed her arms. "This is all a big mess."

Lucian nodded. "It is. But we've handled messes before, and we'll handle this one too."

Lucian took a moment to look around at the faces of his crew. The anxiety was still there, but he knew their capabilities. Without his Orbs, it wouldn't be easy. But they would have to make it work.

"Right," he said, standing from the bench. "We have a day to prepare. Let's use it well. Review the notes. Rest if you need to."

With those words, the crew dispersed.

20

EVERYONE STOOD on the bridge as the moon, cloaked in night but resplendently lit by city lights, swiftly approached. In their timeline, this moon would have been known as Pallas, a world with less than a hundred thousand souls on its surface. But in this reality, Pallas was a metropolis of fifty billion sentient beings, going by the name of Regalia.

As *Tempus* neared, clusters of glowing towers came into view, sprawling out like intricate webs. The planet that Regalia orbited seemed rocky, with thick bands of clouds and vast oceans. Lucian knew from his research that the planet was a great deal larger than Earth, with gravity about twice that of humanity's home planet. It was all but uninhabitable to humans, despite having liquid water. Some of the hardier sentients of the Starsea Empire could live there, but mostly, it served as a source of resources for the moon above.

Regalia was its counterpoint, a haven for life. As they approached, Lucian could hardly imagine how fifty billion souls could fit on one tiny world. Despite the upcoming danger, he looked forward to seeing it.

"All seems clear," Themba said, checking the dash and examining the data readout. "We're passing rather closely to a government satellite, but I'm confident our transponder will keep us safe."

"I hope so," Khairu said.

Themba seemed as good as his word. Within minutes, they were sliding into Regalia's atmosphere, toward the sea of lights below. Lucian, leaning over the bridge's console, watched as the buildings of the moon city came into view. Skyscrapers sprawled in a network of towering iridescence, their nighttime glow casting long, eerie shadows into the chasms of alleys in between. Dozens, perhaps hundreds, of ships flew to and from orbit, while thousands of skycars formed lanes, swooping between massive buildings. Bridges and tunnels connected the urban landscape, while trains screamed along their tracks. Some buildings, Lucian noted, were hovering in the dark nighttime sky, a feat that could have only been accomplished with Gravitonic Magic.

"Rotting hell," Serah said, her eyes wide as saucers. "It's bigger than Nessus! Even bigger than Earth!"

Themba's brow furrowed. "It's often said Regalia is a miniature version of Nai Shairen."

"I can't even imagine," Emma said.

Tempus lowered on its preset course and was soon swallowed by the city's gleaming labyrinth.

As they descended further, the bright mirage of Regalia's upper tiers shifted and was replaced by a grittier reality. The neon hues of the higher cityscape dimmed as they plunged into the shadowy heart of the Deeps. The thrum of skycars continued to echo around them, some zooming perilously close. Pedestrian walkways interconnected the towering skyscrapers in seemingly random patterns. The vertical corridor was barely wide enough to navigate; one false move would see them crashing into one of the many surrounding buildings.

"Feels like we're entering a cave," Lucian said.

"Or an abyss," Serah said. She looked at Themba. "Didn't your notes say this was a water world?"

Themba's red eyes gleamed, reflecting the lights of the ship's surroundings. "Yes. The surface comprises a patchwork of islands. Most of the buildings' foundations penetrate deep into the sea floor. However, we won't be going that low."

After another minute, *Tempus* shifted forward, entering a long tunnel feebly lit with flickering fluorescent lights.

"Ah," Themba said. "We're nearly there."

The Tempus eased into a wide hangar, what Lucian assumed to be the Harbinger's Nest. An array of shabby vessels sat haphazardly in the gloom. Several, Lucian noted, had markings on their outer shielding, most likely from weapon impacts. Dimly lit corners hinted at concealed activities. The walls, covered with graffiti, told silent tales of the Nest's frequent visitors. Overhead, an interlaced network of pipes and conduits snaked across the ceiling, dripping condensation onto the worn metal surface below.

Here, amongst the grime and the shadows, Lucian felt a sense of exposure, a reminder that they were about to exchange the safety of the ship for Regalia's seedy underbelly.

"Remember to let me take the lead," Themba said.

"What if things come to blows down here?" Jagar asked.

"Remember: violence is the crutch of those who can't out-think their problems," Themba said.

"You can't out-think a fist in the face," Jagar said.

"Yeah," Serah said. "Everyone has a plan until fist meets face, so to speak."

"That's a strange way of putting it," Emma said. "But I see what you mean."

"No violence, unless we are truly out of options," Themba said. "Which won't happen. We are having a simple, transactional meeting with Zikhali. Nothing more."

"Should we head out?" Lucian asked.

"The sooner, the better," Themba said. "And remember to have a subservient air whenever speaking to me. People see what they are presented with; if we act the parts of an Ancient noble and five human slaves, that's what others will see."

"Ready when you are," Lucian said.

As they stepped out of the ship, the half-Earth gravity of Regalia made Lucian feel unusually light on his feet. When the door of *Tempus* closed behind them, they followed Themba, who walked at an authoritative pace, signaling to any onlooker that he was the one in charge. The rest of the crew fell into their roles, walking humbly, eyes lowered. For Lucian, resisting the urge to scan the area for threats was a struggle, but maintaining their low-profile disguise took precedence.

Serah, however, seemed to have a different mindset. *Hey, what are those bird-looking creatures? I don't remember seeing them in Themba's notes.*

Despite himself, Lucian looked up to see a group of six bipedal birds approaching them, each with a pair of wide wings connected to lanky arms and hands. They didn't appear capable of flight, but perhaps they could glide, especially in this moon's gravity. They loomed at least two meters high, their dazzling plumage contrasting starkly against the hangar's grimy backdrop. Their obsidian beaks, sharp as razors, glinted ominously. Their black, predatory eyes seemed filled with ill intent.

Lucian recalled the name "Quetzorians" from his studies aboard the ship. *They were the last entry in the notes. These look like trouble.*

Themba hardly reacted, seeming not to care about the incoming threat.

The lead quetzorian's beak opened menacingly, but before it could cause harm, Themba held up a deflecting hand. "We are meeting The Shadowglide. Do not impede us."

The effect was instant; the quetzorians' aggressive posturing deflated. When they stepped back, respect—or perhaps even fear—flickered in their avian eyes.

Without a word, they retreated to the shadows from which they had emerged, waiting for easier targets.

Damn, Serah said to Lucian. *I wonder what it would be like to fight one of those. You see those talons?*

Hopefully, we don't find out.

Emerging from the hangar into Regalia's Deeps, they were met by a narrow, cold street filled with dense, acrid smoke. Shadowy figures passed through winding alleys; the heavy beats of rowdy bars added to the cacophony. In the dim light, things were difficult to make out, but Lucian could see that a diverse array of species populated the street, their many dialects filling the air.

Lucian failed to detect the harsh, yet lyrical, words of the Ancient tongue. No one spared them a second glance; an Ancient and his retinue of human slaves barely afforded notice in such a bustling metropolis.

Stealing a few glances, Lucian was surprised to see humans in one bar they passed. Most served as entertainment—as servers, dancers, or musicians—though humans were certainly in the minority down here.

Though Themba had warned them against curiosity, it was impossible *not* to be intrigued. Their path snaked through a riotous montage of alien life, the likes of which Lucian had only seen in Themba's notes. He spotted a group of small reptilian bipeds with skin shimmering with iridescent scales, their heads bobbing in animated conversation.

Kalari, Lucian thought, remembering that they were known as traders. Naturally, they would be drawn to a busy port world like Regalia.

Almost as soon as he noticed the Kalari, the street vibrated beneath him. Lucian nearly cried out as a gargantuan creature lumbered by, at least three meters tall, hewn from living rock. It moved gracefully for its size, each step resonating in a low, echoing thrum. Other creatures paid it no mind, simply moving out of the way as they went about their business. Lucian couldn't see any eyes on the creature, yet it navigated the crowd with ease. Its craggy face bore three branded marks.

A Vorran. They were supposed to be rare, but at least one existed down here in the Deeps.

As if that weren't captivating enough, Lucian's gaze fell on a pair of elongated, thin creatures standing head and shoulders above the crowd. Clad in flowing robes of shifting colors, these ghostlike beings moved with eerie grace, contrasting with the restless energy of the Undercity. Their alabaster skin glowed with subtle bioluminescence. The creatures seemed to drift past them on three thin, spindly legs. Both creatures' large, ovoid eyes, completely black, seemed to peer into Lucian's soul, both mesmerizing and bone-chilling. One opened its thin mouth, revealing razor-sharp teeth in what might have been a smile— albeit the creepiest smile Lucian had ever seen.

Luminarians, he recalled. He remembered they used their hypnotic eyes to paralyze their prey.

Note to self, he communicated to Serah, steadying his nerves. *Don't look at those creepy tall ones.*

That's nightmare fuel for life.

Lucian felt a similar sense of vertigo as they continued. He couldn't help but be awed by the unimaginable scale and complexity of the reality they were navigating. Here was a universe infinitely more complex than his own, and what was even more mind-blowing was the fact that this divergent timeline was birthed by *their* actions. The weight of this realization hit him harder than ever before.

Who *were* these species, exactly? Had they once existed in their own reality, but had been wiped out by the *Alkasen*? Or did they still exist somewhere in the depths of Dark Space?

The more they moved through the dark and narrow alleys, the more the facade of lively chaos peeled away to reveal a bleaker truth. This was no bustling marketplace of dreams and opportunity, but a desperate struggle for survival, where every moment was a fight to live. The heavy beats of music and laughter from the rowdy bars seemed to mask a deeper pain.

Lucian noticed the desperate gazes of street urchins, mostly human, with eyes wide and hollow. Their faces, smeared with dirt, looked more animal than child. Emaciated figures, human and non-human alike, languished in doorways and dark recesses, their bodies shrouded in tattered rags. Beggars reached out with thin, trembling hands, pleading in various dialects for any kindness.

As they passed a street lined with opulent clubs and bars, Lucian could see, through the open doors, lavishly dressed patrons enjoying decadent feasts while lounging on plush sofas, their laughter shrill and indifferent as they were served by the same species who languished outside their doors.

Themba led them past a dark alley, the odor of waste and decay nearly overwhelming. Lucian couldn't help but glance down at the dimly lit passage, only to see a heap of rags that seemed to shift slightly. He realized it was a person, or perhaps several, huddled together for warmth or companionship.

The divide was clear and unapologetic. There was no middle ground here in the Deeps. You were one of the fortunate, indulging in the excesses of life, or one of the forgotten, scrabbling in the dust for survival. This clash of worlds created an abyss that swallowed any notion of fairness or compassion.

Lucian now understood what Themba had meant in his previous warnings. The Deeps were a dystopian environment where dreams died, a place where the rich feasted while the poor starved, where hope was almost nonexistent. Lucian felt a pang of guilt as he moved through this world, a visitor peering into a reality that was all too real for those who called it home.

With luck, they would leave this place soon. And yet the guilt went deeper, because it was his actions that had birthed this suffering, whether or not he had meant it. He knew that this was just the tip of the iceberg, not just in this world, but in countless others. Trying to stop it was like trying to stop time itself from advancing.

Everyone was silent, apparently having similar dark thoughts. Serah held his hand for a small bit of comfort. Lucian was grateful for at least that much. Some things went beyond words.

Mercifully, they turned from the alley and onto a broader promenade running between a canyon of dark, looming buildings. Lucian looked up, his view impeded by a metal ceiling some fifty meters above. Down here, it would be impossible to see the sky, and living in this place was more akin to dwelling in a giant metal shell than in a city. One could live an entire life down here without ever seeing the stars. Lucian was certain that more than a few had.

As they made another turn, a shining building rose in the distance, as high as the metal shell above them. This massive edifice, resembling an upturned piece of broken glass, could be none other than the Shard. It was easy to see where it had gotten its name. Its resplendent surface stood as a monument of defiance to the surrounding squalor and grime of the Undercity.

As they approached, the beat of esoteric dance music, in a strange, arrhythmic time signature not meant for human bodies, blasted through them. Neon lights cast a dizzying array of colors on the swarm of beings entering and exiting.

Stepping through the Shard's wide entrance, Lucian took one last look at the decrepit city behind him. Regalia was a testament to the darker side of the cosmos, a place where only the fiercest survived.

Lucian had seen many things, especially over the last few years, but nothing quite like this.

We've got this, Serah said. *Get in, get out, and get back.*

Especially that last part.

They, along with the rest, turned away from the menacing cityscape, stepping into the kaleidoscope of lights and sound that was the Shard's dance floor.

The hunt for Zikhali had begun.

21

THEMBA LED them along the periphery of the club, attempting to keep them away from the dance floor's chaos. Without the possibility of using his magic, Lucian felt exposed. He had to trust that Themba could talk them out of any mess.

Just as Lucian had that thought, a large furry creature reminiscent of a bipedal bear bumped into him. It had rounded ears and a long snout that opened to reveal pointed teeth.

"Out of my way, human scum," it hissed in the Ancient language.

Another of the creatures bumped into Lucian from the other direction, obviously on purpose, accompanied by a sniveling laugh.

Themba turned to face them both, seeming to grow half a meter. The two creatures, which Lucian remembered as being called Torlins, drew back, though they kept their threatening posture.

"That's my property," Themba said, his voice carrying despite the dance floor's cacophony.

The first Torlin emitted a low hiss, a snakelike tongue forking through his teeth. "And what'll you do about it, old-timer? I'll tear your flesh before you ever let out a squeak."

"You forget your place, Torlin," Themba said easily.

"You forget yourself. This is the Deeps, and we serve the Shadowglide!"

They rose menacingly, and Lucian took a couple of steps back, standing in front of Serah protectively. A ring formed around them in anticipation of a fight. If this came to blows, Lucian didn't know how he'd survive without his magic. But Themba didn't back down, while also refusing to make the first move.

"That's enough," came a sonorous female voice.

Lucian looked for the source of these words, to find a tall, teal-skinned Ancient with soft features and deep-set jade eyes. Her face was smooth, and she had two short horns protruding from her brow; Lucian noticed the one on the right was broken off. She wore rich, flowing robes, and despite her calm demeanor, exuded a sense of danger.

"Forgive us, Shadowglide," the first Torlin said, bowing deeply. "You told us to alert you if an Ancient entered here."

"Yes, to alert *me*, not to threaten *them*," she said. "Get out of my sight before the Pit finds its two newest combatants."

The Torlins bowed and hastily withdrew into the crowd. Lucian had to assume the Pit was some sort of fighting ring with a high mortality rate.

Zikhali's green eyes quickly took in Themba and the humans with him.

"A motley bunch," she observed, before she settled on gazing at her old comrade. "You've grown old, Themba."

"And you, Zikhali, have not aged a day."

She stared at him for a long moment, as if considering. "Flattery will not get you anywhere, especially given your history. Let's go back to my office."

They followed Zikhali as she threaded her way through the

multi-species crowd. Lucian was surprised to see a tall, rocky Vorran dancing, though most creatures wisely gave him a wide berth.

Zikhali stepped onto another dance floor, this one an elevator that went up the central shaft of the Shard. A scantily clad woman, one of the few humans, danced her way closer to Lucian. Serah, without preamble, sharply stepped on her foot. The woman yelped and seemed ready to fight, but at one look from Serah, she wisely decided not to take her chances.

When the floor arrived at the top level, Zikhali stepped into the outer ring, with everyone following. As soon as they were off, the floor began its descent, along with the dozens of partiers.

"This way," Zikhali said.

Within a minute, they were inside her office. The first thing Lucian noticed were the pulsating neon glyphs etched into the onyx-black walls, their illumination casting long shadows around the room. A large desk of gleaming obsidian sat in the heart of the space, surrounded by strange artifacts that Zikhali had collected over the years.

Encased in protective holo-displays, these included a set of intricately carved crystals, whose soft glow hinted at latent energy within. A holographic star map stood next to the crystals, with each star labeled in the runic script of the Ancients, though from Lucian's knowledge of the language, the words were archaic and completely indecipherable. Finally, a collection of weapons lined a wall, a wide assortment of shockspears spanning from the ancient to the modern.

Several sofas were near the desk, and it was toward these that Zikhali nodded. "Please, sit."

All of them did so. Zikhali herself took a seat behind her massive desk. The humans barely registered; she had eyes only for Themba. Though Lucian knew little about alien body language, the atmosphere in the room was undoubtedly tense. Zikhali's posture was cold and stiff, while Themba's head was slightly bowed, as if in supplication. There was no sound for a good minute, aside from the heavy beats of the club outside.

"So, Themba Makhosi. Allow me to summarize the situation. You vanished from my life without a trace, hunting shadows and legends. And now, against all reason, you've returned, expecting my help. I suppose if you had *any* imagination at all, you would place yourself in my boots and consider how all this makes me feel. But you never had imagination except that which interested you. Even when we were sharing a pod, it was always prophecies, the Time Weaver, and the Chosen. And now, failing your search and on the run from the authorities, as I warned would happen, you've come to me, bowing and scraping for a clean ship to live the rest of your pitiful days in peace." Her green eyes bored into his. "Do I have that right?"

Themba merely looked at her, not contradicting her assessment.

Finally, Zikhali seemed to notice the humans. "Why did you bring these slaves? Bargaining chips? They're completely unextraordinary."

"They're not bargaining chips," Themba said. "They are the answer."

"The answer? To what? Themba, I haven't time for games. It's been over a hundred years. If there's something you came to say, out with it!"

"I thought you told her about the Time Weaver," Serah said.

Both Ancients looked at her sharply before Zikhali regarded Themba once more.

"What's this about the Time Weaver? How does he factor into this?"

Themba watched her closely. "Would you like to learn the truth? Or continue living as if nothing has changed?"

"What are you talking about?"

"Those shadows and legends," Themba said. "They are real. And if the Shadow Emperor discovers as much . . ."

At this, Zikhali's demeanor changed. The light green skin of her face paled to a more subdued hue. "Themba, you've gone completely mad."

"Far from it, Zikhali. It's real. All of it. The Void Cycle is coming. And one of these humans is the only thing we have to fight against it."

"What proof do you have, Themba? In older times, you spoke of the Time Weaver's prophecy, of a human being able to use magic, of wielding a spear of light. Are you saying one of *these* is the Chosen?"

"I am," Lucian said, standing up.

Before Zikhali could say another word, Lucian held out his hand. As he saw it, there was no point in keeping his magic under wraps, at least where Zikhali was concerned.

A line of light materialized, forming Lightspear. Once formed, the weapon seemed to drink in the light of the surrounding office, even dimming the once-shining crystals. Zikhali watched impassively, though her brow twitched slightly at the sight. After a moment, he allowed the weapon to dissipate.

"An illusion," Zikhali said. "If you're truly a sorcerer, as Themba's prophecies say, what am I thinking right now?"

Lucian, not in the mood for theatrics, reached out for her mind. Zikhali was a non-mage and had no defense for his own Psionic Magic.

It didn't take long for him to discover something that made the hairs on his arms rise.

"I think it's best we left," Lucian said. "She's sold us out. The Seraphim are on their way."

Before anyone could say anything, an explosion rocked the room from the direction of the dance floor. Everyone ducked, and amid the thunderous boom, screams of various sentients could be heard.

Zikhali drew a pistol, and Lucian instantly raised a shield. But Zikhali merely stood there, not firing.

"This will be difficult to explain," she said. "Yes, Themba. I told the Seraphim you were coming. All you told me was that you wanted to trade ships. Every word of your message was entitled, no hint of an apology. I . . . was enraged. All this about the Chosen, I never expected . . ."

"We don't have time for this," Lucian said.

He reached out for her mind. He needed to know instantly whether she was lying.

He sensed inner turmoil and confusion. But beneath that, strangely enough, he perceived she was telling the truth. Yes, she'd planned to sell them out from the beginning, and she'd done so out of the vindictive rage that might be expected of an underworld boss.

But even considering this, there had been an unmistakable mental shift. Lucian had trouble believing it was real, but he recognized they were all out of options.

"I have a car," Zikhali said, quietly. "It's our only way out. If we try to go out through the front, it will guarantee our deaths."

"Like hell we're going with you!" Khairu said.

Lucian wanted to yell in frustration. There was no other choice, and he had seconds to decide.

"Lead the way," he commanded, his voice fierce. The others looked at him in shock, but he doubled down. "Go, Zikhali, if you want to redeem yourself."

With no further words, she headed for a side door in her office, the sounds of fighting intensifying outside.

22

LUCIAN DIDN'T HAVE the time, or luxury, to second-guess his decision. He simply had to trust his Psionic Magic, which had yet to lead him astray. This shift from trust, to betrayal, then back to tentative trust, was jarring.

And yet, the fact remained: Zikhali was their only way out.

They were running down a long corridor when, about twenty meters away, a blast tore through the right-hand wall, filling the air with dust and debris. From the smoke, two figures in midnight-black robes emerged, their red eyes blazing with menace.

Lucian's heart pounded in his chest, his instincts screaming danger as a chill ran down his spine.

"Seraphim," Themba said. "Fight with everything you have!"

What followed was a chaotic dance of magic and speed. The Seraphim moved with spectral grace, using Gravitonic auras to glide like phantoms as their shockspears blazed red-hot. They streamed a cascade of fire that roared down the corridor. Several group members formed a Thermal shield just in time to deflect the fiery onslaught.

Themba acted fast, pinning the Seraphim with his Gravitonic Magic, his hands shaking with effort. Emma's Radiant lasers were deflected by the Seraphim's shields, energy crackling and dissipating into the air. Khairu streamed a lightning bolt, but this energy, too, was absorbed by the Seraphim's shields. With a powerful burst of silvery magic, the Seraphim broke Themba's hold on them.

The two sides clashed with a fury that seemed to defy physics. Streams met streams, attack with counterattack, in a relentless back-and-forth that allowed no quarter. Ice spikes from one Seraph's spear were countered by a swift fireball from Lucian's hand, transforming them into a shower of mist.

The Seraphim fought with coordinated elegance, their movements and streams weaving with lethal efficiency. Lucian and his group were no less skilled; their teamwork and shared history allowed them to flow like a single entity. But that two Seraphim could fight so viciously against six experienced mages, including Lucian, only spoke of their martial prowess.

In the chaos, Lucian saw his opportunity. He charged, filling his Focus with ether. After yanking the Seraphim upward with Gravitonic Magic, he also propelled himself, twisting and landing adroitly on the ceiling. The Seraphim's surprise was obvious as they scrambled to regain their balance.

Their confusion was all Lucian needed. With Lightspear in hand, he charged forward, the brilliant weapon trailing light. Lucian entered the Ether, drawing the room's light into Lightspear, shrouding everything else in darkness. The Seraphim hesitated, their synchronization faltering.

Lucian channeled the energy into his spear, a beacon in the dark corridor. He threw it with all his might, and it shot down the corridor like lightning, piercing both Seraphim with a thunderous crash.

When he recalled the spear, the light returned, revealing two piles of ash along with the Seraphim's discarded shockspears.

As the group stood panting, Lucian turned to them. "Everyone all right?"

"We must keep moving," Zikhali urged, her eyes studying Lucian, as if seeing him anew. "There will be more."

"Wait just a second," Khairu said. "You called these Seraphim on us. Why shouldn't we kill you now?"

Zikhali regarded Khairu coolly. "Because I'm the only chance you have."

"Why the change of heart?" Emma asked. "How can we possibly trust you?"

Lucian realized they knew nothing of his mind-reading. "I read her mind. She's telling the truth."

Themba looked at Zikhali strangely. The poor guy had to be suffering from major whiplash. Even if Lucian had seen this coming, Themba obviously hadn't.

Zikhali led them into a compact hangar housing her skycar. She pressed her wristwatch, and the hangar doors slid back, revealing a shadowy alley.

But the moment those doors opened, two Seraphim shot in, propelled by binding tethers. Reacting on instinct, Lucian created his own tether, yanking one toward him and impaling him with Lightspear. The second was dispatched just as rapidly, Themba slamming him through the floor with a powerful Gravitonic stream.

"Come on," Zikhali said.

They climbed into the car, Lucian allowing Lightspear to dissipate. They had barely strapped in before the car hummed to life, roaring out of the Shard and into the alley beyond.

"Rotting hell," Serah said. "I didn't sign up for this!"

"Don't worry," Zikhali said. "My car is fast. And it comes with tricks."

Before Lucian could ask, the car jerked upward, joining a sky lane pointed toward Regalia's upper tiers. Quiet settled for a few seconds until Zikhali's wristwatch chimed.

She glanced at it and cursed. "Our escape ship's been compromised."

"What?" Emma nearly shouted.

"I can set *Tempus's* autopilot to meet us above the city," Themba said. "All of us can escape together."

"You better not be playing us, Zikhali," Khairu warned.

"I'm in as much danger as you," Zikhali said. "Trust me, you're in no better hands than mine."

"We're being followed," Jagar said.

Several speedy skycars, much smaller than Zikhali's, kept pace with her bulkier vehicle, their angular forms cutting through the air, leaving vibrant contrails.

Zikhali veered into a new lane packed densely with traffic, her deft maneuvers taking them through a labyrinth of towering buildings and ever-changing lanes.

"I almost want to take my chance with the Seraphim after this," Emma said, her face pale.

Zikhali said nothing, focusing intensely on the controls. Despite Zikhali's skill, their pursuers were relentless. Bullets and white-hot bursts of plasma whizzed past them, striking the sides of buildings, causing minor explosions. One plasma burst even grazed their car's shield, emitting a burst of sparks.

Lucian and Serah streamed Thermal shields in tandem, their combined strength helping to deflect the barrage.

"Can't we go any faster?" Themba shouted over the roar of the engines.

"Trust me!" Zikhali yelled back, her eyes fixed ahead.

Trust, Lucian realized, was difficult in this situation, but they were out of options.

"Keep shielding," he ordered. "I'm going to knock their cars down."

"Lucian," Serah said, her voice strained. "That'll be tough without an Orb."

"I have to try."

"No need," Zikhali said, her brow furrowing.

Before Lucian could question her, the car darted between two transports, the narrow gap barely wide enough to admit them. Two of the pursuing Seraphim cars weren't so fortunate, crashing into the larger vehicles in a brilliant display of light and debris.

They were in the clear, their vehicle surging ahead. But it wasn't long before even *more* Seraphim closed in from the sides.

"There are so many!" Emma said.

Lucian unstrapped himself from his seat.

"Lucian!" Serah protested. "You're going to—"

Zikhali suddenly shifted the trajectory, and Lucian planted his feet to the ground with Binding Magic. He was pulled in the opposite direction of the turn, but the Binding was secure.

He focused on the pursuing vehicles, two of them veering back and forth across the narrow sky lane.

He summoned Lightspear in his hand and launched it right through the front of the closest pursuing car. It shot in a streak of brilliance, finding its mark. The Seraphim vehicle exploded in a ball of fire, debris sparking onto the buildings below. The second vehicle, directly behind the first, tried to evade, but was too late, getting caught in the blast radius before spiraling out of control.

When the lane ended, they found themselves above the city, with the tinge of dawn lighting the graceful tops of skyscrapers with orange luminescence. It was a beautiful and peaceful view that Lucian didn't have time to admire, because a colossal ship was descending from above, its broad, menacing silhouette blotting out the sky.

"A Seraphim Dreadnought," Themba said. "*That's* the source of the attack."

Zikhali was unflinching, her hands steady on the controls. "Brace yourselves."

"Zikhali," Themba said, "that ship's weaponry will wipe us out in an instant. We must take our chances in the Deeps!"

With a hard yank on the control lever, the skycar shot

forward as everyone screamed. The cityscape was a dizzying blur below them as they flew beneath the underbelly of the Dreadnought, which was now opening fire on the car's pitiful shield. Lucian and the others streamed to augment it, but it was only a matter of time before the ship's firepower overwhelmed them.

With the Orbs, Lucian would have been more than a match for it. It was a hard pill to swallow.

Zikhali barrel-rolled the vehicle and leveled out, flying directly beneath it with just a couple of meters to spare. They were much too close for the ship's guns to do any damage.

"There," Zikhali said. "I can see *Tempus* in the distance."

Lucian could just barely make it out, an insignificant blip against the rising orange sun.

"It's so far!" Emma said. "We'll never make it!"

"This dreadnought will start shooting as soon as we pull away," Lucian said.

"Then shield us with everything you have," Zikhali said. "You're the Chosen, aren't you? Act like it!"

Zikhali didn't know what she was asking. It was impossible for him to create a shield powerful enough without the Orbs. Even if Lucian *could* shield their car, as soon as the dreadnought realized where they were going, it would blast *Tempus* out of existence.

But they were all out of options.

He had one Orb left. The Orb that Arian had said would be useless with no other to power it.

It was a long shot, but better than nothing.

Lucian reached for the Orb of Space-Time, throwing everything he had into it. His will to live. His will to save the others. Their need to escape this reality and return to their own. His desire to live a normal life with Serah in some distant future that seemed increasingly unlikely.

Just a short jump onto the ship. That was all they needed.

With luck, the dreadnought couldn't track them quickly enough given the sudden maneuver.

But try as he might, nothing happened. Lucian could see *Tempus's* hangar bay in the distance, opening up just large enough to accept their car. Bullets and plasma shards glanced off their skycar. The side door came off with a nasty shot from a plasma bolt. The air screamed by.

"Come on," Lucian urged.

At that moment, with the others shouting around him, Lucian's mind retreated to the Ether, to a much calmer time many months earlier, when he had been speaking to Master Lakhmu in the forests of Mako.

The Manifold responds to truth, whatever form that truth takes. When there are multiple truths, the strongest truth wins.

Whose truth was strongest? The truth that he couldn't use the Orb of Space-Time? Or the truth that if he didn't get them out of this situation, all of them would die and all hope would be lost?

It is the nature of reality. And the strongest truth is the one we choose.

Lucian would save them. He didn't *care* if it was impossible.

He was the Chosen of the Manifold, with or *without* the Orbs.

He felt a great welling of energy, and a burst of magic escaped him, a black void surrounding the car that was disintegrating around them.

And when the black void disappeared, the remains of the car came to rest on the deck of the distant *Tempus*.

Lucian blinked, not believing what he had just done. He had used Space-Time Magic on his own, without a single Orb to power it. Something that should have been impossible.

The others scrambled out of the wreckage, startled and amazed, though Themba seemed to have eyes only for Zikhali.

Zikhali, who was sitting still and slumped in her chair. Her wounds were not immediately obvious. Lucian hadn't seen her get hit, but so much had been going on that he must have missed it. His first instinct was to check his own crew, all of whom seemed to be safe.

As Themba unstrapped her tenderly, the others rushed to help.

"Khairu," Themba said, with forced calm. "Get us out of here. There is another world close by, called Ishkah. A gas giant. Find someplace to hide near it. I must see to Zikhali."

"Let me help you carry her," Jagar said.

Themba nodded gratefully.

"Come on," Khairu commanded. "To the bridge."

"This ship's already moving," Emma said. "The autopilot?"

"It's programmed to get us into space and avoid all hostiles," Themba explained. "Once we're in space, it can't help us."

"Come on, I said!" Khairu barked.

All of them ran after her as the hangar bay shut and the ship veered toward the sky.

23

LUCIAN, Serah, Emma, and Khairu sprinted toward the bridge, while Themba and Jagar carried Zikhali to the medical bay. As Lucian ran, the deck vibrated ominously under his feet. He struggled to keep from falling, the inertial forces wreaking havoc on the vessel; even the ship's Gravitonic brand couldn't counterbalance it.

The harsh klaxon of the automated defense system echoed through the ship's corridors, splitting Lucian's ears. Outside the viewscreens, he saw they had already ascended into space. Glowing streaks of deadly plasma raced toward them, burning against the backdrop of the cosmos.

"Brace for impact!" Khairu called out.

Lucian grabbed the wall, and *Tempus* rocked from the collision, the flash of the shield repelling the strike. Several plasma shards streaked perilously close to the hull, the shockwaves making *Tempus* shudder. Lucian doubted the shield could regenerate quickly enough to take many more hits.

Once on the bridge, Khairu leaped into the pilot's chair with a grace born from years of experience. The others took their seats, strapping in for a bumpy ride. Lucian just hoped that Jagar, Themba, and Zikhali would be safe in the medical bay.

Khairu's fingers flew across the controls as she took the stick, starting evasive maneuvers. The stars outside spun dizzily as she reoriented the ship. It didn't matter that it was of Ancient make; she had made it her mission to learn the controls all the same.

"Hang on!" she barked.

Another plasma shard streaked by the port thrusters, and the ship lurched violently to the side, veering back toward the moon city below. Khairu grappled with the controls, steadying the vessel before pushing it forward. The holographic readout revealed a pursuit by at least a dozen ships, including the Dreadnought.

"Next stop, Ishkah," she announced, inputting the coordinates into the navigation system. "Assuming we get out of here in one piece."

"Can you warp us again?" Emma asked Lucian.

"I'm not sure," Lucian admitted. "Just let me focus."

But focus was elusive. As they accelerated out of Regalia's gravity well, the Seraphim vessels gained. Their sleek, menacing forms grew closer on the holographic display. Lucian knew their pursuers had the best engines the Starsea Empire could afford, not to mention the strongest brands crafted by powerful sorcerers.

It was only a matter of time before they were overwhelmed.

Unless he could use the Orb again. Lucian had done it once, so what was stopping him now? What did Arian truly know about the Orb of Space-Time? Perhaps he was wrong.

He stood, and without a word, everyone knew to give him space. Khairu simply kept her attention on the stars ahead, where the navigation system informed them that Ishkah was three hours away.

Entering the Ether once again, sweat formed on Lucian's brow as he prepared to stream Space-Time Magic.

Sorcerer Lakhmu's words echoed in his mind: *Imagination is the beginning of creation. Will what you imagine. Imagine what you desire. And at last, create what you will.*

Drawing upon the raw power of the Ether, Lucian imagined the impossible and willed the ship to bridge the gap.

His hands stretched out, and a vortex of black energy formed around him. The entire ship shuddered, not from an external attack, but from the internal manipulation of time and space.

The magic expanded, enveloping the vessel. Lucian felt as if he were being ripped apart, but his will alone kept him alive. Pain pierced him as he fought to control the energy.

With a final push, he released the magic.

The ship lurched, launching like a cosmic slingshot. Despite the perilous change in velocity, Lucian felt nothing except a sense of stretching over a vast distance.

The Seraphim attackers were left far behind as the ship snapped into position, the navigation system blaring at the sudden change.

Lucian opened his eyes to the sight of a massive gas giant, oceanic blue, ringed like Saturn. He groaned, clutching his chest, before collapsing. Serah was at his side in an instant, calling his name.

"Lucian? Lucian!"

His eyes fluttered shut, and his body went limp, surrendering to unconsciousness.

When Lucian awoke, he saw the sterile tranquility of *Tempus's* medical bay. He couldn't move, such was his exhaustion. He would have slipped back into sleep if not for Zikhali's raspy voice breaking the quiet of the bay.

"You must let go," she managed. "Our life from before is gone, Themba. This moment is all we have left."

"Don't say such things," Themba replied. "With sorcery . . ."

"Don't give me that. You may love me, but your love isn't deep enough." Her words were punctuated by a pained hack, strangely human. "You chose another path. You must see it through."

Themba didn't contradict her. "Forgive me."

"There's nothing to forgive. You've found the Chosen. He's the only one who can stop the Shadow Emperor. Our love was the price you paid. And, as you well know, my hands aren't clean, either . . ."

Themba fell silent, possibly mourning a life that could have been.

"The Time Weaver," she rasped, her voice barely a whisper. "I can't tell you where he is. No one can. But . . . there's an archaeological site . . . my contact tells me it predates the last Void Cycle. Maybe you'll find something there."

"A rumor," Themba said.

"Perhaps. But what else do you have, Themba?"

Lucian turned his head and opened his eyes, struggling to see. Zikhali handed him something, what appeared to be a data stick, or something akin to it.

Themba accepted it solemnly, a silent vow that her sacrifice would not be in vain. "We'll look."

Time seemed to freeze as Zikhali drew her last breath. In the silence of the medical bay, Themba held her hand one last time, his pale gray fingers intertwining with hers.

Lucian could not hold consciousness any longer, and he slept dreamlessly until his eyes fluttered open again to the cold metallic ceiling of the medical bay.

A groan escaped his lips as he tried to sit up, but Serah gently pushed him back down, her concerned eyes meeting his.

"Just take it easy," she said. "We're in the rings of Ishkah now. Lying low. Everything's quiet so far."

"Zikhali . . ." Lucian began, but Serah's look told him all he needed to know. His heart sank, bitter reality settling in.

"Themba and the rest of us oversaw the space burial," she explained. "It was her wish."

Though Lucian didn't even know her, he couldn't help but feel solemn.

"She gave something to Themba before she passed," he said. "A data stick or something. She said it could lead to the Time Weaver."

"So, she *did* know something," Serah said. "It's hard to believe we'd be that lucky."

"Have we discussed what happens next?"

Serah shook her head. "The funeral was not thirty minutes ago. In Ancient culture, it must be performed immediately, out of respect."

"I see. I wonder when I can speak to Themba. He's been through a lot..."

"Give him some space for now," Serah advised. "Looks like we might be stuck for a while. We still need to lose those Seraphim ships."

Lucian realized their situation was desperate. They were fugitives, on the run, cut off from docking at any major port. And the Shadow Emperor, should he learn about them, might start the next Void Cycle, an apocalypse on a galactic scale.

But Zikhali had given them a chance, a lead to explore. It wasn't much, but they had to cling to anything they could.

Lucian rose. Using Space-Time Magic had been impossible until now; even warping the ship had nearly killed him. Even with the Orb of Space-Time, the act should have been impossible.

He realized he had to make sense of his powers. Clearly, there was more to it than he thought.

"Let me help you," Serah said. "Everyone's in the wardroom."

Lucian nodded and allowed Serah to guide him toward the center of the ship.

24

LUCIAN AND SERAH arrived in the wardroom, where they found Jagar, Khairu, and Emma seated at the table. All three looked his way, their expressions concerned.

"Everything okay?" Emma asked.

Lucian nodded. "Yeah. All good."

As he and Serah took their seats, the silence lay heavy. Lucian knew that each of them was grappling with the loss of Zikhali. None had a personal connection, and it was hard to make sense of her brief time among them. She had betrayed them to the Seraphim, but at the last minute, risked everything to correct her mistake. It was hard to know whether to despise or be grateful to her. The flickering stars outside the ship's viewports only added to the somber atmosphere.

"I know things have been rough," Lucian said. "But we might have a lead."

Even this news didn't lift the gloom. Emma's face remained glum, while Jagar sat, drinking deep of his hot *kra* tea, which apparently also existed in this reality.

"What kind of lead?" Emma asked. "Something that'll get us out of this ring system without being detected?"

"I'm not worried about that. Between all of us, we should be able to shield the ship well enough. We'll have to ask Themba about the lead. I saw Zikhali give him something before she passed. Something like a data drive."

Jagar remained withdrawn into silence, his expression grim. Lucian made a mental note to speak to him later. Jagar was unflappable, but Lucian wondered if he had overestimated the stoic man's mental fortitude. Khairu had her friendship with Emma while he and Serah had each other. Jagar was a lone wolf.

As for Serah, she was unusually quiet, too. They had been through so much in the past few hours that it was hard to make sense of it all.

As Lucian fought for something to say to lift the team's spirits, Themba's entrance was announced by the metallic swish of opening doors. His usually vibrant red eyes were resigned, his walk slow as if every step weighed heavily. Yet he held a determined set to his jaw, an unspoken resolve that drew the room's attention.

In his right hand, he clutched the small data drive Zikhali had entrusted to him. Every eye went to it, its importance adding to the moment's gravity.

Themba lowered his head, the heaviness of his brow ridge obscuring his eyes. "There is something we must discuss." His steady voice masked his inner turmoil. "Zikhali left us something. It might be nothing, or it might be everything."

All watched as he came to the table, inserting the drive into a slot on it. Nothing happened.

"Broken?" Khairu asked, her face revealing disappointment.

"No," Themba said. "This drive is from before the last Void Cycle. Over thirty thousand years old. The electronics they used don't calibrate with our own. Thankfully, our holographic projector's software and hardware are polymorphic. Even now, it is learning to readjust and reinterpret the information so we can understand."

Lucian didn't know what that meant, but before he could ask, the space above the table filled with a complex star map, a holographic projection that was startling in its detail. Lucian's eyes widened as hundreds of stars were mapped, along with their connections. The luminous points of light cast an eerie radiance on the room. All watched in wide-eyed wonder.

Yet it wasn't the beauty that held their attention but a dotted line, a path leading from their current position to a not-too-distant point in the cosmos.

"It appears authentic," Themba said at last. "You'll note the positions of the stars differ from our own time. This map shows them as they would have appeared thirty thousand years ago. This map's worth cannot be overstated. There are few enough artifacts from before the last Void Cycle, and their possession is illegal. Zikhali didn't tell me how she came by this, but as a collector, she no doubt went to great lengths to acquire it. To my knowledge, only a few of these maps have ever been found."

A series of runes was illuminated above one system. The script's appearance was like the Ancient language Lucian had learned, but strangely unintelligible.

"The computer is working to decipher the language," Themba explained.

After another minute, the runes rearranged themselves into the Ancient language they all understood.

"The Sigil System," Emma said. "It's hard to tell how the stars correspond to our own time, but unless I miss my guess, it seems to be two Gate jumps away. That would make it the Rune System in our own reality."

Lucian didn't know much about that system, but he knew it was home to a world of the same name. It was the last stop before Terminus, the most Spinward border of the League.

Themba nodded. "Indeed. As you said, Emma, it's a two-Gate

jump away. Encoded on the map are coordinates that lead to an archaeological site, one that predates the last Void Cycle."

The significance of his words hung heavily in the room. They potentially meant answers, assuming all evidence of the Time Weaver had been erased from this reality.

Emma asked a question that seemed obvious. "How do we know this site has anything to do with the Time Weaver?"

"Zikhali didn't get that far," Themba said. "It may, or it may not. We have nothing else to go on. Of course, the Shadow Emperor would want to destroy such a site if he discovered it. That's how he deals with any trace of his previous regimes. He fears if they are discovered, he will lose his grip on the population."

Lucian had a strong feeling there would be answers there. It was hard to tell if that was simply hope welling up within him, or a Psionic premonition.

One thing was clear. The mood had shifted; the gloomy energy was transforming into a new purpose.

"I don't see any reason we shouldn't pursue this," Khairu said. "After all, what else do we have?"

Her question went unanswered, a silent assent that this was the path forward.

And yet, for Lucian, there was no other option. "That's what we'll do, then. We'll head to the Sigil System."

As Lucian glanced once more at Jagar, he couldn't help but notice that his friend's grim demeanor had only deepened. Something was churning inside him, something Lucian was determined to understand.

For now, however, they had a path forward.

———

AFTER THE MEETING, Lucian headed toward the stern of the ship, entering the narrow passageway that led to the engine room. His steps echoed off the cold, metal confines. He could sense the unease among his crew, and Jagar's grim silence had been impossible to ignore.

He had to check in with him, something he hadn't made much of a point of since they'd made that fateful journey through the time gate.

As Lucian suspected, he found Jagar in his usual haunt on the lower deck. He sat alone, watching the stars through a small porthole, his form outlined by the cold blue light from the cosmos outside. Lucian still couldn't get over the younger appearance of Jagar's face.

"Jagar? We need to talk."

The older man turned, acknowledging Lucian with a nod. "I know what you're here for, lad."

"Just checking to see if everything's all right."

Jagar's gaze did not waver. Though his face was younger, his eyes still held all their former wisdom. They were distant now. Troubled.

"You're brave, Lucian," he said, his voice low. "But there are things even bravery can't conquer."

"What do you mean? We're playing the hand we've been dealt."

Jagar laughed bitterly. "No such thing as luck, Lucian. There's only the Manifold. As the Chosen, you should know that. We're in a spiral, pulled by forces beyond our reckoning. I've got a feeling those forces might tear us apart."

"I don't believe that." Lucian's words were firm. "We have to keep going. How else are we supposed to get home?"

"Your optimism is . . . refreshing. But we're going to need more than that."

"That's why we're looking for answers. Something tells me we'll find something out on Sigil. Something big."

Lucian had to fight to keep the frustration out of his voice. It wasn't fair to Jagar, who was fighting his own demons. This reality was so strange that the effects on the crew were bound to be unexpected.

Jagar took a deep breath, his eyes returning to the vast emptiness of space beyond the porthole. "I don't know. Don't you ever think we've tied ourselves in a knot? The Ancient One led us here for a reason. Here, he holds all the cards. He's a clever bastard." He gave a dry laugh. "Beyond clever. We still haven't figured out how this Shadow Magic works yet. Where it comes from. What it can and can't do."

Lucian was quiet for a moment. "That's been on my mind, too. I don't have the answers. But I have to believe the answers are out there."

Jagar was quiet. It felt like talking to a brick wall.

"We can't give up hope," Lucian said. "Whatever comes, we'll face it together. I'd say we've been through much worse, but that'd be a lie. We've got two realities depending on us."

Jagar turned to him, his face almost unreadable. But Lucian could see a glimmer of something profound, something foreboding.

All he knew was he didn't like it.

"I hope you're ready to stand by those words, Lucian," Jagar finally said. "Because what lies ahead of us on Sigil is like nothing we've ever faced before. I'm a Psionic, but I like to stick to the kinetic side of things. Prophecy is too messy. It can rip your mind apart if you mess with it too much. Seen a lot of good people's minds go to rot that way."

"Ansaldra?"

"She, and others. But in this reality, I haven't tried to stop the dreams. And what I dream . . ." He trailed off. "I'll face it, like I always do. I just wanted you to know, Lucian. Something bad is waiting for us. Will there be answers? Oh, I'm sure of that. Just might not be the answers you're looking for."

Jagar turned back to stare at the void of space, his grim words as good as a foretelling. Lucian didn't want to call it that, but it certainly had the feeling of prophecy.

He almost wanted to tell him he was there if Jagar ever needed anything, but the words died on his lips. He ended up just turning around. As he walked, all he could do was wonder whether they were strong enough to withstand the trials they had yet to face.

25

THE FOLLOWING days aboard *Tempus* were filled not just with activity, but with tension. Navigating the treacherous rings of Ishkah was nerve-racking enough without even considering the Seraphim hunting them.

At all times, at least two crew members warded Radiance and Thermalism. Lucian knew the shield wouldn't cover them if the Seraphim were too close, but it would do a lot to hide them from a distance.

Themba had them busy at various roles, so that there was hardly time to even think. And after Zikhali's death and Jagar's warning, thinking was the last thing Lucian wanted.

Themba and Khairu took turns at the helm; the autopilot could not be trusted to make every decision, especially when their pursuers could catch up at any moment. Lucian didn't enjoy being on the bridge, seeing *Tempus'* dizzying path through the icy labyrinth of Ishkah's ring system. Especially concerning Khairu, there was no one he trusted more with the job.

They stayed three days in the rings, opting to play it safe. Themba judged it was the best to get in the proper position for a straight shot to the Eldris Gate. At least, what *would* have been the Eldris Gate in Lucian's own timeline.

But when they ventured out, they would be exposed in the cold dark of space, detectable by any ship that was close enough. If they were truly unlucky, a Seraphim ship, perhaps with the aid of a seeking Radiant stream, could get a lock on them.

There was only one way to mitigate this risk, and it wouldn't be easy.

"We must combine our magic when we leave the rings," Themba said. "For as long as possible, we must hold a confluent shield of both Radiance and Thermalism. We must hold it until the Seraphim can no longer detect us."

"And how long will that be?" Khairu asked.

Themba considered. "As long as possible."

"Well," Khairu said, "we are thirty minutes from the exit point."

"All of you take a break," Lucian said. "Themba and I can take the last shielding shift before all of us have to pitch in. I'll lead the Radiant shield."

"Then I'll shield Thermalism," Themba said. "When I give the signal, Jagar and Serah will join streams with me. Emma and Khairu will join Lucian. That's three per Aspect. With luck, it'll be enough."

That wording made it clear there were no guarantees.

Lucian lost himself in the stream, feeling the ether burn through him. It felt strange that something so comparatively easy took so much effort. Without the Orbs, he was human again. A powerful mage, to be sure, who could delve into sorcery at need.

But limited as he was, the flow of ether was like a trickle instead of the torrent he was used to.

He had to make it work, though. There was no other choice.

The half hour passed quickly, and Themba gave a nod.

"Now."

Lucian felt Emma and Khairu's streams join his, the three

trickles becoming a mighty river. He was in charge of the stream, directing it to strengthen the Radiant shield surrounding the ship. Likewise, Themba, Serah, and Jagar created their own Thermal shield, which would erase *Tempus's* heat signature from the surrounding space.

Unless the Seraphim were within several kilometers of them, they were all but invisible.

"Exiting now," Khairu said.

Tempus streaked into the starry void, its engines kicking into overdrive and its Gravitonic brands struggling to battle the inertia.

"We've got this," Serah said, her gaze fixed on Lucian.

Lucian felt the strain, but he forced himself to smile. He didn't want her to know how weak he had become, how much even *this* task was making him struggle.

But he was far from the only one. Sweat had collected on Jagar's brow, while Emma's cheeks were pale. Khairu ground her jaw, while Themba's eyes were closed as if in deep meditation.

The ship shot through the expanse, its engines roaring defiance against the vacuum of space. They were days yet from the Eldris Gate, but all they had to do was escape the icy clutch of Ishkah and the Seraphim that haunted its rings. If they got enough distance, getting a lock on them would become practically impossible, given the vastness of space.

Lucian's pulse pounded madly from the effort of maintaining the shield. Both Emma and Khairu were flagging, especially the latter, whose primary Aspect was Dynamism. He gave her what he hoped was a reassuring nod.

The star-studded expanse stretched out before them, its tranquil silence contradicting the storm of ether streaming from Lucian's body. Minutes ticked by. At any moment, he expected an alert on the ship's security system, a warning klaxon to signal their doom. Stretched as he was, Space-Time Magic would not save them. Either this worked, or it didn't.

But the expected barrage from the Seraphim was conspicuously absent. No surge of hostile magic rippled through space, no torpedoes, nor did enemy vessels light the navigation screen.

Their carefully woven cloak of magic was holding far longer than Lucian had expected.

How long they stayed like that, Lucian couldn't say. It must have been an hour or more before he gave a frenzied nod. "Enough."

He let out a weary sigh, as did the others. They leaned on chairs, on walls and consoles. Only Themba was in full possession of his body.

Tempus was still accelerating at a steady clip, far beyond the range of any Seraphim ships. If their pursuers knew their location, they would have opened fire by now.

"Four more days until the Gate," Lucian said, looking at the navigation panel. "We did as well as we could have hoped."

"Even better," Serah said.

"Now, we wait," Khairu said ominously.

Jagar remained silent, as grim as ever.

"Our journey has barely begun," Themba said.

The Ancient held the data drive in his hand. While the data it held was no longer needed, as it was safely stored on the ship's computer, it was his only memento of Zikhali.

For now, they had evaded the relentless pursuit of the Shadow Emperor's Seraphim. But Lucian was certain that, at some point, their search would expand beyond the rings of Ishkah, and even beyond this system.

What counted was getting to Sigil before they did.

———

THE SILENCE of the ship's bridge was occasionally broken by the hum of machinery and the distant thrumming of engines. Themba was on duty, and Lucian stood next to him, his eyes lost in the mesmerizing spectacle of stars as the ship raced toward the Sigil System. Themba's eyes were half-closed, as if asleep, but Lucian had learned by this point the Ancient was merely meditating. It seemed to be his default state.

There had been something Lucian had been meaning to discuss with him ever since he had used Space-Time Magic. As a powerful sorcerer, a former Seraph of the Shadow Emperor, Lucian couldn't think of anyone better to ask. The Ancient had more than proven himself in the past few weeks.

"Themba, there's something I've been meaning to talk to you about."

The Ancient's eyes opened, his red-eyed gaze settling on Lucian. "And what's that, Lucian?"

"How was I able to use Space-Time Magic without the aid of other Orbs? Arian said it was impossible, but obviously, it's not. One thing the Prophecy of the Seven said was that the Orb of Space-Time could not be used unless there was at least one other Orb to power it."

"And this prophecy was passed down to Arian by the Seven Oracles of Starsea, from your own reality," Themba said. "I remember." He paused for a moment, seeming to brood over it. "Now, I wonder. Just who were these Oracles, to be so wise in the ways of magic? Did they know everything there was to know? Just because something is spoken in prophecy, does it mean it's true?"

It was a question that had never occurred to Lucian. He had taken everything Arian had said at face value, thinking there was no way that the information could be false.

But if one part of the prophecy was wrong—what about others? Was he even the Chosen of the Manifold?

It wasn't a question Lucian wanted to grapple with. "That's . . . a lot to think about."

"Sorcery," Themba began, "is an extension of oneself and one's will. At its heart, it's the manifestation of your deepest truths, including your fears and desires, and whatever strength you have to face them. It's not about the Orbs, Lucian. It never was. The Orbs are almost like a bypass. A key, if you will, that gives instant access without having to face yourself entirely. This may be difficult for you to believe, but the Orbs are actually a hindrance and a crutch. With them, you never have to stand on your true power. The Orbs, of course, will not consent to be used by one of weak will. But similarly, they are holding you back from your true potential. That is how you used Space-Time Magic. Your desire to save your friends, and to save your timeline, allowed the impossible to become possible. It is the beginning of something new. A blooming of a new truth, perhaps?"

Lucian sighed. "Not the answer I wanted."

Themba let out a small chortle, characteristic of an Ancient laugh. "It is the nature of most sentient beings to believe what they prefer to be true. The important thing is not to run from truth, but to confront it. Your power is only limited by the conflicts within yourself."

"And what if I don't want to confront the truth?" Lucian asked. "I'd rather have the Orbs. It's simpler that way."

Themba paused, weighing his words. "It's your choice, Lucian. But remember, the shadows of the past can only hurt you as long as you let them hide in the dark. Facing them may be painful, but it also allows you to move forward. Mages have the luxury of ignoring their truth. But for the sorcerer, the truth is the entire thing. That will never change. Being a sorcerer is a choice. Every mage is capable of it, but few choose to follow the path."

"That's not what I was taught. I was taught only a few could ever hope to be sorcerers."

Again, Themba chortled. "Then you were taught incorrectly. Most do not choose that way, because it asks too much. More than you will ever believe. But such is the price for the Manifold's power. The Manifold is the ultimate truth, and it only *responds* to truth."

"You remind me of someone I knew," Lucian said, thinking of Lakhmu.

There was a silence as he considered Themba's words. Lucian knew he had a penchant for avoiding conflict when things had the potential to get messy. But deep down, he knew Themba was right. Themba's words resonated more than he cared to admit.

"You're probably speaking from experience," Lucian said.

Themba stared into the void of space. "Leaving Zikhali behind all those years ago was the hardest decision of my life. It meant abandoning the only happiness I ever knew. Many—perhaps *most*—might have let the universe burn as long as they got to live their happy life. But I took the harder path, because when I looked deep down, that was the truth. The smallest splinter in my soul that could not be ignored. If I had lived my life, my happiness, the splinter would have barely been noticeable. And yet, it was there." Themba's red eyes bored into Lucian's. "You must find your splinters, Lucian, as difficult as it may be. We have a few weeks until Sigil. Opportunity enough to meditate on things."

"I'm . . . not sure I could have done what you did," Lucian said. "I don't think I could leave Serah behind. If not for her, I'm not sure this would be worth it. What would happen if I was forced to choose her, or the mission?"

"Did you not already make that choice?"

Lucian had nothing to say to that. He hadn't specifically mentioned choosing to save Emma over defeating the Ancient One, but somehow, Themba had perceived it.

"What are you saying? That I need to sacrifice my friends?"

"Not that. That was my truth; yours will be different. In fact, I hope it will be. Ultimately, the truth is what we choose when the spear is at our throats. Harder still is to pursue the truth when there is nothing forcing you. We stay on our preset paths, striving for comfort. It is how every creature in this universe is wired. To take the harder road is lonely, and that road is only something you can discover."

"Your road was leaving Zikhali."

Themba turned back to space. Ancients didn't have much in the way of facial expressions, but Lucian sensed a deep sadness on Themba's part. It was as if there were a hole in his life, missing decades of memories because he had chosen a different path.

"It is hard to speak of. I knew that finding the Chosen was more important. Even though every fiber of my being yearned to stay with her, to comfort her, to love her, and to receive that from her in kind, I knew I had to leave. And that path I've doubted every single day. Years of loneliness and foolishness. And yet, in the end . . ."

He trailed off, and Lucian noted the deep-set pain in Themba's eyes. Themba had sacrificed his own happiness for the greater good. He was grappling with his own demons, just as Lucian was.

And, perhaps, it meant Lucian might one day have to do the same if the truth called for it.

"But how did you do it?" Lucian asked. "Where did you find the will? How is it possible to let go of someone you love?"

"I never did," Themba answered quietly. "I will carry her with me, always. Just as I carried her every day, from the moment we first spoke to this very moment, mere days after her passing. I cherish our memories, as few and precious as they are, and I know our paths crossed for a reason. Love, Lucian, is not bound by distance or time. It's the most powerful force there is, and yes, love is a part of magic. If mine had been strong enough, perhaps I might have saved Zikhali."

Lucian couldn't help but think of Serah, of how he had saved her from certain death to the fraying. That he had done it at all only proved his love for her. He knew deep down it hadn't been the Orbs.

"If you're honest with yourself," Themba finished, "there's no conflict that can stand in the way of your magic."

Lucian was silent, lost in his thoughts. He had a lot to think about, a lot to confront. He could no longer run. He had to face his conflicts, for the sake of his friends, for Serah, and for himself.

"Thank you," Lucian finally said, meeting Themba's gaze. "You've given me a lot to think about."

Themba nodded. "Take your time, Lucian. Sorcery is not something to be rushed. It's a journey of self-discovery, of learning, and of growth. I have faith in you."

26

AFTER HIS CONVERSATION WITH THEMBA, Lucian found himself in the observatory, taking some time to think things through. As he experimented with the telescope, focusing it in on distant objects, his thoughts kept on returning to his conversation with Serah about Emma.

He kept telling himself it was nothing, that she would get over it in time. That any addressing of the issue was just bound to make things worse.

But this issue could be one of his splinters. Something small and seemingly inconsequential was getting in the way.

"Everything all right, lad?"

Lucian jumped and turned to see Jagar watching him.

"Yeah, everything's fine. Sorry, didn't hear you."

"I can be quiet, but you were pretty focused. Find anything interesting?"

Lucian shook his head, stepping away from the telescope. "Not really. Just . . . trying to think, I guess."

"Good place to think. There's something calming about stargazing. Makes it easy to forget your troubles."

"Something like that."

He almost left Jagar there, but remembering Themba's words, he stopped himself.

"Jagar, I need your advice on something."

Jagar's sandy eyebrows arched. "Oh? What's that?"

Lucian gave him a summary of his conversation with Themba and what he had learned.

Once finished, Jagar watched him curiously. "So, you're wanting to unlock your magic more by removing these splinters, as Themba called them?"

Lucian nodded. "To be honest, there's something that's become something of a sticking point."

"Girl trouble?"

Lucian looked at him strangely. "I guess you could say that."

"Well, if I can help, I'll try."

"It's Serah. And Emma too, I guess."

Jagar's expression darkened. "Don't tell me you've gotten mixed up with both of them. I'll box your ears, boy."

"No, nothing like that. I feel like I've given Serah the wrong idea. She's worried I have feelings for Emma because of what happened."

"You mean when you saved her?"

Lucian nodded. "Yeah. It's this specter that looms up every now and again. I want to reassure her. I just don't know how to make her see it."

Jagar took a moment to digest Lucian's words. "I can understand Serah's perspective. In her position, I'd probably wonder, too."

"Serah's my person, Jagar. I have no doubts about that."

"It's natural for other emotions to get mixed in now and again. Life is complicated and messy."

Lucian was quiet for a moment. "I guess you can say that. If you held a gun to my head, then yeah. Sometimes, old feelings get mixed in I'd rather not have. I just don't know how to make *sense* of them. Emma was my past and was there for me during a tough transition in my life. She was my first friend, I guess you could say, once I found out I was a mage. Serah was there for me on Psyche, and every day after that. She's watched me grow, has been there to catch me when I fell. We've been together almost every step of the way."

"Well, lad, that's some heavy stuff. I'll say this much. The heart isn't logical. It feels what it feels. Anyone with a heart will tell you that."

"What do I do, then? How can I prove to Serah that she's the one for me? Nothing I'm saying is working."

"Well, I don't envy your position. One thing I can tell you right off the bat is that it's important to accept your feelings as they are, without trying to force them into something else. That sounds like what you've been doing these last few years."

Lucian frowned, unsure. "So . . . *acknowledge* my feelings? That would hurt her, and that's the *last* thing I want."

"Lad, I thought I could avoid hurting Ansaldra. I thought I could protect her from everything, including myself. That didn't go as planned. I might even be to blame for how she turned out. Not excusing what she did, mind you. But relationships are complicated. You can't control how others will react to your feelings, but you can control how you communicate. Serah has her own emotions to grapple with, but love is powerful enough to overcome all that."

Lucian sighed. "We have a mission right now, and it feels like this is messing everything up. I can't be distracted. I don't want Serah to be unhappy."

Jagar looked at him kindly. "Look, you can't deny what you feel. It wouldn't be fair to you or Serah. If you try to bottle things up, they'll explode later. Don't be like me, lad. When something bad happened with Ansaldra, I'd go the other way, and that's putting it lightly. By the time I realized what had gone wrong, it was too late."

"What about the mission? We have a reality to save. If any of us are distracted . . ."

Jagar nodded solemnly. "But we're already past that, aren't we? True, our mission is larger than any of us, but addressing your feelings will only make you more focused. Don't you want that albatross off your back? Don't you want to unlock the full potential of your magic? Maybe this is exactly what you need right now."

Lucian stared at his hands. At this moment, Jagar was like the father he had never known. He felt a sense of sadness that he could've had this advice this entire time, if only he'd thought to ask.

"Don't rush yourself," Jagar went on. "Life's not a sprint, it's a long and rotting exhausting marathon." Finally, he clapped a hand on Lucian's shoulder. "Just put yourself in Serah's shoes. She's probably just as confused as you are right now. Aye, scared, too. She's in this storm, too, wishing it would all just go away. You need to be her rock. If you stand by her and don't waver, she'll have no reason to doubt you. And you mention those old feelings . . . you need to work them out for yourself. Sounds like some things were dredged up when you made that decision to save Emma, whether or not you liked it. Just remember: what you feel is not always reality."

"You said I need to accept my emotions," Lucian said. "How can I love Serah if I'm confused like this?"

"You love her by choosing her every day, lad, and letting her see that. That's what you've been doing, and that's all you can do. Here's my advice. You've got to let the feelings come to the surface and settle. And once things have calmed down, have another conversation with Serah, telling her everything I told you. That you're going to stick by her no matter what."

"And what if she won't accept that?"

"There are two people in this, and she needs to go on her own journey. You can't control her reactions, and she needs to learn how to trust. It sounds like she's been betrayed a time or two. Even if you've stood by her every time, well, scars like that just don't go away."

Lucian realized he was right. "She was exiled by her own father."

Jagar nodded. "That would do it. She wants safety. She wants to know you'll be there for her, no matter what. If she sees any threat to that, however small, it's going to set her alarms off."

"How do I stop it, then?"

"You don't. All you can do is love her and be her safe place. Every person has their scars. To accept someone fully, accept that as well."

Lucian nodded. "All right. I'll do that."

"I believe in you. You've got a good head on your shoulders, and you've grown a lot. Serah looks up to you, but she knows you're human. Share your feelings, and respect hers, lad. That's all I've got to say about it. The rest is up to you. Good luck."

Jagar's words hung in the air, heavy with wisdom and experience. He didn't offer solutions, but rather gave Lucian a new lens to view his predicament through.

It was a start, and Lucian felt a small glimmer of hope that maybe there was a way through it.

TEMPUS WAS BUT A LONE SPECK, silently gliding across the vast celestial sea of stars and darkness. They avoided the main travel lanes, so they would not always have to maintain their Radiant and Thermal wards. It allowed them a bit of a reprieve, a chance to focus on themselves and their training.

As the days blurred into one another, a quiet tension filled the vessel, and every day that passed, that tension seemed to grow.

Inside the ship, things were the same as ever. They had settled into the routine customary of deep space travel—maintaining the vessel, training, meditating. It was a rhythm Lucian was familiar with.

He found himself increasingly drawn to the ship's training chamber. It was a place where he could explore his budding Space-Time Magic. This Aspect of Magic returned to him like a familiar friend. The strength was not great, but that it was returning at all was a good sign he was on the right track.

During these sessions, Themba served as his sparring partner, instructing and guiding him to push the boundaries of his magic. Lucian discovered he could phase again when dual streaming Space-Time and Radiance. Under Themba's careful tutelage, Lucian experimented with reverse Space-Time streams, bending the flow of time around him so he could move faster in relation to everything else, at least for a few seconds.

The sessions were intense, mentally and physically. One moment he would stand still, and the next he would phase across the room, dancing between points as if he were in multiple places at once.

But there was a limit to his progress. He was not as powerful as he would have been with the Orbs. Even if Themba said he had the potential to be even *more* powerful, it seemed a distant dream at this point.

After one particularly grueling session, Themba nodded in approval. "You're beginning to flow with the stream, not against it."

And Lucian found this to be true. He no longer felt the need to exert force or willpower to make the magic work. Instead, he relaxed into it, allowing it to move within him and act according to his desires. Sorcery was more about imagination than raw power. Ether molded to Lucian's thoughts, rather than Lucian having to force it to manifest his visions.

Beyond these sessions, Themba encouraged Lucian to meditate, using the quiet hours to unlock new truths. During these moments, Lucian sat cross-legged on the observation deck at the ship's stern, the expanse of space stretching out before him. In these quiet moments, he did not simply look outward into space, but inward into himself. He came to realizations he'd never had the time or mental space to grasp before.

So often, he'd held himself back, retreating into himself out of fear. It was something he constantly struggled with. But with openness, he was capable of change and growth.

Lucian meditated on his bond with every crew member, not just Serah. Serah had been his constant support, his love, his reason for going on. His past feelings for Emma shouldn't be suppressed, but rather acknowledged and understood. They were a part of who he was and did not diminish his love for Serah in the slightest. He was comfortable having her in the role of friend. Jagar had taken on a fatherly role, and it was okay to recognize that for what it was. Themba, too, had his own knowledge to share, while Lucian was fully ready to leave his sometimes-strained relationship with Khairu in the past where it belonged. He admired her resolve and fierce loyalty, for remembering the mission and reminding him of his role in it.

These relationships, as complicated as they were, were not his weakness. They were his strength.

More than that, his magic was not just a weapon, which was how he most often used it. His magic was intrinsically linked to his essence, to the very core of his soul. Power and his role as the Chosen did not define him; instead, he defined his power. His sorcery responded to his truths, his very perception of himself. And his strength came from recognizing who he was and accepting it, not judging or conforming to a perceived role.

He recognized the resurgence of his Space-Time Magic was a response to that. It did not respond to the how's of possibility and impossibility. It responded to the "why."

Each truth faced, each emotion acknowledged, was like a key, unlocking further potential.

The two weeks passed in a continuum of training, meditation, self-discovery. Each day brought them closer to the Sigil System, closer to their destiny.

And each day, Lucian felt more prepared, his powers more honed, his spirit more resolute. Things began making more sense, edified by both Themba's and Jagar's words.

It was time to stop running and revisit that conversation with Serah.

27

THE DAY before they were due to arrive at Sigil, he met with
Serah in the ship's observatory. When he arrived, he found her
staring out of the viewports. When she turned to face him, he
was struck by her beauty framed by the starlight.

"Hey," he said.

"Hey yourself. How's the training going?"

He joined her at the viewport. "Grueling as ever." There was a
silence for a moment before Lucian cleared his throat. "I . . .
wanted to talk about our previous conversation. To put certain
things to rest."

She remained silent, as if steeling herself for him to continue.

"I've been dealing with a lot lately. Facing my emotions and
trying to make sense of them."

"Me, too," Serah admitted.

There was another silence. Lucian had already brought it up,
so there was nothing to do but to finish it.

"I've come to realize that any feelings I have, any confusion,
are just that. They have nothing to do with my love for you.

Nothing to do with us. I don't regret anything with you. It's . . . like a spark against a supernova."

"Except there's still a spark," she said.

"Life is messy. Not everything makes sense all the time, and that's okay. Emma is a part of my past. That's okay, too. My past doesn't define who I am now. It doesn't define us."

She looked away from him, toward the starry expanse outside. "I'm . . . glad you're being honest. But I'm afraid."

He took her hand. "I'm here for you. Always."

She looked at him. "So, you're admitting you have feelings for her, however small?"

"I love *you*, Serah. I choose you every day, because you are my person."

"Rotting hell, can't you just lie to me?"

"No. I can't."

"I know that. And I know I'm being difficult. I'm confused too, you know."

She was silent for a while, still unsure.

"You've said you've been doing some thinking, too," Lucian said.

"I have." She paused for a moment. "I've . . . been thinking about my own faults. I know all this comes from my insecurity. My past. I've been hurt before. I know that's not your fault. That's my past. I'm always looking for threats. It's all out of fear that I'm going to be abandoned again."

He drew her close. "I would never do that to you."

"I know that in my head. The heart is another matter."

He held her like that for a while, and her stance seemed to thaw somewhat.

"We just need to accept each other's pasts, don't we?"

"I accept you, even the parts that drive me crazy."

She had a laugh at that. "I know. There are probably more crazy parts than sane parts. But one thing's for sure. I love you.

Thank you for being so patient. I know she's your friend. She's mine, too. I'm just glad it's all out in the open."

"I'm glad, too."

He held her for a long time, until at last she pulled away with a smile, the light coming back to her eyes.

"I feel better now," she said. "Now, let's try not to get ourselves killed on Sigil."

———

Tempus HOVERED above the atmosphere of Sigil, having already slowed from its long journey from Regalia. After nearly three weeks, they were here. They were about to find out whether Zikhali's data would actually lead to anything.

On the bridge, Lucian watched out the forward viewscreen, which displayed a world that would have been drearily gray, if not for the expanse of iridescent auroras washing over its surface, giving it the appearance of a lustrous pearl.

"Reminds me of home," Emma said.

Themba stood at the helm, the planet's glow reflecting in his red, determined eyes. Lucian watched the others take in the view with a mixture of awe and trepidation. Jagar's face was especially grim, and Lucian couldn't help but remember what the old warrior had said. Something bad down there was waiting for them.

"Look alive," Khairu muttered, her brown eyes staring down at the planet. "It may be empty, but it's dangerous."

"Initiating descent," Themba said.

Immediately, *Tempus* glided through the colorful atmosphere. As they broke through the cloud layers, the ship shook like a leaf in the wind. After another minute passed, a sprawling, broken cityscape came into view, like a ghostly apparition from another age.

The architecture was . . . *dreamlike*, for lack of a better word.

Lucian watched, awestruck, at the immense skyscrapers stretching toward the sky, some of their surfaces glinting with residual ethereal energy. If this site was truly from before the last Void Cycle, then that magic must have been seven-sealed to last this long. Curved buildings wound around each other in a complex dance of organic design, while shattered monuments lay scattered, the silent testament of a once great civilization.

"This is so much more than I expected," Emma breathed. "What is this place?"

The crew was silent, no one having an answer for her.

Everyone seemed to be shocked at the staggering scale of the city. It was remarkably intact, especially if it was greater than thirty thousand years old, as Zikhali's data showed. Even a city like this should have long collapsed from the ravages of time, unless the climate here was mild or tectonic forces practically nonexistent.

Guided by the coordinates from Zikhali's map, Themba steered *Tempus* toward the city's heart. A colossal tower emerged from the urban labyrinth, built against the side of a massive mountain. The construction's pinnacle disappeared into the swirling clouds above, making it impossible to estimate its actual height. Its outer surface glowed with blue iridescence, a sign that Binding Magic had been used long ago to keep its integrity.

Lucian's heart raced as he took in the sight. "That's where we're going, isn't it?"

Themba nodded, his heavy brows lowering. "Indeed. I don't know what we'll find inside, if anything at all. But if a city like this doesn't have answers, nothing does."

Themba guided the ship down, settling it on a crystalline highway that led directly into the entrance of the tower, a wide-open archway. With a final hum, the engines of *Tempus* fell silent, and the quiet stillness of the ancient city pressed in.

Lucian felt a sense of solemnity that seemed to go beyond the foreboding scene. It was like the feeling he had on worlds attacked by the *Alkasen*. It was like a hollow lacking, a silent scream. From the drawn faces of his companions, it seemed he wasn't the only one sensing it. Jagar and Khairu, for their parts, already had hands on the batons of their shockspears.

Themba unfastened his harness, rising from the pilot's seat to stare at the dismal scene. For the first time, in the building's shadow, Lucian saw that something was off. And from the crew's collective intake of breath, it seemed this realization dawned on everyone at the same time.

Hundreds of bodies lay sprawled beneath the shadow of the colossal tower before them, almost impossible to pick out in the gathering gloom. Bodies that were remarkably well-preserved. This massacre had not happened all that long ago.

Lucian swallowed hard at the grisly scene and almost wanted to order them to leave. But they had come too far, and they had nothing else to fall back on.

He was the first to regain his composure. "I know it won't be easy, but we've come this far. We can't leave until we have an answer, even if that answer is to keep looking."

The others nodded grimly around him, unable to tear their eyes away from the horrible sight.

"What happened?" Serah asked, her face pale.

"We may discover that soon enough," Themba said soberly. "We had better get started."

Jagar's usually impassive features were dark. "I agree with Themba. The sooner we're done with this, the better."

His voice seemed to hold hidden meaning. Lucian couldn't help but recall their dark conversation.

Emma was silent, her brown eyes wide and distant as she processed the chilling sight. Even Khairu, who was always so stoic, seemed shaken.

She met Lucian's gaze, her soft voice barely heard over the quiet hum of the ship's systems. "Are you ready, Lucian?"

His answer was a resolute nod.

Emma looked at the data readout on the control panel. "Atmospheric readings show it's breathable. Cold, but we've dealt with far worse."

Themba was already heading for the exit. The others followed behind.

As they stepped off *Tempus*, the surrounding air was eerily still, frigid, and dry, without even the barest trace of wind. The city's beauty was no longer that. To Lucian, it was like an enormous specter of its former glory, a shadow of what had once been. The architecture was stunning, yes, with each building a testament to a once-great civilization. If there was a beauty, it was solemn, and to Lucian, it was as if the city were frozen in a single, tragic moment of time. He couldn't imagine anything happy ever having happened here, especially considering the grisly scene not a hundred meters away at the base of the tower.

A dread built up in Lucian like a rising tide. It was an instinct he knew not to ignore, birthed from his mastery of Psionic Magic. Jagar had to be feeling the same thing. They could either run from it or face it.

Serah placed her hand on his arm. "You okay?"

He forced himself to nod. "Yeah. Let's get moving."

All of them, save Themba, had their shockspears out. Lucian did not summon Lightspear, but he feared he would need it before too long.

"Follow me," Themba said.

Quickening their pace, they followed the Ancient sorcerer as he made his way toward the massive edifice. As they came closer to the bodies, Lucian noticed they were all Ancients, most of them wearing robes denoting their rank as a mage. Some of their robes were even more resplendent, the kind that might be worn by a sorcerer. There were also others dressed in civilian clothing, though that was about a third of the total number.

"Binding Magic is all that's holding this building together,"

Jagar said. "If it's really as old as we think it is, that's some mighty powerful magic."

"That remains to be seen," Themba said. "It denotes that the previous civilization was at least as advanced in magic as ours, if not more so." Themba looked around at the bodies. "These people were no doubt part of an archeological expedition. And the sorcerers and mages tell me that the Ancient One was behind it."

"I thought you said he would want to destroy a city like this," Serah said.

"That is the typical action he takes for this kind of thing," Themba admitted. "However, there may be something here even he wanted to learn about."

"The Time Weaver?" Lucian asked.

"That answer fits, though there could be many reasons. For this city to have survived the Void Cycle, it would have had to be buried. That explains its preservation."

"Buried?" Emma asked, startled. "This city is truly *massive!* How could it have possibly been excavated to this extent?"

"It would have taken decades. Maybe even centuries, even considering the use of magic."

"That's what the mages were here for," Emma realized. "They can't have been dead long. The bodies are hardly decomposed."

"I wonder how they died?" Serah asked.

"We might discover that soon enough," Themba said.

None of them wanted to pass through the high, arched doorway leading into the tower, but they did. Inside, it was lit by a network of glowing light spheres, likely streamed by the sorcerers now dead. Spheres like these could last for years, or even longer, depending on the skill of the creator.

Themba stopped to examine one wall, his fingers tracing the intricate patterns of runes and artwork, his brow ridge crinkling in thought. "Yes, this city is definitely older than the last Void Cycle. This is the same script we saw on the star map."

"Can you read it?" Emma asked.

"With a computer, yes, but we'd have to go back to the ship. But trying to read all this isn't the priority for now. First, we must locate the source of the danger."

"How was this city buried?" Serah asked.

"There is only one answer for that. The city was buried intentionally right before the Void Cycle. Perhaps even in response to it."

"Why would that have been done?" Emma asked.

"My guess is someone, somewhere, wanted to preserve it. Combined with the planet's low tectonic activity and mild weather, there was nothing to disturb it in the intervening time."

"Who wanted to bury it?" Emma asked. "And why?"

"I'm already forming a suspicion."

"The Time Weaver?"

"Again, the answer fits," Themba said.

"Whatever the case," Lucian said, "it means there's something important here, right?"

"Yes," Themba said. "Alternately, the Ancient One himself might have been responsible for the burial, wanting to save the city before unearthing it at a later date. Let's press on."

They continued along the outer edge of the tower, finding more dead Ancients along the way. It seemed they formed a sort of trail, leading down into the building rather than up. The structure seemed to delve deep into the ground. From the central, circular shaft, the bottom could not be discerned. There was only darkness. Lucian had the feeling it was a long way down.

"We should follow these bodies," Themba said. "We'll get to the center of it soon enough."

They descended the wide set of stairs that spiraled around the outer edge of the tower, at each new level finding new rooms, artwork, arcades, and many things the purpose of which Lucian couldn't guess. They were among history, the history of an alternate reality as complex as their own. It was a humbling and haunting experience, almost enough to inspire vertigo in Lucian at his own insignificance in the face of it all.

Themba was examining more artwork in the hallway, seeming to search for something, when his contemplation was broken by a low hum from above.

A surge of adrenaline cut through Lucian. That sound could only mean one thing: a spaceship.

"The Seraphim are here," Themba said. "Run!"

They raced down the stairs, following the trail of dead bodies deeper into the depths of the tower.

28

AS THE TEAM sprinted down the ancient staircase spiraling into the depths of the tower, Lucian summoned Lightspear in his right hand, glancing back for any sign of pursuit. For now, they were in the clear.

"Shield your primaries," Lucian ordered. "Themba and I will cover the rest."

They hadn't been running for thirty seconds when the air above them crackled with energy. A fork of lightning streaked its way down the staircase. Khairu's Dynamism shield was instantly extinguished as it ate the impact.

That was when green lasers sliced the stairway ahead, quickly followed by fireballs exploding above their heads, absorbed by Themba's shield. However, the fires had spread enough to block their passage. Lucian reached out with Thermalism, cooling the flames enough for the team to pass through unscathed.

That was when gravity suddenly seemed to double, a powerful stream that was breaking past Serah's shield. Their legs became heavy, slowing their descent. It was like trying to run underwater, each stride taking immense effort.

Casting a glance over his shoulder, Lucian caught sight of their pursuers. Four Seraphim wearing flowing black robes were floating down the stairs like ghosts, using Gravitonic Magic to skirt the surface of the steps. Their faces were hidden behind ornate masks, while their shockspears were alight with magic—lighting, fire, and even a ball of light.

But he noticed one of the Seraphim standing taller than the rest, whose robes were pure white, with a mask that was more intricate, adorned with dark-glowing gemstones.

"The Grand Seraph," Themba said.

Though his tone was neutral, Lucian noted the fear in his voice through the inflection of his words.

"Come on!" Serah shouted. "Get your heads in the game!"

Her body became surrounded by silvery brilliance, which blasted from her body like a supernova. Just like that, the Seraphim's gravity stream was countered, making them stumble down the steps at their sudden change of weight.

As the attacks continued, Lucian quickly saw that this fight was a lost cause. They had to make it to the bottom of the tower, where the trail of dead bodies was surely leading. But there were still dozens of spirals to make, and trying to fight the entire way down was hopeless.

"Come on, over the side!" he said. "It's our only chance."

To show he meant it, he launched himself over without waiting for the others. Seconds later, he heard the others' screams as they followed his example.

He reached for the Gravitonic and Binding Aspects, knowing that sorcery was the only thing that would save them. First, he streamed Radiance, using its magic to peer into the darkness below. He spied the bottom, about fifty floors down. They rushed down to meet it, time seeming to slow. Lasers and fireballs streamed down the central shaft of the tower, but thankfully, the others were shielding the attacks.

That meant Lucian was the only one who could stop them from making a grisly mess at the bottom.

He entered the Ether and imagined the result he wanted. He wanted everyone to slow about ten meters from impact and land gently on the floor below.

In response to his need, ether swirled around him, setting up the Gravitonic aura that would save their lives.

At the appointed time, he released the stream. A torrent of magic ripped through him, Binding and Gravitonics working as one to lift the entire party up. They alighted on the dusty stone floor below, the shouts of the Seraphim above a distant echo. If they wanted to pull a similar stunt, they would need to organize it first. They had a minute, maybe two, to figure things out.

Immediately, everyone's attention was drawn by a strange, shimmering barrier which seemed to block the only escape, an open archway. It was a wall of magic, its surface dark, almost completely opaque. It was like nothing Lucian had ever seen before, but standing near it, he felt . . . *empty*. It reminded him of the Ancient One when he had faced him on board *Holy Fire*.

There was no question: this was Shadow Magic. None other than the Ancient One himself, or one of his avatars, could be the source.

"No one stream at that shield," Lucian ordered. "It'll be the last mistake you make."

"There's no way out, though," Serah said.

He thought it through. He might marshal enough of his magic to create a Space-Time portal. But their spaceship was almost certainly guarded by the Seraphim, if not destroyed.

"This barrier was created by the Ancient One himself," Themba said. "Shadow Magic, countless years old. It may even predate the last Void Cycle. Conventional magic won't break it."

At that moment, two Seraphim floated down from above, their black capes billowing behind them. Fireballs, bolts of lightning, and shards of ice accompanied their advance as the others threw up their shields in defense.

Lucian, however, took Lightspear and connected with the Space-Time Aspect. He targeted the closest Seraph, phasing forward and planting his spear deep in his torso. The Seraph gave a garbled cry as his magical defenses were shattered, his body quickly disintegrating into ash.

The other Seraph targeted Lucian with a column of fire and electricity, a Thermal and Dynamistic dualstream. Lucian reversed his Space-Time stream, slowing time itself as he made himself a blur against the pyroelectric surge. He danced aside, shooting forward with Lightspear extended. The Seraph tried to dodge it but was far too slow to avoid the thrust of the weapon.

Time resumed its normal course, and Lucian panted, breathless. More Seraphim were circling down the stairs above, perhaps half a minute away. There were dozens of them.

The Shadow shield was still there, a persistent reminder of their impending doom. Lucian knew they wouldn't stand a chance against the Seraphim's increasing numbers.

They had to get that shield down and hope there was some tool beyond that could aid them in their fight.

He looked at the shield, then at Lightspear. He had nothing left.

With a roar, he shot forward with a tether, right for the barrier, plunging Lightspear into it.

The dark barrier immediately reacted as if it were a thing alive, swirling around the blinding spear and seeming to consume it. The Shadow Magic crawled up the spear shaft toward Lucian's hand.

"Lucian!" Serah called out.

He recoiled, trying to let the spear dissipate, but to no avail. The spear was completely wrapped in darkness, becoming a beacon of shadowy magic. Lucian launched it away, and as it left his hand, tendrils of dark energy entered the bodies of both the

Seraphim and the fallen Ancients from the archeological expedition.

The air grew cold, the tower itself seeming to hold its breath.

That was when the corpses rose, their vacant eyes glowing with shadowy luminescence. Shadow Magic pulsated around them. The reanimated bodies moved, attacking the nearby Seraphim that hadn't been touched by the dark stream with ferocity. Several of the shadow beings were eyeing Lucian and his team, and from their collective, deadened gaze, he knew they were not his allies.

But the barrier was gone, along with Lightspear. In the chaos, it had disappeared completely, and no amount of willing it into his hand made it reappear.

Lucian would have to figure it out later. He pointed toward the open corridor. "Go! Now!"

They needed no further encouragement. They raced down the open path, not knowing how long the shadow beings would keep the Seraphim at bay.

As they fled, he kept trying to will it into his hand, but to no avail. Somehow, deep down, he knew Lightspear was gone, like a part of himself was missing.

The weapon he thought invincible had been destroyed somehow, canceled out by the powerful Shadow shield. There was no telling what it all meant. All he knew was that he hadn't just lost his Orbs, but also Lightspear, the only thing that could defeat the Ancient One. How could something like Lightspear fall to a mere shield? There was no way to know, a fact which made hopelessness pulse deep within Lucian.

They ran on, down the long corridor that seemed to go on forever. At last, he and the others sprinted into a vast chamber, a showcase of magnificent architecture with elaborate carvings etched onto every surface. Great pillars towered overhead, supporting a domed ceiling glittering with mineral formations, reflecting a soft, ethereal light. They were stepping into another era, into the heart of an ancient civilization lost to the sands of time.

But what held Lucian's attention was not the resplendent dome above, but the object the shadow barrier had to have been guarding.

A gateway stretched at the end of the chamber, pulsing with a white, radiant energy thrumming with potential. The light of its plane was strange, shifting, twisting into different rainbow hues. This was not another Shadow barrier, but something else entirely. Reaching out for it, Lucian felt the eddying shifts of Space-Time Magic, though its pearlescent appearance made it seem different from the gate on Mako. And unlike Mako, there was no nearby source of power to feed it.

"A time gate," Emma breathed. "Or is it something else?"

"It's our way out!" Lucian said, his voice echoing in the great expanse. "Keep running!"

But even as he spoke, the terrible sound of the Seraphim's magic streaked down the corridor, filling the chamber with violent echoes.

As they ran, he turned to see a host of robed figures floating down the corridor, their shockspears sparking with raw power. At the rate they were advancing, they'd easily cut them off from reaching the gate.

Lucian looked around to make sure everyone was still with him, when he noticed Jagar was gone.

"What the . . . Jagar, where are you?" The others stopped, but Lucian waved them madly on. "Keep going!"

He turned his attention back to the entrance, where Jagar was standing behind a column near the tunnel.

"Jagar!" Lucian yelled. "Rotting hell, get over here!"

He reached for Binding to drag Jagar toward him, but his tether was deflected by a hasty shield. Jagar merely shook his head.

"Go on, boy," he said. "All of you, get out of here! You'll never make it unless I stay behind."

His stony features were set in grim determination. Lucian knew, right then, that Jagar would not be dissuaded. Fear clawed at his stomach.

"I won't let you fight alone."

"Let me fight, or *all* of us die!" Jagar roared. "Go!"

Before Lucian could say anything, Jagar threw his shockspear toward him, guiding it with a tether. Lucian had no choice but to react, using Binding to retrieve it.

"Jagar–"

Jagar gave a grim smile. "Use it well, boy. Something tells me you'll need it wherever you're going."

With a warrior's cry, Jagar charged into the corridor, his entire body aswarm with Binding and Psionic Magic. The Seraphim already were shooting magic missiles of various Aspects, but it wasn't the Seraphim Jagar was hoping to defeat, at least not directly.

It was the corridor itself which, with a thunderous crack, was already collapsing from Jagar's magic, burying the man with it.

"No!" Serah screamed.

And just like that, it was over. The chamber went as silent as a crypt, save for the remnants of the collapsing tunnel and the ethereal hum of the waiting gate.

The spear in his hand felt heavier than it should have, not with physical weight, but with the burden of what it symbolized. It had all happened in less than thirty seconds.

"We must keep moving," Themba said steadily. "That rubble won't hold them for long."

The Ancient's voice seemed to come from another world. Lucian was still reeling. Jagar was more than his friend; he'd been like a father to him, always having sage advice to fit the situation.

His gaze lingered on the rubble, a surge of helpless rage burning within him. It wasn't fair. It wasn't right.

But Jagar had made his choice. And that choice, perhaps, had saved them all.

"Lucian!" Serah's voice was sharp, snapping him back to reality. "We have to move. What would Jagar want?"

His whole body heavy, he joined the others as they sprinted toward the gate. The energy surrounding it hummed and crackled.

But just as Themba predicted, the rubble exploded outward from the corridor. Emerging from the shadows, the Grand Seraph himself floated forward, a ghostly figure of white. His shockspear shone brightly as the other Seraphim floated behind him.

They were mere steps from the gate as the Grand Seraph raised his weapon, gathering Radiant, Dynamistic, and Binding Magic to prepare a shattering laser, a devastating attack against which they couldn't hope to defend themselves.

Lucian and Serah were weighed down with a Gravitonic aura streamed by the other Seraphim, making it nearly impossible to run. Khairu slipped through the portal, followed closely by Emma. Themba remained behind, streaming reverse Gravitonics to give Serah and him a chance to make it.

But it wasn't enough. Lucian, in sheer desperation, reached for his Space-Time Magic. Jagar's sacrifice could not be in vain. He surrounded himself and Serah with a Space-Time aura, warping the short distance to the edge of the portal, where Themba stood.

Just as the Grand Seraph's shattering laser left the tip of his spear, Lucian reversed the flow of his Space-Time stream, making the laser move in slow motion. But even with his magic, it only bought them a few more seconds.

It was enough. It *had* to be enough.

Lucian pushed Serah with a reverse tether. She cried out as she flipped forward right into the portal. Themba, who stood next to its plane, pulled Lucian with his own tether. Together, they fell through the multicolored surface.

Immediately, Lucian was assaulted with a wrenching sensation, as though he were being stretched. The shattering laser entered the portal, but rather than destroy him, its energy diffused in all directions. He felt nothing more than an icy shiver.

He had a moment of weightlessness, of suspended reality, that might have lasted seconds or hours. But eventually, his feet touched solid ground.

He fell to his knees, panting madly for breath. He looked up to find the others all around him, catching their own breath. He glanced over his shoulder to find the time gate on the wall of a cave. He wondered how long before the Seraphim followed them through, when it suddenly retracted to a single speck, winking out with an ethereal hum, leaving them all in pitch darkness.

A light sphere suddenly shone, floating over Themba's head. The cave walls were slick with condensation, reflecting the dim, greenish light of Themba's sphere.

It was terribly silent, aside from breathing and some weeping.

Weeping. The weight of it hit Lucian all at once.

Jagar was dead.

Lucian clutched his friend's spear tightly, feeling the hard weight of that reality settle in. Jagar's death had bought them this escape. The man had always mentioned wanting to go out with a bang, and it seemed as if he had gotten his wish.

It was little solace. But there was absolutely nothing he could do about it. What was done was done.

There was nothing but to go on.

As Serah said, it was what Jagar would have wanted.

29

OTHER THAN THEMBA'S light sphere, the cave's darkness was all-consuming, with not a single pinprick of light to be seen. That told Lucian they were deep underground. If they had emerged in the same place the tower had occupied, they might be in a time before the building even existed.

Or, for all Lucian knew, perhaps they were in a time *after*.

At the moment, he could barely make sense of things. Jagar's death was hard to accept, but there was no way the man had survived all that. Lucian's anger was now being replaced by a numbness that permeated every part of his being. Every step weighed a ton, and from the others' despondent expressions, he wasn't alone.

He looked at Jagar's shockspear, still clutched in his hand. With a thought, he retracted the weapon and pocketed it. That was enough proof that the Psionic brand linking Jagar to the weapon was completely gone. Either that, or Jagar simply didn't exist in this new time period they found themselves in, allowing the weapon to be used by anyone.

It felt wrong to have Jagar's weapon, but Lucian *needed* one, now that Lightspear was . . .

Lightspear. That was another loss, not as grievous to Lucian, but perhaps worse on the face of it. It was the only weapon capable of destroying the Ancient One.

And it was gone, vanished without a trace.

Even now, Lucian held out his hand, attempting to summon the weapon. But as expected, there was nothing.

He just couldn't understand how it was possible. Despite everything, there was always something new to learn about magic.

And sometimes, those lessons were painful.

They walked for hours in silence, Themba leading the way. Lucian doubted the Ancient knew where he was going, though they seemed to be on a general upward trajectory. Perhaps he had a sense that the others lacked, or perhaps he was using magic to guide them.

"The exit is ahead," he said.

As they stepped out of the cave mouth, a new world unfolded before him, lit by a dense star field that bathed the landscape in milky light.

They stood on the slope of a mountain range, verdant with forest and grass, at the bottom of which flowed a wide river. And it was from this river that structures rose, tall towers and bridges of pearlescent material that shone with light, bending and twisting in ways that defied logic. Ships flew silently on the wind, up into the sky, without even the slightest sound. Lucian wondered at that, but for now, he didn't question it.

Lucian felt the cool whisper of the breeze against his skin, filled with the sweet scent of grass and earth. The others stood around him, all looking dazed, each lost in the sheer strangeness of the world before them. A world that hardly seemed like the one they had left behind.

"Is this the same city?" Serah asked.

"Most likely, yes," Themba said. His gaze took in the hundreds of towers and bridges below, almost all of them spanning the river. "Although it's curious that the structure of these seems quite different from what we saw before . . ."

"They *do* seem different," Emma said, her voice worried.

"There is a small possibility we are in a different time period entirely," Themba said. "We will have to see."

Khairu remained silent, her gaze stoic as she stared at the city below.

Lucian wondered what Jagar would have thought of this. He was the only reason they could see this sight. His absence was like a void, an empty echo that could never be filled.

The others looked at him, seeming to want his thoughts on the situation. It was hard to piece any single thought together.

"Jagar's sacrifice will not be in vain," Lucian finally said. "That time gate felt different from the last one. It wasn't created by the Ancient One. It was created by the Time Weaver. That's why it was guarded by that Shadow barrier. The Ancient One was trying to prevent anyone from getting to it."

"Why was there a gate there at all?" Emma asked. "It makes me wonder."

"There's only one reason I can think of," Lucian said. "He wanted us to go through it. He's here. Somewhere. We're on the right track and just need to keep looking."

"It's . . . what Jagar would have wanted," Emma said.

It felt wrong to say that. Some part of Lucian held onto a foolish hope that somehow Jagar was still alive. But they had all seen that rubble go down. And there was no way the Seraphim would have let him escape.

"I can't believe he's gone . . ." Serah said.

The stars shimmered above, bathing them in celestial light. He supposed they would start by going into that strange, ethereal city below, rising from the river like something out of a dream.

But it would have to wait until daybreak—whenever daybreak came on this world.

"We should rest," Lucian said. "We've . . . been through a lot."

He looked at the others' hollow expressions, knowing there was nothing he could do or say to ease their pain.

Without a word, they found shelter within the forest, creating wards for protection from any life forms. No one seemed to have an appetite, so the rations they had taken from the ship went ignored. All were utterly exhausted from the day's ordeal.

"I'll stand watch," Themba said. "All of you, rest. We Ancients don't sleep as much as humans."

It was good enough for Lucian. He laid down and closed his eyes and couldn't think of anything besides Jagar's last stand. The man had been a warrior to the very end.

Lucian's dreams were filled with ghosts of the past and questions of the future. The journey would continue at dawn.

―――

THE NIGHT GREW chilly in the heights of the low mountains. Lucian fell into a fitful sleep, plagued by visions of Jagar giving his life so the rest could continue on.

He jerked awake when he felt a touch on his shoulder. He opened his eyes to see Emma, her face pale in the firelight. Pale glimmers of morning light were lighting the mountain range across the river, beyond the celestial city.

"We need to talk," she said, her voice barely above a whisper.

Just from her mannerisms, he could tell something was off. He followed her away from the camp and deeper into the trees, his senses prickling at her seriousness.

Once they were far enough away, she produced her slate, the screen displaying a complex map of the stars.

"I spent most of the night trying to figure out where—and *when*—we are," she explained. "I've cross-referenced the night sky with the data from our reality's observatories. And I have a near-perfect match."

"What did you find?"

She swallowed, her fingers hovering over the screen. "According to this . . . we are over *ten million* years in the past."

The revelation hit Lucian like a physical blow. His mind raced to piece together the implications. It was an unimaginable stretch. Lucian couldn't even guess what Earth would be like in this time period.

The only thing he knew about ten million years ago was that it was the time of The First Starsea Empire. The Gate Builders. The Dawn of Magic itself. It was the time of the First Immortal and the Ancient One's rise to prominence.

If true, they were in an era far beyond their wildest comprehension, before humans, before even the Ancients. He had expected them to be in a different time, but nothing as unexpected as *this*.

His gaze met Emma's, understanding mirrored in her eyes. "Are you sure?"

"I checked, and I checked again. With such a stretch of time, there is some room for variance, of course. Without the GalNet, my slate can only model so much. But when I plug in observatory data from Rune, which exists in our reality, and run the projection deep into the past, this is the only answer that comes back. I almost gave up after two million years. And then . . . a thought occurred to me. So, I waited until we got to around ten million, and the match became closer and closer." She swallowed. "There is room for error of about one hundred thousand years, but that still places us about ten million years in the past, give or take."

For a long moment, Lucian couldn't say anything. At last, he cleared his throat. "We are in the time of the Builders."

Emma nodded. "Yes. This is where the Time Weaver has led us. But we are completely helpless here. Everything we learned about Themba's reality will be completely useless. There won't be any Ancients here, so we'll know nothing about the Builders' customs, or even what they *look* like."

Lucian pointed to the city. "Anyone who can build *that* is probably way smarter than we are. If we need to communicate, we can use Psionic Magic, just like before."

Emma's eyes widened. "What about the Orb of Space-Time?"

Lucian's eyes widened as well. If they were ten million years in the past, then they were also in a time where the Ancient One had gathered *all* the Orbs, including that of Space-Time.

Lucian reached for his Space-Time Magic, finding he could stream the Aspect readily enough. But that would be expected in a time where all Eight Orbs were gathered.

When Lucian probed for the last Orb, he found it completely absent.

His shoulders slumped. "It's . . . gone. All gone." He laughed bitterly. "What else can be taken from me? Jagar. Lightspear. Now this . . ."

Emma's face was pale. "That's conclusive proof, then. This really *is* ten million years ago."

"I can detect the Space-Time Aspect," he said. "There's a good chance you can, too."

Emma nodded. "Yes. I can feel it."

"That means all the Orbs are gathered. We're in the time of the First Starsea, but before the Ancient One has been defeated. Before he sends the Orbs forward in time."

"What does all this mean?" Emma asked. "Themba's alternate reality and ours have joined. They've both grown from this same tree trunk, so to speak. If we mess anything up here, both our times will be completely erased."

The implications were heavy, but there was nothing either of them could do about it right now.

"We need to share this with the others," Lucian said. "They'll wake up soon."

Emma and Lucian got breakfast ready while Themba got an

hour's sleep. When the sun rose, all of them gathered around, trying to keep warm in the chill air. The mood was somber. Lucian didn't know how he was going to break this news when things were already so bad.

But he had to at some point. He had to trust that they were here for a reason and that this, somehow, was all part of the larger plan.

If it wasn't, then they would be stranded in this reality for good.

Lucian cleared his throat. "Emma made a discovery this morning. It's pretty major, and it's going to shake things up."

"Oh, no . . ." Serah said. "Are we stuck here?"

Emma cleared her throat and shared her findings. Lucian watched the others' faces pale at the news. There was fear. Disbelief. Even anger on the part of Khairu.

Lucian followed up with his own discovery about his loss of the Orb of Space-Time, but also about the general return of Space-Time Magic.

Themba's brow scrunched, his wrinkled face unreadable. "I had my suspicions. The city, the climate, everything differs vastly from the planet we left behind."

"The question is, what do we do about it?" Khairu asked. "How do we even navigate a society none of us knows a thing about?"

"We simply have to try," Themba said. "Lucian and I can both communicate with Psionics if need be. And with Psionics, we can help all of you understand, too. As already mentioned, there are no humans or Ancients here. Not even the ancestors of our kind have come into existence yet."

"We might even be attacked on sight!" Serah said. "For all we know, they'll think *we're* the threat."

"Perhaps," Themba said. "Or they may react with curiosity. There's no telling."

"So, what?" Khairu asked. "We just go down into that city and hope for the best?"

"I don't see what else we *can* do," Lucian said. "I have Space-Time Magic again. I had it before, with sorcery, but being able to use it freely with a simple stream gives us options."

"Maybe you can create a time gate back," Khairu said.

"We have been brought here for a reason," Emma said. "The Time Weaver is the only one who could have made that gate. To create a gate that bridges ten million years would take an unimaginable amount of ether. It's not something we have access to."

"The Time Weaver is here," Lucian echoed. "We need to find him. My guess is, given his name, he might be our ticket out of here. Otherwise, Jagar died for no reason. We have to believe this is all part of the plan. We have something to do here. Or else, why was that gate waiting for us? We have nothing else. Nothing but the Time Weaver. I want to know who he is. I want to know what *he* knows. He has the weapon, remember? Don't forget that. I don't know what it is, or what it does. But it might be the answer. And we won't find him unless we go down to the city and start knocking on doors."

Serah nodded, followed by Emma. Khairu, at last, sighed.

"Fine. I'm usually pretty cool and collected but . . . even *this* is testing me a bit. Seeing Jagar die like that . . ."

She trailed off, not sure how to continue. It was a rare moment of vulnerability from Khairu. Emma touched her arm.

"We'll find something out," Emma said. "You'll see."

"We should get moving," Themba said.

They packed up and within minutes were finding a way down the steep mountain slope. Lucian used his Binding Magic, while Serah used her Gravitonics to speed things along. Within a couple of hours, with the sun high above the valley, they stepped onto the bridge leading toward the towering city built over the river.

30

THEY CROSSED the crystalline bridge and walked toward the city. So far, there was no sign of any creature within, which Lucian found strange. The celestial sprawl spanning the river was unlike anything Lucian had ever seen, an iridescent cityscape with hundreds of towers rising into the sky, while multiple sleek spaceships went to and from the city, making no sound other than an ethereal hum.

Lucian's eyes widened as one ship, which had been plying the serene river below, suddenly rose and headed into the sky.

Whatever this place was, it possessed a level of technology Lucian had never seen before. He wondered if all these ships were powered purely by magic. From their lack of noise, he wouldn't have been surprised.

It was only once they were past the first towers that they saw the city's inhabitants. They were bipedal, like humans and Ancients, wearing lustrous clothing that seemed to have been crafted magically. Their skin was cobalt blue, though upon closer inspection, Lucian wouldn't exactly describe it as *skin*, but a cross between skin and scales. Their forms were long and lithe, with long necks containing gills that fluttered subtly with every breath. Their scales were a dazzling rainbow of hues that flashed under direct sunlight. Their arms and legs contained fins, while their heads almost reminded Lucian of a dragon—somewhat reptilian, with oval eyes, twin fangs, and serrated ears that drooped well past their shoulders.

Just as he was gawking at these beings, they were similarly gawking at him. Some even let out shrill screams, which simultaneously sounded alien and humanlike.

Clearly, these beings seemed to spend just as much time above water as below. Many pools and canals were intermixed with the buildings, and the clear water revealed the towers going well below the river, where even more of these creatures could be seen swimming. He hesitated to describe them as mermaids, because they had legs. But if their legs were pressed together, they would make an effective tool to paddle swiftly through the water.

Before Lucian could even think of what to do, two of these creatures, wearing shining armor and carrying long shockspears alight with electricity, advanced toward them, their bodies rippling with lean muscle beneath their blue skin. Their rounded eyes were narrowed in a universal expression of aggression. Their gills fluttered as their scales shone in the bright sunlight.

They came to a stop about two paces away, their fins twitching as they studied Lucian and his group. Those who hadn't run away now stood at a distance, and the once vibrant city seemed to have come to a standstill.

The two guards pointed the spears forward, and Lucian held up his hands in what he hoped was a placating gesture, though he reached for his Focus just to be ready for anything. Looking at those spears they held, the resemblance to their own weapons was uncanny. Perhaps this place was where the shockspear first came from, or perhaps three separate cultures—his, and that of the First and Second Starsea Empires, had all recognized its potential in breaking shields, magical or otherwise, and had developed them independently.

Before anything bad could happen, Lucian reached out with his Psionic Magic. Instantly, he detected the Focuses of both guards—the first was a Binder, and the second a Thermalist. Before they could react to his use of magic, he created the Psionic ward that would allow them to communicate, and his mouth formed the words of a foreign language that was, thankfully, far less difficult than the Ancient tongue.

"We're not going to hurt you," Lucian said. "I'm only using my magic to communicate. Nothing more."

The guards exchanged a worried glance. It was hard to differentiate the two, but the one in charge seemed to be taller.

The taller one's silver eyes narrowed. "Who, and what, are you? Where did you come from? And how is it your kind can use magic?"

Lucian considered. If the Orbs worked in this time the same way as other times, these creatures—whatever they were called—would be the only magic-users.

He decided not to address that question for now. "We are travelers from another world." He added reverse Thermalism to his stream, using it to calm their emotions subtly. It was a delicate balance; too much calming, and they would grow suspicious of what he was doing. "We've been summoned here by someone called the Time Weaver. Does that name mean anything?"

The guards shared a look, their gills fluttering a bit and seeming to communicate wordlessly. With Lucian's Psionic Magic, he detected they were displaying confusion. The gills, he realized, revealed these creatures' emotional state, while their language merely conveyed words.

The first creature turned back. "We've never heard of this *Time Weaver*. Who is he? Why would he summon you? The

Starsea Empire is large, but we've never seen one of your kind. Certainly not in this sector of space."

Lucian pressed on. "Maybe he goes by a different name here. The Time Weaver is a great sorcerer of Space-Time Magic."

Lucian felt Themba stepping closer to him, the Ancient's calm presence reassuring. "I am Themba, and I think in this case, honesty is the best policy. We don't merely come from another world; we come from another time."

Again, the guards' gills fluttered in confusion. Lucian perceived Psionically that they understood the concept of time travel as a theoretical abstract, but they deemed it to be an impossibility.

"What do you mean, *another time*?" the second guard asked.

"Just that," Themba said. "We are time travelers who have been summoned here by the Time Weaver. It is important that we find him, and just as important that you render aid."

"Impossible," the second guard said, his gills swishing with incredulity. "There is no sorcerer powerful enough to move through time. Though many have tried."

"Are you *Alkasen*?" the lead guards demanded, their grip on their spear tightening.

"No, we are enemies of the *Alkasen*," Lucian responded, picking up on the flash of hostility from the guard's gills. "We've come to offer our aid."

"Aid?" the other guard asked, still suspicious.

"Yes," Lucian confirmed, looking between them and deciding to change tacks. Again, he subtly used Psionics to make himself appear more trustworthy. "We were sent by the Time Weaver to assist you in your conflict with the *Alkasen*."

After a tense moment of consideration, the guards seemed to reach a silent consensus.

The first guard turned back. "If you came to help against the *Alkasen*, you should have simply said so from the start. We have no choice but to take you to the Water Palace. Perhaps, if your story is true, there will be one there who knows about this Time Weaver."

It was progress. Lucian nodded. "That sounds good to us."

"Follow us. And don't even think about wandering off."

"We won't."

The guards began leading them down the street, and life resumed in the river city.

As they walked, Lucian explained the situation to the others, not sure if they had caught everything, despite the ward.

"I don't like this," Khairu said, "but I see no other option. This Water Palace will have higher-ranking officials than these. Maybe we can learn more there."

"This city is *amazing*," Serah said. "None of their ships make any noise. Have you noticed that?"

"Magic," Emma said. "It seems to power all of their technology."

Just like everyone else, Lucian took in his surroundings with a sense of awe. The city was like a living organism, the buildings pulsating with ethereal energy in a network of dizzying complexity. This was a level of magic that would never again be recreated. Not even the Ancients' magic-based society of the alternate reality they came from could compare to this.

This was a civilization where the sorcerers had used their magic not just to conquer, but to build.

They followed the guards in silence, through various crystalline walkways and elevators, rising high above the city streets. Before long, they stood before the Water Palace itself.

It was the epitome of pearlescent beauty. Graceful towers, walls, and archways of gold floated high above the city, accessible only by a long, floating walkway supported by Gravitonic Magic. Waterfalls poured over its sides into the city and river below, the mist creating a tapestry of rainbows. The power of the Gravitonic Magic supporting the palace had to be immense, branded by hundreds of powerful sorcerers. He had entered a universe where the likes of Xara, Vera, or Arian were likely as many as the common mage, if not more so. This would obviously affect society in startling ways Lucian couldn't even imagine or make sense of.

As they entered the building's grandeur, Lucian held his breath. The inside was just as breathtaking as the outside, with waterfalls, alien trees, and rivers, along with walkways and staircases.

The first guard turned to him. "I've received a Psionic message from King Angkasa himself. He wishes to see you personally."

"King Angkasa?" Themba asked.

The guard's gills fluttered. "Yes, a powerful sorcerer, and wise. If anyone knows about this Time Weaver, it's him. This is a great honor, off-worlder. He's curious about you. Two new kinds of sentient beings that no one has ever seen before."

"Word spreads fast," Lucian said.

"Naturally," the guards said. "It's likely by now that every Samikan on Samudraya knows of your coming."

Lucian learned from his Psionic brand that Samikan was the name of their species, while Samudraya was the name of this planet.

They came to the top of the stairs, where a wide waterfall fell like a gentle curtain. The two Samikan ahead of them went through without hesitation, as much at home in water as in air. The others followed with some slight hesitation, unable to see what lay on the other side.

Lucian led the way, pushing through the water to find himself in a vast hall beyond, up to his knees in crystalline, shimmering water. Pearlescent columns rose high on either side, and several dozen Samikan in shimmering robes were gathered in small groups, their clothing seeming finer than most of the creatures he'd seen outside, the colors even more vibrant and decorative. Their conversations stilled as the guards led them forward, through the water and toward the end of the hall where, on a shining throne, sat a Samikan a great deal larger than the others Lucian had seen, which was more or less the same size as a human. This Samikan had to be none other than King Angkasa himself.

The king's robes were pearlescent and luminous, spilling from his high seat and undulating on the waters of the throne room itself. His skin, instead of the characteristic blue, was icy, while his sharp eyes were sea green, glowing with an inscrutable light as he studied the strangers who had walked into his domain.

Lucian's impression of the king was that he was a powerful sorcerer indeed. Certainly, to be at the top in this place required even greater skill and wisdom than in Lucian's time. And in a universe like this, where the fraying was all but absent, the Samikan species would have had centuries, perhaps even millennia, to perfect the mysteries of the Manifold.

As the two guards bowed and withdrew, there was a moment of charged silence between the humans, Themba, and the King. The only sound was the water gently trickling down the columns and from the waterfall behind them. Lucian saw that the water flowed over either side, and must be the source of the falls he had seen from outside the palace.

Lucian took a step forward, only to find himself restrained by powerful Binding Magic. Lucian also felt the weight of Gravitonic Magic press down on him. Hastily, he shielded himself from the block, and for a moment, he and the king were locked in a battle of wills.

Despite the raw power that flowed from the king, Lucian's shield held. The ether that swirled about the room was drawn to Lucian, and less so to the king.

At last, the king relented, his gills agitated as he stared Lucian down. He had tested his strength against the newcomer and had been found wanting.

He hoped the action hadn't sealed their doom. Though Lucian had bested the king, the king still had hundreds, if not thousands, of mages, sorcerers, and soldiers at his command. With one word, they could easily overwhelm them all.

Lucian watched the king for his next move, along with Themba, who stood beside him.

Their fates were in his hands.

31

AT LAST, King Angkasa's gills quivered, a gesture Lucian Psionically knew was the equivalent of uproarious laughter.

The tension went out of the room as the King slammed the butt of his spear in the water, creating a great splash that rained down on Lucian and his companions.

"Pure rains fall upon you," King Angkasa boomed. His voice was a deep tone, almost musical in its resonance. "Be welcome in my hall."

Lucian, understanding the nuances of Samikan customs through Psionic Magic, allowed a smile to grace his face. He lifted a hand, catching some of the falling water droplets, then gently swiped his hand across his heart.

"King Angkasa of Samudraya," he said, his voice echoing across the hall. "May your waters always run clear, and your reign be as eternal as the river's flow. We are honored to stand in your grand hall."

King Angkasa raised an elongated hand, each finger adorned with an intricate ring embedded with jewels that glowed with latent magic. The king's robes shifted colors slightly, showing a ripple of turquoise before returning to their lustrous hue. His wide, sea-green eyes stared at Lucian and his companions with interest.

"You are . . . a *curiosity*," King Angkasa finally said. "I have never seen one of your kind before. Different. Yet not so unlike we Samikan. And you use our language effortlessly. Your Psionic Magic is impressive. I've never known a non-Samikan to use it."

Lucian nodded, knowing Angkasa would understand the gesture, given their Psionic connection.

"Our species can use magic, along with his species," Lucian said, nodding toward Themba. "I'm Lucian. Lucian Abrantes. And this here is Themba Makhosi."

"Strange names," Angkasa said. "And how did you come to the Shining City of Sungmata? It's almost as if you've sprung from the Ether itself. Be warned: despite your power in Psionic Magic, I am adept enough to know when you're not speaking the truth."

Lucian shared a look with the others, and it seemed they all agreed that the truth—or at least a part of the truth—would be the best policy.

He turned back to King Angkasa. "Springing from the Ether would not be too far from reality. We come from the future. We followed someone here called the Time Weaver through a time gate. We are looking for him even now."

For a moment, the king was silent. He leaned back on his throne, his radiant eyes filled with a mix of curiosity and disbelief.

"The Time Weaver," the King finally said. "I don't know anyone by this name. But it is known time travel is impossible. Not even the Immortal himself could do such a thing. The most powerful of sorcerers might slow or quicken time for a moment to give them an advantage in battle. And yet, I detect no lie in your story. A puzzle."

"We didn't know it was possible until recently, either," Lucian admitted. "I can't tell you *how* it happened, except that it *has* happened, twice as far as I know. It seems the impossible has become possible."

"Where is this time gate? Are you capable of creating it?"

"It's gone," Lucian said. "We believe the Time Weaver himself created it and designed it to dissipate as soon as we passed through. As for whether I can create one, the answer is *no*. Only the Time Weaver can."

The Ancient One was also capable of it, but he decided not to mention it.

Thankfully, Angkasa didn't seem to catch this. "A pity." The king seemed to ponder this for a moment, before his gaze rose to encompass the noble Samikan still lingering in his hall. "Leave us."

The nobles dove into the waist-high water, swimming toward the waterfall entrance of the throne room. Only when they were gone did King Angkasa return his attention to Lucian.

"Though I don't think you're lying, there is always a chance you are masking your mind, given your obvious abilities." His gaze became piercing. "You say you come from the future. How far in the future? Who will win this war, Starsea or the *Alkasen*? Did this Time Weaver send for you to help us, or for another purpose?"

Lucian knew exactly how this story ended. In ten million years, the only trace of these Samikan would be the Gates created by none other than the First Immortal using the power of the Orbs. But saying that much to Angkasa risked his wrath.

He didn't know where in the timeline they were. Maybe there were centuries, perhaps even millennia, left for Starsea to fight. Or maybe they just had days left.

Whatever the case, Lucian had to tell the truth. He couldn't risk any deceit being picked up on by the king's sophisticated Psionic Magic.

"In our own time," Lucian began, "we know very little about

your people. We call you the Builders. The only remnant of your civilization is the Gates that bridge the stars. They last ten million years into the future."

As Lucian said "years," it automatically translated into whatever the Samikan equivalent would be.

King Angkasa's gills went still, clearly struck silent by this news. "Then . . . we will fall? Ten million years is a long time. Many things can happen. It is conceivable Starsea itself might be destroyed, if only because of the ravages of time. That is of little concern to me. Is it the *Alkasen* who deal the final blow?"

"As far as I know, yes. I can't say when it will happen, since all knowledge of this time is lost to us. But at some point, yes. It's inevitable."

An eerie silence filled the grand hall, the murmuring waters the only sound. Lucian saw something like grief communicated in the king's posture, as if he had been stabbed with a knife. A resonating sadness pulsated from his being. The waters of the throne room ran on, as if in defiance of that future fate. It seemed impossible that such grandeur could fade. The Starsea Empire was clearly at the zenith of its power.

But all things, Lucian supposed, had to end.

"But you cannot say when, or how this will happen," King Angkasa finally said, his voice carrying a chill. When Lucian shook his head, the king sighed. "That is . . . disappointing. Yet it is the truth I asked for. Though our star shines bright today, I suppose death comes for all, including empires. We hold close what is dear to us, for tomorrow, the sun may not rise, nor the spring burst forth with new life. Not even the stars will survive until the Cycle of Creation begins anew."

"There might be a way to buy more time," Lucian said. "We need to find the Time Weaver. Only he has the answers we're looking for. In our own time, we are also at war with the *Alkasen*. Just as Themba's people are in his time. It is a cycle. The *Alkasen* seek to destroy any species that uses magic. It's their punishment for opening the First Gate. They don't think anyone besides the Ascendant Beings should be able to use magic."

Lucian left unsaid the second part: that they viewed the Orbs as their property and would stop at nothing to get them back. And as soon as they did so, they would seal the First Gate, stopping the flow of ether into the Shadow Realm.

The king shifted at these words. "Yes, we have long known that this is indeed the reason for the *Alkasen's* ire. They have always held a deep resentment toward us. For it was from the First Gate that they first issued and began this endless war."

Lucian realized that since he was here, he might as well get answers he would never find out in his own time.

"May I ask you a question, King Angkasa?"

The king's gills fluttered again, a signal of acquiescence. "You may."

"How was the First Gate created? The Samikan haven't always possessed magic, after all. That only happened when the Immortal got the Orbs. But how did the Samikan get into the Light Realm in the first place, if they didn't have magic?"

King Angkasa watched him closely. "Ah, you seek the heart of our history. This is a tale that dates back two millennia. To the death—and the resurrection—of our people." He paused, his gaze far off as if he were looking into the depths of time itself. "The Samikan, as you rightly noted, weren't always beings of magic. We were once a race who used metal and light to shape reality. Our ships sailed the cosmos using the power of the stars."

"Fusion power," Lucian said. "Much like us."

"Now, our ships move by a different, more efficient means. Those days were primitive, but the Samikan are tinkerers by nature. *Builders*, as you said previously. It is a fitting name for us. However, driven by our thirst for knowledge and power, we experimented with the energy of our sun in new ways. It's said we created an alternate state that opened the First Gate to the Light Realm. I suppose you could say the creation of magic was . . . an *accident.*" He paused for a moment. "At least, that is how the story goes. Who knows if it's really true? So much was lost in the first wave of the *Alkasen* invasion, including our homeworld."

A somber silence filled the room before Angkasa continued.

"Of course, in those days, we were contained in a single system. The Immortal, who then was only known as the Lord of Seas, was the first to enter this Gate to see what lay on the other side."

At Angkasa's hesitation, Lucian leaned forward. "What happened then?"

"Well, it is a legend. But I'll entertain the question. It's said that a great wave of ethereal energy issued forth, all but decimating our home world of Airaruma. Our world, a gleaming cerulean jewel of beautiful islands and rivers, became a charred husk. The Lord of Seas survived, though he no longer had seas to rule. Only a few small space colonies survived, the only remnant to face the dark tide gathering from the First Gate. There is only one reason we ever survived."

"The Orbs," Lucian said.

"Yes, the Jewels of Starsea. The Lord of Seas wielded them, and using their power, he fought the *Alkasen*, allowing our people to flee deep into space as the Immortal created Gates to speed our flight. We escaped far from our homeworld, settling on a new planet that was quite similar to ours. And it was here that he built an empire anew, christening it Starsea. For from the waves we rose, and to the stars we spread. With the Orbs, he led our ancestors to greatness. But never did he forget the deadly stroke of the *Alkasen*, which robbed him of everyone he knew and loved. He swore vengeance, doing everything he could to raise the Samikan into a force capable of challenging the *Alkasen*. Even now, our former home, Airaruma, has been lost in the depths of time. None has ventured into that part of space for centuries. Every few years, a group of intrepid explorers seeks it, but none return."

Lucian remained silent as he considered the king's tale. He

wasn't sure what to make of it. Some of it sounded familiar, like the part about the First Immortal entering the Gate. Apparently, before he had the Orbs, he had another name: the Lord of Seas. But completely unmentioned was the Ancient One, or one like him. Where, and how, did he come into the picture? Were the Samikan aware that the Immortal was actually possessed by something else?"

Lucian kept these thoughts to himself.

King Angkasa looked at Lucian and Themba, his eyes gleaming with curiosity. "I cannot say that I fully believe your story about this Time Weaver and coming from the future," he admitted. "But it intrigues me. For that reason, you will stay here, under my protection, until we determine the veracity of your claims."

Seemingly from nowhere, a few Samikan attendants leaped like dolphins through the deeper water near Angkasa's throne, swimming into the room where Lucian and his friends stood.

"Escort them to our finest guest suite," Angkasa ordered, before turning back to Lucian. "For those who prefer dry land, of course." He turned back to Lucian. "I have much to do today, but I will summon you tomorrow. If there is time."

The attendants bowed, dressed in sheer pearlescent robes that would not be a hindrance in the water.

"Follow us," the lead Samikan said, a being with a graceful, feminine form.

Lucian and the others followed the attendants out of the grand hall and into the opulent chambers of King Angkasa's Palace.

32

THEY WERE LED from the vast throne room by the two richly dressed Samikan servants. It seemed the servants were walking impatiently, knowing they could reach their destination much more quickly by swimming in the various canals of the palace. Much of the complex was underwater, and he could see Samikan teeming below them in various pools and submerged corridors.

"This place is something else," Serah said.

No one responded, either overwhelmed with the situation, or still reeling from what had happened before entering the time gate.

They stuck to the small pathways lining either side of the halls. They seemed little-used, however, as most of the palace's occupants seemed to opt for the clear canals running down the center of each corridor.

Lucian couldn't help but gawk as they were led upward, away from the deep pools to an airier part of the palace. The walls and vaulted ceilings were nothing short of majestic, filled with shimmering lights that reflected off the water's surface like stars.

At last, toward the top of the complex, they stopped before a door that seemed to be made from shell.

"These will be your quarters," the female attendant said, sliding the door back. "There should be room enough for all of you."

Lucian bowed and cupped his hands, one slightly above the other, as if he were holding a small sphere. He knew from his Psionic brand that it was the polite way to dismiss someone. It had something to do with an underwater sport that was popular among the Samikan.

The two attendants left, and Lucian and the rest entered the room, an opulent set of chambers filled with furnishings made of iridescent shells and corals. Detailed paintings depicting scenes of rivers and seas decked the walls, while a wide window displayed the river below, cutting through the verdantly green canyon.

Serah forged ahead, plopping down in a luxurious seat padded with velvet. The others followed behind, taking up their seats as Lucian shut the door. With everything over, at least for now, the events of the previous day were coming back in full force. Lucian couldn't help but notice a space on the sofa next to Emma, where Jagar might have been sitting.

Might have, if Lucian had saved him.

There was a heaviness to the room, a heaviness which struck them all silent. Lucian truly didn't know what to say at this moment to give them hope.

He looked down at Jagar's shockspear, clasping it in his hand. Again, he was hit with a sense of wrongness at having it, even if Jagar had entrusted it to him.

"It doesn't feel real, does it?" Lucian asked.

Everyone remained silent, not having the heart to respond.

He shook his head. "Jagar was a fighter. He died as he lived. A warrior." Lucian gathered his thoughts. "Of course, he was more than that. He was our friend. *My* friend."

Serah and Emma's eyes filled with tears, while Khairu's face was stoic, but Lucian knew her well enough by now to see the sadness in her brown eyes.

"He didn't beat around the bush. He told you exactly what you needed to hear, and no matter how harsh, you were glad he said it. He always had your back."

Serah stood, walking to a nearby table where there were some glasses and a decanter of some liquid. She sniffed and nodded with satisfaction.

"Alcoholic. I don't know how it is elsewhere, but on Psyche, we toast the dead."

No one argued as Serah poured out five glasses. Lucian wondered if the drink inside even agreed with basic human biology, or Themba's, for that matter.

No one raised a protest as they each held their glass filled with the amber-hued liquid. Taking a smell, it reminded Lucian of whiskey, with rich notes that promised a satisfying drink.

"To Jagar," Serah said, raising her glass. Her voice echoed in the room's grandeur, imbuing the silence with a sense of finality. "He fought, he lived, and he was more than a friend. He was our brother, a member of our family." Her voice hitched slightly, but she pushed on. "Here's to a man who faced every challenge head-on, who never wavered, and who stayed true until his last breath."

Their glasses clinked together in a gentle chorus, a promise to keep his memory alive.

Lucian took a sip, letting the sweet but fiery liquid burn its path, a stark reminder of their shared loss.

For a moment they were silent, each lost in their thoughts, the taste of the toast bitter and sweet all at once.

Emma, with her eyes glistening, raised her glass once more. "To Jagar. And to us . . . those he left behind. May we find strength in the coming days and honor his memory with every battle we face."

They emptied their glasses, the alcohol feeling like it was burning a hole in Lucian's stomach. They all shared a look, grief laying heavy on every face.

Lucian stood, walking to the window to stare at the river far below, floating between the green mountains before it was lost to a bend.

Because of Jagar's sacrifice, they had gotten this far. His death could not be in vain.

Sometime later, the Samikan servants came by with a rich banquet of food, alien in appearance but divine in taste. Glistening fruits, vegetables of vibrant hues, and various fish cooked to perfection were set on the table. Exotic aromas filled the air, a melding of the bounty of the river, sea, and land.

Of course, it was hard to enjoy such food given the situation, but all of them ate, not having had a solid meal since coming down on Sigil.

After the meal was done, Lucian felt an exhaustion such as he had never known, and it seemed the others were of a similar mind. There were plenty of beds within the chambers to choose from.

As soon as Lucian lay down, sleep descended on him in a wave.

ALMOST IMMEDIATELY, he went into a dream. Rising in the distance appeared a forlorn, derelict castle, on a high plateau above a rugged landscape beneath a sky rich with stars. The ground was a desolate wasteland of ice and rock, and Lucian knew that there was no air here. Yet, he walked toward the castle, flying toward it using a combination of Binding and Gravitonic Magic.

He sensed something there, calling him . . .

I am here, the voice said.

He landed beneath the yawning entrance of the castle, and in the gloom within stood a figure cloaked by darkness.

Stay thee where thou art, the figure said.

Lucian frowned in puzzlement at the archaic language. He realized the figure was speaking an older version of the Ancient tongue. It wasn't difficult to follow, but it required an extra moment to process things.

Are you the Time Weaver? Lucian asked, wanting to cut to the chase.

I am so. And thou hast come hither at great expense.

Yes. One of our friends sacrificed himself trying to follow you through that time gate.

I am sorry for that. But the Ancient One is a potent adversary. Like thee, he is mine enemy. This is where I had to lead thee. It is . . . needful for the completion of all things. Here, nigh to the very start of it all . . .

What are you talking about?

Even now, I cannot tarry with speech. The Ancient One can hearken, and in this time, his power is most formidable. Like thee, I am a stranger here. But unlike us, the Ancient One knows not what awaits him. Yet we must enact our roles if all of this is to proceed as devised.

What roles?

I cannot speak over so fragile a link. We must meet in the flesh.

Where are you? How are you even speaking to me at all?

The gate bore Psionic Magic, devised to mark thee. Using that mark, I can commune. And what's more, thou can use that very same mark to seek me out.

How?

The Chosen will know the way. There is much to impart unto thee. Not only words, but something thou needest to fulfill thy quest. A mighty armament, as foretold in the prophecy I left for thee. Else, all shall come to naught. Remember. The Chosen will know the way. . .

The dream faded, and Lucian was startled awake, his heart pounding.

He looked around and found, to his surprise, that it was

morning. Serah slept softly beside him, while somehow, a break-fast of unknown fruits and bread sat waiting for them on the table in the main living area.

Serah stirred, having detected his movement. She opened her eyes sleepily. "Everything okay?"

"I've had a vision," he said. "About the Time Weaver."

Serah's eyes widened as her sleepiness was dispelled. "A vision? What happened?"

He quickly explained, and she listened thoughtfully.

"A castle on a barren planet," Serah said. "There can't be too many of those in the galaxy, right?"

"The Time Weaver wouldn't tell me where the castle was. He said the Ancient One was listening."

"He said you'd know the way, though, through the Psionic brand he left on that gate. Have you tried to sense it?"

"Not yet. Wherever it is, it's far from here. This planet is anything but barren. We'll undoubtedly need a ship."

"Then let's get a ship."

"That easy, huh?"

"Where there's a will, there's a way, right?" She eyed the food out in the central area. "Let's talk it out over breakfast."

They woke everyone up, and as they ate, Lucian relayed his dream.

"So, The Time Weaver has branded me," he finished. "He says the brand will lead me to him."

"Sounds like we *will* need a ship," Khairu said. "At least we know the next step."

"I just want answers," Lucian said.

"We'll find answers," Emma said. "Let's just focus on the ship part."

"I know we can't really trust this King Angkasa," Serah said, "but he's probably the only one who can get us a ship."

Lucian knew that much was true. "He was going to summon us at some point. Maybe that's our chance to ask for one. And from what the Time Weaver said, the Ancient One is already looking for him, and he took a risk by appearing in my dream. That cat is already out of the bag. We might as well just ask for the ship. Nicely, of course."

"Do you think he can be convinced?" Khairu said. "And how are we supposed to pilot a ship with such wildly different technology than what we're used to?"

"I don't know," Lucian said. "We just need some way to find the Time Weaver. He's capable of creating time gates. That means after we listen to whatever he has to tell us, and get this weapon, he can get us out of here."

Their conversation was interrupted by the door suddenly opening, revealing the same two attendants from yesterday.

"The King has summoned you," the female attendant said, bowing slightly.

"Speaking of the devil," Serah said.

"We're ready to see him," Lucian said.

"This way, please."

They followed the servants out of their rooms and into the corridor beyond.

33

THE ATTENDANTS LED them back through the palace, through various corridors and stairways, until they once again stood in the water of the King's audience chamber.

This time, he didn't splash them, thankfully. Maybe that was just a one-time thing.

"Lucian," King Angkasa said. "I detected a Psionic fluctuation over the palace during my sleep. I tried to access it, but even my power couldn't make sense of it."

"I had a vision last night. The Time Weaver has summoned me, though I don't know where. It's clearly off this world, and probably somewhere quite far."

"Tell me."

"There was a castle on a desolate planet. I can't say more than that."

King Angkasa's gills fluttered for a moment, as if surprised.

"Does that mean anything, your majesty?"

Angkasa was quiet for a moment. "Describe the castle to me."

Lucian did so in great detail. The high columns, the airy arches, the desolate appearance shaped by years of abandonment. Though he could not read the King's stoic face, he felt his unease.

Once done, Lucian remained quiet. The King sat utterly still, hardly moving save for his breathing.

At last, the King spoke. "What you describe is an old prophecy, often seen by powerful sorcerers. Your description fits the mold. It is called the Castle of Creation, and it's said it's on our long-lost homeworld of Airaruma. Many have sought it, to no avail."

"What is the Castle of Creation?" Lucian asked.

"They say it was the Immortal's home before he became the Immortal, before even the time of the First Gate. In fact, the castles of all the Kings and Queens of Starsea are imitations of the Castle from the sorcerers' dreams."

"Are you sure it's this Castle of Creation? That would mean it's deep in the *Alkasen's* territory."

"It is," Angkasa said. "As for why this Time Weaver would be there, I can't say. In fact, it can be nothing other than an impossibility."

"That would mean the First Gate is nearby," Lucian said, startled at the idea of it.

"Indeed. The very source of the *Alkasen* invasion. Such a place will be highly dangerous."

"How far away is it?"

"Many years of travel, even in the fastest ship," the King said, regretfully. "However, even if you had the time, it would be impossible. No one can survive long in Dark Space."

Lucian found it curious humans had the same name for *Alkasen*-occupied territory as these Samikan did.

Even if the journey would take many years, Lucian knew there had to be a way to bridge the gap. Didn't the Time Weaver insist he would know a way?

"I would only need a ship," Lucian said. "As long as I have that, I think we can make it."

Angkasa seemed to consider for a long while. At last, his gills fluttered as if deciding. "If finding this Time Weaver will aid us in our battle against the *Alkasen*, though it is a hopeless fight, then I have no choice but to aid you."

Lucian blinked in surprise. "Seriously?"

"You seem surprised that it was this easy, don't you? Well, I am the King of Sungmata. A spaceship is a trifle. And if there's even an infinitesimal chance that what you're saying is true, we have no choice. I don't know how you'll ever make it, but you seem determined. And I detect no lie in your words."

"We are grateful, your majesty."

"We have no more time to waste. I will take you to the royal hangar myself."

"Right now?" Lucian asked.

"Yes, right now. You said it yourself; time is limited. We Samikan are practical. There is no reason to delay. All ships come stocked with enough supplies to survive months in deep space. And though your journey will be longer than that, lasting many, many years, it will be enough to give you a strong start."

The king then rose from his throne and beckoned them to follow him from his watery hall, down a back staircase that was previously hidden. They followed him down the stone stairs that spiraled around the floating island on which the castle was situated. The path was narrow, and over the right side was a steep drop well over five hundred meters to the wide river and city below.

Before long, they came to a small entrance that opened into a vast hangar filled with many sleek ships of various sizes. But it was to the closest vessel that the king led them, a ship of such beauty that it took Lucian's breath away. Its curving surface shimmered with an ethereal, magical glow.

"Thank you, King Angkasa," Lucian said.

Angkasa placed an icy blue hand almost lovingly on the ship's ebony hull. "This one is named Garuda."

"How are we supposed to pilot it?"

The King seemed confused by the question. "The ship will take care of everything."

Before Lucian could respond, a gravity settled in the King's eyes, and he stood taller as he spoke, his voice resonant in the vast hangar.

"Children of another time," he began. "Bound to us by the will of the Seas of the Worlds and the Manifold. I bestow upon you this vessel, a creation of my finest shipwrights, imbued with the magic of the greatest sorcerers. May Garuda guide you through darkness, protect you from the unseen and the unknown, and carry you to your destiny with grace and surety."

He then looked at each one of them, his gaze lingering, as if memorizing their faces, before continuing.

"Be brave, for you venture into the abyss, Dark Space long claimed by our ancient enemy. Be wise, for you seek answers lost to our people for millennia. Be vigilant, for enemies lurk in shadows and uncertainty. And most of all, be true to yourselves, for that is the heart of sorcery, the compass which will never fail you."

With a graceful bow, King Angkasa turned and left them, his footsteps echoing in the hangar as the reality of their journey and mission settled upon them. Garuda seemed to shimmer in response, as if understanding the weight of the quest now entrusted to it.

Once King Angkasa was gone, Lucian turned to the others, not knowing what to make of such words. "Come on. Let's board."

In response to these words, the very hull of the ship opened, and a Gravitonic glyph lowered to the floor of the hangar, seeming to wait for them to step on it.

"Fancy," Serah said. She hopped on, seeming to test its strength. "That's some powerful magic there."

The others joined her, and as soon as everyone stepped on, the magical glyph lifted them through the opening and onto the ship, dissipating as soon as its job was complete. The gap in the hull sealed shut, as if it had never been.

They took a moment to navigate the ship's sleek interior. It wasn't too different from most ships Lucian had been on, except for a marked absence of control panels and wiring. Reaching out with his Focus, he could feel the powerful brands built into the very fabric of the ship. It went far beyond anything Themba's ship had, proving just how much more advanced this civilization was than anything they had so far seen.

From the direction of the bridge, Lucian felt a Psionic pull. Knowing it came from the ship, he allowed himself to connect to it. All at once, Lucian realized that this was no mere ship.

It was an *intelligence*, and a magical one at that.

Greetings! My name is Garuda. How might I assist you today?

Lucian blinked. Did . . . you just talk to me?

Yes. I'm Garuda. King Angkasa told me to help you out in whatever way you require. Where would you like to go? What is your name?

I'm Lucian, Lucian responded, a bit dazed. *As for where we're going . . . well, the Castle of Creation on Airaruma. Can you do that?*

There was a moment of hesitation by the ship. *I understand Airaruma is the mythical homeworld of the Samikan people, but I'm afraid traveling there will be impossible. And even if it were, the journey would take four to five years, if rumored locations of the planet are accurate. There are also no safe ports in which to resupply once we're in Dark Space. Given these dangers, not to mention hostile Alkasen ships, any attempt to travel to Airaruma will place you and your crew in grave danger. Is there any other place you'd like to go?*

There is a way to Airaruma. You will just need to follow my exact instructions.

If there is any danger to these instructions, I'm afraid I cannot enact them.

King Angkasa said you have to help us in whatever way we need, right?

Yes, he said this. But in my estimation, placing you in danger is not fulfilling this original instruction.

What if I had a way of getting us there safely?

The ship seemed to think for a moment. *I'm not aware of there being any possibility.*

Follow my directions, Garuda. Can you do that much?

So long as it does not lead us into obvious danger, then yes. I will do so.

Lucian realized that wrangling this ship might be more difficult than had first supposed. *All right. Stand by for further orders.*

"What was that all about?" Serah asked. "It looked like you were really concentrating."

"This ship isn't just a ship," Lucian said. "It's alive, and I've just connected my mind with it."

"Really?" Emma asked. "That's fascinating!"

"That's why there are no controls. You just tell the ship what to do, and it'll do it."

"Remarkable," Themba said. "We've long believed creating intelligence with Psionic Magic to be an impossibility, but it seems these Samikan have figured it out."

"Seems so," Lucian said.

Lucian summarized his conversation with Garuda to the others.

"Can you just feed it your vision?" Serah asked. "Maybe it could confirm that it seems legit."

"Good idea. Let me try."

Lucian returned his Focus to the ship. *Garuda, I've had a vision of Airaruma. Is it possible to feed it to you?*

Yes. Go ahead and transfer it.

Lucian closed his eyes, reaching for Psionics and replaying the contents of the dream as if were a film.

Once done, there was a moment's pause from Garuda, as if considering.

This vision matches the descriptions of many prophecies about the Castle of Creation over the centuries.

Is it Airaruma?

I cannot say that it is. It is possible that it is Airaruma as it exists today, assuming the stories of the death of the Old Samikan civilization are true. Whatever the case, I cannot use the provided vision to fly you there. Such a hypothetical journey would take five of your human years, and once we've passed into Dark Space, there would be no way to resupply or avoid hostile Alkasen vessels.

Don't worry about the how. I can find a way there.

I don't see how that's possible, but for the sake of entertaining hypotheticals, what did you have in mind?

A portal. A very strong one. Using the vision as an anchor point.

There is no mage or sorcerer in the entire Starsea Empire capable of such a feat. And assuming there were, using a vision as an anchor point has never been done successfully, at least to my knowledge.

I've done it before.

That is remarkable, if true! If you can really do this, and assuming you have the requisite magical strength, then yes, creating a portal to this location might be possible. But I do not advise an action that places you in such danger.

I have to make a way. I know it's possible. If I don't, I can't find The Time Weaver and get answers.

The Time Weaver. I'm sorry, but I do not know this entity.

You just have to trust me. Can you take us into space, at least? Somewhere still in this star system, but far away from this planet.

Of course. As soon as everyone is seated, we can be off.

"Strap yourselves in," Lucian said, seating himself.

"About time!" Serah said.

The others found spots around him. There was seating for up to twelve people. The seats automatically adjusted to match each occupant.

I am ready when you are, Lucian, Garuda said.

Lucian nodded. *Let's go.*

Lucian held his breath as the vessel suddenly moved, propelling itself into the sky. It was so fast that Lucian could scarcely believe it. He hardly felt the inertia as the ship soundlessly shot up and away, the world outside blending into a blur of colors as they left the atmosphere. If any ship had attempted this speed in his own time, the g-forces would have instantly killed the ship's crew. It was a testament to the power of the First Starsea Empire's sorcerers.

Within half a minute, they were high above the planet's surface. Before them were a multitude of space stations, crafted in the likeness of castles, far larger than any space installation Lucian had ever witnessed. Hundreds, perhaps thousands of ships, swarmed in a precise flow. It was like a vision of a long-distant future, except that they were ten million years in the past.

Get us away from here, Lucian said. *Far away.*

Acknowledged, the ship said. *Any location you prefer?*

Somewhere we are not likely to be followed.

I know just the place. A little-frequented area of this system far from any space lanes.

Take us there.

At once, Lucian.

Garuda veered course and sped away from the planet below them, into deep space.

34

THE SILENCE of space was familiar, a soothing stillness wrapping around the ship. Lucian directed Garuda away from the gleaming planet of Samudraya. The view was mesmerizing, the world's vibrant greens and blues sparkling against the backdrop of the starry cosmos. The planet receded from the viewscreen with shocking speed before Lucian Psionically changed the display to show the stars ahead of them.

"So, what's the plan?" Serah asked.

Lucian faced them all. "The Time Weaver said the Ancient One could detect the message he sent to me and use that message to find him. He would not have risked that unless he thought I could get to him faster than the Ancient One."

"That would mean a portal," Emma said. "Only how are you supposed to travel to him if you've never been there before?"

"There are two times I've warped to somewhere I haven't been before," Lucian said. "The first was Hephaestus, when I used the vision of the volcano to warp everyone directly there. Then I did it again to reach the Orb of Dynamism. It would be the same with this vision."

Silence fell over the crew. Lucian had never attempted anything as distant as the Samikan homeworld, which was at least five years away by conventional travel methods.

"But that's . . ." Serah started, her voice trailing off.

"Impossible?" Lucian smiled grimly. "Yes, probably. But I have to believe it's possible. Otherwise, the future we came from would have never existed, right?"

"What happens if this fails?" Khairu asked.

Lucian knew a portal of this distance meant he would have to stream a truly insane amount of ether. He wasn't sure how much, exactly, but if he lost control, he would almost certainly die, along with everyone on this ship.

"We won't fail."

"So, that's it then?" Serah asked. "We're doing this?"

Lucian nodded. "I *know* it's possible. We can't risk losing the Time Weaver to The Ancient One. Presumably, he has the same ability I do, and not only that. He also has the benefit of the Orbs. We're racing against him."

"Then we should get started immediately," Khairu said.

Everyone turned to Themba, who had so far been silent. He regarded Lucian with his red eyes.

"You must trust in yourself and your purpose, Chosen," the Ancient said. "You have come far in your abilities. Remember, it isn't about the Orbs. It's your truth that guides your magic. So, remember why you fight. You must endure whatever assault your mind will undergo. If you can do that, then you can bear the impossible."

Lucian absorbed these words, knowing they were true.

"We should get started," Lucian said. "I don't know how long this'll take. I'll need some space to create the stream."

"There's a meditation chamber toward the stern of the ship," Themba said.

Lucian nodded. "I'll go there, then."

Serah took his hand. "You're going to need help. Even if I can't help with the magic, I can at least be there. I mean, if I'm not in the way."

From the steady resolve in her blue eyes, Lucian could see she wasn't going to be dissuaded. And it would be good to have her support. He nodded.

Just as they were about to leave, alarms blared on the bridge. On the viewscreen, dozens of ships materialized from nowhere.

Garuda's voice entered Lucian's mind. *The Starsea Fleet! What could they want?*

Before Lucian could respond, a massive ship materialized before them, far bigger than anything he had ever seen. Such was its scale that it dwarfed even Sol Citadel, the largest space construction ever devised by humanity. It had to stretch for kilometers, its gargantuan form eclipsing the smaller Starsea vessels surrounding it. The ship's hull was a gleaming fortress, shining white against the dark backdrop of space.

Yet, for its monstrous size, the ship glided toward them with speed and grace, its beautiful form radiating menace.

Lucian didn't have to ask who was on that ship.

That's the Buktan, Garuda said, fear palpable in his voice. *The flagship of the Immortal himself.*

"The Immortal's on that ship," Lucian said, explaining Garuda's revelation to the others.

The grand ship of the Starsea fleet loomed before them, advancing quickly.

There was no time to engage, no time to fight. Fighting would have been impossible. A ship of that size had hundreds, if not thousands, of mages and sorcerers on board.

The portal was their only chance.

There was no time to get to the meditation chamber. Lucian reached for his Focus, not allowing himself to doubt or worry about the monumental task ahead.

Serah stood by his side, her presence a comforting anchor. He took a deep breath and closed his eyes, reaching for the Ether as he had countless times before.

But this time, it was different. This time, the stakes were much higher.

And yet, he knew he must do it. That he *had* to have done this already if their time wasn't a lie. That knowledge would have to be enough to bridge the gap.

Already, the power of the Manifold pulsed through his Focus, an intense current of energy setting every nerve in his body afire. He centered himself, homing in on the pulsating energy that powered the Ether itself.

His awareness expanded outward, drawing more and more ether into his Focus. He diverted a small amount to create a warping bubble around Garuda, enabling it to speed away from the Immortal's flagship. He held the aura for only a few seconds, enough to ensure their survival for as long as it took to finish the portal.

He recalled his vision of the Castle of Creation perfectly in his mind, allowing the ether to work according to its will. He was the Chosen, and the Chosen *knew* the way. Every second that passed, the vision became more real.

The portal began forming, keeping pace just in front of the ship. It flickered, mirroring the intensity of his concentration. It was beautiful and terrifying all at once, a doorway to the unknown that demanded even more ether. Ether that seemed to split Lucian at the seams.

And yet, as the portal grew, so did the toll it took. Each moment was agony, as if he were being boiled alive. Such was the pain that he could hardly even scream. His strength was ebbing, each breath a thousand stabbings of a scalding knife. The taste of copper filled his mouth.

The pain grew. And grew.

But he couldn't afford to stop. The Immortal was on their heels, the menacing bulk of the *Buktan* a terrifying reminder of the threat they faced. Already, in the Ether, he sensed the Immortal hot on his tail, homing in on the massive amount of magic Lucian was streaming.

Lucian's mind was divorced from his body, existing purely in the Light Realm. And there he remained, a conduit of an unfathomable amount of ether.

But within the pain, a new sensation emerged. At first, it was like a distant whisper, a gentle balm against the searing agony consuming him. As the fiery pain continued, this softness grew more pronounced, anchoring him back to the reality he had nearly forgotten.

It was a moment before he recognized it for what it was: the familiar touch of Serah's hand.

It steadied him, made him forget the pain, at least for a moment. He opened his eyes to find that he was no longer in the Ether. She was standing before him, her blue eyes filled with resolve. Her presence was a promise that she would be there every step of the way. No matter his pain or suffering. No matter what happened.

With a last surge of energy, Lucian pushed through, the ether within him flaring up to meet the challenge.

In a flash, the portal opened up, for the first time taking full shape and bridging a gap at least ten thousand light-years across. The ship slipped through, and his body lurched, threatening to give in to overwhelming fatigue.

The others gathered around him, holding him steady.

As much as Lucian wanted to sleep, to abandon his consciousness, he knew he had to stay awake, at least for now. Through his blurred vision, a gray world was forming below them.

"The portal's not closing," Emma said.

Lucian looked, and sure enough, the portal was indeed holding. He reached out to close it, but such was his exhaustion that he couldn't manage it.

"Impossible," he said. "I stopped streaming already. It shouldn't be holding anymore."

He watched in disbelief as the gateway refused to close, held in place by a force he couldn't fathom.

At last, the reason came to him.

"The Ancient One," Lucian said, dread settling in his heart. *He* was holding the portal open, and soon, he would pass through it.

"There's no time to worry about that now," Themba said, turning to face the planet before them.

Lucian reached out for Garuda. *Take us to the Time Weaver. The source of the vision.*

Of course.

The ship shot forward, the world before them approaching with surprising speed. As they descended toward the planet, Lucian could only hope they had enough time.

35

GARUDA TOOK them directly to the location of Lucian's vision. There was no need to search. The ship simply headed toward the dead planet's surface, able to scan the entire planet to find the topography that matched Lucian's dream.

As Garuda descended, the thin atmosphere was hardly enough to slow the ship down. There was nothing to bar their view of the harsh terrain below. The warm, watery world of two thousand years past was completely absent. The only evidence of any ocean was thick sheets of ice, frozen in perpetual, near-airless winter under a starlit sky.

Stretching as far as the eye could see was a desolate landscape of monotonous gray, broken by smooth-sloped mountains that might have once been island chains. Frozen craters dotted the icy terrain, while ridges and sharp rocks jutted up from the surface, silent sentinels presiding over the planet's desolation. Distant starlight glinted off the surface, casting a ghostly aura across the landscape.

They zoomed across the surface, rising above a mountain

chain to find the object of their search. The Castle of Creation, the home of the Immortal himself.

The massive fortress loomed on a high plateau across a long, broken bridge. The grand palace, with its proud towers and gentle arches, must have once glittered resplendently in the warm air of Airaruma's gentle seas. Now, those towers slumped in despair, most of them broken. The tall, beautiful spires, their tops still gleaming with gold, were encased in a thick layer of ice. The walls had long since lost their luster, their surfaces a jagged patchwork of crumbling stone and encroaching ice. Covering the entire construction was a sheer, bluish aura, what Lucian knew to be a Binding barrier. It had likely been placed by the Time Weaver to create a breathable atmosphere within.

The castle was as haunting as it had appeared in Lucian's dreams. Perhaps even more so. He couldn't believe it had stood here in silence for almost two millennia.

This was where the Lord of Seas had once ruled the Samikan race. It was all here, the past rising before them like a phantom.

And it was here that the Time Weaver was waiting for them, with his prophecy and his weapon, and the Ancient One not far behind.

Put us down just outside the bridge, Lucian said to the ship.

Of course, Garuda said. *I'm taking you there now.*

Lucian turned to the others. "Stay close. I'll hold the air in around us."

Themba glowed with orange light, signifying he was streaming Atomicism. "I detect a breathable atmosphere within the castle itself. As long as we get inside, we should be safe."

The ship settled in front of the bridge. As soon as they touched down completely, they rushed to the place they had entered.

But before they headed out onto the desolate surface, Lucian directed his Focus toward Garuda. *Garuda, once we're outside, there's no reason for you to stay. Head back to the portal before it closes.*

I'm sorry, but I can't simply leave you here. It is my charge to protect you.

There's nothing you can do to protect us. We won't be coming back. If you leave now, you'll at least escape before the portal closes.

Garuda seemed to ponder this. At least, Lucian supposed that was what he was doing from his drawn silence. It seemed the sentient ship was caught between his instinct to protect his passengers and that of his own self-preservation.

We'll be fine here, Garuda. We have a way back. We can just create another portal, and this conversation with the Time Weaver might take a long time.

At last, the ship responded. *Considering what you've said, it would be best if I returned to Angkasa's castle. But I must do so quickly if I'm to escape the Buktan.*

No worries. We're about to get off the ship. Thank you, Garuda.

It was my pleasure, Lucian. Best of luck with your mission!

The ship was oddly upbeat for Lucian's taste. He supposed the quirk must have been built into Garuda's personality.

Lucian created a magical shield. As soon as it was set, the boarding glyph appeared, and the side of the hull opened to the airless world outside. No air escaped the ship; a Binding barrier immediately powered on to prevent it.

As they stepped onto the glyph, it lowered them onto the planet's icy surface, allowing them to pass through the barrier.

Lucian was still exhausted from the portal jump, but the prospect of being near the end, and perhaps even returning to his own time, gave him the strength to go on.

And truth be told, he sought answers. Answers only the Time Weaver held.

Garuda quickly rose from the ice, shooting toward space. Such was its speed that it only took it ten seconds to get lost in the darkness of space above.

They picked their way carefully across the bridge because of its iciness, and quickly reached the gap in the middle, a good ten meters across.

"We must all run and jump together," Themba said. "I'll use Gravitonics to give us a boost."

"Let's do this," Khairu said.

They lined up, and on Themba's signal, they charged and leaped. Lucian felt himself lifted into the air. He kept his shield strong so that no one was exposed to the hostile environment on the other side.

They came down easily, continuing the rest of the way to wide, open gates, the start of the Binding barrier.

"He'll let us in," Lucian said.

The five of them passed through without incident. Lucian let go of his shield as he took in their surroundings.

High, vaulted ceilings stretched overhead, from which hung decrepit, colorless banners billowing faintly in the cold drafts circulating the cavernous hall. They stood on a mosaic floor, where carefully arranged tiles depicted flowing rivers. In fact, Lucian noticed channels where water had once streamed, but now they were dry and filled with dust. Marble sculptures of the Samikan loomed from pedestals, their aquatic bodies evoking the fluid motion of leaping through what had once been cascading waterfalls falling from upper floors. He got the sense that these had been famous figures in the Samikan's history, but now their names and deeds had been long forgotten.

Lucian and the others took it all in. Their footsteps reverberated through the grand hall, stirring dust from the ornate stonework. Lucian could almost imagine the grandeur of the past, and such was its scale that it would have far exceeded the Water Palace of King Angkasa. Balconies that must have once spilled over with greenery and blooming flowers were now bereft of life.

Emma's voice snapped Lucian from his reverie. "Look!"

On a high balcony above them stood a shadowy figure, his

form obscured by darkness. He watched them, as still as the surrounding statues.

Before Lucian could do or say anything, the figure simply turned and walked away, until the railing of the balcony above hid him from view.

"Hey, he's getting away!" Serah said.

"No," Lucian said. "He's leading us somewhere."

They went to the nearest staircase, with curves reminiscent of ocean waves. They ran up, heading for the landing above where they'd seen the figure. A massive hall stretched before them, seeming to go on forever.

The figure stood at the end, before a set of stone doors that appeared small in the distance, slightly ajar. A glorious light shone from beyond those doors, silhouetting the figure.

They ran until they stood just a few steps before him. Lucian didn't let down his guard, even if he was sure the figure was the Time Weaver himself.

They stopped in their tracks when the being spoke.

"Hold, travelers! Ye have come close enough. Tread no further step."

The voice was sonorous and echoing, with deep and resonant tones. Just as in Lucian's vision, the Time Weaver spoke in an archaic variant of the Ancient language, though up close, Lucian could see the Time Weaver was human, a man of middle-age with unassuming features, brown hair, and gray temples. His eyes shone with a curious golden light.

"You're human," Lucian said, unable to hide his surprise.

"Nay, Chosen. I have merely taken this guise. I can assume any form I desire."

Lucian wondered how that was possible, but he assumed it had something to do with magic itself. "Well, you have to be the Time Weaver."

"Yea, that is so."

"We don't have much time. At any moment, the Ancient One could—"

The Time Weaver held up a hand. "Fret not over him. There is ample time for discourse, though it seemeth not so. This castle is shielded by my concealment magic; we shall remain hidden for a time."

Lucian supposed he must have meant a Radiant shield. "Why have you called us here, Time Weaver? My friend died to get us this far. If we came all this way just to find out there's nothing we can do to stop the Ancient One—"

"—Art thou not the Chosen of the Manifold? Mighty in magic thou might be, but lacking the Power of Creation, thy magic shall avail thee naught against the Ancient One. I've called thee hither for a singular purpose. Thou lackest the weapon to defeat the Ancient One for all eternity. 'Tis I alone, the Emissary of Time, who can grant it unto thee."

"What weapon? I lost Lightspear, all because I was chasing *you*. You're telling me I lost the weapon that can kill the Ancient One, just so I can get it again? Tell me how that makes sense!"

Lucian was getting angry. Jagar had died because of this, and it felt like the Time Weaver was playing games.

"Thou knowest little of that weapon, Chosen. A mighty weapon of profound power, but it was near the twilight of its existence. It had journeyed long ere thy hand ever made contact. But its journey is also a paradox, as thou shalt soon see. Hast thou never pondered from whence it came? Lightspear hath not only traversed time but alternate realities in their entirety. How can thy mind grasp it?"

"Then tell me, since apparently, I know so little. Where did it come from? How did it get destroyed? I thought it was invincible."

"Whence came this conceit? Lightspear is not the ultimate answer. It is the Power of Creation itself. But against the Power of Shadow, even it might wane. The sorcery of the Ancient One is of a fatal kind, unlike any thou hast encountered. Verily, Creation is one of the three Greater Aspects, which only the most potent of sorcerers can command."

"What do you mean, three Greater Aspects?"

"Seven Minor Aspects, Three Major. One thou already knowest as the power of space and time. Only the most mighty of sorcerers may wield it. Sorcerers like thee, and me." The Time Weaver nodded at Themba, and also at Emma. "Them as well. But there be twain more, the Aspects of Creation and Shadows."

Lucian couldn't hide his shock. Two *more* Aspects? That would make for *ten*. If he had known of them before, then in what context had he come across them?

Immediately, the Shadow Magic of the Ancient One came to mind. He had long suspected it to be a new Aspect. Indeed, it explained why the Ancient One seemed to have abilities outside of all the traditional Aspects. The Minor Aspects, as the Time Weaver had called them. That shield on Sigil had also been that type of magic, reanimating the bodies of the dead. This *had* to be what the Time Weaver was calling the Aspect of Shadows. Nothing else fit the description.

The Aspect of Creation, however. What could *that* be?

But then he remembered. The Bond of Creation, which connected all the *Alkasen*. Previously, he had believed the Bond to be advanced Psionic Magic. But something else was going on because the answer was in the name itself.

And Lightspear, too, would have been formed from this kind of magic, since it was the only thing that could counterbalance Shadow Magic.

"I perceive thy contemplation," the Time Weaver said, "but verily, all I speak is truth. The Three Greater Aspects stand apart. Their sorcery is not for the common touch, but to be wielded by the paramount champions of Light and Shadow. Only the mightiest of sorcerers can channel their vast power."

"So, to defeat the Ancient One, I need to use this new magic? How do I access it?"

"It is that which I shall unveil unto thee. I was sent hither by the Ascendant Beings. Thou art the Chosen of the Manifold, the sole sorcerer through countless ages strong enough to withstand the Ascendants' ancient foe. They have bided, Chosen, a vast span of ten million years to find thee. Thou art the only beacon of hope in restoring the Orbs to the Heart of Creation. Thou must answer thy calling."

"You're *Alkasen*," Lucian said. "You have to be, right? You said they sent you."

"Aye. I was forged by the Ascendant Beings as an Emissary to journey through the Shadow Realm. It is . . . a daunting charge, yet the Orbs must be retrieved, come what may."

"Are you in charge of the *Alkasen*?"

"Nay, not so. I am but a herald, an Emissary of their making. Yet, one gifted to traverse both time and space. 'Tis for this they named me the Time Weaver. In the arts of temporal magic, none can match my prowess."

"Do you know another Emissary? Someone by the name of Silumko?"

"I am aware of him. We Emissaries each bear distinct charges laid upon us by our patrons. His path and mine have not intertwined; he stands as the Marshal of War, whilst I operate more from the shadows. That is all thou needest know."

"What is the point of all this?" Serah asked, cutting in. "We really need to cut to the chase here. I know you said your magic can hide us from the Ancient One, but that can't last forever."

The Time Weaver looked at her, as if sizing her up, before returning his eyes to Lucian. "Thou hast staunch friends, Chosen. 'Tis good thou hast allies that will not let thee fight solitary. But as thy friend speaketh, I shall cut to the quick."

"I have one more question," Lucian said. "How did you create that time gate on Sigil?"

"That is naught to me. I have journeyed through time and reality itself. There is no sorcerer in thy Realm of Shadow that can match my power. But back to the question at hand. There is much I must tell thee about thine enemy. Information that will aid thee in comprehending his origins, and how thou can wage battle against him."

"I'm listening."

Lucian had the feeling he was in for quite the speech.

36

THE TIME WEAVER was silent for a long moment, seeming to gather his thoughts.

"The Ancient One, as his name suggests, originates from a time long before this one. He was once an Ascendant, the mightiest of them all. In the Light Realm, they do not utter his ancient name; they instead call him the Fallen. For he was not content to be the strongest; he coveted rulership of the Light Realm as well. To attain this ambition, the Fallen devised a new Aspect of Magic, for naught in the Light Realm had the power to slay an Ascendant.

"Thus was Shadow Magic brought forth. Yet this magic bore a price; if he were to lose his war, he would be reduced to naught but a shadow. He deemed the risk worth it. Rallying the most cunning of Ascendants to his cause, he waged war against those who stayed true to the Light. Indeed, from this war sprang forth the Shadow Realm itself, where thou and thy friends find yourselves. The Fallen and his followers, though few, nearly claimed dominion over the Light Realm entirely. Against the Fallen's Shadow Magic, they could do naught but strive in vain.

"However, in secret, the Ascendant Enkius, the war leader of the Light, known for his resourcefulness and intellect, took a leaf from the Fallen's tome. With the help of his allies, he forged a new Aspect to counter the Shadow. But he did not use himself as the focus of this magic. Understanding it was dangerous to do so, he instead concentrated its power on a companion Orb, the Orb of Creation. He knew that one day, others might need to share in its power to pursue and destroy the Ancient One, wherever he might flee. In the end, the Ancient One and his armies were overcome, and he and his followers of darkness were caught unawares by this new magic. Thus was the Fallen cast from the Light Realm, bound by a decree to never re-enter. They banished him out through a Gate forged by the power of Creation itself, into the Shadow Realm birthed by his treachery. This, the Ascendants of the Light reckoned, would be punishment enough."

"A gate?" Lucian asked. "Was it the First Gate?"

"Yea, verily the same. Yet unknown to the Ascendants of Light, that very Gate could not be sealed anew, not even by the Ascendant Enkius himself. It demanded not only the Aspect of Creation but also that of Shadow, and all the other Aspects combined. The Ascendants of Light could not claim the Aspect of Shadow without pledging allegiance to the Ancient One. This dealt a heavy hand to the Realm of Light. For ether—the very essence of the Light Realm—flowed unceasingly through the First Gate, threatening the very lifeblood of the Light Realm.

"'Twas then that Enkius sought the wisdom of the Foresayer Anlilta, the greatest of the Ascendants at delving the Manifold. After many days, she pronounced the Prophecy of the Chosen. Voicing the intent of the Manifold, she declared that a Being of Shadow, birthed by the Ancient One's deeds, would in due course be his downfall. This *Chosen of the Manifold* would stand as the savior of the Light Realm, and in doing so, rescue all realities by sealing the First Gate. This very Chosen would manifest his fate by wielding the Jewels of Starsea."

Lucian listened to all this, stunned by the revelation. For the first time, he'd learned the names of actual Ascendants of the Light Realm. They were no longer ephemeral, but players on a cosmic field which he could scarcely imagine.

The Time Weaver continued. "Enkius did mock Anlilta's words, for even as they were uttered, the Jewels lay secure within the Heart of Creation. The sayings of Anlilta, laden with paradox, were received with mistrust, not only by Enkius, but by all other Ascendants. How could a Being of Shadow come to possess the Holy Orbs? For no Being of Shadow could walk the Realm of Light without meeting swift doom."

"But that happened," Lucian said. "The Immortal—or I guess, the Lord of Seas—entered the First Gate. And he got the Orbs."

"Verily, 'tis so," the Time Weaver said. "But in due time, we shall delve deeper. Enkius, restless, would not await this improbable prophecy's fulfillment. He sought to gather the strength of the Light to chase the Ancient One into the Shadow Realm. There was but a single path to do so: The Ascendants, sworn foes of the Ancient One, must transform into *Alkasen*, Beings of Shadow themselves. Fettered with a brand of Creation Magic, they might step into the Shadow Realm. Yet such was the impurity of this realm that hopes of returning to the Light Realm were forsaken. The mightiest among these became the Emissaries. They adopted the form and tongue of the Shadow Beings, those bestowed with the light of sentience, to work the Ascendants' will within the Shadow Realm. These Emissaries became the fount of the Bond of Creation, that magic that ties the Shadow Beings unto them. All this, for the singular aim of hunting the Ancient One."

"Is that your fate, too? You're one of these Emissaries, like Silumko."

"Indeed, 'tis true. Yet such is the gravity of mine charge that I would gladly yield my life to see its end achieved."

"What about the Lord of Seas? How did he become the Immortal and survive the Light Realm?"

"The opening of the First Gate went not unseen by the Samikan folk, who dwelt upon this very world. That the Gate manifested so nigh unto this world could be naught but the very intent of the Manifold. Both brave and foolhardy, they journeyed to explore the Gate, led by the Lord of Seas himself. Directly into the maw of the First Gate he ventured, little reckoning the aftermath his choice would bring. Now, the Ancient One did lie in ambush for him. 'Tis at this moment, as the Lord of Seas traversed from Shadow into Light, that the Ancient One possessed him. And thus, the Ancient One found himself within the Light Realm from which he was banished."

"Didn't anyone see him enter?" Lucian asked.

"Nay, he passed unmarked. The Lord of Seas, though ensnared by the Ancient One's Shadow, seemed frail and bereft of magic. Thus, he went unnoticed. Led by the Ancient One's design, the Lord of Seas made his way to the Temple of Light, that veils the Heart of Creation, where the Eight Orbs shone in glory. And there they lay, unguarded, for the Ascendants were distracted by the turmoil at the Gate. Swiftly, he claimed them, and the Ancient One drove his puppet to the portal, clashing with the Ascendants now awakened to the threat. But the Orb of Creation stayed out of the Ancient One's reach, still in Enkius' hold, who harbored hope to heal the rift of the First Gate with its sole might."

That was how it all started, then. The Ancient One was not created out of thin air; he had come from the Light Realm itself, answering a question Lucian long had. It also explained the Ancient One's nature. He took the form of a shadow, and it was his curse to possess others, but to have no form of his own. And *he* was the source of Shadow Magic. No one else could use it unless they swore fealty to him. That had been the case with Xara, Sharo, and Vera.

There was only one way to destroy him—one way that Lucian knew how, anyway.

"I don't understand how I can hope to defeat him," Lucian said. "I don't have Lightspear anymore. That's the only weapon that can kill the Ancient One. I destroyed one of his avatars, but I chased the second one—what I hope to be the last one—into the past. And that road has led me here. I need this Aspect of Creation to finish my mission. If you're telling me I came all this way to find another rotting Orb . . ."

The Time Weaver gave a deep resonant laugh. "Fret not, Chosen. Thou needest not seek it out. Lo, I have brought it with me! Verily, it was my assigned duty to meet with thee herein and deliver it. The Ascendants entrusted unto me its safekeeping. This castle hath served as the utmost sanctuary for it among all the Worlds. Alas, that sanctuary hath been compromised this day."

"Because the Ancient One has followed us here," Lucian said.

"Yea, and the grand fleet of Starsea. But take heart, for at this very moment, a battle such as the stars have never witnessed rages above our heads. The full might of Starsea against the heralds of the Light Realm, the *Alkasen*, led by none other than the Emissary Silumko, of whom you spoke formerly. Thou mayest be wondering why I was confident that we had time to converse. I knew it would require time for the Ancient One to assemble his armadas to confront the *Alkasen* above us. The end of this clash is foreordained, yet we must still play our parts."

"What's going to happen with the battle?" Serah asked.

"The battle encompaseth millions of ships and billions of lives," the Time Weaver said. "And yet, the true battle lieth within this castle. But, Chosen, in thy current state, thou cannot overcome the Ancient One. The time is nigh. I shall confer upon thee the Orb of Creation, the very essence thou requirest to vanquish the Ancient One. Not solely in this present time, but in thine own time."

"How do I use the Orb of Creation?" Lucian asked. "What about Lightspear?"

"Is it not said that the Chosen will know the way? Who thinkest thou uttered these words, which came to the dreams of the greatest prophets born from the stars and creation?"

Lucian was about to say that the Time Weaver had been the source of these words. But then he remembered what the Time Weaver had said about the Ascendant Anlilta, this "Foresayer" of the Light Realm. She had to have been the source of these words, the very one to have predicted Lucian's arrival.

"She will be proven right in the end," Lucian said.

"Verily, thy words ring true," the Time Weaver said. "For none can withstand the will of the Manifold. So, Chosen. How wilt thou proceed?"

Just then, the answer came to Lucian. He took Jagar's spear and extended it, examining it from top to bottom.

"You asked me where Lightspear came from . . ." Lucian said.

But before he could finish his thought, the castle shook mightily, throwing Lucian from his feet, along with his companions. Dust rained from the ceiling far above.

The Time Weaver remained standing, seemingly unaffected by the reverberation.

Lucian waited for the Emissary to give him the weapon he sought. But instead, the Time Weaver gestured toward the room behind him.

"Remember," the Time Weaver said. "The Chosen will know the way. Beyond yon doors, thy prize awaits thee. Go, and take it. And fulfill thy destiny."

Lucian nodded, and walked past the Time Weaver, along with the others, and into the light-filled room beyond.

37

LUCIAN ENTERED the chamber beyond and was immediately struck by an Orb that thrummed with a deep, golden light. It cast a powerful aura, all but blinding despite the vast space. It stood on a pedestal, just like the other Orbs Lucian had found. Being face to face with it, Lucian could hardly believe it was real.

There was a whole other Orb. A whole other Aspect. He was having difficulty wrapping his mind around it.

"You okay?" Serah asked, touching his arm.

The entire chamber rumbled with another impact from the battle above.

He forced a nod. "Yeah. I should probably get moving, huh?"

Lucian approached the Golden Orb, motioning the others to fall in around him. Once he was within reach, nothing impeded his grasp. He took it, and the Orb shone in his hand like a miniature sun, its magic surging into his arms with unbridled power. As its warmth enveloped him, Lucian felt an intoxicating rush of emotions—memories of long-forgotten summers, the gentle caress of a breeze, the smile on Serah's face. It was as if he were connected to every living being that had ever existed. The sheer vastness of this sensation threatened to engulf him, but Lucian held firm, anchoring himself to the present with sheer force of will.

He turned for the door, returning to where they had left the Time Weaver. However, there was no sign of the *Alkasen* Emissary. It was as if he had completely vanished.

Instead, he was greeted with a new sight. That of Samikan sorcerers, dozens of them, all charging forward with shockspears alight. All were streaming magic, but they were moving so slowly. Lucian couldn't tell if they were indeed moving slowly, or if his perception of them was sharpened from his absorption of the Orb.

He was still surrounded by the Orb of Creation's aura of power. With a start, he realized he was streaming, but he wasn't in control of the flow. Somehow, the Orb was fighting *for* him, and Lucian was merely being guided.

And right now, it was clear what the Orb of Creation wanted. These attackers had to die.

A surge of golden magic burst forth, advancing down the great space toward every enemy charging toward them. The wave spread in all directions, and Lucian perceived dozens, and then hundreds, and thousands, of soldiers and ships, all falling to the Orb's deadly magic. Lucian's connection to the Orb of Creation was not a simple wielding of power; it was a communion, a merging of intent and desire. It wasn't a mere stream; it was pure destruction that resonated with the fabric of existence, bending reality itself to his will. The shockwave of golden energy swept through the chamber, and Lucian could feel the lives it touched, sense the panic and confusion in his enemies, perceive the disintegration of everything that wished him and his friends harm. Both awe and terror gripped him at the power he was unleashing.

But one adversary stood resolute, not yielding to the golden tide. He loomed above them all, resplendent in shining white armor, an Ethereal Crown levitating above his head, showcasing the Seven Minor Orbs surrounding an Orb of pure darkness, what Lucian knew to be the Orb of Space-Time. Each of those artifacts thrummed with power, streaming multicolored magic into the dark shield surrounding the Immortal.

But such was the Orb of Creation's power that could not be denied. It pushed against the shield, compressing it ever smaller until it was barely enough to surround the Ancient One.

This is how he dies, Lucian thought. *This is the moment he loses the Orbs.*

And then, as if time had stood still for a breathless moment, Lucian felt the Orb of Creation's energy rise, like a storm preparing to unleash its fury. The sensation was overwhelming: it was a symphony of life, creation, and pure magic. It was warmth, like the sun's rays upon his face.

The Immortal's shield cracked, fractures appearing at its edges as dark tendrils of ether oozed out. He roared in defiance. The very foundation of the chamber trembled under the immense clash of Light and Shadow.

Then, with an explosive force that shook the very fabric of the castle, the shield shattered. The golden brilliance of Creation Magic overwhelmed the Immortal's defenses.

But just before the moment of his demise, the Immortal streamed a great portal of darkness. It happened in an instant.

When the golden wave of magic petered out, there was an emptiness where he once stood.

If Arian's prophecy was true, Lucian knew that the Ancient One had somehow created a time gate through which he had sent the Seven Orbs.

But in accordance with Arian's prophecy, one thing remained; an Orb of midnight black, left where the First Immortal of Starsea once stood. Silence reigned across the cold halls of the castle. Not a soul remained that was hostile to them. Only the empty halls of the palace.

The golden magic of the Orb of Creation had simply . . . *erased* . . . everything that had been loyal to the Ancient One.

"What . . ." Emma began. "What in the Worlds did you just do?"

"Everything's gone," Khairu said, her face ashen.

Even Themba was looking at Lucian with fear, and perhaps even respect, his red eyes inscrutable.

Similarly, Lucian could feel nothing but shock at what had just happened. How could a single Orb be powerful enough to stand up not only to the Ancient One and his Shadow Magic, but to every other Orb in existence? Was the Orb of Creation simply that powerful?

At that very moment, the figure of the Time Weaver appeared near the black Orb that had been left behind. He kneeled and picked up the priceless treasure and made his way across the hall toward them. Unlike everything else, the Time Weaver had survived the golden wave. As an *Alkasen*, perhaps the magic knew to ignore him.

The Time Weaver regarded him, still clutching the black Orb in his hands. "And so endeth an age, the time of Old Starsea. In but a handful of centuries, the empire shall crumble from within and face the onslaught of the *Alkasen*. By thy deeds, Chosen, the cycle is nearly full. A hundred thousand years hence, all traces of Starsea's reign shall vanish from the galaxy's face. Only the Gates shall remain, bearing testimony to the Samikan, the Builders. With them, the Bonded Samikan, the Preserved, and the Devoted shall yield to Silumko's reign. Once they've bested Starsea, they shall withdraw and slumber, till the Orbs stir once again and the Starsea Cycle begins anew. Thus, there is little more for thee to do in this time. The hour is upon thee to leave, taking with thee the Orb of Space-Time and the Orb of Creation. As the Chosen, both are thine by right, by precept of the Foresayer Anlilta, Speaker of the Manifold. The might of the Orb of Space-Time shall prove vital in thine impending ordeal. Though the Ancient One is defeated in this era, thou art keenly aware he is fated to return."

"What was that magic I did?" Lucian said. "How was it so powerful?"

"The might of the Orb of Creation is most potent, chiefly near the First Gate and in this age when magic is new. In thine own time, the force of magic is much diminished, spread thin as a vast ocean over boundless terrain. But in this epoch, it hath scarce had time to diffuse and weaken. Yet, wherever thou art in the annals of time or vastness of space, thy wishes shape the Orb of Creation's intent. Verily, the Immortal had little hope against such force. Yet, things shall change when thou leavest this realm and journeyest to a distant future where magic hath waned, and thou art far from the First Gate. In such a state, it may falter. Thus, thou must craft a new armament, one not bound to the closeness of the First Gate."

"Lightspear," Lucian said, in realization.

"Aye. The time has come, Chosen. The crafting of Lightspear is no trivial feat. It shall demand not only an abundance of ether streamed from the Orb of Creation, but also an extensive passage of time. Yet fear not, for time shall be in abundance for thee. By fate's design, to forge this mighty weapon, thou shalt need to slumber for many epochs. Ten million of thy years shall suffice for this endeavor."

"Ten million *years*?" Lucian said, gasping. "All for one weapon?"

"Indeed, Chosen. The weapon thou shalt inherit shall surpass the one departed from thy grasp. The former Lightspear had nearly spent its power, worn by a long and arduous journey before it found its way to thee. But lo, a new chapter unfolds, and its journey begins afresh."

"How can we survive ten million years?"

"Through the combined might of thy twain Orbs, thou and

thy companions may dwell in a state of stasis whilst crafting thy weapon. As has ever been spoken—"

"—The Chosen will know the way," Lucian finished. He frowned for a moment, something just occurring to him. "The whole reason we came to the past in the first place was to defeat the Ancient One. But if creating Lightspear takes ten million years, that means we would come back out in the alternate reality we just came from. Does that mean that once I defeat the Ancient One ten million years from now, I'll have to create a time gate back to the past to defeat the Ancient One again? And does that mean I'm going to lose the Orbs again?"

"'Tis a curious road thou treadest. But 'tis a road known only to thee. And as for the Orbs' departure, the magic of the Orb of Creation reigns supreme; the Orbs shall not lightly slip from thine hold, even as you travel through time. How such power compares to the Fallen's Shadow Magic is yet to be witnessed. Perchance it'll be a duel to determine who gains dominion over the Orbs. With time, knowledge shall dawn upon thee. Now, the hour is nigh for thee to press on in thy quest. But proceeding without this would be folly."

At that moment, the Time Weaver approached, proffering the Orb of Space-Time. Lucian knew that this was his destiny, his way out. So close to the First Gate, he would have access to the boundless magic necessary not only to travel through time, but while doing so, to create Lightspear.

As Lucian clasped the Orb and absorbed it, he was consumed by a swirling vortex of memories and visions. Scenes from his life merged with glimpses of unknown futures as timelines intertwined and danced before his eyes. He saw not only his own memories, but those of the Orb itself. The sensation was overwhelming, so much so that he could not make sense of it. It was like plunging into a dark ocean and resurfacing into a brilliant, starlit sky all at once. Waves of nostalgia hit him, reminding him of the time when this very power was once an intrinsic part of him. Every fiber of his being pulsed with newfound energy, along with a clarity he hadn't felt in ages. The cold emptiness that had lived in him since losing the Orb receded, replaced by warmth and completeness.

With the Orb assimilated into his Focus, it was like a puzzle that had finally found its missing piece. Yet, along with the euphoria, a myriad of questions clamored for attention.

"What about you?" Lucian asked. "Where are you going after this?"

The Time Weaver gave a knowing grin. "I traverse time not in a straight line, not to nor fro, nor even athwart. My being is a web of realities, hidden from thy sight. 'Tis beyond thee to understand. But I speak too much. Here our ways do part. May the Manifold direct thy course, Chosen, and that of thy fellow travelers. Take heart, for all that hath transpired, yea, even that which hath sown seeds of doubt within thee, hath come to pass for a reason. Thy destiny is to fathom that reason."

At these ominous words, the Time Weaver withdrew, and with the wave of a hand, formed a blue portal into which he stepped. Just a few seconds later, he was gone, off to some new time or reality, the purpose of which Lucian couldn't guess. Lucian was shocked that the Time Weaver could simply step into a new time or reality with a simple waving of the hand. He supposed that was the power imbued to him by the Ascendants.

Lucian looked at the others, their faces grounding him back to this reality. So many bizarre events had happened in the last forty-eight hours that Lucian couldn't believe it. Even now, a part of Lucian thought this was all some strange hallucination. That prospect seemed far more likely.

But he held the Orb of Creation, and he had seen its power. If none of this was real, then they were stuck here in the past. And feeling at his Focus, the Orb of Space-Time was there as well.

Both would be their ticket out of here.

38

AFTER A LONG SILENCE, Serah let out a breath. "I don't even know where to *start* with all that. I could barely understand that Time Weaver guy. But from what I gathered; you're supposed to make Lightspear?"

Lucian gripped Jagar's shockspear. He was already getting the beginning of an idea. "Yeah, that's what comes next. There's nothing left for us to do here. By the time we get to the other side, we're going to be ten million years in the future."

"Themba's future," Khairu said. "We're a long way from home still."

Lucian smiled. "But getting closer all the time."

"What happens next?" Khairu asked. "We would be returning to a time where the Second Immortal still has all the Orbs, except for Space-Time and the Orb of Creation. Right?"

"That's right. We have to defeat him again. Take the Orbs back and use them to finish what we started."

Serah looked at Lucian, her face scrunched with confusion. "So, go forward in time ten million years, kick his ass, then go

277

backward in time one million years, and kick his ass again. Easy enough."

"Another question," Khairu said. "Assuming we did all that, wouldn't it undo Themba's entire timeline? Both of our times stem from the same past. Changing that past would make the alternate reality no longer exist."

Themba cleared his throat. "As for my time, I fear it may be done for, anyway. Almost certainly, the Second Immortal will use his Shadow Magic to usher in a new Void Cycle, as soon as he recognizes the threat to himself. Either way, I have lived my purpose. I found the Chosen. I've learned that *my* reality . . . my life and everything I know . . . was simply a cosmic accident."

Themba seemed solemn, and it was easy to see why. Lucian couldn't imagine his position. And that their present existed was proof that it *was* possible to defeat the Ancient One. Perhaps even inevitable.

Assuming that was true, what became of Themba's reality? Did it go on or would it collapse in on itself?

There was simply no telling. Were the lives in that reality worth any less than the lives in *his* reality? Lucian knew they weren't, but because of his own bias, he couldn't allow anything to jeopardize his own.

Lucian put a hand on the Ancient's shoulder, the latter giving a little jump at the action. Physical touch didn't seem to be a part of Ancient culture, or perhaps it was something highly personal and private. Either way, Themba seemed surprised at the gesture.

"If I can save both, I will," Lucian said. "Maybe there are no hard and fast rules. Maybe your reality will stay the same, even if we were to go back in time. The timelines split rather than getting rewritten."

"*Ours* was rewritten," Khairu pointed out.

"Or maybe it's both," Emma said. "It ceases to exist for us, except perhaps in memory, while it would go on for Themba, if he remains behind."

All eyes went on her as she continued.

"If we were to go to the shared past and destroy the Ancient One, and then return to modern times, we'd find our own world. But if Themba remains in this reality without coming with us, his reality would stay the same. What we observe to be true becomes reality, in the end. And as we've learned, there can be more than one reality. Even infinite realities."

"Maybe so," Lucian said, though Emma's explanation was bewildering.

"It's quantum mechanics," Emma said. "Reality is determined by the actions we take and the specific events we encounter. There can be multiple parallel universes or branching timelines. We've already seen this in our time travel. The act of observation determines which reality manifests."

"Translation?" Serah asked.

"I think I get the gist," Lucian said. "Whatever Themba sees and experiences becomes the truth for him, but not necessarily the truth for us."

"Yes," Emma said. "Of course, I can't be absolutely sure, but that is the most popular interpretation of the theory."

"Either way, it gives me hope," Lucian said. "And it also matches with how sorcery works. What you believe is what becomes possible."

"That's true," Emma said. "From what you've described to me about sorcery, there is a parallel between it and quantum mechanics."

"What I choose to do remains to be seen," Themba said at last. "A part of me wishes to continue traveling with you, Lucian. I have waited so long, and have worked so hard, to fulfill the prophecy laid down by the Time Weaver himself, carried from this Ascendant, Anlilta. And now, I realize the Time Weaver planted that prophecy in my reality so that I would be inspired to find you. It is . . . a challenging mental shift. But if it's required that I stay behind to keep my reality from unraveling, then that is my duty."

"We should get moving," Khairu said. "The *Alkasen* ships could still be up there. If they're anything like the *Alkasen* of our own time, they might not be too friendly."

It was hard for Lucian to make sense of the *Alkasen's* actions. At one moment, they were his enemies. In the next, they were an unexpected ally, giving him a shiny new Orb he didn't know existed. He recalled what the Time Weaver himself had said: everything that had happened, even if it had caused doubt, had happened for a reason. In fact, he realized the Time Weaver had led him on this chase as a way for Lucian to prove himself as the true Chosen.

"Let's go," he said. "We should head back to that room where we found the Orb. It's somewhat sheltered, and we might need that if this whole thing is going to take ten million years. Assuming all this works, we should come out in Themba's time period. Once I've gotten the Orbs back, I can use the Orb of Creation to shield myself from losing them. Then we can travel back in time a million years. With the Orb of Creation, there has to be a way to do that, even without the First Gate."

Serah frowned in thought. "Wait. Wouldn't that mean that both you and the Ancient One will *both* have the Orbs?"

"I'm not sure how it will work," Lucian admitted. "I'm just going off what the Time Weaver said. He said Creation Magic would protect me from losing the Orbs."

"One more question," Serah said. "Why did the Orb of Space-Time get left behind?"

"I'm not sure," Lucian said.

"I'm trying to remember back to the Prophecy of the Seven," Emma said. "Perhaps we can put it together with everything we know now to make sense of things."

"It's hard to remember back that far," Serah said. "Lucian?"

"This is what I think has happened," Lucian said. "The

Ancient One entered the original time gate. Then, he directed Sharo to go where the Orbs would be."

"Wouldn't that be here, just nine million years in the future?" Emma asked.

"The Orbs can't have been in the same spot," Lucian said. "According to the Prophecy, it was found by a lowly slave. But we know that the Ancient One has somehow tied himself to the Orbs using his Shadow Magic. My theory is that as soon as he entered the past, he jumped from Sharo to this slave who had found the Orbs, completing the Joining. In this way, he became the Second Immortal."

"This is twisting my brain around," Serah said. "I'm not good at figuring out this time travel stuff. Let's just go after the Ancient One. Kill him wherever we find him. Simple enough, right?"

"That's the basic gist," Emma said. "Let's not think about it too hard."

"We'll figure it out when we get there," Lucian said. "I can't be the only one ready to get out of here."

But before they could leave, one task remained.

"I still need to figure out how to make Lightspear," Lucian said.

"Yeah," Emma said. "How is that supposed to work?"

"Remember, Lucian," Themba said, "your power not only comes from the Orbs you hold. It comes from yourself. Take everything you've learned and put it into practice. Trust your instincts."

Everyone watched Lucian, apparently waiting for him to make the next move.

"It doesn't really matter where we do this," Lucian realized. "The Time Weaver said the Orb of Creation would protect us. Keep us in stasis, so to speak."

"What if we have to experience the entire ten million years?" Serah asked. "It might make us go crazy."

"I imagine it'll be like being asleep," Lucian said. "Either way, it's the only way out of this."

"We're ready when you are, Lucian," Khairu said. "Let's get it over with."

They gathered around him, and Lucian found there was nothing left to do or say.

At some point, he had to stop delaying the inevitable.

"Okay," he said. "Starting now."

He took out Jagar's weapon, remembering the old warrior's sacrifice. It still seemed unreal he was gone, but Lucian could think of no way better to honor his death. Jagar's weapon would become the base of Lightspear, and with luck, Lightspear would end the life of the one who had been responsible for Jagar losing his. There was a certain justice to it, and he knew his old friend would approve.

He assumed his Focus, entering the Ether and reaching for both of his Orbs, drawing deeply of them.

Instantly, an unstoppable current of magic surged through him. Lucian was no longer in control, though he could sense the Orb of Creation wanting guidance for what to do next.

He willed it to turn Jagar's weapon, his fallen friend, into an ethereal weapon of pure Creation Magic, something strong enough to kill the Ancient One a million times over. He willed the Orb to build the power of that spear for ten million years, all while keeping them protected from the ravages of time and allowing that time to pass quickly for them.

As soon as Lucian was done imparting his will, he thrust Jagar's spear into the air as a stream of golden light encased it.

At that very moment, an aura ensconced him and the others, while time advanced outside their bubble at a blistering pace. Though the hall outside was still, Lucian could tell that years were passing in seconds. And then, centuries. At first, nothing changed. In the near airless environment of the planet, there was little erosion. But as millennia passed, everyone watched with expressions of shock as the castle decayed from the impact of hundreds of micrometeoroids. The sun's unrelenting radiation and temperature extremes bleached the walls white, caused the roof to cave in over the eons. The sky became an endless blur of motion from the dance of stars. Eventually, everything became an endless field of white. All were struck silent, unable to comprehend exactly what was happening.

Minutes passed into hours, and hours, perhaps, into days. As the Time Weaver had said, they were in some sort of stasis, unable to move or speak. There was only the experience.

At last, the stars reformed, and Lucian saw they stood alone in the decrepit halls of the castle. The ruins of ten million years stood around them, the castle about halfway on its journey to rejoining the surrounding icy landscape. The roof had long since collapsed and was open to the stars above. Almost all traces of Airaruma's frozen seas were gone, sublimated to the vacuum of space under ten million years of direct sunlight. They stood on the plateau, now much higher over a gray barren surface that had once been a seabed.

But it was not the surroundings everyone was watching. It was the bright spear that Lucian gripped in his right hand, the same one he had lost on Sigil. Except now, it shone not only with white-hot brilliance. Intermixed within it was a golden aura brimming with vitality. He felt its very power thrumming into his arm, echoing in his Focus like an electric charge.

Before anyone could say anything, he held out Lightspear, using its tip to trace a golden circle. Calling to mind the ruins of the city on Sigil, Lucian stepped through the portal, along with everyone else, leaving the barren castle of Airaruma behind. The action barely took any effort.

Within seconds, they were standing on the road outside the tall tower, where they had entered the time gate that had taken them to the distant past.

Lucian looked around. Same lofty buildings. Same sky. Even

their ship was still there, along with those of the Seraphim, three sleek vessels that surrounded their own.

After everything, Lucian could hardly believe it. They really *were* back to the same moment in time they had left.

He couldn't help but pause and look at the tower, the place where Jagar had fallen.

"We should get moving," Khairu said. "If we're really here at the same moment we left, the Seraphim will still be here."

"And worse," Serah added.

But it was at that moment that Lucian noted a familiar figure standing in the archway of the tower's entrance.

39

LUCIAN SAW A DISTINCTLY human silhouette emerge, tall and lean, dressed in the same humble brown robes Jagar always wore.

But it *couldn't* be Jagar. Jagar was dead.

And yet, as chills rippled down Lucian's arms, he recognized the man standing unbroken, seemingly unharmed from the battle with the Seraphim. Lucian observed him, thoughts racing.

Something wasn't right.

Before Lucian could do anything, an aura of darkness cloaked the man. Just like countless others before him, the Ancient One's Shadow Magic had taken possession of Jagar's body.

The question was, was he dead or alive at the time of possession? Certainly, from where Lucian was standing, his body looked unbroken. Perhaps, if there were no lasting injuries, then maybe —just *maybe*—Creation Magic could cleanse him. Lucian would try anything to save his friend and mentor.

"Stay behind me," he warned the others. "I can handle him."

Upon hearing Lucian's voice, Jagar's face twisted into a feral expression, while his hands conjured a sphere of Shadow Magic.

Memories flashed—it was the same dark force Sharo Khalin had unleashed upon Lucian aboard the *Holy Fire*.

Where once Lucian had been defenseless against this, he now had the Lightspear and the Orb of Creation.

Extending his hand, Lucian thrust the golden spear outward; it flashed as it moved. The sphere of shadow was drawn into it, the weapon effortlessly neutralizing the attack.

Jagar staggered back, hesitating for a long moment.

Then Lucian stepped forward.

With a snarl, Jagar turned and fled into the tower's shadow. As he retreated, the recesses of the tower revealed even more figures, remnants of the Seraphim onslaught. The truth was unmistakable: Jagar, or whatever now controlled him, was their leader.

Among the floating Seraphim was the white-robed Grand Seraph, hanging within the open recess of the entrance. From the depths of the tower, a small army of possessed Seraphim was gathering, along with a wave of darkness far more powerful than the shadow sphere Jagar had streamed.

It was do or die. Lucian tapped into the Orb of Creation's immense power, streaming a counter wave of resplendent golden light. Both attacks, light and dark, raced toward each other and met in the middle.

It was no contest. Lucian's golden wave completely obliterated the wave of darkness, not even diminishing in power or scope as it sped down the avenue.

Before the golden wave entered the shadow of the tower's entrance, Lucian quickly formed an additional stream, surrounding Jagar in a cocoon of golden light. That shell protected him as the Creation Magic swept through the entrance, obliterating the Shadow-possessed Seraphim.

But the battle was far from over. Ephemeral shadows, now devoid of their hosts, darted deeper into the depths of the tower. Lucian soared into the air, using a tether to close the gap quickly. Once inside, he streamed from the Orb of Creation, illuminating every corner of the vast tower. The ensuing brilliance shriveled every malevolent shadow until they were reduced to nothing.

When Lucian let go of the stream, a deafening silence settled.

With potential threats neutralized, Lucian's focus returned to Jagar, imprisoned but alive. Through the barrier's gleaming surface, Lucian could see a face wracked with conflict and aggression. This was not the friend he knew.

But perhaps he could be once more.

Lucian streamed from the Orb of Creation, combining it with the magic of the Orb of Space-Time. He began the painstaking process of extracting the malevolent Shadow Magic from Jagar. Dark tendrils writhed and strained against Lucian's efforts. As Jagar levitated above the ground, Lucian worked tirelessly, using Space-Time Magic to reverse his injuries, mending both physical and emotional wounds.

Time seemed to stretch, but eventually Jagar's form slackened. Lucian cautiously stemmed his stream, lowering him back to the surface. Jagar couldn't take much more, as strong as he was.

It would have to do. Lucian had done his best and could do no more.

As Jagar settled onto the ground, laying utterly still. Lucian reached out with his hand, streaming a brief shock of electricity right onto his chest. Jagar's eyes popped open, and he gave a jolting breath.

Lucian couldn't help but smile as Jagar pulled himself up, panting as though he'd narrowly escaped drowning. Everyone rushed forward, hope and relief shining in their eyes.

"What in the rotting hell just happened to me? Where am I? What is this?"

"Jagar!" Serah said. "You're alive!"

"Alive?" He looked up at Lucian suspiciously. "Where . . . where am I, boy? What's happened? If I'm dead, just tell it to me true."

Lucian let out a laugh. "You're definitely not dead. Seems the Manifold's not done with you yet. And neither are we."

"Rotting hell," he said. "Rotting, *rotting* hell . . ." He looked up at the others almost grumpily. "Why did you save me? I was damned ready to die, and you took that from me?"

"News flash," Serah said. "Whatever *you* were, it wasn't dead. We couldn't just let you be a shadow zombie for the rest of time."

"Huh. I don't quite remember all that, but I guess I'll have to take your word for it."

After a moment, the warrior even had the strength to get to his feet.

"Anyone got water?" he asked. "My throat's drier than the Sandsea."

Emma offered her canteen, and Jagar took a deep pull. After draining the container, he wiped his bearded mouth. "Now I just need some whiskey."

"What the hell just happened?" Serah asked, looking at Lucian. "How did you save him?"

"There was nothing really wrong with him," Lucian said. "The Shadow Magic must have gotten to him before the Seraphim did. It was just a matter of driving it out of him with the Orb of Creation."

"What are you on about, boy?" Jagar asked. "What's this Orb of Creation you're talking about?"

"There'll be time for all that later," Lucian said. "We need to get off this planet. It's time to go after the Ancient One."

Jagar's brow furrowed in thought. "Wait, some of it's coming back to me . . ." He looked toward the ship. "Ah, hell. Well, let's get off this rotting planet while we still can."

———

WITHIN THE HOUR, they were off Sigil and in space. Everyone gathered on the bridge. Jagar sat with a cup of *kra* tea in hand, sipping the beverage gratefully.

While he sat, Lucian told him everything that had happened, with the others filling in the gaps as needed, which took several hours. By the end, Jagar knew as much as any of them.

Jagar frowned as he thought everything through. It was a lot to take in.

"So, we're going after the Ancient One now?" Jagar said.

"That's right," Lucian said. "After we deal with him, we have to go back into the past and deal with him again. That's the only way we can complete the time loop."

"That's a tall order."

"I've got a new weapon now," Lucian said.

"Aye, so it seems. I'm glad you found a use for that old spear of mine, but now I've got nothing."

"I've got plenty of spares," Themba said. "Have your pick."

Jagar nodded gratefully. "In a minute. Let's talk about how we're supposed to get to Nai Elyn. That's where the Ancient One is, right?"

"We have one chance," Lucian said. "I have to create a portal there."

"I thought we couldn't do that because it would be too different," Serah said. "Your memory of Nai Elyn has to match what's actually there for it to work, right?"

Emma smiled. "Who says we have to portal directly to Nai Elyn?"

Lucian looked at her. "You have something in mind?"

"Think about it. Everything is different in this reality compared to ours. Everything, except for one thing."

Serah's eyes widened in realization. "The Gates! Could it work?"

It was an interesting idea. No matter what reality they were in, the Gates were something completely immutable. They would be the same here as in his own reality.

That meant it would be possible to create a portal to it. Normally, Gate passages happened so quickly that it was impossible to get a good look while passing through. But with the First Gate, Lucian had seen it when he had first gained the Orb of Radiance.

He just needed to form that picture, and they would be able to portal to it. From there, it was a straight shot to Nai Elyn.

"If this doesn't work, we'll have a journey of many months on our hands," Themba said. "And when the Ancient One doesn't hear from the Seraphim, he will almost certainly use his Shadow Magic to set off another Void Cycle. If this doesn't work, nothing will."

"No pressure then," Serah said.

"It *will* work," Lucian said. "If it doesn't, the reality we came from wouldn't exist. It's based on us succeeding here."

No one could argue against that.

"The sooner we do this, the better," Lucian said. "We're almost there. Let's take out the Ancient One."

40

AFTER A BRIEF REST, they gathered on the bridge where Lucian wasted no time in recalling his image of the Dark Gate. The picture formed easily enough, and as soon as he held it in his mind, he streamed Space-Time Magic amplified by the power of the Orb of Creation.

Almost immediately, a golden portal sprang up before them, and *Tempus* passed through. The ship's sensors went haywire as they recalibrated to their new position.

"We're here," Themba said, amazed. "We're actually here! You even moved us past the Gate defenses!"

There was a brief flash, a changing of the star field signaling they had arrived in the Nai Shairen system.

Lucian gathered his ether, warping the ship into the far distance to avoid any attack. It seemed the Orb of Creation allowed him to draw ether far more quickly than he was used to.

"They won't even know we were there," he said. "A blip, nothing more."

"We're just a few hours from Nai Elyn," Emma said, looking at the instrument panel. "How is that even possible?"

"Enough time to prepare ourselves, perhaps," Themba said. "We must shield the ship as long as possible. Hundreds of Seraphim sorcerers call the Moon Tower home. And they will be ever vigilant for passing threats."

"This ship is too large to hide," Emma said. "Even if every single one of us was contributing to the shield."

"I have an idea," Lucian said. "I could warp the ship down to the surface as soon as we are close enough. With luck, we won't be detected."

"You think you're up for that?" Emma asked.

"It could work," Lucian said. "We'd just need somewhere to put down the ship where it won't be found."

"I know a place," Themba said. "Assuming it hasn't changed. There is a dense forest to the west of the Immortal City, where the Moon Tower is. It's far enough that we might approach on foot undetected."

"How far is it to the Moon Tower from there?" Khairu asked.

"With magic, a day, perhaps," Themba said. "With Lucian warping us, even faster. It's hard to say just how much has changed and how much has remained the same. There are many things that could go wrong."

"I can close the distance using Space-Time Magic," Lucian said. "It's important to get there undetected. If the Ancient One is tipped off, it's over."

"Then we'll try to land in the forest," Themba said.

"And if we *are* detected?" Khairu asked. "What then?"

"There are no guarantees," Serah said.

"I suppose not," Khairu said.

"I don't like winging it, either," Emma said. "But in this situation, it seems we have no choice."

"We're almost close enough to be detected," Themba said. "I will need help with the shield."

"Khairu can continue to pilot," Lucian said. "As for everyone else, help Themba keep the shield strong. I'll warp the ship once I lock us in on a good warping point."

"I'm updating our trajectory to point us toward the forest," Themba said. "No action will be required Lucian, other than warping us toward the moon."

"I can handle that much."

It went quiet after that, everyone lost in their own thoughts. Lucian could feel the urgency in the air. Despite this, there was also a sense of unity. After waiting so long for this moment, Lucian was almost glad it was finally here. He didn't feel nervous at all, only ready for the trial ahead.

Themba began the Radiant shield and others joined in. Meanwhile, Khairu sat at the helm, her face filled with steely resolve.

There was no room for mistakes. One error, and they could lose everything they had achieved so far.

Already, the blue dot of Nai Shairen, as well as the smaller dot of its orbiting moon, was well-formed in the forward viewscreen. Still, they remained undetected, a testament to the power of the shield streamed by Themba and the crew.

The central terminal logged dozens, and soon hundreds of spaceships. And just half an hour out from the planet, they were logging *thousands*.

"It's so much busier than even Earth," Emma said, her features strained from maintaining the shield. "It'll be hard to keep us completely off LADAR."

Lucian thought about adding his strength to the shield, but already he knew the time was coming when he would need to warp the ship forward. He would need all his strength.

Now, both the planet and the moon were in clear view. The scene was exactly the same as when they had approached it in their own reality. The only difference was that the nighttime sides of both floating spheres were lit with the lights of the cities below. Nai Shairen's landmasses were completely flooded with lights, while Nai Elyn was darker, except for the location of what had to be the Immortal City.

Lucian reached for his Focus. "About to complete the first warp. Standby to strengthen shield."

Reaching for both the Orbs of Creation and Space-Time, Lucian focused on a spot quite close to the surface of Nai Elyn, where he knew the forest to be. He streamed.

Instantly, they were there, being pulled into the moon's atmosphere.

Lucian added his own strength to the Radiant shield, more than doubling its power. The ship shook violently as it surged through the moon's thick atmosphere. Lightning slashed from a storm, the winds buffeting their descent.

The ship slowed as it approached a thick forest below. Khairu scanned the ground, looking for a suitable landing spot. In the far distance, Lucian could see the iridescently shining Immortal City, with its thousands of bright skyscrapers. A single tower in the center rose above the rest, dwarfing all the others. It could be none other than the Moon Tower, the home of the Immortal himself.

"Going in for the landing," Khairu said, her voice tense.

She lowered the ship into the only visible clearing in the dense forest. Almost as soon as the ship landed, Lucian felt the deck lurch beneath his feet. Thinking quickly, he covered the deck in a Gravitonic disc that allowed everyone to remain standing.

The ship floated for a moment, bobbing up and down on the surface.

"Khairu, you landed us on a lake!" Serah said.

"How was I supposed to know? It's dark!"

"Get off the ship," Themba said. "Now!"

They rushed to the exit, Lucian keeping gravity pulling toward the deck so that it was easy to navigate. Themba opened the door.

"Outside," he said. "Hurry!"

One-by-one, they climbed out of *Tempus*, Serah boosting everyone to the top of the ship with Gravitonics. When Lucian stood on the upper hull, he found the vessel was rapidly sinking into the murky depths.

Emma created a powerful light sphere above their heads, which revealed that they had landed in a swamp.

To make matters worse, massive snail-like creatures floated toward them, their gaping mouths filled with serrated teeth. There were *hundreds* of them.

Even in the face of the nightmarish scene before them, Lucian didn't falter. He saw the monsters were shying away from the light emanating from Emma's sphere. Those furthest from the glow were already beginning to creep onto the hull.

"Emma," Lucian commanded, "brighten that light!"

As she intensified the light, the surrounding monsters recoiled with a collective hiss. Suddenly, the ship lurched, nearly making Lucian lose his balance. Jagar slipped off the ship's side, sliding toward the writhing tentacles of a nearby monster. Lucian quickly streamed a tether to pull him back to safety.

Themba, with a swift raise of his hands, unleashed a stream of fire against the monster horde. High-pitched shrieks echoed as the fire clung to their shells, burning hot despite the damp environment. Lucian noticed an oily tinge to the flames and wondered if Themba had used Atomicism along with Thermalism to create some sort of incendiary mix.

The flames spread across the swamp's surface, reducing their available standing space. As the ship's descent slowed, an equilibrium formed between the vessel and the swamp beneath. However, not all the monsters had been reached by the flames, and Themba appeared to be running low on ether, his flames petering out.

"Lucian," Serah called out, "Over here!"

Lucian turned his attention from the inferno to the ship's

opposite side. Down there, the tentacled monsters were growing increasingly bold. Dozens were now flinging their spiked appendages onto the ship's hull.

Drawing upon Thermalism, Lucian conjured a storm of ice shards and hurled them forward. The shards struck with deadly precision, driving the monsters back with hisses of pain.

Meanwhile, Khairu, who had been gathering her ether, unleashed a storm of orange death lightning—a potent mix of Atomicism and Dynamism. The lightning crackled across the water, instantly reducing any creature it touched to ash. By the time her attack ceased, several dozen monsters had been completely vaporized.

Above them, Emma's light sphere shone with incredible intensity, and its brightness grew with each passing moment. To Lucian's surprise, luminous arrows began raining down from it, targeting any creature that dared approach. Each arrow struck with the potency of a laser, piercing flesh and shell alike. With each arrow, the sphere lost some of its luster, only to be refreshed by Emma.

Lucian realized the real reason the ship had stopped sinking—Serah was streaming a reverse gravity aura that was slowing the ship's descent. Her face was strained with the effort.

By now, only a few creatures were persisting in the attack. Lucian dealt with these by guiding Lightspear with a Binding tether. The spear instantly vanquished everything it touched.

As Lucian fended off the remaining monsters, the rest of the crew joined Serah's stream, halting the ship's sinking deeper into the swamp. For the first time since landing on the moon, the forest fell silent save for the calls of a few nocturnal creatures.

As the silence settled in, Serah brushed a loose strand of hair from her eyes. "That's the last time we let Khairu pick the parking spot."

Khairu was nonplussed. "Always quick with the punchlines, aren't you?"

"Well, *someone* has to lighten the mood."

"Try to focus on lightening the ship," Khairu said, a small smile tugging at her lips.

"Speaking of the ship," Lucian said, "this one's not going to last long. Where we're going, though, we won't need it."

"Well, how are we supposed to get through the forest?" Emma said. "Especially with these . . . *things*."

"Swamp-maws," Themba said. "They're plentiful here. Why do you think I told you to land here? No one would ever voluntarily come into this place."

"This is worse than the Shadowed Forest on Psyche," Serah said. "At least that one had solid ground. How are we supposed to get to the Moon Tower if we can't even walk?"

"We don't walk," Lucian said. "We fly."

"I can't shield that amount of ether from detection," Emma said. "Even if Themba and I are working together."

"Well, maybe *flying* was the wrong word," Lucian said. "I just planned on tethering everyone to the treetops."

"What about once we're in the city, though?" Khairu asked. "It'll be harder to escape detection."

"Well, let's focus on getting everyone up in the trees and away from those things. I'll go on alone. Once I find a way inside the Tower, I can portal everyone else in."

"Seems like a good plan to me," Serah said.

"From there, I assume we go after the Ancient One?" Khairu asked.

Lucian nodded. "Look, we should really get moving. This ship might appear stable right now, but anything could change."

Lucian found a nearby tree that looked tall and sturdy. He began by tethering everyone to the top branches. Once he joined the rest of them, he could see clearly across the mist-shrouded forest to the glittering city in the distance. The Moon Tower rose tall and resolute, while the planet of Nai Shairen formed a backdrop against the starry sky. The scene was enough to take his breath away.

Reaching for Radiance, he could clearly see beyond the city itself.

"This tree seems safe enough," he said. "I'll head toward the Tower. Once I'm inside, I'll open the portal right here, close to the tree trunk."

Lucian pointed and formed a mental picture for later.

"Be careful," Khairu said.

"Good luck," Emma said.

Lucian locked eyes with Serah, who looked worried.

"This won't take long. Promise."

"Do you need someone to shield your magic?" Themba asked. "I know the city, and I won't slow you down too much."

Lucian considered for a moment. "All right. Themba comes, too."

Themba created a powerful Radiant shield that would make them all but invisible. "Ready when you are."

"Be back soon," Lucian said.

He sought a large tree in the distance and tethered Themba toward it. With a last glance at the others, he tethered himself after him.

41

LUCIAN AND THEMBA journeyed through the lush treetops, their shadowed forms dancing against the backdrop of the starry sky. The forest's thick canopy provided them with cover as they made their stealthy advance toward the Immortal City. With every leap, Lucian's heightened senses kept them on track.

Themba moved with fluid grace, keeping pace just behind Lucian, their movements almost mirroring each other. They navigated the night, guided by the soft glow of the Immortal City and the luminescence of Nai Shairen in the distance.

Once they were close, Lucian halted. Their tethers would be easily spotted this near, especially with the Seraphim on guard. He scanned the lofty Moon Tower, which dominated the city skyline, its peak stretching at least three kilometers into the sky. Tapping into the Space-Time Aspect, Lucian anchored his focus to a building approximately a third of the distance into the city.

In an instant, they reappeared atop the selected structure, granting them a sweeping view of the sprawling city below.

Lucian's voice was urgent. "We need to go higher. I need a vantage point to see inside that wall."

Themba gestured to the city's second highest structure—a magnificent tower that pierced the sky. "That might be our answer."

Lucian warped them to a balcony of the skyscraper. From there, they had to ascend the building's sheer face. Themba streamed Radiant Magic for protection, while Lucian manipulated the tethers for both of them. Their ascent was swift, and soon they overlooked the Moon Tower's formidable outer wall. Beyond it, Lucian discerned a lush courtyard.

Themba's voice was low. "The shield surrounding the tower is eight-sealed. Not only with the Seven Aspects, but with Shadow Magic. It will destroy anyone without the right Psionic brand. Only the Immortal can give such a mark."

Lucian glanced at him. "Do you still have it?"

Themba shook his head. "Once, but its power has faded."

Lucian pondered the problem. "I have the Orb of Creation. Maybe a Creation shield can neutralize the Shadow barrier. Though bypassing it without triggering its defenses is risky."

Assessing the immense shield, Lucian noted its complexity— a testament to the Immortal's prowess. However, Lucian had something the Immortal lacked: mastery over Space-Time Magic.

Maybe it would allow them to skip the shield entirely.

"I'll reinforce every Aspect when we warp," he said. "There's no other way."

Themba nodded. "Your call."

Lucian reached for his Creation Magic, reinforcing it with other Aspects, and crafted a formidable shield. Then, zeroing in on a secluded corner of the courtyard beneath majestic trees, he started the warp.

Suddenly, they stood amidst the verdant garden, their arrival seemingly undetected.

Lucian turned to Themba. "Are we good?"

Themba nodded. "Seems we're safe."

But as soon as he spoke, three Seraphim, adorned in opulent black robes, descended rapidly from above. Lucian deftly summoned Lightspear, deflecting a deadly lightning bolt hurled by the lead Seraph.

The garden erupted in chaos. Trees went up in flame, lightning forked from the sky, shockspears stabbed and sliced relentlessly. With their backs pressed together, Lucian and Themba defended against the onslaught. In the storm, Lightspear moved like a living entity, dispatching one Seraph effortlessly. As more enemies closed in, Lucian unleashed a forceful blast, fending off three more.

Themba held their flank as Lucian opened a portal back to the safety of the forest. Serah, Jagar, Emma, and Khairu rushed through, reinforcing their defenses with shields of their own. By the end, the courtyard bore the ashes of the fallen Seraphim.

"Quite an entrance," Serah said, in between breaths.

Lucian's eyes darted to the tower's pinnacle where a malevolent force pulsed, causing a chill to run down his spine. "He's up there."

"We can't waste time," Khairu said.

Jagar and Emma nodded in agreement.

They sprinted toward the tower's entrance, but two more Seraphim blocked their path, shockspears poised with spheres of green Radiant Magic collecting on their tips. Twin lasers shot forth, but Emma's shield absorbed them. Lucian warped directly behind them, taking them down with a swift strike from behind.

Now inside the main atrium, Lucian was surrounded by four more Seraphim. Four tethers simultaneously grappled him, each threatening to pull him in a different direction with dismembering force.

Using another warp to dislodge the tethers, Lucian appeared right behind one of the Seraphim and stabbed him through. To dispatch the rest, he created a point of intense gravity between the remaining defenders for just a split second, causing them to crash into each other in a bloody pulp. He streamed reverse Gravitonics in between the gravity point and his companions so they would not be similarly affected.

With the next obstacle cleared, they took to the crystalline stairs that rose along the tower's periphery. There were at least two thousand meters left to climb before reaching the top.

"Stay close to me!" Lucian called out.

Lucian entered a trance of nonstop streaming and sorcery as they ascended flight after flight. From doorways, ceilings, and hallways, more Seraphim emerged. Almost as soon as they appeared, they fell.

Lucian was completely numb to the killing. His companions shielded all the magical attacks while he dealt devastating blows with his Space-Time Magic, against which the Seraphim had no counter.

It was a slaughter, the most powerful sorcerers in the Starsea Empire falling like wheat before a scythe.

Anytime there was a reprieve, he would warp everyone as high as he could, only to fight once more. The Moon Tower's halls echoed with the Seraphim's garbled screams and the clash of shockspears, the din punctuated by powerful streams of magic. Deadly streams of fire, ice, and lightning created a storm within the tower's halls.

They moved efficiently, with every action coordinated. Lucian would sometimes open a quick portal, allowing them to step through and launch a surprise attack from a different angle.

Never did the Seraphim flee. No matter how hopeless their plight, their dedication to their master was unwavering. They fought as if they were possessed, not holding anything back. But so quick and devastating were Lucian's attacks that they couldn't hope to fight back.

The Orb of Creation seemed to pull him ever upward, toward its counterpart embodied in the person of the Ancient One.

As they ascended higher, waves of pure Shadow Magic blasted downward, obliterating all in their path, including the Seraphim. Lucian shielded everyone with the golden light of the Orb of Creation. Soon, there were no more Seraphim, only hostile pulses of dark magic.

Finally, after hours of fighting and climbing, they reached the end of the stairs, along with a short landing leading to a pair of heavy doors inscribed with runes. Lucian blasted the doors off their hinges to reveal a room filled with pure darkness. Drawing on the power of the Orb of Creation, he and his companions entered, a single light in an ocean of pressing darkness.

Lucian knew the true fight was just beginning.

It took a moment for Lucian to realize that this wasn't a room, but the very top of the tower itself. He could hear the wind howling around him, but so potent was the Ancient One's Magic that all was dark outside the aura of golden light.

But there was another light, or rather, *seven* lights, glowing in a septagonal shape in the distance. Lucian immediately recognized what they were, and his heart lurched at the sight.

The Seven Orbs shone with resplendence, in the form of an ethereal crown floating above a shadowed and malevolent form, what could be none other than the Ancient One. His visage could only be seen as a deeper darkness staining the surrounding black. Here, the Ancient One had clearly abandoned having a body in favor of this more ethereal state.

A wave of coldness pulsated from his aura as a wave of chilling laughter unleashed a haunting chorus. Each Orb in the Ethereal Crown pulsed with immense, otherworldly energy that distorted the surrounding darkness.

Lucian struggled to hold not just the darkness at bay, but also the raw power of the Orbs that threatened to overwhelm both him and his friends.

"Pitiful fool," the Ancient One said, his voice cold and sharp as frosted steel. "You think you could stand against *me*? Against this?"

The Seven Orbs set in the crown glowed brighter with a new discharge of magic. A beam of light, powered by all Seven Aspects, nearly shattered Lucian's Creation shield. Beneath the crown, Lucian could see twin baleful eyes, red as coals in the darkest part of the night.

As much as Lucian quailed to meet that gaze, he also felt a surge of defiance. "We'll never stop fighting, no matter *what* you throw at us!"

"Futile," the Ancient One hissed.

The Ancient One's dark form eddied, releasing a brutal wave of multicolored magic. It crackled through the air, a storm of swirling colors and inky black racing toward them.

Lucian and his team reacted instantly. As he edified his own Creation shield, the others added their own streams, as paltry as they were. Their collective magic converged in a brilliant shield, all the colors of the rainbow joining the golden aura and lending it a pearlescent light. The Ancient One's magic crashed against their defenses, each pulse threatening to shatter their protection.

Unyielding, Lucian retaliated with a potent stream of Space-Time Magic. A swirling vortex of energy rippled from the tip of Lightspear, racing toward the Ancient One. To his left, Themba unleashed a torrent of white-hot fire, while on his right, Emma's laser was bright enough to create a flash of dazzling light that was instantly snuffed out by impending darkness.

But their attacks were ineffectual. The Ancient One merely stood, absorbing each stream with a shield of darkness to match their own shield of light. His cruel laughter echoed all around them. Even as they redoubled their efforts, the streams seemed to curve away from him, losing their ferocity as they were sucked into the unseen void beyond.

With a wave of his hand, the Ancient One intensified his attack. The rooftop shook as another shockwave of raw power radiated outward from him. The attack threw them back like leaves in a tempest. They clung to each other to remain standing.

"His power . . . is so much," Emma said.

Themba gasped out, his face wrinkled from the strain.

"Don't give up," Serah said. "This isn't over!"

The Moon Tower echoed with their clashing streams, the very stones groaning beneath them under immense pressure. Each attack they launched was met with harsh resistance, while the Ancient One countered with ruthless precision. Their streams of fire, light, shadow, gravity, and electricity illuminated the grim scene.

Darkness spread in all directions, a darkness so complete that it was pushing against Lucian's Creation Magic. The Void Cycle was spreading, and they were fighting at its epicenter for the fate of this reality.

Lucian's heart pounded in his chest. Desperation threatened to choke him. He could last much longer, but what about his friends? Their faces were filled with despair, their streams flagging in intensity. How long had this fight gone on? How much longer could he expect *them* to fight?

Even his own golden shield was threatening to buckle as the Ancient One's Shadow Magic grew ever more powerful. It was as if the larger the Void outside became, the more powerful the Ancient One's magic.

"Now, Chosen," the Ancient One taunted, "your story ends. You'll go to a place beyond death, beyond hope. Such is the fate of those who dare to challenge me!"

Before Lucian could react, the Ancient One moved with a speed that blurred the darkness. His form slammed into the Creation shield surrounding Lucian and his friends. The sheer power sent Lucian spiraling backward, the shield shattering into a million fragments of golden light quickly snuffed out by the darkness, like sparks dying on a frosty night.

All he heard was Serah's scream echoing through the ominous void before all went silent.

42

THE SCENE FROZE FOR A MOMENT, time coming to a standstill as Lucian's figure was entrapped by an engulfing darkness. He was in a cocoon of black, through which there could be no escape. It was so quiet here that even his scream was eaten by the void.

He could hear nothing. Nothing, save the taunts of the Ancient One.

This is your doom, Chosen. For all eternity, you will float in stasis with nothing but your memories for company. With no companion but your own failure.

Lucian shook his head. "No."

Against my Shadow Magic, none can prevail. Every moment that passes, it grows stronger. Not even Enkius's Orb can hope to stand against it!

Lucian knew better than to believe the Ancient One. He recalled an image of Serah's face, something the Ancient One could never take from him. Combining the powers of the Orbs of Creation and Space-Time, he streamed.

He appeared before her; she, too, had been isolated in the darkness.

"Lucian!" she said.

He drew her close. "We need to find everyone else. Get the shield back up."

"Right," she said. "I saw the Ancient One turning before he blasted us out here. I think he's trying to get away and trap us!"

Lucian immediately saw the danger. While he had access to Space-Time Magic and the Orb of Creation, they could not escape this reality without first dealing with the Ancient One.

He needed the Orbs. *All* of them.

Holding onto Serah, he next warped to Emma, then Khairu, and finally Jagar. Last of all, he found Themba. He strengthened the golden shield to encompass them all.

Now that he was no longer actively fighting the Ancient One, his shield of Creation Magic could expand and banish the surrounding darkness. The top of the Moon Tower revealed itself, including the far end, where the Ancient One stood revealed for a moment, a shapeless shadow with the Ethereal Crown of Orbs floating overhead.

Instantly, the Ancient One's Shadow Magic pushed back, meeting Lucian's golden light halfway across the tower. Light and darkness danced. With his friends beside him once more, Lucian felt his determination grow.

Just as Lucian felt victory was near, the Ancient One sneered. "I tire of this game."

A shimmering portal of darkness formed before him.

"We can't let him escape!" Emma said.

Themba lunged forward, well out of the protective reach of Lucian's golden aura.

"Themba!" Lucian shouted.

But the old Ancient was heedless of Lucian's warning, fighting the darkness with every step to make it to the Ancient One. He moved in a blur, and Lucian realized their guide was doomed from the moment he stepped outside Lucian's shield.

At this desperate moment, all Lucian could do was help him along.

Lucian redirected some of his magic to form a sort of tunnel of golden light toward the Ancient One, even as overall, the shield weakened. At any moment, the Ancient One could strike a mortal blow against that shield, but he had committed himself to creating his gateway, and would not be dissuaded. Everything hung on Themba reaching the Ancient One in time, finding some way to distract him long enough for Lucian to finish the job.

"What is this?" the Ancient One asked. "A slave who dares to challenge the master? Don't think I've forgotten you, honorless worm!"

Just as the Ancient One swiped with a shadowy arm, aiming to strike down Themba once and for all, the gateway fully opened. The Ancient One abandoned his attack, deciding instead to escape. He was seconds away from disappearing forever.

Streaming with everything he had, Lucian reached out with Space-Time Magic, warping himself between the Ancient One and the gate, opening a second shield of Creation Magic and branding the shield protecting his friends to continue on without him. The branded shield would not last forever, so Lucian needed to make this quick.

The Ancient One roared his defiance, stabbing with a spear of darkness to match Lucian's own. The two weapons met in midair, letting out a high ethereal shriek. Behind the Ancient One, Themba withered from the Shadow Magic. Meanwhile, the golden aura surrounding Lucian's friends was also weakening, having seconds left.

Themba was already melting into the surrounding darkness, his gambit buying precious seconds. Just when Lucian thought all hope was lost, Themba's long fingers, stretched out and warped by the encroaching darkness, barely brushed against the powerful Crown levitating above the Ancient One's head.

This action did little except make the Ancient One cry out in rage. But it was the distraction Lucian needed. He blasted forward like a shooting star, Lightspear extended. He aimed the golden-white spear right at the Ancient One's heart.

Realizing his mistake, the Ancient One whirled around, a powerful shield of darkness countering Lucian's attack. For a moment, Lightspear and the Shadow shield battled for supremacy. But in the struggle, the magic binding the Ethereal Crown to the Ancient One's form was coming loose.

Enough for Themba, withered and nearly absorbed by the darkness, to grasp it and pull it away.

The Ancient One emitted a discordant scream. A desperate magical blast sent what was left of Themba reeling backward into the darkness, but amazingly, the Crown was still clasped in his hands, even as the rest of his body was cast in different directions, absorbed by the encroaching Void.

The Ancient One abandoned Lucian, his shadowy form racing toward the Crown that was spiraling into the darkness. A kinetic blast sent Lucian downward, away from the Crown.

But to Lucian's utter amazement, the Crown began coming *toward* Lucian. Right before his death, Themba must have branded it to fly in his direction and away from the Ancient One.

This action, Lucian realized, gave him nothing more than a chance. It was up to him to make sure Themba's sacrifice was not in vain.

The Ancient One shot forward, changing trajectory, as Lucian did likewise. The Crown continued on its path toward Lucian, but the Ancient One was much closer.

Behind the collapsing golden shield, his friends were streaming, too, apparently slowing the Ancient One's advance. Even a second or two could make all the difference.

Lucian was getting closer. He was going to get there first.

A kinetic blast thundered against Lucian, but he had prepared himself with a shield. The Ancient One screeched his dismay as Lucian reached out for the Crown, just a hand's grasp away.

As Lucian's hand closed upon it, he felt its power enter him. The strength of all Seven Minor Orbs, plus that of Space-Time and Creation, were now his to command. It was as if his very veins ran with lava, all that power needing an outlet.

Around them, the Void Cycle continued its merciless advance, the growing darkness consuming everything in its path. But now, armed with all the Orbs, Lucian streamed everything he had into Lightspear. In a golden explosion, the darkness retracted immediately. The stars reappeared, while the sphere of Nai Shairen itself formed in the distance. There was only one spot of darkness, a single island surrounding the Ancient One.

His form sputtered, shrinking every moment as he tried in vain to retreat to the portal behind him. But an isthmus of golden magic separated the Ancient One from his only form of escape, and without the Orbs, all he had was his Shadow Magic.

Lucian's gaze fell on the Ancient One, whose figure was wavering before the onslaught. Lucian gathered all available ether, channeling it through the Orb of Creation into a single sphere of concentrated energy at the tip of Lightspear.

"You haven't won yet," the Ancient One said. "This . . . is only a battle."

Lucian didn't dignify him with a response. Fortified with Creation Magic, he plunged Lightspear directly into the Ancient One, who screeched his pain and dismay. He shriveled, jerking back and forth, until he was nothing more than a splotch of pure darkness. That darkness retracted into a small sphere that suddenly winked out and disappeared entirely.

As soon as the ball of shadow disappeared, silence reigned atop the Moon Tower. The surrounding city was in chaos, towers crumbling and fires burning. More orange light, what seemed to be similar fires, could be seen on the surface of Nai Shairen far in the distance.

But the Ancient One's portal was still formed, having been branded there with the power of every Aspect. It would only close when used.

Lucian turned to his friends, who were all staring at him wide-eyed. All of them stood panting and exhausted, but unharmed.

"Themba..." Khairu said.

All of them were silent as they thought of their unexpected friend and guide. Lucian could hardly believe he was gone, that he had done so much against the Ancient One's encroaching darkness.

Without him, they surely would have failed.

"He gave everything for us," Lucian said, his voice strained.

Emma swallowed hard, her eyes shimmering with unshed tears. "He didn't deserve this..."

"Death in battle is a warrior's honor," Jagar said quietly, his gruff voice filled with an odd mixture of sorrow and respect. "He knew what he was doing, just as I did. While I live to fight another day, we can't say the same about him."

Serah was quiet, her gaze lowered. Her hands clenched, her knuckles turning white. "Themba was always full of surprises. His bravery ... his *sacrifice* ... won't be in vain. It *wasn't* in vain. Without him..."

There was a moment of silence, a brief interlude where they allowed themselves to mourn their fallen friend. Themba, the stoic and steadfast Ancient, was gone, consumed by the Ancient One's Shadow Magic. And with the dissolution of that magic, he was now in the Ether itself, Lucian supposed.

But his spirit, his sacrifice, would live on with them as they continued their temporal journey.

Lucian turned to the others, his gaze taking them all in. "We honor him by finishing this. Against all odds, we have the Orbs.

We have the power. The Orb of Creation won't let me lose them again." He nodded toward the gate. "That's the next step."

"Where does it go?" Emma asked.

"The only place it *can* go. It will take us a million years into the past, where Themba's reality and ours meet. This alternate reality we're in now was born by our actions, but a soon as we go through that gate, we'll get another chance to stop the Ancient One. It's time to close the loop."

There was a collective nod of agreement, a shared resolution that hardened their expressions. Losing Themba was a painful blow, but it had also ignited a flame of resolve. They had a universe to save, a mission to accomplish.

And a friend to honor.

They would fight the Ancient One again on a different battlefield.

They would win.

And they would always remember Themba.

43

"GET READY!" Lucian ordered.

Lucian surrounded himself with Creation Magic. As the Time Weaver had said, the Orb would keep him safe from losing the others. He wasn't sure how it worked, or what would happen when he occupied the same time period as the Ancient One. But he had to take the Time Weaver at his word.

They had nothing else to go on.

As they crossed the plane of the gate, a swirling maelstrom of temporal energy consumed Lucian's vision. Temporal tides ebbed and flowed around him, a feeling that was now strangely familiar. Each swell and dip of power carried them further and further away from the alternate timeline they had saved.

But now, it was time to finish the original job they had come back to accomplish. The Ancient One in this past was the one they had chased through the original time gate on Mako. And Lucian would have to defeat him again. It was strange to think that this Ancient One would have no memory of the future battle that had just taken place.

Lucian felt vertigo, his stomach lurching as the dark tides

around him blurred, stretched, and snapped into place. The sensation was like stepping off a fast-moving carousel. As reality reformed, Lucian stood on a high plateau overlooking a vast, primeval landscape. Verdant foliage spread across the sprawling expanse beneath a sky painted with purples and blues. The untouched landscape was beautiful, full of wild, untamed power.

Lucian knew this could be none other than Nai Elyn, given that Nai Shairen was visible above the low mountains in the distance. They must have come out on another part of the moon, since the Moon Tower would have existed in this time period.

But the intricacies of time travel were not Lucian's concern at the moment. It was the strange pull he felt from the Orbs. His Focus seemed to twist within him, as if the Orbs wanted to come loose. But the golden shield around him refused to let the Orbs escape his grasp.

"Where is he?" Serah asked.

Before Lucian could answer, a burst of powerful golden magic shot from his body, heading directly into the sky. There was nothing Lucian could do to control it. He vaguely realized what must be happening: in this reality, two sets of Orbs existed—his and the Ancient One's. Neither could exist separately, and yet, Lucian's Creation Magic forbade him from losing his own set.

His Creation Magic was seeking the Ancient One. As the Time Weaver had suggested, perhaps the Orbs had to decide who would control them.

He didn't have to wait long. The golden thread retracted, and not a moment later, it created a golden portal on the other end of the plateau. From this portal, an aura of darkness emanated, and within that darkness stood a tall and powerfully built Ancient, wearing robes of pure white with a billowing cape of shadowy darkness. As Lucian had guessed, it seemed the Ancient One had discarded Sharo Khalin's body entirely in favor of another. The Ethereal Crown, with its seven attendant Orbs, hovered ominously above his head.

Unbidden, Lucian's Orbs also manifested as a Crown, but only the Seven Minor Orbs. Those of Creation and Space-Time remained locked within his Focus, apparently deciding that there was no contest on this front. Those two Orbs were his to command, probably because the Ancient One didn't possess them in this time period.

A sudden, disorienting force pulled at Lucian, a paradoxical snap as the universe—or perhaps the Light Realm or the Ether or the Manifold itself—tried to resolve the contradiction of two separate manifestations of the Jewels of Starsea. In the next moment, the Orbs hung suspended between Lucian and the Ancient One, a golden thread connecting them to Lucian, while a thread of pure darkness connected them to the Ancient One.

The Ancient One's red, baleful eyes locked with Lucian's, cold and cruel.

For a split second, silence hung heavy in the air, charged with anticipation. It was a stalemate, a silent confrontation, as they faced each other across the small distance.

"Get somewhere safe," Lucian said to his friends. "This isn't your fight."

"No," Serah said. "We won't let you fight alone."

"If you don't go, he'll use you against me."

With a stray flick of the hand, he created a portal that opened onto a distant mountain.

"Get inside, now!"

"Come on," Jagar said. "Into the portal!"

The Ancient One manifested his spear of shadow magic, aiming it right for Lucian's friends.

Lucian threw Lightspear toward it; his aim was true. The golden spear clashed with the spear of shadow, breaking the latter apart.

"Go!" Lucian said.

Jagar ushered everyone through the portal, and thankfully, no one argued. Serah looked at him helplessly for a moment before

Lucian pushed her through with Psionic Magic. It was the only way she would have gone.

The Ancient One reformed his spear. It seemed to be made from pure Shadow Magic, the counterpoint to Lucian's. Even if it was no match for Lightspear, he knew one touch would kill him just as surely as Lightspear could kill the Ancient One.

"So, we meet again, Chosen," the Ancient One taunted, his voice echoing across the barren plateau. "But this time, not even the power of Creation will avail you."

"That's what you just told me," Lucian said. "Or rather, that's what you *will* tell me."

The Ancient One stood still, trying to make sense of Lucian's words. "I was blindsided. I never expected that fool Enkius to send that Orb of his using the pitiful Time Weaver. What a fool! Now, the Orb of Creation and the Orb of Space-Time will *both* be mine. Your doom is sealed."

Lucian met the Ancient One's gaze with steely resolve. His grip tightened around Lightspear, a tangible reminder of the battles fought and this battle to come. Although Lucian thought his position was unassailable, he could not underestimate his opponent.

Shadow Magic swirled around the Ancient One's form. "A duel then. For the mastery over the Aspects. Let us see who the Orbs truly favor."

"That has already been decided by the Manifold," Lucian said. "Are you ready to play your part?"

"Such arrogance. You think you know so much, but perhaps you know nothing at all."

"Enough talking."

With those words, both Lucian and the Ancient One shot toward the Orbs. As Lucian and the Ancient One made contact with the Crown, the air crackled and flashed.

Lucian found himself in the same environment, only everything was painted in vibrant hues of red. The Orb of Thermalism in the Ethereal Crown above shone so brightly that it overpowered the others. When Lucian reached his Focus, Thermalism was the *only* Aspect he could access.

Intrinsically, he knew what was happening. One-by-one, the Aspects were going to choose who would be the master.

It didn't take long for the scene to erupt in a fiery spectacle. Lucian extended his hand and a whip of flame sprung from his fingers, a molten, living creature at his command. The Ancient One countered with a shield of frigid ice, turning the surging fire into harmless steam that hissed into the air.

The Ancient One retaliated, hands moving with a fluid grace. He summoned a barrage of ice shards that flew toward Lucian with deadly intent. Lucian streamed a wall of pure flame, melting the ice before it could reach him.

The two circled one another, a dance of red and blue leaving the plateau scarred with the aftermath.

Lucian pressed the offensive, creating a massive vortex of fire that roared toward the Ancient One. The Ancient One wreathed himself in ice, sidestepping the incendiary wave, and countered with his own stream of frost that stopped the fire cold, solidifying it into a wall of glittering ice. The wall shattered, raining shards of ice that threatened to stab Lucian through.

Lucian, once again, created a wall of flame; as soon as the ice made contact, it melted and hissed as it turned to steam.

The battle raged on, neither gaining a decisive advantage. Sweat trickled down Lucian's brow from the intensity of the duel, but he remained resolute, locked in this test of wills.

Once more, they faced off with each other. Lucian created another vortex of flame, strengthening it beyond any he ever had before. The Ancient One countered with a freezing tempest. The collision of hot and cold energies created a shockwave that threw both of them back.

Yet, Lucian was undeterred. With a final, desperate move, he reached for the Orb of Thermalism with his Focus. But rather than purely draw from the energy of the Orb, he also drew from the sun burning in the sky above. A sharp infusion of ether entered his Focus, the surrounding heat intensifying as hot as a living star.

The Ancient One hurriedly tried to counter with another wave of freezing cold, but Lucian charged forward, throwing himself at the Ancient One. His shield of ice broke, and the Ancient One screamed as Lucian's fire consumed him.

———

INSTANTLY, everything reset, and the brilliance of the Orb of Thermalism faded, to be replaced by the molten orange glow of the Orb of Atomicism.

Lucian and the Ancient One squared off again, now entering the realm of Atomic Magic.

Lucian felt the stone beneath his feet shift, transmuting into an acidic liquid. He pivoted away to safe ground. He targeted the air around the Ancient One, solidifying it into crystal.

But before the stream could complete, the Ancient One dodged, leaving behind an empty chrysalis.

Again, Lucian felt the ground shift beneath him, first into sand, and then into water. Lucian sublimated the water into hydrogen and water, falling a short distance into the cavity beneath. He tried to use Gravitonics to get out, but this Aspect was barred to him. He reached for the solid earth in front of him, blasting it into the air with a small chemical explosion to create a makeshift ramp.

But the distraction allowed the Ancient One to fill the hole with heavy, yellow gas that Lucian fought hard to reverse. By the time he'd transmuted it into breathable air, he was stumbling out of the hole, coughing, his skin and throat feeling as if they were being stabbed.

He retaliated against the Ancient One by morphing the surrounding air into a solid wall, boxing him in.

Yet, the Ancient One was not so easily ensnared. He turned the solid air back into a gaseous form, and with a flick of his wrist, sent a shockwave of orange Atomic energy toward Lucian, a wall of pure radiation that would cause the very skin to fall off his bones.

Lucian shielded the attack, barely surviving the blast. He could scarcely draw breath from the aftereffects of the poison gas. He only had a few minutes before he completely suffocated.

It was all Lucian could do to defend himself against his adversary. Lucian let out a blast of concentrated radiation toward his opponent. The Ancient One encased himself in a temporary shell of super tensile metal.

Lucian realized that his knowledge of Atomicism was limited; it had always been his weakness, and it had been his mistake to not develop it to its full potential. The range of attacks he was forced to defend against was nothing short of astounding.

If he was to have any shot of winning, he had to bring the fight in close.

Lucian ran forward with Lightspear, finding that thankfully, this weapon wasn't barred to him. He used Atomicism to infuse oxygen into his very blood, so that his wasted lungs no longer had to breathe. The surrounding air was now laced with carbon monoxide and even more deadly poisons. He shielded himself as he met the Ancient One in the center of the plateau, Lightspear and Darkspear clashing in a cascade of shimmering sparks.

Lucian transmuted the air around the Ancient One into an unstable isotope of oxygen, which immediately caused a blinding explosion that sent his adversary hurtling backward.

But the Ancient One was far from defeated. He rose, a shell of

Atomic Magic around him crackling ominously. He was gathering the energy for a finishing blow, a pure nuclear explosion.

Lucian manipulated the atomic structure of the soil beneath the Ancient One, turning it into quicksand. The Ancient One struggled, but the more he moved, the more he sank. He abandoned his stream and attempted instead to undo the quicksand.

But Lucian had counted on this. He changed his own attack, solidifying the quicksand back into solid stone to lock the Ancient One in place. He set the brand with all of his power, and there was nothing the Ancient One could do to undo it.

With the Ancient One immobilized and defenseless, Lucian charged forward. The Ancient One no longer had the time to complete his original fission stream and had to settle for a wave of toxic radiation. Lucian easily countered, stabbing Lightspear.

The Ancient One parried, but could do nothing as Lucian circled around for a backstab. He cried out his dismay as his body disintegrated into ash.

The scene once again shifted. As the yellow Orb shone from the crown above, Lucian knew the next match was going to be Dynamism.

ONCE AGAIN, the battleground on the plateau was reset. Lucian drew a breath and was relieved to find that he was completely healed for this next bout.

Storm clouds formed overhead, mirroring the conflict on the ground. Lucian felt electricity coursing at his fingertips. The Ancient One, with his dark cape flying in the wind, threw up his hands and sent a whirling vortex of electricity spiraling forward.

Lucian responded instinctively, creating a magnetic sphere in front of him to attract and diffuse the incoming storm. Sparks sprayed off in a dazzling display of light.

Lucian redirected his stream to manipulate the magnetic field of the moon itself, repurposing it to surround the Ancient One, binding him with a confining force. In response, the air around the Ancient One crackled and warped, ionizing into an electric cocoon that absorbed and dispersed Lucian's magnetic constraints.

The plateau transformed into an electric battlefield, lightning bolts dancing across the expanse as they took shots at each other, leaving behind a mosaic of electrified destruction.

Lucian, drawing upon every ounce of his ether, ripped a blinding electromagnetic pulse through the turbulent air. The sheer force of it tore through the Ancient One's magnetic defenses, throwing him back and leaving him sprawled on the ground. The very force of it seemed to have stunned him.

Now was his chance. He gathered his remaining strength and summoned a devastating wave of electrical energy that washed over the Ancient One, staggering him once again.

He brought forth Lightspear and stabbed directly into his dazed foe.

———

As the electrical sparks dissipated, the battle shifted to the Radiance round, a green light emanating from the Crown above.

Lucian wasted no time in creating an intense sphere of pure, dazzling light designed to blind the Ancient One. The Ancient One staggered backward, hastily conjuring a reflective barrier that threw Lucian's searing brightness right back at him.

Lucian only endured the light for a moment, countering by bending it around him, masking his form. He kept the stream active, trying to approach the Ancient One while he was still invisible.

But the Ancient One retaliated with a cunning move that Lucian would have never expected. He manipulated light to create an army of illusions, at least five other phantasms among which he mixed in. So fast did the illusions move, and so convincing were they that Lucian quickly lost track of his true enemy.

One of these ethereal ghosts charged at Lucian, and he shattered it with a laser, causing it to scatter in a kaleidoscope of surreal colors.

Lucian felt panic welling up. He didn't know what would happen if he lost one of these engagements. Did he need to win all of them? The majority? He didn't want to take the chance.

He needed *something* that could counter these illusions, but what?

A green laser shot toward Lucian's position; he raised his shield to find that the attack was real. He tried to keep track of the Ancient One, the real one, but he was already lost among the projections again.

Lucian reached out, crafting a wall before him that did not allow light to pass through, thus allowing him to pass without being seen. He ran from his position, setting up in a nearby crater before allowing the stream to dissipate.

Quiet fell over the battlefield, though light shone down brightly from above as the Ancient One began his search.

All this time, Lucian gathered his ether, readying it to create a massive attack that would guarantee the Ancient One's demise. Lucian only had one shot, though. He couldn't aim his stream at an illusion.

He had to pick the right one.

At the crunch of nearby footsteps, Lucian rose and came face-to-face with the Ancient One. His enemy fired a laser, and it took every ounce of willpower for Lucian to allow it to enter him.

The laser passed harmlessly through. An illusion.

Lucian turned to see another visage of the Ancient One. Was it fake, or reality?

Again, he allowed it to attack him, and nothing happened.

Acting on instinct, he looked above to see the Ancient One

falling down on him, Darkspear extended. That had been the Ancient One's mistake; the raw shadow magic emanating from the weapon could not be faked.

Lucian unleashed a concentrated beam of light, and the plateau was lit with blinding brilliance. The laser struck true, hitting the corporeal form of the Ancient One directly in the chest, disintegrating him into ash.

Lucian stood ready, meditating to reorient himself for the next duel.

———

THE RADIANCE ROUND left an afterglow of shimmering light, the last vestiges dissolving into the Ether as the duel shifted to the Binding Aspect.

The very air around them crackled with potential, radiating unimaginable power that threatened to tear the atomic fabric of existence asunder, or meld it together.

This power was both Lucian's and the Ancient One's to command.

The Ancient One stretched forth his hand. A crushing force, like an unseen black hole, swirled around Lucian, seeking to squeeze the surrounding space and compress him into a singularity, an inescapable prison of atomic compression. Lucian had never known magic like this; he realized there was so much more to Binding Magic than even he had imagined.

Lucian, gritting his teeth, felt the pressure, but refused to bend or break, reversing the power of the stream with a cocoon of opposing Binding Magic. With a defiant roar, he channeled against his adversary's power. A beacon of blue, volatile energy pulsed from within him, spreading in a shockwave of raw, unstable decay. The plateau trembled as Lucian broke free from his Binding prison.

"Your strength will wane, Chosen!" the Ancient One snarled,

his voice carrying over the Binding storm he'd conjured. Once again, he attempted to crush Lucian with a compressing Binding shell.

Marshaling his strength, Lucian seized control of the Binding, reversing its iron grip. A brilliant flash of blue energy burst from within, the blue shockwave hurling the Ancient One backward. The ethereal Binding chains snapped in the wake of Lucian's stream.

The Ancient One, recovering from the surprise reversal, lashed out with renewed vigor. He streamed a torrent of Binding energy, a storm of blue lightning of such intensity that it threatened to tear the fabric of reality itself apart. If that storm contacted Lucian, the very atoms of his body would disintegrate.

But Lucian was ready. He streamed a field of repelling energy that met the oncoming storm head-on. The energies clashed in the space between them, creating a tumultuous maelstrom of intertwining forces.

"Is this your future, Chosen?" The Ancient One's mocking voice echoed above the cacophony. "A reality torn apart by your weakness?"

"Weakness?" Lucian shot back. "You've lost four times so far. Or have you lost count?"

With that declaration, Lucian reshaped his repelling force into a series of tethers, four strands of vibrant blue. With a sweeping motion, he cast them toward the Ancient One, who, surprised by this sudden change in tactics, was ensnared by them.

The Ancient One cried out in dismay as Lucian yanked him forward, disrupting his control over the Binding storm. Before the Ancient One could center himself, Lucian reversed the stream, pushing the Ancient One away with an unreal force, sending him arcing through the air.

As the Ancient One fought to regain his balance and control, Lucian took a moment to gather his own Binding storm. Once the

Ancient One had recovered enough to create a tether back to the plateau, Lucian unleashed his fury. A storm of Binding tethers, pushing and pulling, tore into the Ancient One, breaking him apart piece by piece. Once the Binding lightning ceased, there was nothing in the air but charged static.

Again, Lucian stood victorious.

———

THE CLIMACTIC BINDING STORM SUBSIDED, giving way to a calm that was both serene and unsettling. With a flicker, the next Aspect came into play—Psionics. Its violet light spread over the plateau, which was now basked under the glow of evening.

Lucian drew upon the power of Psionics, commanding everything that could be a weapon to strike. Pebbles, dust, rocks, anything that wasn't bolted down became a weapon, whirling toward the Ancient One in a blinding storm.

The Ancient One, however, parried with a barrier, his mind's fortress repelling Lucian's kinetic onslaught.

"Feeble," he said with a sneer.

The Ancient One retaliated by grappling anything in Lucian's vicinity, creating a chaotic whirlwind of debris. Lucian dodged an incoming boulder, propelling himself away with a kinetic push.

Lucian recalibrated and launched a psychic assault, his thoughts a barrage aimed to penetrate the Ancient One's mental defenses.

A grunt of surprise escaped the Ancient One as Lucian's psychic attack landed, causing a crack to appear in his previously impenetrable psychic wall. He staggered but swiftly recovered, his red eyes glowing with an eerie intensity.

The Ancient One struck with a double-edged attack, using both psychic and kinetic streams. A mental assault aimed at overwhelming Lucian's mind, while a barrage of physical debris shot toward him.

Lucian rolled to evade the physical attack, his Psionic shield flickering as he resisted the psychic invasion. He needed to end this round, and quickly.

He shouted defiantly, unleashing a torrent of magic to repel the Ancient One's kinetic attacks, redirecting the debris back at him while unleashing a psychic blast.

A grimace twisted the Ancient One's features as he met Lucian's counterattack. He skidded back, the psychic attack throwing off his concentration and allowing the redirected debris to crash into him, piling him so deeply in rubble that Lucian knew there could be no possibility of escape.

All the same, Lucian didn't let up. He kept piling more and more debris on top. He didn't stop until the duel moved to its next Aspect—Gravitonics, the confirmation that his tactic had won him this round.

———

As the dust from the Psionics round settled, the final round was set into motion. The battleground became a distorted landscape, hills rising and falling as if in a surreal dream. All evidence of Lucian's mountain of rubble was gone. Everything had once again been reset.

Lucian, despite his exhaustion, knew he could not stop now. He suspected he had to win every round to truly prove his mastery. If he lost, it was all over.

He was the first to strike. He increased his gravitational pull, firmly anchoring himself to the ground as he sent a crushing Gravitonic wave toward the Ancient One. The distorted air raced toward his adversary.

The Ancient One met the attack with a wave of his own, the two gravitational forces clashing midway, twisting the very fabric of space around them.

"You tire, Chosen," the Ancient One mocked. "To have won every battle, only to fail this one . . ."

Lucian gritted his teeth against the strain, the physical toll of the battle and the words of the Ancient One like a weight on his shoulders.

Yet, his spirit remained unbroken. "It's not over. Not even close."

The Ancient One, with a cruel sneer, opened a Gravitonic aura. The ground under Lucian's feet cracked from the pressure. The Ancient One lessened his own gravity, allowing him to leap into the air.

Lucian created a reverse gravity barrier just as the Ancient One crashed down from above, pushing his foe in the opposite direction. He redirected the stream to counter the aura he was in, stepping out of its grip.

By now, the Ancient One had landed right in front, swiping Darkspear with fury, weighing down the spear to strike hard and fast. It was all Lucian could do to defray the intense pressure.

The Ancient One loomed above, his expression triumphant. "It ends now, Chosen."

It seemed as if the Ancient One's prediction was about to come true. Lucian was kneeling, struggling against the intense gravity streamed by the Ancient One, which his own shield could hardly counter. It felt as if his very atoms were being crushed.

But then, in the depths of his despair, he remembered how far he had come. The friends he'd made. The impossible obstacles he'd surmounted, all because he'd had the audacity to never give up.

And he wasn't about to give up now.

Lucian pushed himself to stand, his legs shaking beneath him. With a surge of raw power, he leaped high into the air, breaking free of the broken ground beneath him.

"You can't escape!" the Ancient One called from below.

Lucian didn't intend to. He gathered all the ether he had left, shaping it into one decisive counterattack. With a swift motion, he reversed the gravitational pull around the Ancient One as well.

Surprised, the Ancient One was sent hurtling upward. Lucian didn't waste the opportunity. He increased his own gravitational pull, falling toward the Ancient One who was racing up to meet him. Lucian pointed Lightspear down, while the Ancient One stabbed Darkspear upward. Even Lucian didn't know, at that moment, which would emerge victorious.

With a thunderous crash, Lightspear and Darkspear collided in mid-air, and the Ancient One went crashing down. For good measure, Lucian increased the gravity pulling on the Ancient One, causing him to crash through the hard rock of the plateau itself, flattening in a grotesque display. There was no question. The Ancient One's body was beyond all repair.

As Lucian landed lightly, a wave of relief washed over him. He had won the final round.

The Ethereal Crown came toward him, each Orb now shining to its fullest brightness. It joined with him, entering his Focus and joining the Orbs of Space-Time and Creation.

The Gravitonic battlefield dissipated, revealing the original broken landscape of the plateau.

Kneeling in the distance, no longer bound to his corporeal form, was the Ancient One. Though stripped of his Orbs, he had one trick left: his Shadow Magic, which Lucian could only dispel with the power of Creation.

The Ancient One regathered, levitating above the rocky, scarred ground of the plateau, Darkspear pointing toward Lucian. Despite having access to none of the Orbs, he wasn't going down without a fight.

The unimaginable power of the Aspects, not just the original Seven, but those of Space-Time and Creation, coalesced within Lucian, intertwining and resonating within his Focus. Each pulse of power was a testament to the journey he'd endured, a symphony of triumph and tragedy ringing in his soul. The broken landscape around him was a stark contrast to the celestial radiance now emanating from him.

In the middle of the shattered plateau, the dark, formless mass of the Ancient One had been reduced. But even in this diminished state, his malevolence burned fiercely, and he wasn't to be underestimated.

Lucian had to admire his grit. Against all odds, he was going to fight this out to the end.

But Lucian could not forget the hundreds of mages who were now a part of the Ancient One's Focus, their power now his.

The Ancient One lashed out, attempting to enshroud Lucian with his possessing Shadow Magic. But with the power of the Orbs coursing through him, Lucian was more than ready to face the Ancient One's desperate assault. With a swift motion, he countered with a brilliant beam of pure Creation Magic, casting away the darkness with the sheer force of golden light.

Lucian's attack ripped through the shadowy form of the Ancient One. He flew forward and landed a hit with Lightspear, causing the Ancient One to recoil.

But each blow he landed was met with an almost instantaneous regeneration, shadow knitting itself back together with stubborn tenacity.

If Lucian wanted to end the Ancient One for good, he had to stab Lightspear and keep it there until the Ancient One was good and dead.

The Ancient One thrust his shadow spear toward Lucian. But Lucian parried with Lightspear, severing the shadowy weapon, reducing it to mere wisps of darkness that vanished.

"It's over," Lucian said, his voice resounding across the plateau. The Creation Magic around him intensified, radiating waves of golden power that rippled against the Ancient One's cowering form.

"Never," the Ancient One hissed.

In a final, desperate lunge, he hurled himself at Lucian. But Lucian, embodying the Aspect of Creation, stood his ground. To Lucian's surprise, the Ancient One's form made decent headway through his shield. But the Ancient One being slowed allowed Lucian to drive Lightspear into his opponent's center.

A brilliant explosion of light emanated from the point of contact, illuminating the entire plateau. The Ancient One emitted a high, terrible shriek as the shadow fought to be loosed from Lightspear's hold. Lucian did not waver, gripping Lightspear with an iron strength as the Ancient One weakened and retracted.

At last, after several minutes of this, Lucian stood alone, every trace of the Ancient One dispelled. His clothing, a simple cloak of the Ancient style he had found aboard *Tempus*, fluttered in the rising wind.

As difficult as it was to believe, the Ancient One no longer existed in the Shadow Realm.

Exhausted, Lucian lifted his gaze to the sky. Though the Orbs were returned to him, he hardly felt any different. This didn't feel real.

Unless there was another avatar of the Ancient One unknown to him, then this really meant he was gone.

He allowed a slow smile to form on his lips.

"Finally," he whispered to the wind, his heart brimming with relief. "Rotting finally."

44

LUCIAN CREATED A PORTAL, allowing the others to get back to the plateau. They watched the battle-scarred landscape with wide eyes. It was as if the remnants of every battle had been mixed in the same place. Lucian wasn't sure how that had happened, but it was the only thing he could figure.

Serah ran up to Lucian, embracing him. It was only then that he allowed himself to relax.

"He's dead?" she asked.

Lucian nodded. "Yeah. He's a goner."

"The Orbs?" Khairu asked.

Lucian let go of Serah and looked at Khairu. "I have them all."

"Not all," Jagar said.

He stood off in the distance and was looking at something on the ground. Something Lucian had missed in the darkness. Lucian frowned, walking over to join him.

Right at Jagar's feet was another Orb, one that was a dark violet, subtly glowing but hardly discernible from the surrounding darkness.

"What the hell?" Serah asked. "Which one is that?"

Lucian probed at his Focus, finding that every Orb was accounted for.

"I can only think of one thing," he said. "That's got to be the Orb of Shadows, or something to that effect."

"An Orb of Shadows?" Emma asked. "But the Time Weaver said the Ancient One never made an Orb. He *himself* was the Orb, so to speak."

"Maybe," Lucian said. "But also, when an Orb-holder dies, they leave behind whatever Orbs they had. While he didn't have an Orb, maybe his magic had to go *somewhere*. So, it created *this*."

All of them stared at it, trying to understand the implications.

At last, Serah broke the silence. "We need to chuck that thing into the nearest black hole."

Lucian considered for a moment. He was at a loss for what to do. The Time Weaver hadn't warned him of this. But then again, did the Time Weaver know everything?

"I wonder if it's possible for me to pick it up without absorbing it," Lucian said. "I'm not sure what would happen if I touched it."

"You *definitely* shouldn't touch it," Emma said. "It's the embodiment of the Ancient One. I'd hazard a guess that as long as that thing exists, there's a chance he could come back."

"Maybe," Jagar said, grimly. "But neither can we leave it here."

"Maybe we can hide it," Serah said. "Take it somewhere where no one will find it. Somewhere where *we* can pick it up when we come back to our own time. And then, we can safely take it back to the First Gate."

"We have all the Orbs right now," Emma said. "Theoretically, if we could somehow scrounge up a spaceship, we could begin our journey right now to go back to the First Gate. Change the timeline."

"That would alter history in such a way that it would mean nonexistence for all of us," Lucian said. "And not only us, but everyone we've ever known. My mom, Fergus, and all the rest. Everything we've ever known will be different."

"Wait," Serah said. "I thought Emma said the timeline would still exist, even if we acted differently. As long as someone is there to experience it."

"It will exist for them, but not for us," Emma said. "It could lead to a paradoxical situation where we would cease to exist because all of us are cut off from that reality, while they would continue to go on."

"Maybe Lucian could stop us from fading by using the Orb of Creation," Serah said.

"Maybe," Lucian said. "But I won't have the Orbs anymore once we return them, right? And we're forgetting something important. What are we even fighting for? Right now, we're a million years in the past. Humans haven't even come on the scene yet. If we end magic now, we'd be saving the universe. And creating an entirely new reality where humans will develop with no form of magic at all. Everything in our timeline will be exactly the same until the point of magic arrives. And then it will diverge . . ."

"That's assuming the Ancients die out," Emma said. "And that's assuming that they don't do anything to mess with Earth with their new lease on life."

"That's the humanity we would save," Lucian said. "But it's not *our* humanity. *Our* reality. Maybe on paper, the Ancients matter as much as us, or that future version of humanity. But we can't fight for every reality, every possibility. We can only fight for the one we know. Otherwise, what's the point?" Lucian shook his head. "Of course, all this is just speculation."

"So, the vote is going back to our own time with the Orbs," Khairu said. "And from there, returning them to the Heart of Creation?"

"Not exactly," Lucian said. "The Orbs can't come back with us."

"Why not?" Serah asked.

"Because the Ancient One's death—or the Second Immortal —doesn't match with our own history. Way back on Volsung, when I first got the Orb of Binding, remember what Rhana said? The Second Immortal was overwhelmed by both the *Alkasen* and internal rebellion. She said nothing about a Chosen defeating him."

"What does that mean, then?" Emma asked. "How do we save the timeline?"

"I imagine history falsely remembers the Second Immortal's death," Lucian said. "The Orb of Creation drew him here because the Orbs could not exist in two places at once. I'm willing to bet that the Immortal was busy fighting a battle, maybe even in this very star system, either against the *Alkasen* or against an uprising of his own subjects. Maybe even at the same time. His sudden disappearance would have led to chaos. Perhaps that battle is still going on. Either way, with him disappearing altogether, it's likely his soldiers think he's dead."

"So, you want to find out where the Second Immortal was before he got taken *here*?" Khairu asked.

"We wouldn't need to do something so exact. We would need to leave the Orbs somewhere. Somewhere they can be found by the right Ancients."

"But how would you know you were leaving them in the right place?" Emma asked. "Any wrong choice could create the wrong timeline."

It was a quandary, and one Lucian didn't know the answer to. "That's why I have to seek answers from the Manifold itself. I'll have to delve the future. There's no other way."

"Okay, what about the Orb of Space-Time?" Khairu asked. "Arian has to discover it at some point, though he never explicitly mentions *where* he discovered it."

"He finds it in the Moon Tower," Lucian said. "He mentioned it in that recording I found on Nai Elyn."

"Okay," Serah said. "So, how does the Orb of Space-Time end up there? That's the real question. Any solution will be rotting convoluted," Serah said.

"There's a missing piece," Jagar said. "The Dark Gate."

Lucian frowned. "What about it?"

"Don't you find it strange that Nielsen and Arian could find Nai Elyn, when its only access point is the Dark Gate?"

"Why is that strange?" Serah asked. Her eyes widened in realization. "Oh, because Lucian was the only one who's supposed to find it, right?"

Jagar nodded. "It's something that's always bothered me. Of course, maybe they stumbled upon it with blind luck, but something tells me they had some help."

"Some help?" Lucian asked. "What do you mean?"

"Well, maybe the Dark Gate wasn't *always* dark. Maybe they found it because someone drew some attention to it."

"Someone like me," Lucian realized.

"How would you have done that, Lucian?" Serah asked.

"You're asking me as if I've already done it."

"Well, you *had* to have done it already for the original Orb to have been found by Arian. Right?"

"A brand, maybe," Emma said. "A powerful signal that wouldn't go dark when The Starsea Cycle ends and magic dies out. That won't come until a few centuries from now, when the Oracles decide to protect the Orbs from the *Alkasen*."

"They don't *decide* to," Khairu said. "They are *driven* to."

"Another thing we have to do?" Serah asked.

Khairu nodded. "The Prophecy of the Seven was originally the impetus for them to protect the Orbs. But the one thing we never asked was where the Prophecy came from."

"The Manifold, I've always assumed," Emma asked. "Maybe this Anlilta figure the Time Weaver mentioned."

Khairu shrugged. "I'm thinking that maybe Lucian himself is the source of the Prophecy. He has access to the Orb of Space-

Time. Using it, plus the power of the other Orbs, he can communicate everything necessary to get the Oracles to do the right thing."

Lucian realized she was right. With the Orb of Creation, and perhaps Psionics and Space-Time, it would be possible to do. He wouldn't need to speak every word of the Prophecy; he simply had to transfer his thoughts and memories into the Orb itself, allowing them to enter the Ether. From there, he could access those same thoughts and memories through the Orb of Space-Time, along with Arian, when he came to possess it.

"Add it to the list," Serah said.

"It's a lot," Lucian said. "But it's necessary. I need to think about this. Everything has to be done in the proper order, or it could mean disaster."

Lucian reached out, surrounding the Orb of Shadows with a powerful Binding brand. He sealed it with every Aspect at his disposal, including that of Creation. He imposed his will upon it, ensuring it would remain completely untouchable until he unraveled it.

He picked up the blue-enshrouded Orb, finding there was nothing to fear. He placed it in his pack.

"We should move out," Lucian said.

"Back to Mako, right?" Serah asked.

Lucian nodded. "Yes. I want a safe place to delve the future. And eventually, I'll need to use the Source of Power and the Orbs to create the time gate back."

"I wouldn't be surprised if our camping supplies are still there," Emma said. "Assuming we came back at the same time we left."

"That would be a trip," Serah said.

Wasting no more time, he created a portal to the cave, finding no issue with the connection. They went through, ready to enact the first part of their plan.

45

AS THEY ENTERED the portal and into the Mako cave, a wave of exhaustion such as Lucian had never known hit him in full force. He created a powerful Radiant ward, enough to block out their presence to any Ancient mages lurking nearby. They then went right back to where they had set up camp all those weeks ago. Placing his hand near the ashes, Lucian found they were still warm.

They scanned the perimeter with Radiant Magic, finding that whatever Ancient mages had been here were long gone. A few hours must have elapsed since the original battle.

Whatever the case, the coast was clear, and Lucian was confident they wouldn't be interrupted again.

There, they slept for what seemed forever. They hadn't gotten a wink of sleep since waking up in Angkasa's palace nine million years in the past. And Lucian wasn't counting the time shift as a rest.

Lucian swam through dreams and awoke to find the interior of the cave dark, with nothing but a star-filled sky outside the wide cave mouth. Jagar tended the fire over which he cooked a pot of stew from what few supplies had been left behind.

Lucian helped himself. He was ravenous. As the light outside grew, the others woke up and joined him.

The events of the past few weeks had been so insane that Lucian got the feeling that maybe it was all some strange dream, and that he was simply waking up for the first time since coming to the past.

But the Orbs in his Focus quickly put a dash to that notion.

"I think it's time," he said, breaking the silence.

"Do what you need to do," Khairu said. "We'll be here, so take your time."

"Well, maybe not *too* much time," Serah said. "Those Ancients could be back at any moment."

"I don't think they'll be bothering us," Lucian said. "And if they come back, we can handle them this time."

"All the same. Be careful."

He headed off into the darkness, using Radiant Magic to see. Within minutes, he was back near the Source of Power, a shining sphere of energy floating in the cave's darkness, a rending between the Light Realm and the Shadow.

Lucian reached for it, along with his Orbs, and began his work.

Instantly, he was pulled into an intricate web of futures. Multiple realities spun out before him like threads in the cosmic loom, each a unique tapestry of events, decisions, triumphs, and tragedies.

But among this entanglement of potential futures, certain threads stood out, glowing with an undeniable sense of destiny.

It was toward these that Lucian directed his will. In the swirling Ether, he entered a trance, and began speaking in the Ancient language, his mind somehow knowing how to form the words of the tongue of this era rather than the alternate future version of the language. He knew his words would one day inspire the Oracles to protect the Orbs from the *Alkasen*.

How long Lucian spoke, he couldn't say. He was a conduit of the Manifold, enacting its will on the Shadow Realm.

By the time he finished, every word resonated within the Ether, and more than that, within the Orb of Space-Time itself. When humanity reached out for the stars, his words would find their way to Arian when he came to possess the Orb of Space-Time.

He then switched his Focus to the next task; what to do with the Orbs he now had.

Again, possibilities outspread before him. He searched for hours until he found the right path that would lead to a future that was his own.

The answer came to him in a flash. Could it be so stunningly simple?

He doubted this insight for a moment, but he remembered that the Manifold was showing him this.

If this was the way, then he had to follow it.

He reached through the Ether, toward the only other being that could help him.

Time Weaver . . . I'm here.

Lucian felt the message connect, along with a general acknowledgement. The Time Weaver had heard him.

Lucian opened his eyes, knowing that the moment to create the time gate had arrived.

Guided by the knowledge of the Orb of Creation, Lucian formed an image in his mind not only of this location in his own time but also of all of his emotions and associations with it. It took hours before the picture was completely painted, but once done, he knew he had everything he needed.

He channeled the ether held within the Source of Power toward a single point, every Orb working in tandem. A golden time gate opened before him, a tenuous line of ether connecting it to the Source. This one appeared different from the one streamed by the Ancient One; it was bright, the plane of its surface lit with a golden sheen rather than opaque darkness.

Lucian branded the stream. He was confident his Creation Magic would keep it open until it was ready to be used.

Lucian was utterly exhausted from the effort. He hobbled back to camp, finding the others waiting anxiously for him, and evening light outside the cave.

"The gate is open," he said.

The others cheered this news, but Lucian was far too tired to join in.

"Now, we need to figure out what to do about these Orbs," Emma said.

Before Lucian could respond, a visitor entered the cave and walked in their direction. As the others rushed to get up, Lucian held up a hand.

"Don't worry. I invited him."

Before they could ask anything, they could clearly see who it was: the same middle-aged man they had met on Airaruma nine million years in the past.

"The Time Weaver?" Serah asked. "What's he doing here?"

The Time Weaver came to a stop and regarded them all a few paces from the fire. His eyes went up to Lucian, brown and friendly, and perhaps mischievous.

"I was wondering when thou would summon me. Fret not, for all this is according to the plan. Knowest that I alone hold the power to accomplish this mighty task."

"What mighty task?" Serah asked. "Sounds serious."

Lucian took in the group. "The Manifold has revealed its will to me." He nodded toward the Time Weaver. "*He's* the one who's supposed to take the Orbs."

There was a collective gasp from the group at this news.

"Not all of them, surely?" Emma asked.

Lucian shook his head. "No. Not all. I'll keep the Orb of

Creation and the Orb of Shadows. By the time we return to the present, I'll have all the Orbs again. If everything goes according to plan."

"So, he's supposed to divvy out the Orbs?" Emma asked. "Make sure they get into the right hands?"

Lucian nodded. "More or less."

"That's . . . *crazy*."

"Is it, though?" Lucian took everyone in. "There's no way we could untangle this knot. Plus, the Manifold revealed that this was the way. This is the last step."

"Can we trust him?" Serah asked. "He's *Alkasen*, after all."

"There's no other way to make sure this job actually gets done," Lucian said. "We need someone to not only distribute the Orbs to the right Ancients of this time period. We also need someone to make sure Arian finds the Orb of Space-Time in the right place and time. The Time Weaver is the only being in the Worlds who can do it. Unlike any of us, he can create time gates at will."

"Like Serah said," Emma said, "he's *Alkasen*. How do we guarantee he doesn't just take the Orbs back to the Heart of Creation?"

"Because I will still have the Orb of Creation and the Orb of Shadows," Lucian said. "He won't return the Orbs unless he has these two as well. And I'm not giving them up unless the Time Weaver plays his part."

The Time Weaver broke his silence. "Yea, I'm the only one who can do this. There is no time unknown to me, and I have beheld all this within the Manifold. Yet, there remains another price thou must pay for mine aid, which I bestow not lightly. For my mission is no simple task, even with my powers."

"What price?" Lucian asked.

"It concerns the Orb of Shadows. When you return it to the Light Realm, you must bring it to the Ascendant Enkius himself."

"What is this Orb?" Lucian asked. "We were wondering what to do with it. And what does Enkius want with it?"

"The Orb of Shadows is the very essence of the Ancient One, and any soul that wields it shall assume his Aspect. It doth taint and defile all other Orbs, and whilst it endures, the Orbs can never be truly purged of his presence. The Orb of Shadows is a gateway to ruin. It must never be wielded by thee! Thou must vow this unto me if thou desirest mine aid."

"Why would I ever use it in the first place?"

"There may come a time when thou art sorely tempted to do such a deed. Be not taken aback, Chosen, however unfathomable this appears now. Thou must vow not to lay a hand upon it, or else all is vanity. I can undertake naught unless thou swearest this unto me by the Manifold itself."

Lucian hesitated. Of course, right now it seemed a fine thing to promise. He was fully committed to never using the Orb. He knew doing so would risk himself to being possessed by the Ancient One.

But he couldn't help but feel he didn't have all the information. Yet, he could not risk the Time Weaver not fulfilling his end of the bargain. The Manifold was clear that he had a part to play, both in distributing the Orbs and making sure Arian found the Orb of Space-Time later on, instigating a new Starsea Cycle.

"I promise," Lucian said.

The Time Weaver smiled. "Fear not; what you ask is already accomplished. Dost thou remember? We are all bound to enact our roles. And remember thy vow; the Ether itself binds thee to it, and to go astray would be a grave error, not merely for thee, but for all creation."

All were silent at these ominous words, and yet, Lucian could not see any other way to get the Time Weaver's help without making that promise.

"When thou art prepared, Chosen, I stand poised to receive thy offerings."

Lucian steeled himself for what came next. It felt wrong to give up these Orbs he had fought so hard for. And yet, he knew that there was no other path forward.

He had to trust what the Manifold had revealed to him. Nothing he had seen by his magic was a lie.

"All right," he said. "Here goes nothing."

His Creation Magic would keep the time gate open by the Source of Power; he wasn't worried about that. He was just worried about being wrong, about messing something up.

This felt . . . *wrong*. And yet, he knew beyond a doubt there was no other way forward.

So, he gathered his courage and imagined the Ethereal Crown. It manifested above him readily enough, only in the center floated the Orb of Space-Time. The Orb of Creation he kept within his Focus. The Orb of Shadows was still safe in his pack, though he felt a powerful pull from it akin to magnetic attraction. It wanted to join with the others in the Crown.

"Make haste, Chosen," the Time Weaver said. "Hand over the Crown!"

The longer Lucian waited, the more powerfully the Orb of Shadows was attracted. There was no more time to lose.

He thrust the Crown toward the Time Weaver, who took it with reverence. The Emissary did not absorb them into his own Focus. He merely placed it into his leather satchel, not even tempted by the godlike power that would be his. Perhaps he didn't need that power. He seemed powerful enough without the Orbs.

"I must take my leave," the Time Weaver said. "May the Manifold look favorably upon thee, Chosen, and guide thy steps. Thy fate lies at the very Heart of Creation."

With that, an aura of dark Space-Time Magic surrounded the Time Weaver, causing them all to jump back. He was gone in a flash, with nothing but a swirl of dust to prove he was there.

"That was . . . *something*," Emma said.

"Are you sure you did the right thing?" Khairu asked.

Lucian nodded. "I know it was right, but it feels wrong. If that makes any sense."

He puzzled over the intensity of the Time Weaver's words, and why he had been so pushy about securing a promise about the Orb of Shadows. Lucian couldn't think of any reason he would ever need, or want, to use it, especially when he knew doing so would cause the Ancient One to possess him outright.

And yet, he couldn't help but feel suspicious. Maybe the Time Weaver sensed some danger in the future that Lucian wasn't aware of.

"The gate is waiting for us," Lucian said.

"Let's get the hell out of here," Jagar said.

46

AS THEY PACKED everything up and headed for the time gate, Lucian felt a pulsating emptiness. After he had regained the Eight Orbs that were once his, it felt as if he'd gotten a part of himself back. Maybe even *most* of himself.

Now, there was only a hollow void. Everything inside him told him he'd made the wrong choice, and yet, unless the Manifold was lying to him, he'd made the *right* choice.

There was one condolence; he still had the Orb of Creation, not to mention the Orb of Shadows, Bound and safe inside his pack. The Orb of Shadows he had sworn not to touch.

He would return both to the Heart of Creation, and hopefully, get conclusive answers. From the Ascendant Beings themselves, if possible.

Lucian breathed a sigh of relief to see that the time gate still stood. It was stable and continuously fed by the Source of Power. As soon as they all went through, it would close behind them. If all went according to plan, this entire ordeal would soon be over.

"Time to see if it worked," Jagar said.

"If not," Serah said, "it was an honor and a privilege to serve."

"Something like that," Emma said.

Khairu remained silent, her eyes reflecting the golden-white light of the gate. Unshed tears shone in her eyes.

"It'll be like we never even left," Lucian said.

"I'm ready," Khairu said. "Let's go back home."

They made their way back, walking in a line so all would pass through at the same time. As soon as they passed the temporal threshold, Lucian once again had the strange feeling of being stretched. For an indeterminate amount of time, he hung in limbo, drawing ever closer to the opening through a muddled non-linear chaos.

At last, he found the other side, along with the others, dizzyingly stumbling out of the other side. Lucian blinked to find they were in the same cave in which they had started. The gate snapped closed behind them, leaving them with nothing but the Source of Power for company.

Everything looked and felt the same. The features of the cavern were more decrepit, having a million more years to erode compared to the past. But Lucian had the strong feeling that he was not only in the right place, but at the right time.

But the next test was still to come. Did he still have the Orbs? Had the Time Weaver fulfilled his end of the bargain?

He reached for his Focus. Psionics. Gravitonics. Thermalism. Atomicism. Dynamism. Radiance. Binding.

And, last of all, Space-Time and Creation. A quick peek in his pack revealed the Orb of Shadows was still there, thrumming with dark violet potential.

All were there and accounted for.

"I have them," he said. "Every single one."

"It worked!" Serah said. "It rotting *worked*! I can't believe it!"

"That was . . . *insane*," Emma said, nodding toward the empty spot the gate once occupied. "He's really dead, then? The Ancient One?"

Lucian looked at the Source of Power, the Ancient One's vain attempt to create a Second Gate to the Light Realm. Through it, he had imbued his very Focus onto Xara, Vera, Ansaldra, and Sharo. As long as this Source existed, then anyone with the power could conceivably take on the Ancient One and become his avatar again.

It was unlikely, but it would always be an issue.

"You're going to close that?" Emma asked, seeming to guess his thoughts.

Lucian nodded. "It's too risky to leave it open. If another mage came here, it would allow the Ancient One into our reality again."

"That begs the question," Khairu said. "Just *how* do you close it?"

"I would have to read the magic behind it. It's a brand, one of great power and complexity. So much so that not even the Ancient One could finish it right. If it *had* been completed, then there would be a Second Gate to the Light Realm right here instead of this rending in reality. I'm suspecting the reason he failed."

"How?" Khairu asked.

"He was missing an ingredient."

"Creation Magic?" Serah guessed.

"That's what I'm thinking. Again, I'd have to read the brand to be sure. According to the Time Weaver, it was Enkius who created the original First Gate with Creation Magic. It might be the same here."

"This will be a massive undertaking," Khairu said. "If the Ancient One used nine different Aspects of Magic to create this, it could take you days to go through the whole thing. If not longer."

Lucian knew she was right. It was enough to make him second-guess things a bit. There was always the possibility that it might take even longer than that.

Yet, the risk of this staying open was unacceptable. And with that, Lucian's mind was made up.

"I know this is the last thing we want to do," he said. "We're home. We want to relax before starting the next part. But for my mind to be at ease, this needs to be done. I'm not sure how long it'll take, but we can't leave this planet until this is taken care of."

The others nodded, not liking this news, but unable to argue against Lucian's logic.

"We have plenty of supplies on the ship," Khairu admitted. "It would be a shame to go through all that pain just to have to fight the Ancient One again."

"Are there any risks to this?" Jagar asked. "I imagine trying to close this Source would be dangerous. Is there a way the Ancient One can fight back?"

"It's a door into our reality, and an imperfect one," Lucian said. "He can't do anything unless I accept his invitation, so to speak. Just like Xara did. That said, you can bet he'll know exactly what I'm doing, but be powerless to stop it." Lucian smiled at the picture. "It'll give him something to think about while we're on our way to the Heart of Creation. Once we're rid of the Orb of Shadows, he'll be gone for good."

"I hope so," Emma said.

"Let's get started," Serah said. "The sooner we get it over with, the sooner we can party, right?"

Within the hour, they were back on *Blood Wyvern*. It was surreal being back, like coming home. Checking his slate, Lucian was surprised to find that only a couple of hours had passed since they'd left. What had been weeks for them had been mere hours for everyone else. And checking the newsfeeds, it looked as if everything was the same as before. The news from Nessus hadn't had time to travel this far.

Jagar shook his head, marveling. "Rotting hell, we did it, didn't we?"

"Seems so," Lucian said.

"I was worried we might shift the timeline irrevocably," Serah said. "Like giving everyone an eye in the middle of their fore-heads or something."

"Should we let Mira and Fergus know we're okay?" Emma asked.

"By the time our message finds them, we'll probably be done here," Lucian said. "Besides, there'll be plenty of time to explain later. If we did everything right, the Shadow Magic on Nessus should have stopped by now."

"Right," Emma said. "I wonder how the Ancient One pulled that off, anyway? It's the last big question."

"My guess is, he used whatever crew he had left from the Siege of Earth. He came here and used the Source of Power to turn them into conduits of Shadow Magic, so to speak. I know the terminology is crude, but with enough of them in a crowded spot, it had the potential to spread to millions of people. It's like the Bond of Creation, except in reverse. Whatever the Orb of Creation can do, the Orb of Shadows can do as well in the oppo-site way. If that makes sense."

"A Shadow Bond," Emma said. "Yeah, I could see that. It seems similar to the Bond of Creation."

"This next part I need to do alone," Lucian said. "The ship is the safest spot, unless you want some nasty critters in that cave for company."

"No thanks," Serah said. She looked at Lucian. "Please be careful, all right?"

"I will."

Lucian headed out of the ship. Rather than walk the entire way to the cave, he simply completed a short warp, finding himself standing directly in front of the Source of Power.

After a few centering breaths, he extended his Focus toward it. He entered a deep trance as he accessed the Ether.

First, he started off by making sense of the brand created so long ago by the Ancient One. The Ancient One's magic was convoluted, the complexity far beyond anything Lucian had encountered so far. Sifting through the tangle of raw streams, Lucian traced all nine Aspects used to build the Source of Power. The Seven Minor Aspects, along with the two major Aspects of Space-Time and Shadow. They intertwined into a vast, chaotic tapestry. But in that chaos was a beauty and order that defied words. The streams existed not only in three-dimensional space, but in the fourth dimension as well, extending forward and backward in time.

But he also found something else—a gap, a void where Creation Magic *should* have been. This was the missing ingredient, the ultimate piece that would have solidified the Ancient One's Second Gate. Lucian could almost feel the Ancient One's disappointment, his rage, upon realizing that he could not complete his grand design. It was a chilling insight into the mind of his enemy.

Lucian knew then that, if he wanted, he could complete the Ancient One's vision. All he would have to do was fill in the gaps with Creation Magic. But intrinsically, he also knew that doing so would give the Ancient One unfettered access to the Shadow Realm, his own reality. The First Gate, he presumed, was guarded by the Ascendant Beings and the Ancient One couldn't hope to pass through it.

A potential Second Gate was an escape route. Completing it would be folly. Lucian wasn't sure how the Ether and the Light Realm related, or if they were, in fact, the same thing. All he knew was he didn't want to take the risk.

Lucian began the intricate process of unwinding the twisted brand. He worked slowly, cautiously, knowing that a single misstep could cause a disastrous backlash. He disconnected one stream of magic, then another, meticulously untangling the knots that held the Source together.

He worked for hours, perhaps even days, his sense of time distorted by the intensity of the task. The Ether itself was his sustenance, his fuel.

With each severed thread, the Source of Power dimmed ever so slightly. Eventually, its once-blinding light was reduced to a mere flicker. And yet, the Ancient One's influence remained, a shadowy specter lingering in the background. Lucian could feel that presence marking his every move, but he was so intent on his task that it faded to the background.

After everything he'd been through, such a minor thing wasn't going to affect him.

Finally, only one stream remained—the stream of Shadows. It pulsated menacingly, resisting Lucian's attempts to sever it. He could feel the Ancient One's gaze upon him, a malevolent force wishing him to fail.

But Lucian was not deterred. His hand trembled as he reached into his pack and pulled out the Orb of Shadows. He could feel its chill seeping into his bones, a dark counterpart to the warm light of Creation. If he could not cancel out the power of Shadow Magic, the entire brand would rebuild itself from the bottom up. Somehow, he knew using the Orb of Shadows could easily give him mastery over this stubborn stream. He could also undo it with the Orb of Creation, but it would be a tougher fight.

Lucian decided he had come too far to risk himself by using the Orb of Shadows. Perhaps he could hold the Ancient One at bay and still use it. But he had made a solemn promise to the Time Weaver, a promise that was sealed by the Manifold itself.

If it was a battle, then he had to face it head-on, just as he had with everything else.

Lucian reached for the Orb of Creation, sending a raw infusion of golden light that interwove with the Shadow Magic. With all the other Aspects disassembled, the action would no longer complete the Second Gate. Instead, the two threads battled one another for supremacy. The Aspect of Creation for dismantling the brand, and the Aspect of Shadows for not only reestablishing the brand but subverting the Aspect of Creation for its own ends.

For a long time, Lucian streamed. The exhaustion of this

work was wearing him down. Hours could have passed, or perhaps even days. He could not lose patience.

Finally, with a last surge of will, Lucian severed the Shadow stream. He opened his eyes to see the Source of Power collapsing in full, its ethereal light extinguished.

For the first time in ten million years, the cave fell into an eerie darkness.

He swayed a bit, exhaustion nearly causing him to pass out. It was all he could do to gather the ether to complete a warp back to the ship.

As soon as he did so, he collapsed on the deck.

47

WHEN HE CAME TO, it was in *Blood Wyvern's* clinic.

He sat up, finding Serah sitting by his bedside.

She leaned forward, reaching for his arm. "How are you feeling?"

Lucian nodded. "Alive. Barely." He ripped out the IV in his arm and smiled at Serah. "How many times have I woken up with you sitting there like that?"

Serah laughed. "This had better be the last time."

Jagar and Emma entered the clinic, apparently drawn by the commotion.

"What day is it?" Lucian asked.

"Tuesday," Serah said. "About a week after we got here."

"That long?"

She nodded. "We went in there to check on you several times, but we quickly realized we needed to give you space. We didn't want to interrupt anything."

"Well done, lad," Jagar said.

"I'm glad you're safe," Emma said.

"I can get you some soup from the galley," Serah said. "I'm sure you're hungry."

Lucian was indeed. He was still tired, but he didn't want to stay in there for another moment. "I'm ready to get out of here. I want to check in with everyone. They need to know everything that's happened."

"Get some rest first," Emma said. "Khairu is already getting the ship ready. You shouldn't create any portals until you're one hundred percent."

Serah returned with the soup, along with a cup of coffee. Lucian ate and drank gratefully.

"I'll leave the two of you to it," Emma said. "We'll be up front when you're ready."

Emma and Jagar left as Lucian finished his meal and coffee. With food in his belly and the caffeine kicking in, he felt more than good enough.

"Feeling better?" Serah asked.

"A lot better. I'm ready to head back and see everyone."

"You sure?"

He got up from the bed and felt quite steady on his feet. Serah watched him, her expression worried as she held him close.

"I've missed you," she said. "I don't want you pushing yourself too hard."

What had been a week for Serah had only seemed like a few hours to him. And yet, as he held her close, he recognized he had missed her, too. Without the long journeys in space, there hadn't been much time to talk about anything other than the mission.

"I've missed you, too. I want to get away from everything for a while. Just lay on a beach somewhere."

Serah smiled. "That sounds grand. I'd really like to visit my dad on Psyche. If we're really not coming back from the First Gate . . ."

Lucian didn't really want to think about that, but it was a

genuine concern. They had to get all their last meetings in before they went off again to finish the job.

"One thing at a time," he said. "Let's head up front."

Serah wrinkled her nose. "Not before you've had a shower."

Lucian couldn't help but laugh. "Kind of forgot about that."

"Shower. Now."

Lucian did as he was asked, changing into a clean pair of clothes. He couldn't stomach wearing his Sorcerer-Ascendant gear, since he wasn't leading any fleets for the foreseeable future.

Once up front, Khairu straightened in her seat. "News says the League Fleet is orbiting Nessus now."

"I guess Mwangi and the Sentinels created a portal," Lucian said.

"They're very capable," Emma said.

"Okay. We'll be there before you know it."

Lucian formed a picture of Nessus and took a moment to gather his ether. The portal opened before them, and in the next instant, they emerged from beside the planet.

Almost immediately, they received a hail from *Mekong*. Khairu accepted the transmission.

"*Blood Wyvern*, welcome back," Mira said. "We've got a lot to talk about."

Lucian smiled. "Yes, we definitely do. How is everything?"

"Still chaos. But whatever happened with those Shadows, it seems to be gone now."

"Good. We did everything right, then."

"Right? What do you mean? Did you find the Ancient One?"

"In a manner of speaking," Serah said. "Let's just say he won't be a problem anymore."

"Seriously? That's amazing news!"

"We'll be docking with you soon," Lucian said. "Be sure to clear your schedule. This might take a while."

"Where's Fergie?" Serah asked. "I've missed that old stickler."

"I'm right here," Fergus said, "and you *know* I don't like you calling me that."

"Just making sure you're there," Serah said. "We'll be there soon."

"What about Linus and Plato?" Lucian asked. "How are they?"

"I've sent them down to the planet with the Mage Division," Fergus said. "Keeping the peace."

"We're on our way."

Within the hour, everyone was reunited in the fleet admiral's stateroom. A polished desk, cluttered with data slates and various trinkets, occupied one corner beneath a softly glowing holographic star map. The center held a conference table, surrounded by ergonomic chairs, a place to have private meetings. An antique liquor cabinet took up another corner, filled with liquors found from all over the Worlds. The entire cabin was bathed in the celestial glow of stars pouring in from a massive viewport, painting the room with the ethereal light of the inner bands of the Milky Way.

Here, within this epicenter of decision-making, Lucian and his team recounted their extraordinary journey over drinks and a hearty meal carted in by one of the fleet's serving droids. Fergus and Mira listened slack-jawed at their mind-bending journey through space and time, only interrupting with a minor question here and there.

By the time they had concluded, it was deep into night hours. Neither one of them could find a word to say.

"I know," Lucian said. "It's a lot."

"Is he out there right now?" Fergus asked.

At first, Lucian thought he was referring to the Ancient One. And then he realized he must be talking about the Time Weaver.

"I don't know. Possibly."

"It's like he was engineering everything to happen a certain way," Mira said. "Though we can't guess everything he has done behind the scenes. He obviously moved all the Orbs around in the right way . . . otherwise, we wouldn't be here talking about this."

"We should check the latest reports from Nessus," Fergus said. "It's been long enough for another info dump."

"Let's hope for good news," Mira said.

Fergus projected a series of video feeds before them, along with news reports painting a different picture from when they had left. Things had remained quiet on the planet, confirmation from Lucian that the Ancient One had truly been defeated.

Lucian closed his eyes in relief.

Fergus took a swig of his cognac. "So, this might be a bit too soon, but what's next?"

Lucian pondered the question for a moment. "Sleep. Lots of sleep."

"Well, your old room is still there," Mira said. "In the meantime, we'll keep cleaning up. And of course, I'll continue running interference with the Hegemon. She already knows you're not responsible for this."

"That's good," Lucian said. He was far too tired to dwell on it. "There's one more thing I was wondering. Last week, we saw Transcend White, and she was very ill. Has there been any news?"

Fergus shook his head. "None to speak of. We received a light-message from the Academy shortly after you left. We've heard nothing since."

"I'll have to check in on her," Lucian said.

"Not before you've had a rest," Serah said, taking his hand. "I'd say we've earned it."

Lucian realized she was right. "I've been doing too much."

"Yes, you have," Mira said. "Have a rest, Lucian. That's an order from your mother. I'll have food sent to you two in the morning."

"Sounds good."

"As for the rest of you, your usual rooms are ready."

Lucian and Serah left. Whatever the details were left, Mira and the fleet would see to it. All he wanted was a moment of peace with Serah, a chance to get away from everything.

As soon as his head hit the pillow, he was asleep.

———

THE NEXT MORNING, everyone on the Mage Council who was present gathered in the conference room on *Mekong* to discuss the next steps, including Linus and Plato, who had been recalled by Fergus.

Lucian began the meeting by unceremoniously dumping out the Orb of Shadows. Wrapped in its Binding brand, it simply floated toward the center of the table, drinking in the surrounding light of the room, pulsing with deep violet potential. Mira, Fergus, Linus, and Plato all drank in the sight with widened eyes.

"This is all that remains of the Ancient One," Lucian said. "It's our job to return it, along with all the rest, to the Heart of Creation. I don't know exactly how far it is."

Everyone was quiet as they considered this.

At last, Mira cleared her throat. "I don't really know how all this works. But assuming the Samikan homeworld is untouched in this reality as the alternate one, it would look the same, right?"

"You're thinking we can portal directly there?" Serah asked.

Lucian could see the logic. In theory, that meant they could get to the First Gate with absolutely no trouble at all. The Time Weaver's original vision had worked ten million years in the past, but Lucian wouldn't have to use that.

He already *had* a memory of Airaruma, and his mother had said, assuming nobody had messed with the Castle of Creation, it would look exactly the same. Of course, there was no telling whether it would work until they tried it.

"The question is, how do we find the Gate itself?" Emma

asked. "It'll be in the same system, yes, but we still need to find it."

"The Seven-Fold Path will lead the way," Lucian said. "In theory, we could probably be there tomorrow if we really wanted."

There was a long silence as they all considered this.

"So," Mira said, "when do we start?"

"As soon as possible," Lucian said. "It's time to finish this. No one can stop us now. Silumko went to the past with his fleet to deal with the Ancient One during the time of the First Starsea. The Time Weaver could be anywhere; my gut is, he's fulfilled his role. So, all that's left is just finishing everything up."

"So, who all's going?" Fergus asked.

Lucian looked at everyone around the table, all the people who had become his friends over the years. He could never have imagined his road would lead this far.

"This will be volunteers only," Lucian said. "No reason to be a martyr."

"I'm going," Serah said, with no hesitation.

There was silence after that. It seemed the others had to think about it longer than her.

Jagar shifted in his seat. "This is a journey I won't be going on. This last one . . . nearly broke me. I inherited some land on Alsan. I think it's best I get everything squared away there."

"You have land?" Serah asked. "You never told us!"

He shrugged. "No reason to bring it up. Anyway, even with my younger body, this journey has been a rough one. I'm ready to live out my days in peace. No offense, Lucian. I gave you that spear and told you to use it well." He gave a small smile. "Well, you certainly did. I hope to never have to use a weapon again."

"You've earned your rest, Jagar."

"I have to agree," Linus said, coming out of his silence. Every eye went to him. "Sorry. I'm a little out of my depth here. I've no interest in going to this rotting Heart of Creation place. I don't want to go eye-to-eye with the bloody gods of the universe, or whatever you call them. They sound rotting mad, if you ask me. I'll stay right here where I belong."

"I'm not going, either," Plato said. "I couldn't keep up with you guys even if I tried. Besides, I've got my own things to take care of. I tracked down some of my family, and if the universe only has a few weeks left, or even less, I want to spend it with them."

"I don't blame you," Lucian said. That was three who didn't want to go.

"You'll need a pilot," Khairu said. "But unfortunately, it won't be me. Like Jagar, this last trip was hard on me. I . . . can't go through something like that again. And with Transcend White ailing, I'm going to be needed."

"Of course," Lucian said.

Not having Khairu as a pilot would be a rough blow, but they would find a way.

"We've gone too far together now," Emma said. "We must finish this out and hope for a way back. That's how I see it, anyway. I'm going. But before I do, I want some time to rest at home, if that's okay."

Lucian was glad she made that choice. "That's fair. But I don't want to wait too long. Even a few days can make all the difference."

"Ah, rot it," Fergus said. "I'm not going to miss this."

"Fergus?" Mira asked. "What do you mean?"

He seemed torn, looking between her and the others. "Look. Call me crazy, but I don't think this is a suicide mission. There's a way back, I know it! Like Lucian, I think there are answers. Answers we can't even imagine sitting where we are right now. Everything we've been told about the Heart of Creation isn't the full story. Who's saying what'll it be like? That's like asking someone what it's like to die. Nobody knows. All we ever hear about it is stories of tunnels, or feelings of peace and acceptance and being one with the universe. What lies beyond that door? Hell, don't tell me you're not curious, too!"

"Of *course* I'm curious," Mira said. "We just have responsibilities here. *I* have responsibilities."

"Give the reins to Thorin and come with us, then! I'm sure he'd love it. The power-mad fool. Sure, some *Alkasen* might be out there, but nothing the likes of Thorin can't handle, especially with the mages at his back."

Mira seemed conflicted. Finally, she looked at Lucian. "I'm not a mage. What'll happen to me when I go in there? From the Time Weaver's story, it sounds like someone who isn't a mage can't last there very long. For all I know, it'll kill me as soon as I step inside!"

"I can protect everyone with my Creation Magic," Lucian said. "Nothing will happen to you."

"Son . . . are you sure about this? This is crazy!"

"I'll be right beside you," Fergus said, taking her hand. "Come on. Don't tell me you don't want to go. Besides, they'll need a pilot. And you're one of the best."

"*The* best," Serah corrected.

At last, Mira smiled. "Damn it. Fine, I'll go."

Lucian smiled. "I couldn't ask for a better crew."

"Five in all," Emma said. "Seems like a good number."

"All this is happening so fast," Mira said.

Lucian nodded. "Given how hard everything has been, let's take a week for some R&R. Go anywhere you want in the Worlds. I can portal you there and pick you up later. For those of you who are parting paths with us . . . no hard feelings. Really. We understand, and too many people might gum up the works, anyway. So, those of you coming with, let's meet back here a week from now. Sound good?"

"I'm glad I'll get to go home one last time," Emma said.

"I'd like to go back to the Academy, if you'll portal me there,

Lucian," Khairu said. "I think I'd like to say my own goodbyes to Transcend White."

There was a moment of silence. He'd already said goodbye and Transcend White would probably just berate him if he tried to do so again.

"As for me," Jagar said, "I'm eager to see how Alsan has changed over the years." He gave a small chuckle. "Guess I'm going to find out."

"Fergus and I are going hiking in the Rockies," Mira said. "Aren't we, Fergus?"

"Oh, of course. Nature and all that."

"Colorado is so beautiful. Being in nature is *just* what we need. One more day in space and I'm going to scream."

"Well, *we're* going to Miami," Serah said. "Sunshine, beaches, mojitos, Cuban food . . . and a visit to my father on Psyche once we're rested up. If time allows."

"We should also make time for the mountains," Lucian said.

"Psyche has mountains," Serah said. "Plenty of them. You can see your mountains, and I can see my dad. Two wyverns with one stone."

Lucian smiled. "I can concede that point."

"I take it this meeting is done?" Khairu asked, standing up.

"I would say so," Fergus said.

Mira nodded. "All right. I'll see that *Blood Wyvern* gets stocked up. Packed to the brim."

"Meeting adjourned," Lucian said. "Have fun and be back in one week."

EPILOGUE

THE NEXT DAY, Mira made the arrangements to resign her position, explaining the situation to the Hegemon. Admiral Thorin was promptly appointed as her replacement. Thankfully, the Hegemon accepted without too much fuss, given the risk of the *Alkasen* continuing their attacks until the Orbs were returned. And, of course, Thorin was more than happy to assume the role.

Lucian helped the others get to their chosen vacation spots. He was sad to see Jagar go, but the man had earned his rest. He couldn't imagine what he'd gone through in the tower on Sigil, but maybe peace and relaxation was what he needed most.

Once done with the goodbyes, Lucian and Serah booked a private island in the Miami Archipelago. For a few amazing days, there was nothing but food, drinking, and lounging on the beach. For Lucian, it felt strange to be back. He'd never really had the money to enjoy much of what his home city offered. Most of the joy came from showing Serah all his old haunts.

A few days later, they joined Fergus and his mother on one of their hikes. During the more difficult bits, he couldn't help but use his magic to get the best views, even if Fergus said he was cheating. With a few days to spare, Lucian and Serah visited Elder Ytrib and his wife, Gia, on Psyche, who were both busy at work trying to reform Kiro Village.

The time went all too quickly. When everyone came back, *Blood Wyvern* was outfitted for a journey of many months, just in case the portal to Airaruma didn't work. Linus and Plato were the only ones there to see them off.

"No worries," Linus said. "We'll hold down the fort. Just do your jobs, and we'll do ours."

"Good luck," Plato said. "I know you'll set everything to rights, Lucian, my boy. Just follow your moral compass and everything will turn out right."

"If there's a way back, we'll find it," Lucian assured him.

This wasn't going to get any easier, so he nodded at everyone to board the ship. Once everyone was strapped in, Mira piloted *Blood Wyvern* out of its berth and into the space surrounding Nessus.

"Ready?" Lucian asked.

At the others' nods, he formed a picture of the desolate landscape of Airaruma from the alternate reality. He had made a portal of similar length ten million years ago without the benefit of the Orbs and by his own power as a sorcerer. As long as the surface of the Samikan's homeworld was the same as it was in the alternate reality, it would work.

He took his time in gathering the requisite ether to ensure the job was done right. The Orb of Creation allowed him to pull far more quickly than he was used to, but even considering this, it took about half an hour to have enough. At last, a golden portal opened, and Mira eased the ship through, right into the nearly airless atmosphere of the Samikan homeworld. The plateau rose before them, along with the icy, decayed castle beaten down by time.

But the castle was not his concern for now. Mira angled the ship upward, back into outer space.

Once above the planet, Lucian reached out to sense the Seven-Fold Path. He easily found it, its presence far more powerful than he had ever felt. It was an overwhelming sensation of being pulled. Once he homed in on the path's source, he used Radiance to transfer the data to the ship's navi-comp. It took a moment to calibrate before estimating their destination to be just a few hours away.

"So close," Emma said.

Lucian nodded. "Let's finish this."

They had one last meal together, talking about old times to deal with their nervousness. With just an hour left, they all gathered on the bridge, suited up and ready for whatever was to come.

A bright point appeared in the distance. It looked like an ordinary star at first, except it grew brighter and brighter as they drew closer. The screen tinted itself to block out the radiation, but the pinpoint of light grew ever brighter. It was like the Source of Power on Mako, except far more intense. He could almost see the Ether rushing past him in a swift current as it dispersed through the cosmos.

No one said anything, completely rapt, as the light grew with alarming speed.

Mira started the ship's deceleration sequence, not sure what exactly would happen when they passed through.

Space itself seemed to stretch as they drew to the First Gate. Reality around them brightened until there was nothing but an endless field of white spreading in all directions.

Lucian streamed a Creation shield around every one of them, branding each to ensure no one came to any harm.

The ship flew on before suddenly stopping. Despite the drastic shift of speed, there was no expected inertia. There was a brief flash, a switching in the gears of reality itself. In the very next moment, everything had changed.

Lucian blinked, looking through the viewscreen to find that

they were in a strange, ethereal forest, with trees stretching upward into infinity. A low fog hung on the ground, circling around the bottom of the ship. Everyone watched open-mouthed.

"Is this real?" Emma asked.

"Maybe we died," Serah said.

"No, we're alive," Lucian said. "This is it. The Light Realm."

Fergus and Mira were both staring out of the viewscreen, completely rapt.

"This is . . . *weird*," Serah said. "I don't know how else to describe it."

Lucian switched the camera to look behind, only to see a golden portal surrounded by yet more fantastical forest. The portal hung suspended, far smaller than what he would have guessed.

His eyes were drawn by the surrounding foliage. It was hard to describe, but the colors here seemed more . . . *colorful*. The objects more solid. He looked around, amazed. It was as if he had been partially blinded his whole life and was just now seeing fully.

"Let's head outside," he said.

"Readout says the atmosphere is breathable," Emma said. "This seems like it might be another planet, perhaps inside the First Gate itself."

It was an interesting theory, but right now, Lucian was more concerned with checking things out for himself.

They removed their suits and descended the boarding ramp. Going outside just made the colors that much more intense. And not just the colors. The sweet, earthy scent of the forest was far stronger than what he'd expected, the air cool and wet upon his skin. It was as if he were in a state of intense mindfulness, and yet that feeling was present all the time. It was almost overwhelming, and he hoped he would get used to it, because it was distracting.

Lucian couldn't help but marvel at the strange flora surrounding them. Trees shimmered with silver trunks and reached for a golden sky, their leaves a radiant shade of blue that seemed to pulsate with an inner light. Fluttering about them were creatures that seemed like a blend of butterfly and bird, their wings scattering specks of luminescent motes as they moved. The air was thick with the scent of flowers that resembled bells, emitting a soft, harmonious hum that only added to the forest's enchanting allure.

Not only that, but every one of them was surrounded by a subtle, glowing aura. Lucian assumed it was the brand he'd placed on them all, though he hadn't expected it to manifest so powerfully.

This would take some getting used to.

"I feel . . . *different*," Mira said. There were tears in her eyes, and she wasn't the only one. "It's hard to explain. Like the thing I've been missing and searching for my whole life . . . is finally here."

Lucian turned to her and was shocked to see how different his mother looked. She looked younger, about his age, with her wrinkles smoothed. Fergus also had a slightly younger appearance, as if ten years had been erased off his life.

Both she and Fergus looked at each other, crying out at the same time.

"What *is* this place?" Mira asked. "What's going on?"

Emma and Serah looked different, too. While they weren't de-aged, there was a subtle aura surrounding them, radiating power and beauty. From their reactions to him, it was clear Lucian had undergone a similar transformation.

"We have Light forms, and Shadow forms," Lucian said. "The Light Realm is said to be the base reality from which everything else comes from. Maybe this is just how we appear here. The manifestation of our Focuses if you will."

Mira frowned, confused. "But . . . I don't *have* a Focus. I'm not a—" At that moment, she gasped. She held out her hand and produced a flame above it.

Everyone watched in awe.

"Mira, you're a mage!" Serah said.

"Yes," she said, dazed. "It would appear so. I can see these colors in my head, and when I reach for them . . ."

"That's your Focus," Lucian said, hardly believing this was happening. "Well . . . welcome to the club."

"Amazing," Fergus said. "Whatever's happening, this must be part of the plan."

Lucian took another look around their environment. Just because this area was beautiful didn't mean it wasn't dangerous. The First Gate would be something that was likely watched. And not every being here would be their friend.

"We should get moving," he said.

"So, where's the Heart of Creation?" Emma asked. "That's where we need to go, right?"

Again, Lucian reached out to sense the Path. A prismatic stream speared, leading off into the forest.

"Somewhere off that way," Lucian said, nodding through the trees. "That's the best I can figure."

"Maybe we should explore, then," Fergus said.

"Very sensible," Serah said. She frowned. "This world seems a bit . . . mundane, for lack of a better word. Don't get me wrong. Colors are brighter, sounds are sharper, smells are smellier, if you know what I mean. But it's *real*. Realer than real. I expected it to feel more like a dream, I guess."

"Maybe *our* world is the dream," Emma said. "If the Light Realm is the true reality, that means we are the reflection. That's what the great mages say, anyway, but until now, the idea was always hard for me to wrap my head around."

At that moment, Lucian heard a gentle voice in his head that he interpreted as feminine. It was in a language both beautiful and lyrical, and strangely, he understood every word without having to learn it.

Well-done, Chosen. Long has your journey been, and truly have you walked your path. You have suffered great pain to fulfill your quest. But your road is not done, and some might say, it is even starting.

Who is this?

Do you not know? I am Anlilta, Speaker of the Manifold.

The Time Weaver told me about you. You are the source of the Prophecy of the Chosen.

No, not the source. I am but a Speaker of the Manifold. But never mind that. You must listen to me. You have come during a time of great turmoil, as you will soon see. The Light at the Heart of Creation fades. At any moment, all could be lost, and with the loss of our Realm, yours too will fade. Without the Orbs to heal the Heart, I fear there is little time left.

What do you need from me?

You must find me, Chosen. Just know that not everyone here can be called a friend. This is a very dangerous place. More dangerous than you know. I know it must be beautiful to your eyes, but therein lies the peril. It is not only the Ascendants who make their home here, but many beasts and monsters the likes of which you've never seen or even imagined. The armies of the Ancient One have yet to be vanquished, and their power here is great. They want to do everything to stop you from fulfilling your quest. Here, you will be tested as never before. Just as there is unending beauty, there are horrors beyond knowing. These dangers are the reason that I cannot meet you where you stand. Instead, I must trust that you can find your way to me. Your path is fraught with danger. Over each side is a treacherous drop, so you must walk a balanced path if you ever hope to finish your mission.

That sounded ominous to Lucian. Whatever the case, he needed to figure out what exactly was going on.

I'll get moving, Lucian said. *I have questions of my own.*

And they will be answered. Be wary of the Dark Orb you hold. Even now, the minions of the enemy want nothing more than to take it from you, by force or by trickery. And some who appear fair here, even among the Ascendants, are foul in heart. A great many of the Fallen's acolytes would love nothing more than to assume his Dark Aspect. And such a grievous blow would only serve to tip the balance in favor of the Shadow. You must trust no one.

Does that include even you?

Yes. Even me. For none can complete your path but you, Chosen. This Realm will be strange to your Shadowed eyes, and you have much to learn about how things work here. But I cannot explain as much in a message. Even this taxes me, for the forces of the Fallen are strong, and we lost control of the First Gate long ago. I can say this much before I depart. Find me in the City of Anshar, in the Court of the Lord-Ascendant Enkius. The Seven-Fold Path will lead you there.

Before Lucian could ask anything more, the connection severed.

"What was that?" Serah asked. "Someone talking to you?"

"That was Anlilta. She wants us to find her."

He quickly explained the rest until they knew as much as him.

"What about the Orb of Shadows?" Emma asked. "Or the Dark Orb, as she called it. The Time Weaver said we needed to give it to Enkius, but Anlilta wants us to find her first. Are we sure she can be trusted?"

"I have no idea."

Fergus chimed in. "Emma's right. We're in unknown territory where everything is different. I get the impression that maybe she and Enkius don't see eye-to-eye on things. We must remember there are two sides to every story, or even more. We can't be too careful."

Both were solid points. "Of course. The only people I trust are standing around me right now."

Lucian reached out his hand. Lightspear formed as true as ever. At least that much was the same.

"Is it weird to say I'm afraid?" Serah asked.

Lucian drew her close. "Not at all. I'm scared, too. I mean, just look at this. Voices in the head and all this doom and gloom isn't a promising start."

"It's a lead," Fergus said. "But if there are truly monsters here, then we must find more defensible ground before nightfall."

"If this place even *has* nightfall," Serah said.

It was a good point. They wouldn't know what they were dealing with until it happened.

With nothing but the clothes on their backs and as much supplies and food as they could carry, and their weapons, they left *Blood Wyvern* behind. Lucian just had to hope the ship would remain safe there for them next to the First Gate.

He considered using the ship to cover more ground, but instantly saw the folly of the idea. For one, he knew the ship wouldn't work; it had stopped completely as soon as they'd passed through, so whatever quantum stuff it did to propel itself in their reality wouldn't work here. Second, it would just make them a target. Moving quietly was the key to avoiding detection.

Lucian led the way into the strange, mystical forest, and the others followed behind toward an uncertain future.

The Heart of Creation was waiting.

THE END OF BOOK NINE

THE STARSEA CYCLE CONCLUDES IN BOOK TEN:

THE HEART OF CREATION

KYLE WEST
THE
HEART
OF
CREATION
THE STARSEA CYCLE BOOK TEN

ABOUT THE AUTHOR

Kyle West is the author of multiple science-fantasy series, including The Starsea Cycle, The Wasteland Chronicles, and The Xenoworld Saga. While his fiction is set on strange and alien worlds, he strives to write characters that are human and relatable.

He enjoys the outdoors, hiking, and all things sci-fi and fantasy. He lives in Oklahoma City with his family.

Please visit kylewestbooks.com to learn about his books and stay in the loop with future releases.

ACKNOWLEDGMENTS

Special thanks to the Beta Team for their hard work hunting typos: Cindy, Jeremy, Barbara, Krzysztof, and Mark. You guys are the real MVP's!

Despite best efforts from everyone, typos *always* find a way of slipping through. This is inevitable when hundreds of people read the same text. Any errors left behind are the fault of the author.

If you believe you've found a typo in this text, please email kylewest@kylewestbooks.com.

www.ingramcontent.com/pod-product-compliance
Lightning Source LLC
Chambersburg PA
CBHW010547170726
48285CB00011B/2799